THE TIGER'S CAGE

Linda J. White

Cover design: June Padgett, Bright Eye Designs

First Printing March, 2016
Tiger's Cage 14-Paper c3.pdf
Printed in the United States of America

Scripture quotations are from the ESV® Bible (The Holy Bible, English Standard Version®), copyright © 2001 by Crossway, a publishing ministry of Good News Publishers. Used by permission. All rights reserved.

White, Linda J., 1949-
The Tiger's Cage / Linda J. White

ISBN 978-0-9912212-0-2 paperback
ISBN 978-0-9912212-3-3 ebook

For Amelia, whose generosity and patience
changed the course of my life.

The Tiger's Cage
Character List

Kenny Donovan, 18, a high-school senior in Fairfax, Virginia, a wrestler, and the son of an FBI agent, Tom.

Tom Donovan, 47. A door-kicking FBI agent. Originally from Boston, he's fighting drug gangs in Northern Virginia.

Angel Ramos, early 40s. A Salvadoran, and Tom's current nemesis. He's using kids to help sell his cocaine.

Miguel Camacho, 30s. Ramos's right-hand man and Tom's best hope to snare Ramos.

Cathy Donovan, Tom's wife. She has spent most of her adult years quietly, as a mom at home, while Tom chases bad guys. She has a part-time job at a library.

Jack McRae. Tom's partner and best friend. Hired by the FBI as a forensic geologist, he got tired of being in the lab and applied to become an agent. He's a West Virginia country boy and Tom's Dr. Watson.

Ryan Douglas, a Fairfax County police officer.

Lee Burnett, the supervisor of Tom's and Jack's squad at the FBI.

Alex Cramer, Special Agent in Charge of the FBI's Washington Field Office.

John 'Fitz' Fitzpatrick, Assistant Special Agent in Charge. He's Cramer's right-hand man, well-respected and experienced.

Trish, 49, Cathy's sister who lives in Chester, PA. She's an interior designer and Cathy's polar opposite.

Terry McDaniel, early 30s. He's the leader of the Fairfax Fellowship of Athletes and a mentor for Ken.

Rachel, Cathy's friend who lives down the street.

Amanda Whittaker, a young FBI agent investigating

Ken's assault.

Bill Adams, an FBI agent investigating Ken's assault.

Caryn Wheeler, an FBI agent investigating Ken's assault.

Maria Aguilera, Ramos's girlfriend and sister to Luis.

Luis Aguilera, one of Ramos's older gang members.

Pablo Ramos, Angel's younger brother.

Edmundo, a member of Ramos's gang.

J.D. McRae, late 30s; he's Jack's brother, and a teacher in Spotsylvania County, Virginia.

Brenda, an FBI agent who accompanies Cathy on the train to Philadelphia.

Tracy, daughter of Trish and Cathy's niece. Tracy spent summers with the Donovans and she's practically a sister to Ken.

Chip, a cop on duty at the Donovans' house.

Gregory, Trish's husband; Tracy's father; Cathy's brother-in-law.

Dr. Peter Montgomery, 50-something, an English professor at the university where Gregory teaches. He's charming, handsome, and sophisticated.

Rodriguez, a member of Ramos's gang. Tom and Jack confront him in a bar.

Spark is one of Tom's informants. Tom has special phone numbers he uses for these "sources." Spark calls Tom "Mick," which is an ethnic slur for Irish people.

Marie works with Tracy at Hope House, a shelter for crack babies.

Mary, night manager at an IHOP in which Cathy takes refuge.

Coach Hall, Ken Donovan's high school wrestling coach.

David Perez, Ken's opponent in the District wrestling meet.

Roberto, a gang member.

Kate, an FBI agent.

Carlos Ramirez, a young gang member.

Dave Borsten, head of the elite FBI Hostage Rescue Team.

Santini, bartender at Chico's.

Smitty, an agent on Tom's squad.

Officer Patrick Donovan, Tom's father. An Irish cop in Boston.

Mrs. Ramirez, Carlos's mother. Her husband was killed in a construction accident.

Alicia Menendez, an FBI agent who speaks Spanish and acts as a translator.

Miguel Ramirez, Carlos's younger brother.

Mike Cornell, a young agent.

Ed McLaughlin, an older agent who has a remote office serving Fauquier and surrounding counties.

James Finn, soil scientist for Fauquier County.

Edmund Perez, Ramos's lawyer; David's father.

Billy Sears, an old Fauquier County farmer.

Brad Everett, an agent with nerves of steel.

Frank Littleton, an FBI agent who is also an EMT.

CHAPTER 1

TUESDAY, JANUARY 12, 1993

"RIDE, Kenny?"

"No, thanks. It's a good night to be outside."

"See you tomorrow at school, then."

"You bet." Kenneth Patrick Donovan turned toward his home, just a mile away. His suburban Northern Virginia neighborhood was quiet, peaceful, softly illuminated by lights from living room windows spilling onto front yards in gentle squares. Four inches of snow from yesterday's storm lay on the ground, fluffy and clean, like a down comforter shaken and re-laid on the earthy bed.

No one was out, not even the neighborhood dogs, and Kenny drank in the solitude like a tonic. He couldn't get the meeting out of his mind. Amazing. He was learning so much. Shoving his hand in the pocket of his high school letter jacket, he fingered a little metal cross. He looked up at the starry January sky, and it seemed he could see forever.

He didn't notice the white Chevy van as it came down the street. He heard a noise. A small alarm went off in his head. He started to turn around, too late.

They grabbed him from behind. Kenny's head snapped back and fear exploded in his belly. He pulled against their hands, and sucked in a panicked breath as someone shoved a bandanna in his mouth. He couldn't breathe! The night disappeared under a knit hat.

"Hurry!"

They pushed him toward the street and he braced his legs,

resisting, until a sharp crack on his head impelled him forward. He stumbled. They grabbed him by his collar and threw him onto the ribbed metal floor of a van.

He tried to get up. They held him down, forcing his hands together behind him. "Tighter!" he heard one of them say, and zip ties tightened around his wrists. A new wave of terror ran through him. No, no! He fought wildly, like an animal in a trap, the plastic cutting into his flesh, and he made it to his knees. Then a blow to the back of his neck made him collapse and he lay helplessly on the floor, trembling with fear and exertion.

The side door slammed shut. Kenny felt the van accelerate. A musty, heavy tarp dropped on top of him, suffocating him. He moved around, trying to find an air space. He got a sharp punch in the ribs.

"Stay still!" a voice commanded.

Oh, God, he thought, help me! Who are these people? And every muscle in his eighteen-year-old body began shaking uncontrollably.

✞ ✞ ✞

Night had fallen like a magician's cape over the streets of Alexandria, Virginia. The bright lights were scattered like multi-colored sequins over the darkness. As FBI Special Agent Tom Donovan worked his way through the congested downtown, he looked at the glittery night with a jaded eye. He stood close enough to the stage to see the magician's tricks, to know that behind the shimmering lights were dark pools of despair—shadowy alleys and dirty streets where twenty minutes of euphoria could be bought in a vial for ten bucks and paid for, forever, with your soul.

As he drove along, Tom rehearsed the details of his testimony for the next day's grand jury over and over in his mind. Catching Angel Ramos's right-hand man, Miguel Camacho, with a kilo of coke was a stroke of luck even he couldn't have anticipated. An indictment would up the odds of flipping Camacho. His testimony against Ramos could bring the drug kingpin down once and for all.

Satisfied at that thought, Tom flipped on the radio to a sports-talk show. Callers were re-hashing the Buffalo Bills game against Pittsburgh on Sunday. He had no dog in that fight, and changed stations. "Today, President Bush announced that ..." yada yada. Punching that off, he inserted a cassette. Upbeat Celtic music. Perfect.

Twenty minutes later, Tom pulled into the garage of his Fairfax County home. As he did, he felt a vague uneasiness, confirmed by Cathy's glare as he walked into the kitchen. "Hey!" he said.

"Where's Kenny? I expected you both to be home when I got here."

Tom's mind began racing. Where was he ... when was he ... was he supposed to ...

"You were supposed to pick him up!" she said. "You forgot, didn't you?" She had dark hair, like him, but her eyes were blue. When she was angry, they seemed to develop flecks of gold, like sparks from a blacksmith's hammer.

"Tonight?"

Cathy rolled her eyes and turned away.

Tom cursed under his breath. "Sorry. I'll get him now. Where is he?"

"He gave *you* that information. You were the one who was supposed to get him."

"Oh, right." Tom began patting his pockets, searching until he found it—a scrap of paper with an address. "Got it! I'll be right back!"

But when he arrived at the house on Littlefield Street, the two-story white Colonial looked dark except for one small light in an upstairs bedroom. Puzzled, he jogged up to the front porch and rang the bell. A minute later, a man in a plaid bathrobe answered it. "I'm Tom Donovan," he said to the man. "I was supposed to pick up my son, Kenny. I guess I'm late."

A teenaged boy came partway down the stairs. "Mr. Donovan? Kenny said he'd walk home."

Tom frowned. "What time did he leave?"

"All the kids were gone by, what, nine, Jason?" the dad asked his son.

Tom glanced at his watch. Nine-twenty-five.

"Yes, sir. Coach said we had to be in bed by nine thirty, so Terry kicked everybody out at nine."

"Thanks," Tom said. "Sorry to bother you." He turned

and stepped off the front porch. The door closed behind him. How far was he from home? A mile? Two? Shouldn't Kenny be home by now?

✞ ✞ ✞

Kenny struggled to stay calm. Within minutes, the van stopped, the door slid open and strong hands jerked him to his feet, pulling him out. He twisted again, trying to get away, but the grips holding him tightened. Heart pounding, Kenny tried to see, tried to hear, tried to figure out where he was. He could feel pavement under his feet, and a little loose gravel. The knit hat covering his eyes seemed a little floppy and by twisting his head just the right way, he could see just a bit of the ground.

What now? He was breathing hard. He heard a car door slam and footsteps, and then he smelled something. A cigar? He looked down. A pair of cowboy boots appeared right in front of his feet. A shiver went through him.

The cigar smoker pulled Kenny's wallet out of his back pocket. "Donovan. Muy bien."

That voice ... did he know that voice?

The man laughed. "Your father will be missing his boy, no?"

Kenny could smell the cigar, so close.

Then the man jerked open Kenny's letter jacket. He ran his hand down the young man's ribcage. Kenny reacted, pulling against the hands holding him. He twisted his head right and left, finally dislodging the bandanna in his mouth. He sucked the cold night air into his lungs. "What do you want?" he cried out, his chest heaving. "Who are you?"

The man hit him, hard, across the mouth. Kenny's head jerked to the side and he felt his lip split against his teeth. He swallowed blood.

"Shut up." The man grabbed Kenny by the throat, pressing his thumb into Kenny's neck. "Just shut up." He released his hold. "My muchachos, they are bored." He switched to Spanish. "Haz lo que quieras." Do whatever you want.

✞ ✞ ✞

The snakes in Tom's belly were starting to slither. He drove slowly through the empty neighborhood, then pulled into the garage and entered the house. "Cathy!" he bellowed. "Is he here? Did he come home?"

Cathy emerged from the family room. "No. He wasn't at that house? Where is he?"

"I have no idea. He told them he'd walk home."

"That's ridiculous! Where could he be?"

The anger in her voice masked fear. Tom knew that. "I don't know." He ran his hand through his hair. "Where does he go? What does he do? McDonald's? Where do I look for him?"

Cathy turned. She crossed her arms. "He doesn't go anywhere, not during wrestling season."

"Except for this group."

"That started just a few months ago. You'd know that if you were ever around!"

"Does he have a girlfriend?"

"Not that he's told me." Cathy raised her chin, and in that small gesture, Tom saw vulnerability.

"Look, Cathy, there's probably some good explanation for all this. Kenny's a good kid." They'd gone through some tough times with their son when he was younger, but Tom thought those were behind them. "Maybe he stopped to help someone with homework. I'll go back and get the names of the kids he was with. Then I'll check around the neighborhood."

"I'm going to look, too."

"No. You stay here." His voice sounded firmer than he intended.

Cathy's mouth tightened into a line. At first, Tom thought she was going to argue with him. "Someone needs to be here when he shows up," he added. "You can page me."

She glared at him. "Fine. Do it your way. Just find him, Tom!" Her voice caught, and she walked swiftly out of the room.

✞ ✞ ✞

Kenny sensed several men around him. Five, maybe six guys. What were they going to do?

The first blow slammed into his gut, and Kenny's breath exploded out of his lungs. Then came another, higher, and to the right, and pain screamed through his ribs. Another blow landed, and another. He felt himself slipping, sinking to his knees, and the blows became kicks against his body, his face, his legs. "No!" he breathed. "No!" And then the blackness began to envelop him. He collapsed and fell, the loose stones of the parking lot studding his face.

He was a little boy again, on his first bike with hand brakes, a silver Columbia five-speed. He was so proud! He whizzed down the hill past his grinning, clapping father, his hair blowing in the wind. He owned the sidewalk! He was king of the hill!

But he was going too fast. He squeezed too hard, locked the brakes, and sailed over the handlebars, his mouth wide with surprise. He hit the ground hard.

He was hurt. Crying. Scared. His dad ran up. "Kenny. Son. You okay? I'm here. It's all right." He felt his dad's hands touching him, saw his steel-gray eyes grow soft with caring. "You're going to be fine, son."

Dad's here. He was safe now. His father's strong love could fix anything.

Kenny Donovan turned his head. Asphalt. Stones. Ice. Dad wasn't here. He was on his own.

✝ ✝ ✝

Tom steered his car back to the house on Littlefield Street, parked, rang the doorbell, and apologized when the dad in his robe answered again. "He's not home yet. I need to know who my son was with," Tom explained. "I need names."

The dad motioned him in and, with Jason's help, compiled a list of eighteen kids and their phone numbers. "Thank you," Tom said, as he stood up to leave.

"I hope he shows up soon," the dad said. "I'm sure he will."

Tom nodded. Then he looked Jason's dad in the eye. "Why was he here, anyway?"

"FFA."

Tom blinked.

"Fairfax Fellowship of Athletes."

What kind of … when did Kenny get hooked up with them? His jaw tightened. "Thanks." Tom started to leave then asked, "Do you mind if I use your phone?" He'd have the office page his FBI partner. There was no one he'd rather have with him right now than Jack McRae.

CHAPTER 2

"SO, WHAT ARE YOU THINKING, Tom?"

Tom looked over at his partner, seated in the passenger seat of his car. Jack was a West Virginia country boy, a descendant of the hard-working, hard-fighting Scots-Irish immigrants who filled the hollows of Appalachia with strong whiskey and sweet music. He was shorter than Tom, barrel-chested, and solid as the granite he'd grown up on. Jack had joined the Bureau as a forensic geologist. But he soon discovered he didn't like being stuck in a lab all day, so he transferred to a job as a street agent and used his geology when he could. He met Tom at the scene of a gang-related murder at a quarry. Their collaboration on that case had led to a partnership, unusual for the Bureau, but it had worked for them now for more than ten years.

"Something's up," Tom said. "It's not like Kenny to disappear like that."

"You want to call it in?"

"This neighborhood ... it doesn't get much safer than this." Tom stared out of the front window. "If I call the county, you know what they'll say: Give him twenty-four hours. They'll figure he's a runaway, or irresponsible."

Jack said, "Girlfriend?"

Tom shook his head. "Not according to Cathy."

Jack stroked his chin. "You know, if someone wanted to keep you from testifying before the grand jury tomorrow, this'd be a way to do it."

Tom frowned. "No way. They'd never go after a fed's family. The whole Bureau would be down on them. Ramos isn't that stupid."

Jake nodded. "Yeah, you're right."

"Look, you drive around, okay? Try a couple of different routes back to the house. I want to look a little more, ten minutes, maybe. If he still isn't home, we'll start calling these kids."

"Got it," Jack said.

✞ ✞ ✞

Kenny lay on the ground, shaking with cold and anxiety. Then something sent a chill down Kenny's back. A sound? A change in the tone of the men's conversation? Or just the increased tension in the air, like static electricity building up a charge? He heard a noise, the crunch of boots on ice, and the acrid smell of cigar smoke drifted toward him. His stomach tensed and the back of his scalp tightened. Okay, God, he thought. This is it. This is where I really need you. He clenched his cuffed hands behind his back.

He heard the boss issue a few sharp commands in Spanish and suddenly strong arms grabbed him and jerked him to his feet. Searing pain streaked through his left shoulder and Kenny cried out. He knew the boss stood straight in front of him, and every bone in his body begged him to run the other way.

"We let you go this time. But take a message to your daddy," the boss said. His voice sounded oily and smooth, and it sent chills down Kenny's spine.

Kenny set his jaw. "Don't bother."

"We'll have to convince him we're serious, no? That he needs to back off?"

"He'll never stop." Kenny's breath came harder now.

"You know," said the boss, "I always wonder about those feds, how macho they really are under those nice suits." He ran the back of his hand up and down Kenny's ribcage, and the hair on the back of the young man's neck stood up.

"You, muchacho, are not a fed, but you are the son of a fed. His blood runs through your veins, eh? How tough are you, kid?"

Kenny heard a click, and then he felt the flat side of a knife slide across his cheek. It made a rasping sound as it scraped backwards against the stubble on his face, and

Kenny felt fear begin to swirl inside him. What was this guy going to do? What?

Suddenly, the boss grabbed Kenny's shirt. He sliced the shirt right down the front, and Kenny felt cold air hit the skin of his chest. The two men holding him tightened their grip.

"Let's see what you can take. Are you ready?"

Then Kenny felt the knife slicing through the skin on his chest. He caught his cry of surprise and pain in his teeth as it left his throat. Another slice. He gritted his teeth and choked back the acid rising from his stomach. The pain, the feel of his skin separating, the smell of the cigar combined and swirled around him, nauseating him, intensifying the fear that sucked at him. He became dizzy, and panic rose within him. "Oh, God!" he heard himself cry out.

"How's that? Mas? You can take more?"

Flashes of orange and yellow appeared in Kenny's mind's eye, like a popping, snapping fire. He squeezed his eyes shut. His back arched in pain and his voice became tangled in a web of outrage and fear. He twisted helplessly against the hands that held him. He felt his chest grow wet with the warmth of his own blood. He desperately sucked in air.

"We got a strong man here!"

Kenny's chest heaved, his knees buckled and reality began slipping away. Somewhere in the distance, he heard a voice screaming. Finally, everything went white, the voices receded and Kenny lost consciousness. It was a blessed escape, a gift from God.

☩ ☩ ☩

Tom drove swiftly through the neighborhood, checking cross streets and one small park several blocks over. Then Cathy paged him, using the 911 code. He raced home. She had her coat on and her car keys in her hand.

"Fairfax Hospital took in a John Doe, a young man about Kenny's age, fifteen minutes ago," she told him.

Tom checked his watch. 10:13. "They called you?"

"No, I called all the hospitals."

Smart.

"I'm going!" Cathy shoved past him.

"Wait, no, wait."

Jack pulled up.

"Come with me. Or let Jack take you. Please, Cathy." He was afraid she'd have an accident.

She hesitated, then yielded. "I'll go with Jack."

CHAPTER 3

THE SKY LOOKED AS BLACK and hard as polished rock, the moon like quartz as Tom ran across the parking lot of the emergency entrance to Fairfax Hospital. He flashed his FBI credentials to the woman at the desk. "You have a John Doe that came in here tonight?"

The receptionist studied him. "I'll get the officer."

Fairfax County Police Officer Ryan Douglas emerged from the back just as Jack and Cathy arrived. "Where is he?" Cathy asked.

The cop had a high school letter jacket in his hand. "You recognize this?"

"It's his! It's my son's," Cathy said.

Had she seen the blood on the front? Tom couldn't tell. His heart felt like a ping-pong ball jumping around in his chest.

"I'll take you back," the cop said. He fell into stride next to Tom. Cathy trailed behind. "Looks like your kid was in the wrong place at the wrong time."

Tom's jaw shifted. "Yeah?"

"He's beat up pretty bad."

"Did he know them?"

"Said they spoke Spanish. That's all." He pushed open a door. "First room on the right."

Tom had braced himself but as he rounded the corner, the world seemed to drop away.

He was barely recognizable, this son of his. Kenny's face was swollen. His left eye was closed, his right eye open only a slit. An angry red and purple bruise, the color of a plum, covered the left side of his face. A cut on his lip gaped open.

Tom felt strangely detached as he watched Cathy move to Kenny's side. She took his hand, and her son looked up at her with his one good eye. Tears dripped down her cheeks.

Kenny shook his head and whispered, "Don't." He raised his right hand to touch her.

Tom's eyes locked onto the swollen, cut area on Kenny's wrist where the marks of a zip tie remained in his skin. He felt his face flush with anger. Handcuffs? Why handcuffs? Then he saw a large white bandage stained with blood covering a wound on Kenny's chest and Tom wanted to lift it, to see it, but he didn't want to do it in front of Cathy. "Who did this? Do you know?" Tom asked.

Kenny's eyes shifted from his mom to his dad. He tried to sit up. A fresh rivulet of red blood trickled out of his mouth.

Tom reached for tissue and wiped Kenny's face. "You have any trouble at school lately?"

Kenny shook his head.

A nagging thought dogged Tom. "The kids you were with tonight—one of them holding a grudge?"

"No." Kenny reached toward his dad, starting to say something else, but then his stomach clenched and he rolled onto his side and began to throw up. Tom jumped to his feet, grabbed a basin and held it for him. "You're all right. You're all right," he said, his hand on Kenny's shoulder. Behind him, he heard Cathy softly crying.

Kenny fell back onto the bed.

"Excuse me." A nurse appeared. "We're ready to take him back for tests."

"He just threw up a lot of blood."

"We'll be checking for internal injuries." She held out a clipboard holding a sheaf of papers. "If one of you could fill these out."

Tom took them. His hand shook.

"Wait down the hall. Consultation Room 1, on your right. Your friend is already there. Someone will collect the forms in a few minutes."

✝ ✝ ✝

The tension between them felt like an iron bar as Tom and Cathy walked down the hall to the consultation room. Tom held the door open for her and Cathy walked in. She dabbed her eyes and Tom watched helplessly as she easily slipped into Jack's embrace and began to sob.

Tom fought back his feelings, sat down, and began filling out the forms. By the time he finished, Cathy had settled into one of the blue vinyl chairs in the room, Jack next to her. She held his hand and leaned her head on Jack's shoulder, dabbing her eyes once in a while. Strange that the difficulties he and Cathy had been experiencing hadn't killed her trust in his best friend.

"Did you talk any more to the county?" Tom asked his partner, setting the clipboard aside.

"A guy found him after his dog started barking, in a parking lot behind an elementary school."

Tom shook his head. "Did he see anything, hear anything before that?"

"Apparently not."

A nurse came in and Tom stood up and handed the forms to her. "County having street gang problems?" Tom asked when she'd left.

"Not that I know of," Jack said. "I put in a call to the gang coordinator."

"What'd they do with Kenny's clothes?"

"They have them, but they may be compromised. I called someone to pick them up and take them to the lab."

"Pictures?"

"Some." Jack stroked his chin. "You think we better call Lee?" Lee Burnett was their squad supervisor.

Tom rubbed his neck. "Why?"

"You think you're going to make it to the grand jury tomorrow?"

"Of course! It's over."

Cathy looked up, her cheeks wet with tears, her eyebrows raised in disbelief. "What makes you think it's over? Didn't you see his face?"

Tom swallowed. "That'll heal, Cathy. He'll be fine! He's a tough kid."

"Really? Just like that? How long do you think it will be before Kenny can walk down the street at night by himself without jumping every time a car drives by?"

How could he make her understand? "Cathy,..." he began.

"Don't start with me, Tom. Not everyone thinks assault is an everyday affair."

Tom shook his head and stared down at the floor. He turned and walked toward the window, his emotions engaged. He didn't want to fight. Not here, not now. Then he heard the vinyl chair squeak, and sensed Cathy right behind him. His jaw tightened.

"Let me ask you this, Tom."

He turned and looked at her.

"How many times have you forgotten a court date?"

He felt his face grow hot.

"How often have you missed a meeting with an informant? I'll bet," Cathy said, "that in your twenty-one years with the Bureau, you have never once failed to be where you were supposed to be when you were supposed to be there." Tears filled her eyes. "Your son worships you, you know. Your priorities are messed up." And with that, she turned and started for the door.

✞ ✞ ✞

Before Cathy could open the door, Officer Ryan Douglas entered.

Tom approached him. "You got a gang problem here in the county?"

The officer cocked his head. Douglas was too nonchalant for Tom's taste. Or maybe Tom was just angry.

"Not really," Douglas said. "This stuff happens. They're kids."

"My son doesn't fight. He said they spoke Spanish." Out of the corner of his eye, Tom saw Jack's eyes cut toward him.

Douglas shrugged. "They probably figured he had some money. I mean, I've seen kids assaulted for their shoes."

A doctor walked in, interrupting. "Mr. Donovan?"

Tom's gut tightened. "Yes."

"Your son did fine." The doctor sounded fatigued. "He took quite a beating tonight."

Tom flexed his jaw.

"What do you mean?" Cathy asked. "Will he be okay?"

"He's all stitched up," the doctor said, continuing. "I asked him what day it was and he had trouble coming up with 'Tuesday.' So we are keeping him overnight. But I really think he'll be okay. He's got a massive bruise on the side of his face, but none of the underlying bones appear to be broken. His rib may be bruised. I don't think it's cracked or broken. We found no internal injuries, although we will watch for signs of concussion."

Tom nodded.

"It's the cuts that really ..." the doctor shook his head.

"Cuts?" Cathy said.

"On his chest. It's like somebody knew just how deep to cut to hurt him without killing him."

Tom stiffened.

"Give us a few minutes and we'll let you see him." The doctor started to leave, then turned back. "Oh, your son asked me to tell you something."

"What's that?" Tom asked.

"He wore boots. The guy who cut him wore gray alligator-leather cowboy boots."

Tom's anger ignited.

"Ramos!" Jack said under his breath.

Cathy turned to Tom. "This is because of you?"

Eyes narrowed, face hot, Tom turned toward Officer Douglas. He gestured with his index finger. "I want a uniformed guard on my son 24/7. Beginning now!" Off to the side, he could see Jack using the phone.

Angel Ramos had just declared war on the FBI.

CHAPTER 4

JACK HUNG UP THE PHONE. "Lee's hit the ground running. He'll be here as quick as he can."

"He'll call the boss?" Alex Cramer, the Special Agent in Charge of the Washington Field Office, would be at his home at this time on a Tuesday night.

Jack nodded.

"Tom, what does this mean? What's going on?" Cathy's eyes flashed.

Even when she was angry he felt attracted to her. He glanced around to make sure they were alone and he lowered his voice. "Ramos runs a gang over in Alexandria. He uses kids to move his cocaine. We caught his right-hand man coming off a plane with a kilo of coke. That's what the grand jury is all about tomorrow. If we get an indictment, odds are we can flip this guy Camacho, and take Ramos down."

"Wait. So Ramos goes after Kenny to get at you? I thought you said criminals wouldn't touch an agent's family."

Tom felt his face flush.

"You have always said that!"

"There's an unwritten rule …"

"Unwritten?"

Jack stepped in. "Cathy, these guys know if they touch an agent's family, the whole force of the FBI is going to come down on them like a boot on a bug. That's just what will happen now." He touched her shoulder. "Don't worry. Your boy will be safe and so will you."

Cathy wouldn't be coddled. She spat her words at Tom:

"You expect me to believe that? After tonight?"

✝ ✝ ✝

"You've got your boy in a safe place?" Lee Burnett sat across from Tom in a hospital security guard's office. A few years younger than Tom, he'd taken over as squad supervisor six months ago.

"He's been admitted under a false name, and there's a uniformed cop outside his door. Cathy's with him. He's fine." Tom's knee jiggled.

"We'll want to interview him as soon as we can."

"He's out of it right now." Tom rubbed his hand across his thigh, willing his muscles to relax.

"Jack's gone to the scene?"

Tom nodded.

The door opened and the Assistant Special Agent in Charge of the Washington Field Office stepped in. Tall and fit, John "Fitz" Fitzpatrick's gray hair testified to his decades with the Bureau. His years on the street earned him high credibility with the agents and his calm wisdom gained him respect with their families.

Tom and Lee rose to greet him.

"Why'd they do this, Tom?" Fitz asked, as they all sat down.

"I've got grand jury in the morning. We caught a break on a case we've been working on for two years."

"You want to go through with testifying?"

"You bet. I'm not letting Ramos win this one."

Burnett nodded. "The AUSA thought you'd say that." The assistant U.S. attorney prosecuting Camacho had been working with Tom. "So that's at what, nine o'clock?"

"Right."

"Alex Cramer has asked me to head up a special task force on the assault on your son," Fitz said. "He wants to get this guy almost as badly as you do. We have to get the message out—nobody touches an agent's family. Nobody."

Tom nodded. "Yes, sir."

"For the grand jury appearance, I'll want two agents with you and I want you in a different car going to and leaving the courthouse."

"Yeah, good."

"I'll take care of that," Lee said.

"What are we doing to connect Ramos to this? Has your son identified him?"

"No, sir. He doesn't know him. But he said the guy who cut him wore gray alligator-leather cowboy boots." Tom took a deep breath. "And that's Ramos."

"There's more than one pair of those around."

"The boots, the fact I've got grand jury tomorrow—it fits. I got a list of everybody at the meeting Kenny was walking home from. I think there's a connection. Somebody told Ramos my kid would be there."

Fitz frowned. "Give Lee the list and we'll check it."

Tom pulled the crumpled notebook paper out of his pocket and handed it to Lee.

"What else?" Fitz asked.

"I've got agents doing a door-to-door on the street where Kenny walked and we have his clothes going down to the lab," Lee said.

"Okay. Get someone establishing a timeline for Ramos. I want to know where he was every minute yesterday. I'll interview Kenny tomorrow morning ..."

"I want to be there," Tom said.

"I'll interview him at eleven, assuming the doctors okay it. I don't want to wait longer than that. So if you're there, fine. If not ..." Fitz let that hang in the air.

Tom took a deep breath.

"Cramer wants to see you at one tomorrow afternoon. You and Jack. Probably you, too, Lee."

"Okay."

"Let's get this guy," Fitz said, standing up. "If this was really him, Ramos stepped over the line. Big time."

☩ ☩ ☩

Tom spent the night at the hospital with his son, leaving just in time to get to the courthouse in Alexandria. Despite his lack of sleep, his testimony before the grand jury felt like a slick ride down a snow-covered hill. Smooth as glass. Camacho would be indicted. He was sure of it.

He would have been elated had his mind not been preoccupied by the stark images of his beaten and battered son lying in a bed in Fairfax Hospital. Ramos would pay.

He'd make sure Ramos paid.

He checked his watch. With a little luck, he'd make it to Fairfax before eleven when Fitz would interview Kenny. Tom wanted to hear every word his son had to say.

✞ ✞ ✞

As Tom walked into the room, he saw a nurse hand Kenny a small plastic cup with a straw in it. Fitz sat in a chair next to the bed. Two other agents stood off to the side next to a Fairfax County detective.

Kenny looked up and smiled a crooked smile. "You look terrible!" he said to his dad.

"Yeah? Well, you look great," Tom responded, forcing a grin. "Gentlemen," he said, nodding to the others.

"We haven't started yet," Fitz explained. "You're in good time."

Tom wanted to wrap his arms around Kenny, grab him in a big bear hug, tell him how sorry he was he'd been attacked, and how he'd never let it happen again. Instead, he sat down in the chair the detective had yielded to him.

"Jack coming?"

"He's parking the car," Tom said.

Fitz nodded. "Let's get started."

Some agents had a hard time turning off the command voice, even with victims, even with their families. Not Fitz. He was everybody's grandfather, everybody's friend. He gently carried Kenny back to the night before, to his meeting, to his decision to walk home, to the abduction and beating. "Tell me, Kenny, what happened. Begin with the meeting. What group was it?"

Jack came in. He leaned against the wall, his face impassive.

Tom focused on his son. He'd heard a lot of stories over the years, and he'd been hoping to listen to this one objectively, as an investigator. But as his son recounted being assaulted, the details of his story clicked into Tom's brain like bullets being loaded into a magazine, until he thought his head would explode.

"And what happened then, Kenny?" Fitz asked.

As he spoke of this new man, the one they called "El Jefe," arriving, a line of blood and saliva began seeping from the corner of Kenny's mouth. He reached toward an empty tissue box.

"Here." Fitz took his own handkerchief out of his pocket.

Kenny wiped his mouth, and leaned back again, staring at the ceiling.

"And you didn't recognize his voice?"

"No, sir. But he knew Dad. He called me 'Donovan's son.'"

Tom looked away, tense as a coiled spring. He could hardly sit still. The muscles of his jaw ached and his hands were wet with sweat.

"What else, Kenny?"

Tom wished it were over. He leaned forward, resting his elbows on his knees, and focused on a black square floor tile, trying to stop the swirling inside.

"He cut my shirt." Kenny's voice quavered, "and then ... then he began cutting me across my chest. I remember feeling blood running down." His voice dropped to a whisper. "He kept cutting and cutting. Then, I must have passed out. That's all I remember."

When he finished speaking, the room was completely still, like the dead calm before a storm.

Tom looked up, his anger burning in his belly. He glanced over at Jack, whose face was rock-hard.

"You're okay now, Kenny," said Fitz. "We've got a guard on you. They can't get to you. Do you understand?"

Kenny nodded.

"You get some rest. You've helped us a lot." Fitz turned to Tom. "Cramer wants to meet with us at one o'clock."

"Yes, sir."

The men began to leave. Jack stopped, leaned over Kenny's bed and said something to him. Tom saw tears well in Kenny's eyes. Jack patted his shoulder and shot Tom a look as he left.

Tom moved toward his son. He reached over the bed and awkwardly hugged him. "You're safe now. They won't get you again." He tried to keep his voice confident, even, but he could feel Kenny trembling.

"It was bad, Dad."

Part of him wanted to explode out of that room. Join the

other agents. Find Ramos and kill him. Instead, he sat down in the chair and gripped Kenny's hand. "I know it was hard, but you survived it. You're safe now. I'm just so sorry. If I'd been there, this wouldn't have happened." He kept talking. "Soon as I get Ramos locked up, we'll go on a vacation. You and mom and me. Someplace warm. It'll be all right, Kenny."

Gradually the shaking stopped.

"Can you stay with me for a while?"

As much as he loved his son, it was all Tom could do to keep himself in that chair. "Sure." Tom squeezed his hand. "We're going to get these guys, Kenny. I promise you, we will."

Kenny closed his eyes. Tom sat, his body as tight as a clenched fist. He'd never let Ramos get away with this. Never.

And then he heard Cathy's voice in his head: *You can't even protect your son?* He gritted his teeth. Ramos was no longer his case, he was his career.

CHAPTER 5

ALEX CRAMER'S OFFICE STRUCK TOM as plush. The light-blue carpeting offset the FBI seal woven into the center. Red accents around the room repeated the theme. The wooden desk, though, is what really captured Tom's attention. Huge, made of walnut, the desk looked solid. Quite a contrast, Tom thought, to the battered gray metal desks the field agents used. But then, a good field agent didn't use the desk a whole lot anyway.

Cramer was standing behind the desk talking on the phone when Tom, Fitz, Jack, and Lee walked in. He wore a dark blue suit, a white shirt with blue stripes, and his FBI tie. He nodded toward the chairs, silently telling them to sit down, as he finished his conversation. He cradled the phone against his shoulder and fiddled with one gold cufflink. "Yes, sir, Senator, we'll see what we can do about it." He rolled his eyes as the men looked on. Sometimes being the Special Agent in Charge of the Washington, D.C. Field Office had its drawbacks. A Congress full of them.

He hung up the phone and came around the desk, extending his hand toward Tom. "Donovan? How's your son?"

"He'll be just fine, sir." Tom shook his hand. "He's a tough kid."

"What's the latest, Fitz?"

Fitz filled him in on the details. Tom only half-listened. He was too busy thinking about his game plan. He'd been working on it since he heard Kenny's story.

"Agent McRae took rock and soil samples from the

parking lot where Kenny was found and the street where he was abducted." Fitz nodded at Jack. "Tell him the rest."

"I did a little nighttime mission over in Alexandria. Found two of Ramos's vans on the street and I took soil samples from tires on all of them. We got 'em going down to the lab. Not sure if we'll have a match, but if we do, it'll give us a way forward."

Tom's eyes widened. When did Jack do that? While he was with Kenny? He silently thanked his partner.

"Tom," Cramer turned back to him, "since it appears Ramos is behind this assault, the Bureau's going to transfer you immediately. We've got several cities open. You want to give me your input?"

Tom's heart thumped. "Transfer?" He glanced at Jack.

"As soon as your son can travel."

Tom's mind raced. He hadn't anticipated this. "Sir, I don't want a transfer."

"That's not your option. Headquarters doesn't want to take chances. The Bureau can't guarantee your safety. So they're moving you."

"Wait." Tom felt his heart pounding. "We don't need to uproot my family. This is a personal vendetta. One man, Ramos, against me. As soon as we lock him up, it's over."

"And the rest of the gang?"

"They do what he wants. They're dope dealers, not the Mafia out to defend the family's pride. The problem is one guy. We take him out and that's it."

Cramer stood in front of his desk, leaning on it, his eyes narrowed. He crossed his arms.

Tom stood up, unable to sit any longer. "Look, Mr. Cramer, sir: No one knows Ramos better than me. You want Ramos arrested? I'm the best person for the job. And it's not just Ramos's gang. I've got fifteen other drug cases I'm dealing with, hot cases. I've been here eight years. I've got seven productive informants, and more convictions than any other agent in the office."

Cramer looked at Lee, who nodded.

Tom continued, "I don't want to leave all that just because one thug crosses the line. It'd be like, like running away."

Lee Burnett spoke. "It's true, Alex. Tom's a very effective

agent. And he's in the middle of a lot of big cases right now."

Cramer walked back toward the windows, tapping his hand against his leg. He turned to face Tom. "And your family?"

Tom sat down. "My son's in the middle of wrestling season. He's finishing his senior year. He's been accepted at Virginia Tech. He's not going to want to leave." *And your wife*, a voice screamed inside his head. *What about your wife?* Tom fought to ignore it.

Cramer leaned on his desk with both hands. "You really don't want to go."

"No, sir!"

Cramer shook his head. He blinked his eyes and took a deep breath, weighing his options. "I have no idea how I'm going to explain this to headquarters, but okay. You can stay."

Relief flooded Tom.

"But here's the deal: Your wife and son leave town until Ramos is locked up. Is there a place they can go?"

"Yes, sir." He'd find a place.

"Second, I want you off the street. You can help from the office but I don't want you out there where Ramos can get at you. I don't want you directly involved in the investigation. It's too personal. You be the consultant, help all you want, but let the others work the case. Don't handle any evidence. I don't want the case jeopardized. And I don't want you in danger. Got it? Stay off the street."

"Yes, sir. Thank you, sir."

Everyone stood up to leave.

"Oh, and Tom," Cramer added, "take the rest of the week off. Spend the time with your family, okay? And talk to an employee assistance counselor."

"Yes, sir," Tom said, shaking Cramer's hand. "Thank you, sir."

✝ ✝ ✝

The men all left Cramer's office together. They were waiting for the elevator when Tom walked away from the group. "I'll see you," Tom said with a wave, and he disappeared into the stairwell.

Fitz, Lee, and Jack stopped talking and watched Tom,

their minds turning like twin wheels on a paddleboat.

"Yeah, he'll take the week off," Lee said.

"I'm sure he's going to talk to a counselor right now," Jack added. "That's why he was in such a hurry."

Fitz shook his head. "Jack, why don't you stick close to Tom for a while?"

"My thoughts exactly," said Jack, and he took off after Tom.

✞ ✞ ✞

The wind was whipping up whitecaps on the Potomac River as Tom crossed the 14th Street Bridge into Virginia. A jet roared overhead on its way out of National. Eleven years before, in 1982, a similar jet, weighed down by ice, had slammed into the bridge on takeoff. More than seventy people were killed, including some in cars. That was one miserable January day.

He felt like he'd just avoided a close call in Cramer's office.

No way did he want a transfer. No way. Tom zipped down I-395, past the Pentagon and the Army-Navy Country Club, took the exit for Glebe Road and headed east. A little side trip wouldn't hurt.

He parked the car in north Alexandria, and walked down Mount Vernon Avenue toward a Mexican restaurant. A guy who hung out there always seemed to have something for him. The air was cold, but he was used to it. Growing up in Boston did that to you. The sun felt warm on his back. Suddenly, he sensed someone just over his left shoulder.

"I could've done you five times since you left your car," Jack said.

Tom turned.

"You lost, Tom?"

"No, why?"

"I thought you were s'posed to be home, in Fairfax. This is Alexandria."

Tom started walking again. "You followed me?"

"Yeah, it was easy. You were the one making the stupid moves."

A bitter gust of wind buffeted Tom. He hunched his shoulders against the cold.

"We had a cow like you once," Jack continued. "Never

could find her way home. She was always just one hill over from where she was supposed to be. Momma usually sent me to find her. The trouble is, in the mountains, being one hill over can get you killed."

"We're not in the mountains, Jack."

"That cow was not that smart."

Tom stopped, squinting in the bright sun. The flag on the post office across the street snapped loudly in the wind, its pulley clanging against the metal pole. "Look," Tom said, "this is my case. Ramos has made it real personal. And I can't just sit it out, I've got to make it happen. That means working the street."

"And Cramer? All that stuff he said about taking the week off and staying off the street and not putting yourself in danger? Working from the office? You think he'd like it if he saw you right now?"

Tom rolled those thoughts over in his mind. "I've got to do it, Jack." Tom shook his head. "This one time, I'd rather beg for forgiveness than ask for permission."

"One time?"

Tom turned and walked on. Then he stopped, and looked back at Jack, shading his eyes with his hand. "You going to turn me in?"

Jack sighed. He walked up to Tom and lowered his voice. "What good would that do? Cramer'd get mad and lift your creds and your gun. You'd get another gun, and then be out here like a common criminal. Something would happen between you and Ramos and you're the one they'd prosecute." He shook his head. "No, Tom, I won't turn you in. But tell me what you're doing. At least let me cover your back!"

Tom didn't answer.

Jack squared off with him, his wise brown eyes focused right on Tom. "Look, Kenny needs you alive. After what they did to him, having Ramos kill you would really mess him up."

"Ramos isn't going to kill me."

"And Ramos wouldn't hurt the son of a fed, either, Tom. We both said that. But there's a boy lying up in Fairfax whose face has been rearranged and who'll have scars for the rest of his life to prove we were wrong."

Tom looked down at the sidewalk and kicked a small rock with the side of his shoe, tapping it toward Jack.

"You trying to distract me with a rock?" Jack grinned, then got serious again. "Tom, you don't want to mess this up. You don't want Ramos to get off on some technicality. I'll help you keep it clean."

Reason and emotion vied for control. Finally Tom spoke. "Okay, Jack. You're right."

"We had to buy a bell for the cow."

Tom smiled. "You're in the city now, boy. We use beepers."

CHAPTER 6

CATHY SAT NEXT TO HER only child, listening to him breathe, still shaken by his injuries. Anger and fear had formed a toxic mix in her soul and naturally her fury flowed toward just one person.

She had been a college student, an English major at UMass, when Tom Donovan had stolen her heart. He was four years older than she, and already in line to be an agent. Compared to the pot-smoking, directionless hippies that populated the campus in 1972, Tom seemed sharp, organized, driven, and caring. Now she saw him as compulsive and obsessive, hyper-focused on his job, indifferent toward her.

And look what he'd brought into her life.

Her son blinked his eyes, breaking her thoughts.

He stared at the ceiling, squeezed his eyes shut again, and re-opened them. Then he turned toward her, wincing as he did. "Mom?"

Cathy touched his arm. "How are you?"

"Okay. Dizzy." He tried to sit up.

"That may be the painkillers."

"Can I have a drink?"

"Of course." Cathy handed him the cup of ice water at his bedside.

Kenny drank deeply, then handed the cup back. "Bet you were scared," he said, settling back in the bed.

She nodded. "I was."

"I'm sorry."

She shook her head. "Not your fault." Her blue eyes

ranged over his face, cataloging every bruise, every cut. "Would you tell me about it?"

He hesitated.

"I need to know," she asserted, reading his thoughts.

He ran his tongue over the sharp stitches in his lip, and then told her what had happened.

She couldn't help it—by the end, she was trembling. Now at least the nameless, shapeless fear that had scraped her heart on a metal grater had been expressed in words. "Were you scared?" she asked.

He nodded. "Terrified. Why would they think they could intimidate Dad?"

Cathy reacted viscerally, and opened her mouth to retort. Then she thought better of it. She'd let him have his hero. He'd realize the truth about Tom sooner or later. She patted his arm. "Keep talking about it, Kenny. Tell the story over and over, as many times as you need to. It'll diffuse the power of it, and help you work through the feelings. It's when you try to bury the feelings that they start to eat you alive."

"Thanks, Mom." He shifted his position in the bed. "Hey, do I have any clothes? When are they letting me out of here? I've got a match in, like three days."

Wrestling! How could he be thinking of that? Cathy took a deep breath, started to tell him he wouldn't be wrestling any time soon, then chickened out. Let the doctor tell him. Or Tom. "We'll have to ask, Kenny," she responded. "We'll just have to ask."

✝ ✝ ✝

Tom walked down the hospital corridor, his mind devising Plans C, D, E, and F. The trip to Alexandria had been a dead end. Jack had gone home to get some sleep. Tom had promised him he was just coming to see Kenny, then he'd go home himself.

He rounded a corner, and saw Cathy sitting in a chair in the hallway, within sight of the officer outside Kenny's room. Her head was back, her eyes closed. She had on jeans and a chambray shirt with a burgundy turtleneck underneath, and for a minute he saw in her the college girl he had taken out for bacon pizza in the days before anyone cared about cholesterol.

He walked over to her, touched her arm lightly, and she opened her eyes. He started to kiss her gently on the cheek, then thought better of it. "It's just me, Cathy. How are you doing?" he asked, squatting down.

"Oh, Tom," she said, surprised. For a moment, the animosity was missing from her voice. For a moment.

Cathy sat up and looked around. "What's going on?"

"I finished up downtown," Tom said. "How's Kenny doing?"

"He's sleeping. I moved out here for a change of scene."

Tom nodded. Glancing around first to be sure they were alone, he said, "Listen, Cathy, Alex Cramer wants me to send you and Kenny somewhere safe until we get Ramos locked up."

"Of course. I'd planned on it."

Tom fought to keep the surprise off of his face. She'd already planned to leave? With Kenny? He forced himself to keep his voice even. "It shouldn't be for long, just until we get enough on Ramos to arrest him."

"Which could be forever. You don't have any physical evidence on him, right? Nothing to positively link him to what happened to Kenny?"

"Well, that's true, but …"

Cathy pressed her lips together. She waved her hand. "We're not staying here."

He cleared his throat. "Where'd you like to go? I'll set it up."

"It's all set. We'll go to Trisha's. She has a big house …"

"A big, empty house." Tom didn't think much of his wife's sister.

"Trisha has a big house," Cathy persisted, "and she'll let us come. I've called her."

She'd called Trisha already? Tom fought frustration.

Cathy lifted her chin. "Kenny's already started about wrestling."

"Wrestling?"

"You need to tell him it's not happening. Not even for the districts."

"When's that?"

"A little over three weeks."

"And you don't think …"

"Don't be ridiculous!" Cathy adjusted her position. "He won't be here anyway. I just didn't want to tell him. That's your job, Tom. This is your mess. You fix it."

✟ ✟ ✟

The doctors wanted Kenny to spend one more night in the hospital, so Tom stayed with him. The next morning, Cathy showed up around eight, and Tom headed into D.C. Clouds had slipped over the mountains in the night. It looked like it might rain.

Tom started seeing brake lights as he approached the perennial traffic jam at the mixing bowl at Springfield. He flipped on the radio, listened to stories of two murders and one congressional hearing, and flipped it back off. The Paul Simon song, "Fifty Ways to Leave Your Lover," came to his mind and he thought, there must be fifty ways to catch a bad guy. He just had to come up with them.

First, he thought, you get in Ramos's face, let him know you're not going away, that what he did to Kenny had the exact opposite effect of what he wanted. Second, you press Camacho until he begs for a deal. Third, you go after Ramos's money—that's what most of this was about anyway. Ramos had gotten a taste of the big money to be made in drugs.

Strategies came to Tom one after another like automatic weapon fire and he listed them on the notepad that he kept on the front passenger seat, keeping one eye on the stop-and-go traffic. Finally, the bottleneck broke loose. He made it to the office, parked his car, and went upstairs. His supervisor, Lee Burnett, caught him coming in the door.

"Hey, Tom. Did you hear?"

"What?"

"Big ruckus at the jail last night. Camacho got caught up in it."

Tom's stomach clenched. "Camacho?" Their best chance to get Ramos?

"He's dead."

"Dead?" A rush of anger coursed through Tom and he swore. "That was no accident." He swore again. "There is nothing Ramos won't do!"

Lee hesitated. "We don't know that ..."

"It was Ramos. I guarantee it!"

✟ ✟ ✟

Tom pulled up to his house, automatically trying to predict what he'd find inside. The marked police car outside told him Cathy had brought Kenny home from the hospital. Jack's car occupied the driveway. When he entered the house, his partner was sitting on the couch in the family room.

"Well, Tom. Been out have you?" Jack said. He wore tan cargo pants and a plaid shirt and had his feet propped up on the coffee table. He juggled a rock in his hand. "Weren't we s'posed to stick together?" He sat up and put the rock down.

"Y'know, Jack, you'd make a good mother." Tom pulled off his parka, but left his gun on his belt. He felt better having it close at hand. "I just ran into the office for a minute."

"Lee paged me. You do that again and I'm putting you on restriction."

"Sure, Mom." Tom shifted his weight. "I guess he also told you about Camacho."

"Yes. Tough break."

"Unbelievable." Tom looked around. "Cathy in the kitchen?"

"Upstairs."

"Okay. I'm just going upstairs. In my own house. To see my own wife. That okay with you, Mom?"

"I guess so. Just don't be gone long. And be careful," Jack said in a falsetto voice.

Tom went out to the foyer, and hung up his coat. Next to the closet, on the wall, hung a control panel for a new intrusion alarm system, installed by the Bureau.

Tom took the stairs two at a time. Passing Kenny's room, he looked in. The kid looked asleep. Tom went on back to his bedroom. He could hear Cathy moving around.

"Hey, Cath." Tom's stomach tightened as he surveyed the scene. Drawers and closets were thrown open. Cathy was pulling things out of her dresser and sorting them into boxes that sat on the bed. The cherry four-poster bed was full of stuff. "Everything all set?"

"Yes," Cathy's voice sounded crisp as an apple. "Trish is expecting us Monday. I told her I'd ship our clothes so it wouldn't be obvious that we were leaving town."

"You shouldn't have to be gone long," Tom suggested.

She didn't answer him. Tom ran his index finger down the edge of the flap of one of the boxes. "You're taking an awful lot of stuff."

"I just want to be prepared."

Prepared for what? Tom thought. Eternity? "Did you tell Kenny?"

She stopped. Then her eyes shifted behind him and Tom turned to see what she was looking at.

"Tell me what? What's going on?" Kenny stood in the doorway. He had on a T-shirt and gray sweatpants, and he had a tissue in his hand. His eyes looked tired.

"Oh, hi, Kenny. I thought you were asleep. Your mom and I were just talking. You two are going to your Aunt Trisha's for a while." Tom's stomach quivered.

"Aunt Trisha's? Why?"

Cathy moved over from the dresser to where she could see Kenny better. "It's not safe for you here, Kenny, not as long as those men are out there. So you and I are leaving. Aunt Trisha has plenty of room and she said we can stay there as long as we want."

Tom could see the black and blue skin of Kenny's cheek moving as he flexed his jaw.

"I don't want to go."

"It's just for a while," Tom said. "Just 'til we get Ramos locked up."

Kenny wiped the saliva from the corner of his mouth with the tissue. The stitches looked like black wire. "That could be months. What do you have on him? Nothing, right?"

Tom looked down.

Cathy picked up a shirt from the bed and began to fold it. "You'll be safe at Trish's. We'll work out something with the school so you can get your diploma." She looked back at Kenny and smiled. "It's all fixed. Trisha said she's looking forward to it. And Tracy will be there, too!"

"I'm not going." His words dropped like a stone off a bridge, sending almost tangible ripples through the room.

"What?"

"I'm not going."

"You don't have a choice. You have to go!"

"Oh yes, I do have a choice, Mom. And I'm not going!"

Whoa. Tom hadn't expected this. He looked at his wife and his son. Cathy's eyes were flashing with anger, but Kenny's back was up, too.

Kenny's eyes remained focused on his mom. "This is my senior year. The District meet is in three weeks. I've got four months of school left to be with friends I've had for eight years. I'm not leaving all that because of some jerk gang!"

"They're not just some jerk gang, Kenny. Look what they did to you! Now they've threatened to kill you."

"I know who they are, Mom. Better than you. And I'm not running from them." He looked at Tom, then back at Cathy. "They held me hostage for forty minutes. I'm not letting them hold me hostage for the next four months. No way." Kenny hit the doorjamb with his fist.

"Kenny, don't be bullheaded," Cathy said, almost shouting. "You can't possibly think you can stay here. Those men could come after you again. And who knows what they'll do the next time?" She looked at Tom, who avoided her eyes. "Tom, tell him!"

"Did anyone think to ask me? Before you made all these plans for my life? Did you think to ask what I'd like?" Kenny exploded

"Look, son. Your mom's right." A prickly feeling ran up the back of Tom's neck as he reluctantly waded into the fray. "It's really best if you get out of town. As a matter of fact, the Bureau wanted to transfer me." Tom scratched his head. "I talked them out of it. But Cramer is insisting that you and Mom leave, until we get Ramos."

"I don't work for the Bureau, Dad. They can't tell me where to live. They don't own me." Kenny's face was red and his hand trembled as he wiped his mouth again.

"Kenny, you're not staying here," Cathy said, "and that's final!"

Tom couldn't remember the last time he heard Cathy yell at Kenny.

"I'm eighteen, Mom. I can stay anywhere I want."

Tom stepped in. "Hold on, Kenny. Let's just cool down." He moved toward him. Kenny's eyes were still on Cathy. "Kenny, stop. Try to see where your Mom is coming from. She's concerned about you, that's all. Me, too."

"You think about it, Dad, as long as you want," Kenny snapped. "I'm not going anywhere. I'm going to wrestle in three weeks. And I'm going to finish my senior year." He dabbed at the saliva trickling from his mouth. "You don't want me here, fine, I'll go to a friend's. Or Terry McDaniel's. But there's no way, no possible way, I'm going to Pennsylvania!" He glared at both of them, turned and left the room.

Tom shook his head. He hadn't seen that temper in a long time. He hadn't expected it. Wow.

Cathy glared at him. "This is your fault!"

CHAPTER 7

TOM WAS STILL SHAKING HIS head when he left the bedroom. He was surprised to see Kenny standing right outside the door, leaning against the wall. His face was drawn and pale, his right hand was holding his chest. Tom could hear his breath coming in short, shallow gasps.

"What is it?" Tom asked.

"My rib."

"Can you make it to your room or do you want to lie down here?"

Kenny nodded toward the room.

Tom put his arm around Kenny's waist and together they moved toward the room. They were almost to the bed when Kenny suddenly stopped, and Tom saw his lip turn white as he bit down on it.

"If you can make one more step, I can get you into bed."

Kenny nodded and took the step, and Tom eased him gently onto the bed. He could see Kenny's eyes watering from pain. "Just move around until the pain lets up. You've got something out of place."

Kenny turned to the left, then over to the right, and sighed when the pain suddenly dissipated. Tom watched him. The kid had been through a lot. "You going to be okay now?"

"Yeah. Thanks, Dad."

"I'll come up and check on you later."

"Dad?"

"Yes."

"I'm not going to Trisha's. Don't try to make me. Please."

"Okay, son. We'll talk later."

✤ ✤ ✤

Jack was still sitting in the family room when Tom walked in. He lowered the *Sports Illustrated* in his hand. "Sounds like somebody tried to light the stove with gasoline."

"That kid can be so stubborn!" Tom dropped onto the couch next to Jack.

"The apple does not fall far from the tree."

Tom took a playful swing at him and Jack defended himself with the magazine.

Cathy came in the room. "Tom, you've got to do something."

"I know, I know." Tom sighed.

"What's his problem?" Jack said.

Tom picked up a paper clip off the coffee table and began straightening it. "He doesn't want to go away. He wants to be here to wrestle in three weeks. Plus, he doesn't want to miss the rest of the school year. He says it would be like running away."

"It's ridiculous ..."

"It's not ridiculous, Cathy," Tom said. "He doesn't want to feel like a wimp. And school is important to him."

"Teach him to be macho some other time, Tom. We're not talking about a high school bully. It's a drug gang. *Your* drug gang." Cathy sat down in the chair, and pulled her knees up to her chest. "Why does he have to be so bullheaded? Anyone can see the danger!"

"Wait a minute." Jack leaned forward. "Aren't you being a little rough on the boy? All he's saying is he's not going to let these thugs ruin his life, which to him is wrestling and school." He looked at Tom. "Sounds pretty gutsy to me."

Tom shrugged. In his heart, he agreed.

"It's stupid!" said Cathy. She abruptly got up and left the room.

Tom blew out a breath and leaned back on the couch. How was he going to work this out? The Bureau and Cathy were insisting Kenny leave. Kenny was intent on staying. He could see Kenny's point but still, what a mess. The snakes in his belly were at it again.

Jack got up and walked around the room, his hands on his hips. He went over to the window and pulled the curtain back, looked outside, then turned back and faced Tom.

"What if Kenny leaves here but stays in state? What if he gets away from Ramos, but still stays close enough to wrestle and do the other stuff he wants?"

Tom looked up. Jack was rubbing his chin. "What are you thinking of?"

"You remember my brother, J.D.?"

"In Fredericksburg?"

"Spotsylvania. Sixty miles and a world away, but still in Virginia."

"Yeah?"

"He's a teacher at a high school. Kenny could stay with him, work out with the wrestling team, even go to classes there if he needed to. And Ramos'd never look for him there."

"Would J.D. take him?"

"I don't know. I could ask. He's got three kids of his own. What's one more?"

"That just might work!" Tom scratched his head. "He might have to get special permission to wrestle in the districts. But hey, we can try!"

Jack stood up. "I'll go call J.D. You talk to Cathy. See what she says. If it looks good, you can try it on Kenny."

"You know, Jack, now and then you come up with a good idea."

"I'm glad you noticed." He grinned. "By the way, we still on for the game on Sunday?"

"Why don't you just cancel your cable? You're here all the time anyway."

"I was plannin' on it. Thanks."

✞ ✞ ✞

As Tom stood at the kitchen counter he could hear the pre-game chatter. The NFL AFC Championship game was about to begin. His mind went back to Friday. He had wanted to go into the office, but Jack had talked him into going to the county police headquarters to see a new cop, an expert on Salvadorans, who'd just come from Houston. Tom thought the whole thing was a waste of time. Angel Ramos was not a typical Salvadoran refugee. He'd been in the U.S. for twenty years. So Tom had sat fidgeting while Jack asked one irrelevant question after another, and as they were walking out to the car, he had given Jack grief for blowing the afternoon.

"Hey, I'm sorry," Jack had responded. "Even good dogs get on the wrong trail now and then."

Tom took two tall glasses out of the cabinet, and filled them with ice. Then he opened a two-liter bottle of Coke and poured it into the glasses. He watched the ice snap and crack, little spritzes of liquid popping like fireworks. Tom rummaged in the fridge until he found the maraschino cherries, put two in each glass, and added a little cherry juice. He stirred each one, grabbed both glasses and a bag of potato chips, and headed for the family room.

But as he turned to leave, Cathy came into the kitchen. She wore jeans and a soft yellow sweater. She had just showered, and he could smell her shampoo, and for the first time he noticed a wisp of gray in her hair, right at her temple. It was attractive to him, an ornament, like a fine silver earring.

"Hey, Cathy!" he said.

"I'm going over to Rachel's for a while."

Rachel. Her friend down the street. Tom barely knew her. "All right. Everything okay?"

"Well, I know you and Kenny and Jack are going to be watching the game, and I thought I'd just go talk."

"Fine. Fine. I'll be here, so you take the deputy with you."

"If you think that's necessary."

"I'd feel better."

"Okay." She cocked her head. "I called your mother."

Tom felt his face flush.

"She needs to know these things, Tom. She cares about her grandson. And you."

Tom nodded. "Thanks."

"I'll be back later."

He wanted to touch her, to put his arms around her and kiss her goodbye, but his hands were full and before he could move, she turned and walked away. He watched her go, a little pang corkscrewing into his heart. "Bye, Cathy," he said, but she must not have heard him.

CHAPTER 8

RACHEL LIVED IN A TWO-story, Southern colonial, complete with tall white pillars that went from the concrete porch to the very top of the house. Inside, the decor was simple: American country. Wood crafts and baskets were everywhere, holding bunnies and bears and placid-looking Holsteins. The walls were covered with country landscapes and wildlife prints, and some of Rachel's own needlework. In the foyer was a country pine table that held an old wooden bread bowl and a spatterware milk jug filled with dried flowers. Cathy and Rachel had found the table in a junk shop on one of their antiquing jaunts.

Rachel opened the door as Cathy and the deputy approached, before they even had a chance to ring the doorbell.

"Come on in!" Rachel said. She was wearing navy slacks and a long-sleeved chambray shirt. Her honey blond hair was pulled back by barrettes, and she wore the ceramic sheep earrings she and Cathy had found in a shop in Occoquan.

Cathy and the deputy walked into the house. Rachel took their coats.

"We're going to talk in the family room," Rachel said to the deputy. "Why don't you come back to the kitchen? There's coffee there, and a TV, so you can watch the game if you want."

While Rachel ushered the deputy back to the kitchen, Cathy went on into the family room. She paused at the stone fireplace. On the mantel, Rachel always set up a winter scene of a small village. There were miniature sand-cast houses and shops, and a church. There were little trees and gas streetlights. And there were tiny people walking around, ice skating on the mirror-pond or looking in shop windows. Perfect little people. Perfect little town.

Rachel came into the room with a tray of tea which she had made for the two of them. Tea and sympathy. A good combination.

"So how's Kenny?" Rachel asked as they took their places on the couch.

"Kenny's fine. Really good, in fact. He's up and around more now. He's really anxious to start working out again, but that's got to wait. He's very impatient."

"But what a good sign, that he wants to get on with his life!" said Rachel. "What does the doctor say?"

"He says he can start limited workouts after his appointment on Wednesday."

Rachel stirred a packet of sweetener into her tea. She asked about his injuries, and about the progress in the investigation. Then she looked at Cathy. "And how are you, Cathy? How are you doing?"

There was a long pause.

"Rachel," Cathy finally said, "I'm thinking about leaving Tom."

There. The words were out. Let them float around, shape themselves, gain their own form and direction. Cathy was glad. The words were out.

"Leaving Tom? You mean going up to your sister's, right?" Rachel asked, surprised.

Cathy put down her teacup. "No. I mean for good." She put her elbows on her knees and rested her chin in her hands.

"Why?" Rachel asked.

"I just don't feel anything for him anymore, Rachel. Well, unless I'm angry. But most of the time, it's like I'm dead inside."

"How long have you felt this way?"

Cathy shrugged. "I'm not really sure. But seeing my son bruised and battered ..." She hesitated as tears began to flow. "It's pushed me over the edge." She took the tissue Rachel offered and wiped her nose. "I don't know if I can take it anymore."

"Take … ?"

"The violence. The guns. My husband never being at home. My son in danger."

"Have you talked to Tom about this?"

Cathy shrugged "Nothing ever really changes."

Rachel put her cup down and sat back. "Men can be pretty dense. Does he know how serious this is? Have you told him you're thinking of leaving?" she said softly.

"No. He knows I'm going to my sister's. He doesn't know I'm planning to stay."

"Cathy, I don't know what to say. You've caught me by surprise."

Cathy felt like she was hovering on a precipice. She changed the subject, as if she were afraid to take the leap, or having Rachel talk her out of it. "Tell me, Rachel, how's Jen doing at school?" Jennifer was a college freshman.

That safe subject led to another. Two hours and two cups of tea later, they circled back.

"I hope you can relax up in Pennsylvania," Rachel said. "I assume the library's letting you take some time off?"

"Well, it's not like I'm essential personnel!" Cathy got up and went over to the mantel. She turned and looked back at Rachel. "It's crazy. I'm 43 years old, and what do I have to show for it? For over twenty years I've been someone's wife and someone's mother and for what? I took that little, part-time library job so I'd have time for the guys, but now, I'm alone all the time. And I'm unhappy. I feel like I've wasted my life!"

"Being a wife and mother is not a waste."

Cathy shrugged. "The guys don't care." She walked back to the couch. "I need to make some changes," she said finally. "I need to get away—away from Tom, away from the guns and the beepers and the bravado. I need to find out if there's any 'me' left."

"Oh, Cathy." Rachel suddenly sounded tired. "I can understand why you feel like getting away. I can even understand why you feel so empty. But," she hesitated, "do you want my opinion?"

Cathy thought for a minute. Finally she nodded.

"Go if you have to, Cathy. Get away. Relax. Think about your life. Decide to make some changes, maybe decide to go back to school and finish your master's. But don't be too quick to divorce Tom. You've got too much invested in him to throw it away. Too many years, too many memories. If you walk away now, you'll be walking away from an important part of yourself, and the ripping and shredding will tear you apart. Not to mention Tom. And not to mention Kenny."

"You don't know what it's like."

"No, I don't. And all I'm saying is I'd hate to see you throw away something valuable—your marriage— just because you're not seeing it that way right now."

Cathy stood up to leave. "Thanks, Rachel. I appreciate your concern. I'll think about what you said." She hugged her friend goodbye. She'd miss her.

☦ ☦ ☦

That night in bed, Tom could see she was still awake, staring at the ceiling in fact. The digital clock said 11:25. In a little more than six hours, she'd be on the train, headed north. This was the last time he would sleep with her for who knows how long. Tom sighed deeply. This was wrong.

At least the situation with Kenny had been resolved. Their son had come to them right before bed, and said he would agree to go to J.D.'s, provided he could come back and wrestle in three weeks. Tom thought that shouldn't be a problem. Ramos should be in the can by then.

Tom stared at the ceiling for a while, then turned on his side and raised himself on one elbow. Moonlight streamed in the window, highlighting the left side of Cathy's face. He could see her long, dark lashes, and the whites of her eyes, and he wanted to kiss her, on the mouth, but instead he gingerly brushed a lock of hair off her forehead, traced the line of her jaw with one finger, and let his hand come to rest gently on her shoulder.

He took a breath and began. "I'm really sorry, Cathy, about all this."

No response.

"I'm sorry Kenny got hurt. And I'm sorry you have to leave. I'm going to miss you."

She looked toward the window.

"The house is going to seem empty without you."

She turned to him. "It's empty all the time. You're just never here to notice."

"I'm sorry."

"Sorry doesn't help a whole lot, Tom. It doesn't fill your seat at the dinner table. It doesn't give me any companionship. And it certainly doesn't change what they did to our son."

"Cathy, I don't know what to say to you."

"There's nothing you can say. I'm sick of the whole mess. I'm sick of you being gone all the time. I'm sick of the guns. I'm sick of the macho attitude. I'm sick of drug dealers and kidnappers and seeing my son bruised and beaten because of you!"

"That's a little harsh, isn't it?"

"Oh, is it, Tom? You are the reason they beat up Kenny. You can't dispute that." She looked away again and Tom saw her blink back tears. They looked like crystalline drops in the moonlight.

"You know, Tom, most of my friends actually do things with their husbands. They go to plays or out to the movies. They work together around the house. They even have dinner as a family every night."

"I don't have a job I can just leave at five o'clock, Cathy."

"You're right. You have a job that is with you twenty-four hours a day. In fact, it's so much a part of you I can't separate you from the job. You work until ten or eleven every night, expecting me to sit here by myself while you track down just one more lead, or sit in some smoky bar with an informant that sees more of you than I do. How can you do that? How can you just ignore me like that? And Kenny?"

He had no answer.

"And even when you are here, Tom, you're not really here. I'll be in the middle of telling you something, and I'll see your eyes drift. Before I know it, you're on the phone to one of your buddies because you just put two and two together and it equaled the name of some suspect. And I say to myself, why am I here?" She turned back and looked at him. "I hate it, Tom. I hate your job, I hate the Bureau. And sometimes I'm afraid I'm even beginning to hate you."

"Cathy, I don't know how else to do my job. Drug gangs don't operate on a forty-hour week. You knew what I wanted to do. You knew you weren't marrying a bureaucrat."

"But I had no idea I was marrying someone who was so totally self-centered, so obsessed with his own life that he'd make no room for me."

That did it. His anger ignited. Tom rolled over onto his back. Self-centered, he thought? Really?

"I don't understand you, Cathy. I'm not a drunk. I've never been unfaithful to you. I don't abuse you. I do my best to be a good father, a good provider. What more do you want?"

"I want a husband who will relate to me." She paused. "I can get about three inches into your soul before I hit The Wall. You've shoved all your deep feelings, all your passion, behind this ... wall. The only thing you let out is your anger. Everything else about you is untouchable, sealed away behind the bravado, the 'I can handle it' attitude. You don't let me get close to you. I hate surface relationships, Tom. I hate being alone all the time. I hate the guns. And I hate violence."

"So, let's see. You hate everything about me, and everything about my job. Is anything else bothering you, Cathy? Or is that it?" Bitterness edged his voice.

"That's all, Tom. Just that." She turned away from him.

He could have responded but chose not to. He sighed heavily, exasperated.

They were both silent for a long time. She was trying to hide her tears, but he could hear by the pattern of her breathing that she was crying. His stomach felt alive with snakes. He didn't want to lose her. He really didn't want to lose her.

"Look, Cathy," he said finally. "As soon as Ramos is locked up I'll ... I'll see about a transfer. To Headquarters." Oh, how he would hate being a bureaucrat! He thought again. "Or the Academy. To something with more normal hours, anyway."

She reached toward the night table, got a tissue, and blew her nose. He didn't wait for her to respond. He pulled her back against his chest. She felt stiff next to him.

"I love you," he said. "I really do. And I don't want to lose you."

"You're a little late, Tom. Years late."

☥ ☥ ☥

Low, thick clouds hung over the area in a sullen clump, coloring the day gray and damp.

Cathy had left that morning on the early Amtrak Metroliner. Tom didn't want her to drive, didn't want any chance she'd be followed. Brenda Jones, an agent in Tom's office, had volunteered to ride the train with her to Philadelphia. They would look like two anonymous women on an excursion.

Now that she had gone, Tom knew his job: Get Ramos in so he could bring Cathy back and fix the problems in their marriage. And he was determined to do it.

Tom swung into the concrete parking garage, locked up the car, and took the elevator up to the third floor. He went straight to the conference room where the squad investigating Kenny's abduction and assault was meeting at eight thirty.

"Okay, ladies and gentlemen," said Fitz. "Where are we?" He took off his half-glasses, put down a file, and looked over the group.

There were twelve agents seated around the walnut table. Notepads and file folders were everywhere. The room smelled like fresh coffee and aftershave.

Tom sat next to Jack near the end of the table. He restlessly drummed his thumb against his leg, and silently assessed the strengths and weaknesses of the agents in the room.

"Let's start with the crime scene. Any leads from the place he was found?" Fitz looked down the table.

A young agent, Amanda Whittaker, spoke up. "We've done a door-to-door of the whole neighborhood. No one saw or heard anything, Fitz. Everyone was inside."

"And the place where they grabbed him?"

"Nothing definitive. We've also done a door-to-door there. We found the exact place he was abducted. We found a pin from Kenny's letter jacket and some disturbance in the snow.

Nothing we can even get a clear print from. And we can't put a vehicle there."

"And no one saw any strange cars in the neighborhood in the days prior?"

"No, sir."

"Vehicles—any ID on the van they used?" Fitz asked.

Bill Adams, the agent across from Tom, spoke up. "Kenny remembers being put in a van, uncarpeted, possibly a Chevy by the sound of the engine." Adams tapped his pencil on the table. "Teenage boys sometimes pick up on details like that." He glanced down at the table. "Ramos owns three vans, registered to his construction company. One is a Chevy. We took a sample of dirt from the tires, right, Jack?"

"The lab couldn't make a significant match," Jack said. "They found common gravel and dirt, not enough to suggest a link between any of the vans and either the two site where Kenny was abducted or where he was found. A botanist is looking at the samples now to see if anything clicks."

Adams picked it up again. "We're hoping maybe the lab will come up with a paint chip off Kenny's clothes. Even having a color would help."

"How about those kids at that meeting?" Tom asked.

"Nothing there, Tom," Amanda Whittaker responded. "We checked the whole list you gave us. They're just normal, suburban high school kids. Even your son didn't think they were involved."

Tom fought to keep his mouth shut.

Fitz looked down at the file in front of him, pursing his lips. "The question remains, how did Ramos know where Kenny would be?"

"That group, the Fairfax Fellowship of Athletes, is open about where its meeting are going to be. There are flyers posted all over the school," Amanda said. "All Ramos had to know was that Kenny was part of that group. And that wouldn't be hard: Tom's son is one of the officers."

Fitz nodded. Tom looked unconvinced.

Someone coughed. Fitz looked up. "What's the status on the wiretap authorization on Ramos?"

"It's up at Headquarters, Fitz. They're looking it over. But the Principal Legal Advisor doesn't think we have probable cause. So as of now, it's going nowhere."

"I'd sure like to tap his phone. We'll just have to come up with something else." Fitz looked around. "How's the surveillance going?"

Tom's mind started to wander. Everyone seemed to be making so little progress. His eyes scanned the light blue walls of the room, stopping at the bulletin board where over three hundred shoulder patches of different law enforcement agencies were displayed. All kinds of cops, all putting their lives on the line trying to make a difference, trying to stop the bad guys and make their communities safer. And not getting very much support from anyone. His eyes skimmed over the place names on the patches, until he came to the one from Boston, then looked away quickly and tuned back in to the meeting.

"How did the interview with Ramos go on Friday, Caryn?" Caryn Wheeler had been at WFO just six months.

Tom looked at Jack. So that's why Jack had insisted on that wild goose chase on Friday! Just to get him out of the office. Jack grinned and shrugged.

"Ramos has an alibi," she said. "He attended a Latino community party at the big church there on Trembley Street that night. The party took place between seven and eleven. Many witnesses saw him there, including the priest."

"Was he there the whole time?" Fitz asked.

Caryn looked at her notes. "He received a beeper message around nine, left to make a phone call, and got back a few minutes later."

"*Around* nine?" Tom asked. "Can you get more specific?"

"People didn't remember."

"Yeah, I'll bet they don't remember." Tom leaned forward.

Fitz interrupted. "Caryn, when did Ramos leave for the night?"

"Ten forty-five, he says. He went home with a woman. She agrees he spent all night with her."

"Who's the woman?" said Tom.

"Maria Aguilera, sister of Luis."

Fitz nodded and made a note.

Tom jumped back in. "How far is that church from the elementary school?"

"Oh, I don't know. I'm guessing, half an hour, at least."

"What was the traffic like that night? When was the last time he was definitively seen? Could they have beeped him when they had Kenny? Could he have driven there and back by ten?"

"They said he was gone for a few minutes."

"How do they define 'few'?" Tom tapped his pen on the table. "We need details, Caryn, details on the period from nine to ten Tuesday! Where was Ramos every minute? And where was his knife?" Tom's face felt hot. He knew he should be quiet. He opened his mouth to say more but Fitz stopped him.

"Caryn, did you do a polygraph?" Fitz asked.

"Ramos refused."

"Okay. You did well. Please continue to develop those timeline details for the period between nine and ten. And Tom's right—check the traffic reports. See if Ramos could have made it to the elementary school and back."

Tom thought his head would explode. "Fitz," he said. "Excuse me. I want everyone to see this." He held up a computer printout with just a few words near the top. "This is Ramos's rap sheet." He pointed to the words. "One minor traffic violation. I don't know about anyone else here, but I'm getting sick of this guy weaseling out from under stuff."

"You're right, Tom. It's time to get him. Now where do we go from here?" Fitz looked around. "Everyone who has work in progress, keep going at it. Any of you that are dead-ended, I think it's time to work on the gang members. We know a bunch of them were there. Who should we target?"

"Who wasn't at the church on Tuesday night?"

Caryn looked at her list. "Luis, Edmundo, Ramos's younger brother, Pablo ..."

A young, dark-haired agent spoke up. "There's a possibility."

"No good," said Tom. "For three reasons. One, you won't get him to flip. Pablo worships Ramos. Two, he's too young. He's only eighteen. He won't stand up under the pressure. Three, it'd be like throwing a match on gasoline. You start screwing with Ramos's little brother and he'll institute a scorched earth policy that'll wipe out everyone and everything that could help us."

"Well, who then, Tom? Who do you suggest?"

"Go for Edmundo. Luis is too tight with Ramos. Edmundo might flip and he's dealing a lot. He was our second choice, after Camacho."

"Okay, Edmundo's our man." Fitz looked around the table. "I'll get an undercover guy on that. Everybody else, back to work. We meet here next Monday, same time. Unless we crack this case first, of course."

There was a room-wide scraping of chairs and shuffling of feet as everyone got up to leave.

Tom grabbed Jack by the arm. "Hey, man, you owe me one."

Jack laughed. "Okay, okay! What do you want?"

"Let's go check out Chico's." Tom often stirred up some mud from the bottom by going there.

Jack frowned.

"For lunch, Jack. We've got to eat lunch somewhere."

"You're worse than a rat terrier on crack. Fitz is gonna wring your neck."

Tom grinned. "Eleven o'clock. I'll drive."

CHAPTER 9

CATHY NESTLED IN THE HIGH-backed seats of the Metroliner, allowing the rhythmic clicking of the wheels and the gentle swaying of the train to diffuse the tension that had permeated her body over the last week. She rested her head back and read an Anne Tyler novel.

North of Baltimore, the train began crossing the long bridge that spans the Susquehanna River. The bridge marked a transition for Cathy. Ten years before, she and Kenny had made the trip together, just the two of them. It had been raining when they left D.C., and raining through Baltimore, and even raining when the train started over the bridge. But at the other end, when they reached the north bank of the Susquehanna, the rain changed to snow. It felt like crossing a magic bridge into a different world.

And that was sort of what she hoped to do now, Cathy realized, cross a magic bridge, and leave her world behind.

"You doing okay?" Brenda asked. The agent's assignment was to accompany Cathy as far as Philly.

"Yes, I'm fine."

"I'm sure all this frightened you." Brenda spoke discreetly, in case anyone around them was listening.

"Yes, it did."

"Tom will take care of it. I can promise you that."

Tom. If it hadn't been for Tom, none of this would have happened. But Cathy knew better than to respond. Anything she said would get back to Tom, for sure. Besides, what could Brenda, a single woman, know about marriage?

At Philadelphia, Brenda insisted on walking Cathy out to

the parking lot, where her niece, Tracy, waited for her in her battered old Honda. "Thank you," Cathy said to the agent. Brenda would return to Washington on the next train.

Happy to be free, Cathy threw her bag in the back and climbed into the passenger seat of Tracy's car. Maybe now she could forget about the FBI. "Tracy, honey, thank you for coming to get me," she said. She reached over and hugged her.

Tracy was twenty now, truly a young lady. Her Kelly green wool coat was buttoned high against the cold, and she had on worn jeans and sturdy, serviceable boots. Trish always complained her daughter dressed like a tramp, but Cathy thought she looked charming. Her shoulder-length, strawberry blonde hair fell in soft waves around her face.

"Oh, Aunt Cathy, I'm so happy you're here!" Tracy started the engine. "How are you? And how's Kenny?"

"Kenny's a lot better than he was a week ago," she said, buckling her seatbelt.

"I just couldn't believe it. That was so awful, so scary." Tracy shivered.

"He's safe, or he will be on Wednesday. He's going to stay with the brother of one of Tom's friends. I wanted him to come here ..."

"I know, I know. He told me on the phone. It's the wrestling. He really wants to wrestle."

"I don't get it. But what can I say? They overruled me." Bitterness crept into her voice.

Tracy glanced over at her. "How are you doing?"

How much should she say? "I'm happy to be gone from there. I just wish Kenny had come, too." Her voice caught in her throat.

At the next stop light, Cathy remembered something. "Oh, Tracy, Kenny sent you something." She turned and found a gift bag.

Tracy looked inside and pulled out a six-inch stuffed brown bear wearing an FBI T-shirt. "Oh, cute!" Tracy said. She found a note in the bag and laughed out loud. The light turned green. She handed the note to Cathy.

Don't worry, Trace, the note read, *G-bear always gets his man! Love, Kenny. Rom 8:28*

Cathy didn't understand it. "What?"

"G-bear is our name for Tom," Tracy explained.

"Oh."

"He'd play with us and pretend he was a bear and chase us. He was so much fun!"

Cathy had treasured her niece's summertime visits and the adventures they'd had. But she didn't remember them playing with Tom. She changed the subject. "How's your mom?" Trish worked as an interior designer.

"Busy," came the response. "She has several very wealthy clients who think they own her. And they pay so well she feels like she has to respond immediately every time someone breaks a vase or gets tired of the wallpaper. She's making a lot of money, but she has very little free time."

"And your dad?"

"He's lost in his world of European history. He can tell you the seventh in line for the throne of Spain in 1450 but he can't tell you what Mom likes in her coffee or the names of any of my friends. It's weird."

"I'm sorry, Tracy."

"Hey, I'm used to it! But it sure was fun being with you and Tom and Kenny all those summers. It was like being part of a real family."

Cathy looked out of the window. A real family?

Chester Springs, where Trish lived, was a little pocket of country in the middle of the suburbs. Large, old stone homes sat like dowager aunts on expansive lawns. Horses, covered in blankets against the cold, nibbled at the dormant grass. The stone fences marking off the fields made Cathy think of Robert Frost's poem, "Mending Wall": "Something there is that doesn't love a wall."

Something in her certainly didn't love a wall. Tom's wall. Good fences may make for good neighbors but they don't do much for a marriage.

Tracy swung the Honda into the circular driveway in front of the house, modest by the standards of the area, though still huge to Cathy. Circa 1820, it, too, was made of beautiful tan stone.

"We're home, such as it is," said Tracy.

✞ ✞ ✞

Tom felt rushed. He was running a little later than he had wanted. Lunch at Chico's had given him some new ideas, which he spent the afternoon pursuing. And now it was dinnertime, and with Cathy gone Kenny would be by himself, except for the cop. Tom wanted to be there with him. He drove as quickly as he dared through the streets of his neighborhood. He had to make the most of these last couple of days before Kenny went off to Spotsylvania.

The cop stood on the front porch, getting some fresh air. Tom waved as he pulled into the garage and parked the car. As he entered the house, he heard voices in the kitchen.

Kenny sat at the kitchen table. He had on his burgundy Virginia Tech sweatshirt and gray sweatpants, and in the light Tom could see that the bruise on his face had begun to yellow. Seated across from him was a young, clean-cut man with dark hair. He was wearing a Carolina blue sweater with a white shirt underneath. A fancy digital sports watch covered his left wrist. Between them, on the table sat two empty glasses and an open Bible.

Tom tensed up. Kenny and the young man both stood when he entered.

"Dad!"

"Hey, Kenny."

"This is Terry McDaniel. From FFA." He turned to the young man. "This is my dad."

The young man's handshake felt firm. His skin was tan and he had the beginnings of a five-o'clock shadow on his face. He was slim, like a runner. "Nice to meet you, Mr. Donovan," he said. "I've heard a lot about you."

Tom cocked his head.

"You must be proud of your son."

"He's a good kid."

"I've enjoyed getting to know him. He has a strong faith."

Tom jammed his hands in his pockets. "Kenny has guts." His eyes were on Kenny when he said it. When he looked back, Terry was looking at him intently.

Terry smiled. "I'd better go. Kenny, I'll talk to you later." He gave Kenny a pat on the arm. "Mr. Donovan, it was good to meet you." He shook Tom's hand. "See you again sometime."

Tom didn't respond.

"I'll let you out," Kenny said, moving toward the door. "We've got an alarm system now." His voice trailed off.

Tom heard his footsteps returning. "Who is this guy, Kenny?" Tom paced over to the counter and leaned against it.

Kenny sat back down at the table. He grabbed a tissue and wiped his mouth. "He's the advisor of FFA—Fairfax Fellowship of Athletes."

"Don't you realize I think someone in that group ratted you out? It could have been him! I can't believe you let him in the house."

Kenny ducked his head, "Not Terry, Dad. It's not him. He's helping me."

"Helping how?"

"Helping my faith. Helping me understand how God knew ..."

"God knew what?" Tom walked over to the table. He flipped the Bible closed and then he walked away.

Kenny squirmed. He looked up at Tom. "He knew where I was. And what was happening. He was in control of my situation. Dad, I could have bled to death if that dog hadn't alerted his owner. "

"So God woke up a dog to save you? Why didn't he stop Ramos to begin with? Then he wouldn't need a stupid dog!" Tom turned around, opened a cabinet door and took a glass out. He filled the glass with water and took a long drink. He emptied the glass into the sink and set it noisily onto the counter. Then he looked back at Kenny. His son was tracing the wound on his left wrist with his right index finger. "Kenny, you have courage. Fight. That's how you survived. Your own strength. God had precious little to do with it."

Kenny looked down and shook his head. "I disagree, Dad."

Tom felt a stab of guilt but he continued. "The dog barked because that's what dogs do. It was coincidence. Maybe luck. But it was some combination of that and courage that got you through this. Don't go giving God credit for stuff that just happens. Don't get moon-faced on me, Kenny."

Kenny looked up at him. Their eyes connected and for a second Tom saw someone else, a man whose Irish eyes flashed with laughter as he swung Tom high over his head. Tom took a quick breath.

"I was scared, Dad, most of the time. Terrified. I've never been that scared before. I felt so completely helpless. And the only thing, the only thing that kept me from falling apart, was knowing that God knew where I was and he was in control, even when it didn't feel like it."

Tom threw up his hands in disbelief. "In control? In control?" His voice shook with anger. "Was God in control of Ramos's knife? Did he decide just how many times you'd be cut? If God's in control of your life, he's sure doing a lousy job!"

"He allows things to happen but he promises it'll all work together for my good."

"Whoa! There's some fine double talk! Whatever happens, God's off the hook."

"It's not double talk! It's real."

Kenny looked hurt. Tom saw it and knew he should stop but he couldn't. "Real? You want to know what real is? It's innocent boys being hurt by drug dealers. It's babies born addicted to crack. It's thugs winning most of the time, Kenny, because there's nobody on Earth or in heaven stopping them, except a few tired people with badges in their pockets and ulcers in their guts." He grabbed a breath. "That's what's real. Not some invisible Being who stands by to take the credit for some good that comes out of something that, if he had any compassion, he would never have allowed in the first place." Tom slammed the cabinet door shut. "It sounds like you're mixed up with a cult."

Kenny's anger ignited. "It's not! It's classic, orthodox Christianity. Ask anybody. Ask Fitz."

"It's crazy, Kenny. There are lots of things that just happen in life, good and bad. If you start depending on God bailing you out of stuff, I can guarantee you one thing." He pointed his finger at Kenny. "He won't be there when you need him. He won't be on the dark streets when a drug gang comes cruising down. He won't be there when someone decides to carve you up. He won't be in the alley when some

SOBs …" Tom stopped, his heart pounding, his words catching in his throat. "He won't be there, Kenny. That you can count on." He turned his back, and started to leave the room.

"Forty years is a long time to hold a grudge, Dad."

Kenny's words hit him like an explosion at the base of his skull. He felt himself grow hot, then cold. He clenched his fist and his jaw dropped open as he turned to retort. But his eyes got snagged on the stitches on Kenny's mouth, and tripped over the bruise on his face, and he closed his mouth and turned and walked away.

CHAPTER 10

TOM WENT UPSTAIRS, PUT ON his sweats and his Nikes, and left the house. He began running, sucking in the cold air until his lungs ached. He ran a mile to the high school, then ran around the track. He ran past the bleachers where he had sat in the hot sun, sweat running down his neck, watching Kenny run track. He ran past the steel bars, where every year for the past eight years he had challenged Kenny to a chin-up contest, and where every year for the past three years Kenny had easily beaten him. He ran until the buzzing in his head began to fade, and then he ran some more. Finally he stopped running and walked under the one floodlight on the field, his chest heaving, his heart pounding. He looked at his watch. He'd been gone almost an hour. And he realized he didn't want to be gone at all, that he really wanted to be at home, with his son.

He jogged back toward home and walked the last three blocks to cool down. He'd forgotten his key, but Kenny must have seen him coming. He opened the door.

"Dad ..."

"Kenny, I'm sorry."

"I'm sorry, too." They hugged, which didn't happen very often any more. "I shouldn't have said what I did."

"I'm just glad you're safe."

Kenny let go of him, backed up and looked at his father. "I thought about you that night, Dad. I thought about you a lot."

Tom felt his throat constrict and he looked down. "I love you, Kenny." He looked back at his son. "And the rest is just something ... just something we disagree on." He slapped Kenny on his shoulder. "What do you say we call out for pizza?"

Kenny nodded.

"You go find out what—who's on duty? Chip? Go find out what Chip likes on his pizza and I'll call it in."

"No, Dad. I'll call it in. You go take a shower," said Kenny, grinning.

"I get no respect," said Tom, pulling at his collar.

"Just like you said. In life, you get what you earn."

"You little smart-mouth." Tom struck out playfully at Kenny who dodged him and moved toward the family room. Tom started up the stairs to shower.

"Hey, Dad, one more thing," yelled Kenny.

"Yeah, what?"

"Where's your money?"

Tom laughed. "Up here." Then his voice got serious, and he came halfway back down the stairs. "Hey, Kenny, you never told me. What made you finally agree to go to J.D.'s?"

Kenny walked back into the foyer. The lamp overhead lit up his face. "It was Terry, Dad. Terry McDaniel. He said I ought to go along with you, respect your authority as my father."

Tom felt his face flush. "Yeah, okay."

✝ ✝ ✝

Cathy changed into the extra clothes she had stuffed in her tote bag and then went downstairs. She was fixing a cup of tea in Trish's enormous kitchen when she heard the front door open. She walked to the hall and looked into the foyer.

"Oh, Cathy, my poor sister!" Trish stood in the doorway, cold air sweeping past her, the brass foyer lamp swinging in the breeze. She wore black boots, a challis skirt, a royal blue silk blouse, and a cashmere coat. A black leather briefcase occupied one hand. The other held a black leather tote bag spilling over with fabric samples.

Cathy walked over to hug her and Trish squeezed her awkwardly without putting down either bag. "How are you, honey?" Trish said.

"Okay, fine," said Cathy, feeling suddenly tacky in her black slacks and red wool sweater.

"Well, none of us could believe it," said Trish, swinging the door shut with her elbow. She put down her bags, took off her coat, and hung it in the closet. "Of course, we should have known something like this would happen, Tom being who he is and all."

Tom being ... what? What does that mean, Cathy wondered.

"I've never been able to understand how you tolerate living with a cop." She began walking back to the kitchen, expecting Cathy to follow. Which she did. "It used to make me so nervous, letting Tracy visit you, knowing there was a gun in the house."

Tracy walked into the kitchen. She caught Cathy's eye and smirked.

"I can't imagine living with that violence all the time."

"Well, Kenny's safe, anyway," said Cathy. Her sister hadn't even asked.

"Yes, well, that's great. I am positively beat. I cannot *wait* for this decorator's showcase to be over."

"You have one coming up?"

"Yes, in just a little over two weeks. I'm in charge of the whole thing and I am exhausted. Between the decorators who weren't happy with their room assignments and the publicity person who can't write a press release without me holding her hand, I'm worn out." Trish turned to looked at Cathy. She had colored her hair, adding some red, since the last time Cathy had seen her. "I envy you, Cathy, having nothing to do all day."

Cathy felt herself flush with anger but her sister had turned away. Over in the corner, Tracy was choking back laughter. That's right, Cathy thought. I've got to lighten up and treat it like a joke if I'm going to survive around her.

Cathy had always been overwhelmed by Trish, even when they were little. Trish (her name was Patricia then) was three years older, and outgoing to the point of flamboyance. She loved to dress up their pet dogs and cats, creating unwilling characters for her childish plays. She would stage elaborate tea parties for neighborhood children, with real china tea cups borrowed from their mother's kitchen and tiny sandwiches made of ham and cucumbers or tuna salad.

There was always a flower or two stuck in a jar in the center of the table and always, always cloth napkins.

During the tea parties, Cathy was usually off somewhere by herself, sitting under a tree, lost in one of her many books. She lived in the land of Nancy Drew, "The Black Stallion," and the wonderful Sunnybank collies. She thrived on her imaginary world and considered her sister an unwelcome intrusion at best.

When their parents died in a horrible automobile accident, Cathy realized Trish was all the family she had left. She tried to make her peace with that but she still felt like a penciled stick figure next to Trisha's fully drawn, colorful self.

"Oh, by the way dear, did Tracy tell you? Gregory is bringing home a friend from the University. Peter Montgomery. *Doctor* Peter Montgomery, an English professor. You two can talk books all night."

✝ ✝ ✝

In the formal dining room, the polished mahogany table, the Chippendale-style chairs, and the sideboard glowed in the candlelight. The Spode china, its deep red design richly echoing the color of the wood, lay ready and waiting. A crisp, white linen napkin sat at each place.

Cathy stood in the doorway, admiring the room. Trish really did know how to make things beautiful. But Kenny had always said the dining room looked like a scene in a murder mystery.

Cathy had changed back into her skirt and blouse but she still felt vaguely uncomfortable. Trish always seemed, well, costumed, rather than simply dressed. And Tracy wasn't even there to rescue her—she had gone out for pizza with some friends.

Cathy heard voices approaching and met Gregory, her brother-in-law, in the hallway. He was fifty, short, paunchy, bespectacled, and he had a gray beard that he had grown in an attempt to hide his weak jawline. Cathy always thought he looked through her as if she were in a fog, and his real objective lay right behind her.

"Hello, Cathy," he said as he gave her the requisite peck on the cheek.

"Gregory, good to see you!" she responded.

"Oh, yes, Cathy," he stepped to the side, "this is Dr. Peter Montgomery, an English professor at the University. Dr. Montgomery, my sister-in-law, Cathy Donovan."

"How nice to meet you."

Cathy blinked. Peter Montgomery was a George Clooney lookalike. George Clooney, with the perfect, salt-and-pepper hair. George Clooney, with those unforgettable eyes. George Clooney, star of Cathy's only can't-miss TV show, "ER."

Dr. Montgomery wore a tweed sports jacket and a white shirt, open at the neck, and gray flannel slacks. When he held out his hand to shake Cathy's, she noticed he had the long, slender fingers of a concert pianist.

"Nice to meet you, Dr. Montgomery." She felt a shiver run up her spine.

"Peter, please."

"Peter."

Dinner was filet mignon, cooked to perfection by an elderly German cook who muttered while she worked and wielded a knife with alarming expertise. Gregory and Trish were collectors of wine, and their selection for the evening left Cathy feeling drowsy and warm all over. By the time they adjourned to the library, Cathy had almost forgotten she was less than twelve hours departed from her own turbulent home.

✝ ✝ ✝

"So, tell me, Peter," Cathy said, "what are you teaching this semester?" She was sitting on a leather couch in the library after dinner, her second glass of red wine in her hand.

He sat on the couch as well, half-turned so he could see her. The firelight reflected off his face, making his skin look bronzed. Where did he get a tan like that in the middle of winter? Cathy thought. The rich colors of the Oriental carpet on the floor seemed like segments of a stained glass window in the flickering light. The walls—hunter green—were the perfect backdrop for the brass horn, the foxhunt prints, and the myriad of books with which Trish had decorated the room.

Gregory sat reading in the leather chair nearest the fire. Trish had gone off to bed. Cathy and Peter were left to entertain each other.

"The department gives me quite a lot of latitude," said Peter. "My specialty is the English Romantics—you know, Shelley, Blake, Wordsworth, Coleridge. This semester, I have three undergraduate classes and one graduate. So in one class we're looking at the spirit of man under oppression, in another the twin themes of innocence and experience, and so on."

"Sounds fascinating."

"Oh, it is, absolutely. And being surrounded by all the young, impressionable minds—it's exhilarating, and at the same time, sobering when you think of the responsibility to mold them."

"I can imagine," said Cathy. When was the last time she had talked to anyone in depth about literature? About William Blake's "The Tyger," or Coleridge's "Kubla Khan"? Twenty years? Was that how long it had been? Twenty years?

They talked on about his work, about his students, about his research. Lulled by his sonorous voice, Cathy lost all track of time. Around midnight, Peter said he had to leave and that he had enjoyed the evening. As the door closed behind him, Cathy marveled. How refreshing. And so different!

CHAPTER 11

TOM HEARD THE SOUND AND it merged with his dream until it shocked him awake. His eyes snapped open and he raised his head, listening intently.

Kenny! Tom jumped out of bed, his heart leaping, and ran into Kenny's room.

Kenny stood next to the bed, his back to Tom, clearly agitated. The streetlight outside cast just enough light into the room that Tom could see him. The lamp on the table was tipped over, and the covers were half-pulled off the bed. The digital clock said 2:37 a.m. Tom ran over to his son.

"Kenny?" Tom said, reaching out to touch his shoulder.

But Kenny reacted to the touch and swung around violently, his fist headed straight for Tom's jaw. Tom ducked, parried the blow with his left hand, and grabbed Kenny's wrist.

"Kenny! It's me, Dad!"

Kenny tried to twist his wrist away, and Tom gripped harder. Tom could see that his eyes were wide and full of fear. Kenny struck out with his left hand. Tom grabbed it, and forced Kenny over to the wall, pressing him tightly with his legs and body.

"Kenny, stop it! It's Dad. Stop!"

Suddenly the overhead light flicked on and Kenny reacted with surprise, his eyes blinking and widening and finally coming into focus. Tom glanced over his shoulder. The officer on duty stood in the doorway.

"It's okay, Chip," Tom said. "He's had a nightmare. I can handle it."

Chip looked at the two of them for a minute. "Call me if you need me."

Kenny was breathing hard. His face looked flushed and Tom could see the arteries in his neck throbbing. His eyes still darted around the room. His T-shirt was soaked with sweat.

"Let go of me," Kenny said, his voice tight with anger.

"Take it easy." Tom kept a firm grip on him.

Kenny looked into his dad's eyes. "Let go of me!" He struggled against Tom's hands.

Tom calculated his response. "Okay," he said finally. "I will. But if you take a swing at me again, I'm putting you on the floor. Do you hear me?"

Kenny blinked away a drip of sweat.

"Do you understand me, Kenny?"

He nodded.

Tom let go of his son and stepped back. Kenny moved away from the wall, and turned toward the window, rubbing his face with his hands as if to wake himself up. He was trembling. Tom reached out and gently touched his arm.

Kenny jerked away.

Tom backed off. He stood watching as Kenny restlessly moved around, trying to shake the tension that gripped him. He saw him clench and unclench his fists, then Kenny pounded his fist into the wall.

Finally, he turned around. "I'm sorry, Dad."

"It's okay, it's okay," Tom said. He moved forward, and touched his son. Kenny flinched, but stood still "Your heart's running a thousand miles an hour," he said, his hand on his son's chest. "That must have been some nightmare."

Kenny looked away.

"Sit down on the bed. I'll go get you a drink."

When Tom returned, Kenny sat on the edge of the bed, his elbows resting on his knees, his face in his hands. Tom touched his shoulder. "Here you go."

Kenny took the glass, drained it in a matter of seconds, and set it on the table.

"You want to tell me about it?" Tom asked.

"No."

"Let's get that T-shirt off," said Tom.

Kenny pulled off the clammy shirt, wiped his face and

neck with it, and threw it into the corner, in the general direction of the laundry hamper.

Tom's throat tightened when he looked at Kenny's chest. Years of working out and lifting weights had made his muscles strong and well-defined, but they were now defaced by scars, as obscene as graffiti on a beautiful brick wall.

Kenny looked up, caught his stare, and as their eyes met, Tom said, "You're safe now, that's the important thing. The rest of it will heal."

Kenny ducked his head.

Tom stood up, went to the dresser, opened a drawer, and pulled out a clean shirt. "Here you go," he said, handing it to Kenny.

Kenny pulled on the shirt and got back into bed. Tom helped him with the covers. He studied his son. Kenny's eyes still looked disturbed.

"You want me to stay for a while?" Tom said.

Kenny looked up at him. "Yeah."

"You have to promise not to punch me again." Tom muttered. Kenny smiled slightly.

He moved two chairs opposite each other, next to Kenny's bed. He got a quilt out of Kenny's closet, and turned off the light. Then he sat down in one chair, propped his feet up in the other, and covered himself with the quilt. He was facing Kenny, and could see him staring at the ceiling.

"Will they go away, Dad? The dreams?"

"Yeah, they'll go away." Tom sighed. "I think of them like snakes. They like to wiggle out of the box sometimes, but you just pick 'em up, shove 'em back in, and clamp the lid on 'em. After a while, they settle down and leave you alone." Until you least expect it, Tom admitted to himself. Until you let yourself get vulnerable somehow.

Gradually, they drifted off to sleep.

They both woke up at about the same time, as daylight filtered into the room. Tom grunted a little and stretched. He felt stiff and sore from sleeping in the chair. He tapped Kenny's foot. "Better get up. You have a doctor's appointment at nine and Jack's coming to get us at eleven to take you down to Spotsylvania. I sure hope his brother knows defensive tactics."

"Funny, Dad."

Tom started to leave the room.

"Dad?"

He turned back. "Yes?"

"You are going to get those guys, right?"

"You bet, Kenny."

"So I can come back and wrestle?"

"Count on it."

Tom started again to leave, but his eyes caught sight of something on Kenny's night table, something he hadn't seen in the dark. He walked back. It was a small gold cross with a tiny ring at the top. Tom felt his heart turn as he picked it up. "What's this?" he asked.

"It was your dad's," Kenny said, his voice suddenly soft. "Grandma sent it. She thought I might like to have it. She said he used to wear it on the chain of his pocket watch."

"I know," Tom said quietly. He took a deep breath, put the cross down quickly, and turned and walked away. When he got to the door, he looked back at Kenny. "Get up now, okay?" he said, his voice thick with emotion.

"Sure, Dad," Kenny replied, but Tom was already gone.

✟ ✟ ✟

Tom's world felt excruciatingly empty with both Cathy and Kenny gone, one gray day blending in with the next until he was enveloped in a thick cloud of loneliness that he ignored with Herculean effort. He immersed himself in his mission, convinced that the solution was within his reach, if only he worked a little harder. He had talked to Kenny twice and he sounded good. Cathy was harder to reach. Seemed like nobody ever stayed home at Trish's house.

On this Sunday, almost two weeks since the assault, he and Jack sat in Tom's family room, feet propped up on the coffee table, a bowl of popcorn between them on the couch, and two open cans of beer on the table, half-watching an NBA game. The Celtics weren't playing, so to Tom it was a throwaway game.

Outside, the sun lay impotently behind a thick shield of dark clouds, held hostage by a front that had settled in like a visit from an icy neighbor. It wouldn't rain, it wouldn't snow, and either would have been preferable to the gloom. Time sat like a slug, bloated and heavy, imperceptibly moving.

"I talked to J.D. yesterday," Jack said. "He really likes your kid." He picked up his beer.

"Kenny likes him, too."

Jack continued. "J.D. said you must be a great dad to have such a fine son. I told him even a blind hog gets an acorn once in a while."

"Thanks for your endorsement," Tom said.

The game resumed after a commercial break.

"Hey, Jack, does J.D. have a name?"

"What do you mean? That's his name: J.D."

"No, I mean, does it stand for anything? Like 'John David'"?

"I swear, you Yankees are so ignorant." Jack sighed. "His name on his birth certificate is James Dulany McRae. But nobody ever called him anything but J.D."

"Kenny told me your brother goes to church."

"Well, don't look at me like it's a social disease."

Tom shrugged.

"He is involved, I will say that."

The buzzer signaling half-time sounded. A series of beer and car ads began. "What do you think of all that, Jack?"

Jack's voice became uncommonly serious. "I don't know. I think Mark Twain said it: 'Religion's a dangerous thing if you don't get it right.'"

Tom nodded and sat up, resting his elbows on his knees. He picked up his empty beer can and began pressing dents in it.

"Thing is," Jack continued, "I think it is possible to get it right."

Tom stopped and looked at him. "What do you mean?"

Jack took his feet off the table and sat up. "I'm like you, Tom. I don't understand it. You give me a rock that I can categorize, measure, and date, something solid I can hold in my hand and I understand that. But religion? I can't figure it out. Sometimes I think that's because, deep down, I don't want to." Jack paused. "Problem is, my brother's solid. So's Kenny and so's Fitz. They're smart, strong men. They get it, somehow. I'm thinking they know something we don't."

Tom didn't say anything for a long time.

"House seems pretty empty, doesn't it?" said Jack.

Tom looked down at the floor. "Yes," he answered. Then he looked at Jack. "Do you miss Cheryl?"

Jack leaned back on the couch and stared at the ceiling. "Every day," he said, "and every night. Especially at night. When that drunk crossed the road and killed her, he killed part of me, too. Maybe the best part." He coughed. "It's especially bad when the kids both go back to college. House just seems so daggone quiet."

An awkward silence followed. Finally, Jack slapped Tom on the knee. "Hey," he said, "I'm sick of this game. Let's go down to the range and shoot some flat white guys. How 'bout it?"

"That's a good idea," said Tom.

"See," Jack replied, standing up and stretching, "anybody can have a good idea if they live long enough."

✝ ✝ ✝

With his shirt-sleeves rolled up, Fitz looked a little like a newspaper editor as he looked out over the assault investigation squad. Tom figured he probably wouldn't like that comparison.

It was Monday morning and it felt like it. The day had begun with a cold, freezing rain that always meant a disastrous commute. Washingtonians held fast to a tradition of panicking at the first sign of slipperiness on the road. Some slowed down, others sped up, and together they created Gordian knots at intersections and on the freeways.

Tom hated the traffic. But he had finally made it into the office and as he sat at the conference table and sipped his black coffee, he found himself perking up.

"I'm going to start with the bad news. Our undercover agent has had to back off. He was talking to Edmundo in a bar in Arlington. A guy he arrested in Southeast D.C. six months ago walked in and saw him. The UC's sure he made him. Why that guy was in a Latino bar in Virginia is beyond me and I'd like whoever is in charge of teaching proper bad guy procedure to correct that problem." Everyone chuckled. Except Tom. "At any rate, Tim's out. We'll get someone else and we'll have to pick another crew member to target."

Tom sat back and shook his head. He drummed his thumb

against his leg. "Not Pablo," he said.

"Right, Tom. Ramos's little brother is off-limits." Fitz raised his eyes. "Now for the good news."

Tom sat up.

"Angel Ramos packed up his car this morning and headed north on I-95 with Maria Aguilera. He has a proper federal escort, and we've alerted New York. He may be headed up to make the connection with Jose Alvarez, a heroin dealer." Fitz looked up. "At least, that's what we're hoping."

Murmuring followed.

This could be it, Tom thought. This could be the chance to bust him. He felt excitement jump in his stomach. Even if it was just a drug bust, they might be able to keep Ramos locked up. And if they took someone else, like Maria Aguilera, down with him, they just might be able to get something on the assault on his son.

Jack looked at Tom across the table and raised his eyebrows. He gave him a subtle thumbs-up.

"We'll keep you all updated on that," Fitz continued. "In the meantime, what else do we have?"

The rest of the meeting seemed inconsequential to Tom. His mind was already fixed on the possibility of a drug bust. Yeah, this was good. They were going to get this guy. Like all lowlifes, Angel Ramos would eventually make a mistake. This could be it.

After the meeting, he took Jack aside. "Hey, let's hit Chico's again for lunch, what do you say?"

"I'd say you were a pit bull in a former life."

"C'mon, Jack. Ramos is out of town. Let's go."

"All right, all right. Eleven o'clock. This time, I drive."

CHAPTER 12

CHICO'S RESTAURANT & BAR SLOUCHED ON the street like a man out of work. The decades-old, dirty stucco had flaked off in places, revealing plain cinderblock underneath. It was a step down to the entrance, which allowed a muddy trough to develop outside the door. The door itself was solid oak, scratched, worn and braced with multiple locks. A neon *Miller* sign glowed in the one small window.

Tom and Jack stepped through the door, shaking the rain from their coats. Dark and warm, the bar smelled like onions and garlic and cigarette smoke all mixed together.

Tom automatically scanned the men sitting sullenly at the bar—the usual mixture of truckers, construction workers, and a few yuppies in search of ethnic flavor. Or something.

He moved down past the bar toward the booths in the restaurant section. Jack stayed a couple of paces behind him. Suddenly, a young Latino man got up from a booth and turned as if to leave, nearly colliding with Tom.

"Sorry," he said, without looking up.

"Hey, Rodriguez. You're just the man I'm looking for." Tom grabbed the man's arm and forced him into an empty booth, sliding in beside him to block his exit.

"Hey, man! What you want? I didn't do nothing, man!"

Jack slid into the other side of the booth.

"I just want to buy you a drink," Tom said.

"I'm not thirsty, man. Look, man, I gotta go."

"Just sit!" said Tom. "This isn't going to hurt you."

Trapped, the man looked down at the table, avoiding eye

contact with both Tom and Jack. Tom ordered a round of Cokes and a bowl of cherries. Rodriguez left his untouched. They sat there for a half-hour getting nowhere fast.

"Look, man. I'm telling you. I don't know nothing."

"You're telling me," said Tom, "that you see Ramos nearly every day, that you work for his construction company, that you were at that big community party, for crying out loud, but you don't know anything?"

"I never saw Ramos there, man. Never saw him leave. Never heard of no one who helped him with beating up a kid. I don't know nothing, man. Now let me leave!"

Frustrated, Tom blew out a breath. Jack looked at him and shook his head. "Guess the man doesn't know anything, Tom," he said.

Tom tapped his spoon on the table.

"Y'know, Jack, I oughta just stand up, shake this man's hand, and say, real loud, 'Thanks for all your help, Rodriguez.' Real loud, so everyone can hear."

Jack smiled and looked down, snorting softly. Rodriguez squirmed in his seat.

Finally, Tom said, "Okay, Rodriguez. You win. This time. But you better not deal where I can see you. You better not need to rely on my good nature. 'Cause this is the only time you're gonna see it."

Tom got up and Rodriguez scrambled out of the booth and immediately left the bar.

Jack looked at Tom. "I think I just lost my appetite."

"Me, too," said Tom, and they got up, paid the bill, and left.

✞ ✞ ✞

Tom couldn't resist calling Cathy. He had to tell her about Ramos going to New York. He'd only talked to her once since she'd left. And now he had good news! He dialed Trish's number. Fortunately, Tracy answered.

"Hey, Skinny!"

"Tom!"

"How's the little freckle-faced kid? I missed you last summer."

"I know. I thought I ought to work. But I really missed you guys, so this year I'm coming down, regardless."

"Kenny will like that. And the rest of us will put up with it."

"Oh, Tom!"

"Hey, Tracy, my wife seems to be missing. You seen her around anywhere?"

"What's the matter? You can't keep track of your things?"

"First I lost my mind. Then I lost my wife. Or vice-versa, I really can't remember."

Tracy laughed. "Oh, Tom! She's here, but she's not here. I don't know where she is, frankly. You want me to tell her you called?"

"Yeah. Nothing special. I just called."

"How's Kenny?"

"He's doing okay. He's down with Jack's brother. I talked to him yesterday. He's a pretty tough kid."

Tracy's voice got serious. "And how are you?"

"I'll be great once we get this one guy locked up."

"Just one more? That'll do it?"

He thought he could hear the smile in her voice. "Yep, just this one."

"Take care of yourself, Tom."

"Always!" He hung up the phone and smiled. Tracy was a good kid, the closest thing he ever had to a daughter. How such a terrific person could come from two such ditzy parents was beyond him. So much for nature and nurture, he thought.

He'd wait for Cathy to call him back. Maybe by then he'd have even better news about Ramos.

✝ ✝ ✝

Cathy didn't call back, and when she hadn't called by Thursday, Tom felt mildly concerned. But he told himself he didn't want to push her. He really didn't know what to do and so he did the easiest thing, which was nothing. He spent his time ignoring the problem, blocking the fear that nibbled at the back of his brain with more and more work.

The day started out well enough. The sun finally broke through the clouds and a warm front from the southwest blew in. The temperature would top out at fifty degrees. Tom was glad to leave his topcoat at home. After he arrived at the office, Fitz called him in and things started going downhill.

Ramos' trip to New York had resulted in nothing. He met with Alvarez in a restaurant, dutifully observed by agents at two separate tables. He showed Alvarez something—money? —in a briefcase. Then Ramos and his connection went to a room at a fancy hotel and ordered champagne from room service. At midnight, Ramos and Maria left New York, heading south.

With only their suspicions, and hopes, to go on, the agents tracking Ramos had no probable cause to stop him. So reluctantly they enlisted the help of the New Jersey police. Just outside Trenton on I-95, the police managed to catch Ramos doing 62 mph in a 55 zone and they pulled him over. The agents following him stopped too, and questioned him while others thoroughly searched his car. They even brought in a drug dog. But after two hours of searching, they found no traces of drugs, not even a personal supply. Frustrated, they had to let Ramos go with only a warning ticket.

As Tom listened to the story he felt his neck tighten. How could they have read this wrong? Why would Ramos go all the way to New York for dinner and champagne? Someone else had to be muling for him. Or he'd ship the stuff some other way. Or he just wanted to tweak the FBI.

Regardless, Ramos had jumped off the hook, as usual.

Tom was standing behind his desk, trying to rebound from that disappointment, when his pager went off: 5545. His informant, Spark's, special number. Tom picked up his desk phone and called the number of a pay phone at a bar where they often met.

"Spark?"

"Mick, how's it going?"

Spark loved using the ethnic slur. "Okay, Spark. You?" Tom sat down. Jack sat several desks away, bent over a report of some kind.

"I'd be better if the Lakers had won. You see, Mick, I know this guy, and he says to me, 'Spark', he says, 'how many points ya wanna give me on the Lakers?' and I says…"

"Uh, Spark …"

"You don't want to hear it, do you, Mick?"

"I'm pretty busy, Spark."

"It's okay. I understand. What with the kid and all. How is

the boy, by the way?"

"What do you have, Spark? Why'd you call?"

Tom heard a pause at the other end of the line. He picked up a pencil and tapped it restlessly on his desk. C'mon, Spark, he prompted mentally.

"Well, remember the other day, when you and your friend were in Chico's?"

Tom sat up. He wished Jack would turn around. "Yeah, Spark."

"Remember the guy you talked to?"

Tom picked up a little box of paper clips and threw it at Jack. The box opened mid-air, sending a shower of silver all over Jack and his desk. He looked up, surprised. Tom signaled him—4-6—and Jack silently picked up his extension, keeping his eyes fixed on Tom.

"Yeah, Spark. Let's see, Rodriguez, I think. The guy we saw in Chico's."

Jack nodded. Now he was up to speed.

"That's him. Well, yesterday, after Rodriguez left in the morning, somebody broke in his house and did a number on his wife. Terrorized her for about three hours."

Tom fought to keep his voice level. "Who do you figure did that, Spark?"

"Someone who didn't like him talking to you."

"He didn't tell me anything!"

"Doesn't matter, Mick."

Tom couldn't think of anything to say.

"Just wanted you to know, Mick, so you'd understand why, if you walk in a place, everyone else just may walk out."

"Thanks. I appreciate the information."

"Okay. You take care. By the way, Rodriguez says you come near him again and you'll leave with a knife in your back."

"Thanks, Spark."

Tom hung up the phone. Jack came over.

"Ramos sure has a way of getting messages to people," Jack said.

"That man doesn't deserve the label 'human,'" Tom responded. It had been a long day. A really long day.

They sat there for a while, talking and thinking. Finally,

Jack said, "Tom, why don't we take some PT time and a couple hours annual. Go home, jog for a while. Maybe catch a movie or the Celtics. What do you say?"

"Okay."

"And then why don't we call J.D. and see if we can meet him and Kenny in Fredericksburg on Saturday for lunch?"

"Let's do it."

CHAPTER 13

ON SATURDAY, TOM AND JACK left the house, switched cars in a busy parking lot to be sure they weren't followed, and got on I-95, headed to Fredericksburg. The winter sun lay in the south. The trees of the hardwood forest that lined the interstate stood bare and gray, braced against the winter. A buzzard circled slowly overhead, looking for a possible meal, and once Tom saw a red-tailed hawk go after something on the shoulder of the road.

As they crossed the Rappahannock River at Falmouth, Jack said, "Look over there, Tom. You know what that is?"

"A river."

"What's it look like?"

Off to Tom's right, water boiled around large rocks and boulders. "A river full of rocks."

"Not just rocks," Jack said, "that there's the fall line."

"The fall line."

"To the left of us, the river looks deep. That's because we're at the fall line, the place where the underlying rock changes. Once upon a time there were mountains along here. Wore down over time, but left hard bedrock. That's what you're seeing. East of here is the coastal plain and soft, sandy soil. West is the Piedmont, and harder rock."

Tom settled back in his seat. "And that's significant because ..."

"Because it's why Virginia developed like it did. Colonists came up from the east, and their ships couldn't go any farther than the fall line. So cities grew up there: Alexandria, Fredericksburg, Richmond, and Petersburg."

"And your point is ...

Jack looked over him. "Rocks matter, Tom!"

Tom grinned. "I remember pitching a few that did." He tapped the passenger side window with his knuckle. "Hey, what's the name of the restaurant?"

"The Irish Brigade." Jack glanced over at him. "You know about what that is, right?"

"Nope. Never been there."

"No, I mean the real Irish Brigade."

"Jack, riding with you is a real education."

"A bunch of wild-eyed Irishmen from New York and Massachusetts recruited by the Yankees in the Civil War made up the Irish Brigade. They were here, in the Battle of Fredericksburg, December 1862. The Yankees were on the Stafford side of the river. The Rebs were over in the town and up that hill.

"The Yankees were slow to attack, and by the time they did, Lee had secured a good position. The Yankee general, Burnside, stupidly sent his troops up after 'em, across a broad, open area. The Irish Brigade was part of the second wave to try to cross that killing field. Their general, Thomas Meagher, had 'em put sprigs of evergreen in their caps to remind them of who they were, and some people say he filled them with whiskey. They went screaming up that hill, following their own green flag with a Celtic harp on it, stepping over the dead and wounded as they went. They knew they'd been ordered into a slaughterhouse but they went into it with the courage of men who'd spit in the eye of the devil himself."

Jack shook his head. "At the end of the day, there were only two hundred and fifty left of the fourteen hundred Irishmen that went into battle. Nobody, Yankee or Reb, ever forgot the courage of the Irish Brigade. After the war, a Richmond newspaper editor said they were brave not because they were Yankees, but because they were Irish." He looked over at his friend. "Wild-eyed Celts. Could've been your ancestors."

"How do you know all this stuff, Jack?"

"I read, Tom. You should try it."

Jack parked and together the two men crossed the street to

the Irish Brigade Restaurant. The large-paned glass windows were scrubbed and shining under the green canvas awning. Jack pulled at the brass door handle.

They stepped inside and Tom smelled fresh bread. A young waitress showed them to a table near the windows. Made of maple, its warm, brown wood reminded him of a well-oiled rifle stock. In the middle, a small amber lamp glowed. Brass and wood ceiling fans turned slowly overhead.

After a few minutes, Kenny and J.D. walked in. One look at the boy made Tom realize again how much he'd missed him, and he got up quickly, walked over to him, and hugged him. "Kenny!"

"Hi, Dad!"

Tom held his hands on Kenny's shoulders and looked him over from head to toe. "You look terrific! What's this man been feeding you?" He turned to J.D. and stuck out his hand. "How are you, J.D.?"

J.D. looked like a younger version of Jack, same brown hair, same brown eyes. He was two inches taller than Jack, but he had the same husky, strong build. He had on jeans and a plaid flannel shirt, and his grip felt strong as he shook Tom's hand.

"Great, Tom. Good to see you. Hey, Jack."

"He does look like somebody let him out in the tall grass," Jack grinned.

Kenny smiled. Tom noticed that the bruise had almost completely disappeared from his face. Only a small area around his ear still remained discolored.

"Well, come on over and sit down," said Tom.

"Tom," Jack said. "I think J.D. and I will take a hike and let you two have some time together."

Tom nodded, grateful.

"We'll come back in an hour or so."

They left and Tom and Kenny sat across from each other at the table, hardly knowing where to begin.

Kenny looked around the room. "Hmm, 'The Irish Brigade.' What is this, Dad, an attempt to return me to my ethnic roots?" He grinned.

"I have to do something to make up for not raising you in Boston." Tom scrutinized him. "So how are you, Kenny?

How are you feeling?"

"Really good. Honestly."

"Pain?"

"Almost all gone. I have headaches once in a while, but that's about it."

Tom nodded. "How are your workouts going?"

"I'm almost back up to the weights I was lifting before. And J.D. and I are jogging every night. We did three miles last night. I want to get back to five as soon as I can. You know Coach Hall came down?"

"Yeah, I talked to him."

"Guess he wanted to check me out for himself."

"He's just being careful—nobody wants you to overdo it."

"The doctor said ..."

"I know, I know," laughed Tom.

The waitress came and they ordered bowls of Irish stew and soda bread.

Tom looked at his son, who was dressed in a blue sweater with a light blue shirt underneath. Kenny's neck looked normal again, the swelling gone so he could once again see the clear definition of his jaw. His skin had good color. He really looked healthy.

Kenny played absentmindedly with the salt shaker. He looked up and their eyes met.

"How about the dreams?" Tom asked.

Kenny took a deep breath. "They're going away. I don't have them every night now. And I haven't punched anybody out recently."

Tom smiled.

"J.D.'s been real good, Dad. He keeps me talking. And the youth pastor from their church has been out a lot. They're having a Super Bowl party tomorrow and I'm invited." Kenny took a drink of water. "It's been just what I needed, Dad. Thank you for setting it up."

"It was Jack's idea." He hesitated. "I miss you."

The food came and they both dove into it. "Hey, this is good!" Kenny said when he came up for air.

"Aren't you glad you're not English!"

"I appreciate you more every day, Dad." Kenny grinned and Tom noticed again how blue his eyes were.

They talked and ate until their bowls were empty and they had exhausted their supply of easy topics. Kenny looked at Tom with those clear blue eyes and said, "Dad, I'm worried about something."

"What's that?"

"I'm worried about you and Mom."

Tom looked down. Why this? Why now?

"She's been really distant lately, Dad, and it bothers me."

Tom looked up and mustered up as much confidence as he could find. "Don't worry about us Kenny. We'll be fine. You've got enough to take care of just getting yourself back to normal." He tried his best to smile reassuringly.

"How long did she expect to be gone, Dad?"

"I don't know. A few weeks. Just 'til it's safe, that's all."

"Did you see how many clothes she sent up there?"

"Women like to have options, Kenny."

"Is one option leaving you?"

"Clothes, Kenny. Options about clothes." Tom shifted uncomfortably in his seat. It seemed to be getting hot in the place.

Kenny leaned forward. "I think she's drifting away and you're not acknowledging it."

Tom sat back in his chair, stretching his legs out under the table. He stuck his right hand in his pants pocket and felt the comfortable bulge of his gun under his arm. "Kenny, your mom's going through a rough time. What happened to you was hard on her. She'll be okay. She just needs some space." Tom looked around, hoping someone would rescue him.

But Kenny wouldn't let up. "Why don't you take a week off, go get Mom, and go away somewhere? Just the two of you? I'll be fine at J.D.'s."

"That's a good idea. Just as soon as I get Ramos in."

"There's a hundred agents that can get Ramos, but you're the only husband she's got."

"I know, I know." Tom sighed. "Look, Kenny, there are just some things you don't understand. Mom and I have been married a long time. We'll get through this. Just relax, okay?" He picked up the dessert menu. He never ate dessert, but he had to do something.

Kenny watched him carefully, let him read for a minute,

then hit him again. "When's the last time you talked to Mom?"

"Oh, I don't know. I tried calling earlier this week, I guess." The snakes were slithering.

"Did you know she's looking into master's degree programs?"

"Oh really? Good for her!" He felt genuinely pleased.

"Up there?"

Up there? That fact hit him like a well-placed slug to the gut and took his breath away, although he tried not to show his reaction. The fear that had yawned like a gaping hole just to the left of his conscious mind slid into his peripheral vision. He forced it away with the same intensity that he drove the snakes in his belly back in the box when their writhing became unbearable. He set his jaw and stared Kenny down.

"Don't worry about it, Kenny. It's going to be all right."

"Call her, Dad. If you don't call her, she'll think you don't care."

"Look, Kenny. I promise you. I'll call her. I'll talk to her. Before I pick you up next Saturday. I promise. Now knock it off." He tried to smile. He glanced beyond Kenny and saw Jack and J.D. come in. Rescued. Just in time.

Jack pulled out a chair and sat down. "What I want to know is," he said, "is this boy ready to wrestle one week from today?"

"You bet," said Kenny.

"Well let's just find out." Jack began taking things off the table while the others stared at him. "Switch chairs with me," he said to Tom, and they moved so that he sat across from Kenny. Then he propped his elbow up on the table, in the traditional arm wrestling position. "Let's go, boy!"

Kenny smiled. He pulled off his sweater and rolled up his shirtsleeve. "I think I can beat both you and Dad!"

"Both of us? What's the bet?" Jack said, his eyes dancing.

Kenny looked around. "A hat," he said finally, nodding toward the Irish Brigade hats in the display case near the register.

"You're on."

They gripped right hands and stared each other in the eye

until Tom said, "Go!" and then the contest began. Kenny's forearm was slightly longer, giving him a small advantage, but Jack gave him a run for his money. They were both sweating by the time Kenny put together one superior push, and Jack's hand crashed to the table.

"All right!" said Tom.

"Who were you rooting for, partner?" said Jack.

"Blood's thicker than water."

"Yeah, but I'm the one's got your back most days," said Jack. He looked at Kenny. "Think you can take your old man?"

"Not a problem," Kenny answered, and everyone laughed. He gulped down a glass of water and unbuttoned his shirt. His sweaty undershirt stuck to his chest.

Tom got up, took off his sports jacket, and rolled up his sleeve. Then he sat down. Kenny took his seat across from his father and raised his hand. "I'm ready."

Tom positioned his elbow and grabbed Kenny's hand. They were a good match, the same size. It would be a test of strength and of will.

"Go!" said Jack.

Gosh, he's strong, Tom thought. He countered Kenny's push. He shifted his weight and felt the muscles of his back straining with his effort. Tom could see the sweat beading on Kenny's upper lip.

"C'mon, Kenny!" J.D. said.

Tom felt a slight move in Kenny's hand and he pushed, hard, and started to move his arm over.

"Yes, Tom! Go for it!" said Jack.

Kenny didn't flinch, his eyes never left his dad's. He took a deep breath and pushed, and Tom fought him, but gradually their hands moved back to the upright position.

A drip of sweat rolled down Tom's forehead and over his eyelid. He shook it off. He could feel his heart pounding, feel the blood pumping in his chest. Kenny's eyes were intense, focused, and Tom could see how someone would find him a formidable opponent.

"J.D., were you there when Ol' Man Beckley's pit bulls got into a fight?" Jack asked.

"No."

"Man, they locked their jaws onto each other's necks, grindin', goin' for the jugular. Neither one of them would give up. I feel like I'm seein' it again. Two pit bulls in a fight to the death."

They'd been wrestling nearly four minutes and suddenly Tom's age was catching up to him. The ache in his arm had extended itself up to his shoulder and down his ribs. He looked at Kenny for signs of tiring. There were none. The fire in his son's eyes was undiminished.

Tom took a deep breath and gave it one more push. He thought he started to move Kenny's arm, but then Kenny reacted and slowly he started pressing Tom's hand to the table. Even a waiter was involved, now, standing over the table, watching. Tom was sweating and his vision was getting dim around the edges. He struggled, but the end was inevitable. His arm hit the table with a thud.

"Yes!" Kenny let him go immediately.

Tom stood up. "Congratulations! You're the better man!"

"Maybe just the younger man," Kenny laughed. "You okay, Dad?"

"What'd you expect, cardiac arrest?"

"You never know, at your age."

Tom cuffed him playfully upside the head.

They gathered up their things. Kenny downed his third glass of water.

"Let's get you that hat," said Jack, and he took him over to the register.

Tom smiled as the two walked away. He turned to Jack's brother. "Thanks for taking care of him."

"He's a neat kid. My kids love him. We all do."

They walked out to the street, Kenny in his new hat, and said goodbye. Tom slipped him a fifty-dollar bill. "What's that for?" Kenny said.

"Just in case you need something."

They started to shake hands, then Kenny hugged him. "Thanks, Dad. I love you. Call Mom."

"See you in a week!" said Tom, and then he was gone.

"What are you going to do," Jack asked, "if Ramos is still on the street next week?"

"I've got to let him wrestle," said Tom grimly.

"Yeah," Jack agreed, "you've got to."

"He jumped through hoops to get special permission. They made all those exceptions for him."

"It took a lot."

They were quiet for a while, thinking, then Tom said, "We'll just pick him up, early Saturday, let him wrestle, and bring him right back down. The tournament's at another high school. Ramos'll never know he's in town."

"It'll be fine," Jack said.

CHAPTER 14

WHEN HE GOT HOME SATURDAY night Tom, faithful to his word, tried calling Cathy but she was out. Sunday no one answered the phone, even though Tom called before, during, and after the Super Bowl.

On Monday, Tom attended another non-productive meeting and he chased a couple of dead-end leads. When he tried calling, Cathy was out. As usual. By Tuesday, Jack had noticed the dark mood that gripped Tom, so on Wednesday, Jack suggested going out to dinner. That seemed fine to Tom, since the one thing he didn't want to do was go home to his empty house.

But he was hung up now, almost obsessed, with getting in touch with Cathy. While they were waiting for their food he excused himself and used the pay phone. It was dinnertime, for crying out loud. Certainly she would be at Trish's now.

But she wasn't and he felt both irritated and confused when he arrived back at the table.

"Did you get her?" Jack asked.

The way Tom snapped up his napkin gave him the answer. "No," Tom said coolly. "She's probably out with Tracy."

Their food came, a hot roast beef sandwich for Tom, and blackened chicken for Jack. The food was delicious, as usual, but Tom just picked at his.

Three times Jack tried to get a conversation going. Tom seemed only half there. Finally Tom gave up trying to eat. He told Jack he was going to hit the men's room. He felt Jack's eyes on him as he walked to the back of the restaurant.

Where is she going all the time, Tom wondered. He

pushed in the door, and as he stepped into the bright fluorescence of the restroom he could not believe his eyes. There, alone, in front of the paper towel dispenser, wiping his hands, stood Angel Ramos.

Tom's heart began pounding. He swung the door shut and kicked a tall metal trashcan in front of it. "Well," Tom said, "it's amazing what kind of scum you find in public restrooms these days."

"Get out of my way, Donovan. I'm leaving." His black hair was combed neatly back, his white shirt open at the collar. He wore a gray tweed jacket and black pants. His hands were large and strong, but it was his eyes that transfixed Tom. They were small and black and had seen too many things. Every bit of innocence had been burned out of them. All that was left were smoldering embers of cruelty and hate.

"Not so fast. Not so fast." Tom shoved Ramos back against the wall. "What you been up to lately, Ramos? Been rolling over any kids? Engraving your mark on peoples' chests, just for fun?" He thumped Ramos on the chest with the back of his hand.

"I don't know what you say. I'm leaving."

"I said 'not so fast.' We got a little business to take care of first." Tom grabbed Ramos' shirt and threw him up against the sink.

Ramos caught himself, his hand slipping on the wet porcelain. He turned slowly and glared at Tom, his black eyes gleaming. "Call my lawyer."

"No, no. Personal business. A little score to settle." Tom felt the muscles in his diaphragm tighten.

"Get off my back, Donovan." Ramos turned his shoulder and started to shove past Tom.

But Tom grabbed him and spun him around. "You touch my kid, Ramos, you got to deal with me."

"You can't prove nothing."

"It give you a thrill to work over kids? Make you feel like a real man? When they're blindfolded and handcuffed? Does that turn you on?" Tom's fists were clenched, his face hot. He breathed hard and strong, getting ready. "Are you into killing kids?"

Behind him the door opened. "Tom?" The trashcan clattered to the floor as Jack pushed into the room.

"Hey, your amigo here is a little too hot. You should cool him off, you know?" Ramos said.

"Tom, let's go," Jack said quietly, keeping his eyes on Ramos.

"You afraid to deal with a man, Ramos? One on one?" Tom shoved him, hard, and Ramos' head hit the wall with a thump.

"There are many ways to deal with a man, you know? Sometimes you deal directly with him, sometimes not," Ramos shrugged.

"Tom ..." Jack put his hand on Tom's elbow. Tom shook him off.

"It's real macho to cut a kid, Ramos, especially one that's tied up. You're real tough."

Ramos looked straight at Tom, his eyes narrowed. "I don't know what you talk about, Donovan." He cocked his head and smiled. "But I tell you one thing. If I did get my hands on your kid, I'd do him slowly ... methodically ... and I'd make him scream." And then he laughed.

Tom cursed and jumped at him. He had his left hand on Ramos' collar and was just about to let his right fist fly when Jack grabbed his arm from behind.

"Tom, no!" Jack yelled. He twisted Tom to the left, catching him off balance, and he pushed him back into an open stall. The door crashed against the wall.

Tom was fighting mad and Jack had to use all his strength to keep him contained. Ramos stood, hands upraised, laughing.

"Ramos, I'll kill you! There's no way you're going to get away with what you did. No way!" Tom struggled to get his balance back, to get away from Jack.

Jack leveled his eyes on Ramos. "Get out of here, Ramos. Now!"

"You better leash your dog, eh? This would not look good on his record, harassing a citizen?"

"Get out of here. You understand? Get out!"

"Ramos, you punk!" Tom's cursing echoed off the walls.

"Shut up, Tom. Shut up! Ramos, out."

"See you later, Donovan. Say hi to your kid for me, eh?" He laughed.

Tom's curses bounced off the walls. His heart was pounding, hammering against his chest. Sweat poured down his back, and his head felt like it was bursting as Ramos left.

Jack relaxed his grip a little. "You're taking the curve too fast, Tom."

"Get off me!"

"Calm down!" He gave Tom an extra push. "Don't be stupid."

"Get off!"

Jack hesitated, then let go. Tom started toward the door. Jack grabbed him. "Stay here!"

Tom cursed and kicked the overturned trashcan as hard as he could. He ran his hand through his hair, and hit a stall door, hard. He cursed again.

✞ ✞ ✞

Working with Tom the rest of the week was like trying to put a choke chain on a rogue elephant, and Jack could only hope that watching Kenny wrestle would help Tom focus on more positive things than Angel Ramos. Saturday could not come too soon.

But before Saturday they had to get through Thursday, and Thursday night when Tom called Pennsylvania he was in no mood to fool with Trish, who answered the phone, so he simply asked for Cathy without identifying himself.

"She's out with her professor!" Trish said. "Who is this?"

"Tom."

"Oh, Tom!" she giggled. "Oh well, you'd find out eventually anyway."

He hung up the phone with an angry slam, and a minute later it rang.

"Tom?" Tracy's voice. "I'm sorry. Mom's a jerk sometimes."

"Yeah," was all he could muster.

"Tom, look. I don't know what's going on."

He grunted.

"And I don't want to get in the middle of it," Tracy said.

"I understand."

"But why don't you try calling tomorrow evening just

before six? She's going with me somewhere during the day. And I happen to know she'll be home until six-ish. Or better yet, come up here."

"I can't come up, Tracy." He sighed. "Kenny wrestles on Saturday."

"Yeah, that's right. Well, just call her."

"Okay, Tracy. Thanks."

CHAPTER 15

"THANKS FOR COMING WITH ME, Aunt Cathy," Tracy said early Friday morning. She brushed her hair out of the collar of her coat, started the car, and pulled out onto the road. "This work is really important to me. And it's something most people don't want to see. Namely, my parents."

"I'm happy to come," Cathy replied. The crystal blue, cloudless sky cradled a bright sun, its light streaming through the leafless trees. Cathy shielded her eyes. "How did you get started doing this?"

"We had a choice of three things to study for a psych class. I chose crack babies, and for a whole semester I went to Hope House once a week. When the semester was over, I found I couldn't just walk away. I've been volunteering there ever since."

"And you've declared psychology as your major?"

"Yes. My parents don't care what I study as long as there are multiple degrees attached. So I'm going to go all the way, get my Ph.D., and then, well, I'll see where I'm led."

"Where you're led?" Cathy raised her eyebrows.

Tracy swallowed. "Yes." She turned toward her aunt, and for the first time, Cathy noticed she was wearing a gold necklace. A cross.

Cathy adjusted herself in her seat.

"There's an awful lot of people out there who need help, Cathy. You know that, from listening to Tom's stories."

"I try not to listen to Tom's stories," Cathy replied dryly.

Tracy glanced at her. "Is something wrong between you

and Tom?"

"Why do you ask?"

"I'm just getting a bad feeling."

"Let's just say I'm re-evaluating."

"Re-evaluating?"

"We've been married a long time. It's time to re-think it."

Tracy hesitated. "As crazy as my parents are, I'm glad they're still together. I think it would tear Kenny up if something happened to you two."

Cathy waved her hand. "He's practically out of the house. He won't care."

Tracy had no response.

When they got to the outskirts of Paoli, Tracy pulled into the parking lot of what looked like a large, old brick home. Ancient oaks stood like sentries in the yard, and a deep porch hugged the front of the house. A wooden sign reading "Hope House" hung next to the carved oak door.

"Tom ever talk to you about what cocaine does to people?" Tracy asked.

"No."

"You're about to see some of it."

Tracy and Cathy entered. The door opened into a foyer and a long, dark oak staircase leading to the second floor. The wide hallway to the right of the stairs led to the back of the house. All of the interior doors and trim were beautiful, dark oak. "Hello!" An older woman carrying a tiny baby came out of one of the rooms. "Oh, hi, Tracy!"

"Mary, this is my aunt, Cathy Donovan. I wanted to show her what we do here."

Cathy couldn't keep her eyes off of the baby in the woman's arms.

"Well, of course! Feel free to show her around. We just got a new baby, a little girl."

"Thanks, Mary."

Tracy led Cathy into the front room on the right side of the house on the first floor. It had probably been the parlor originally, but it now contained four cribs, two rockers, and two changing tables. The walls were painted mint green, and a green, pink, and white wallpaper border of bears and bunnies ran around the wall near the ceiling. A woman in a rocker was attempting to bottle feed a small baby while another woman loaded supplies into a cabinet. They looked up and smiled as Tracy and Cathy came in the door.

In one crib, a baby slept. In another, an infant lay on his side, staring at the wall, his arms and legs jerking erratically. "They come to us through Social Services," said Tracy in a low voice. "The mothers have tested positive for drugs, usually crack. Or they've just confessed to doing drugs because they feel guilty."

"They are so tiny!" said Cathy.

"They're often premature or have low birth weight. This little guy," Tracy walked over to the baby, "is typical. He's jittery. He doesn't like to look you in the face. He reacts poorly to stimulation. But he's much better now than he was two weeks ago when they brought him in." Tracy touched his hand lightly with her forefinger. "He's even beginning to grasp my finger," she said. "That's it, little guy!"

Cathy gently stroked his face. He reacted by turning away.

"We have three rooms like this," Tracy continued. "Let's go find the new baby."

Tracy led Cathy upstairs and into a small, dark room. The crib farthest from the door held a baby lying on her back. She had blond hair and fair skin and a mark above her right eyebrow. She was dressed in a pink terrycloth sleeper, and Cathy thought she looked like a doll. Periodically, a shiver would run through the baby's body.

"When they come here, they're very sensitive to light and sound," Tracy whispered. "Some of them don't like being touched. Many of them have withdrawal symptoms—jitters, sneezing, tremors, cramping, and sometimes breathing disturbances." Tracy leaned over the crib and picked up the baby. "Hello, precious," she crooned. She handed the baby to Cathy.

She couldn't have weighed six pounds. Cathy felt like she was holding an empty envelope. "Hi, baby," she said. She cradled the baby in her arms and looked into her eyes. The baby wouldn't look at her.

"You have to be careful of too much eye contact," said Tracy. "They can't handle it."

She looked so perfect. Cathy held her close, turning her

body to rock her gently, humming an old lullaby softly.

Suddenly multiple babies across the hall began to cry. Cathy looked at Tracy, who stood quietly, listening. After a few more minutes, someone called out, "Can anyone help?"

"I'll be back in a minute," Tracy whispered, and she left the room.

Alone with the newborn, Cathy's arms fell naturally into position. She spoke softly to the baby. "Hello, sweetheart. Do you know how beautiful you are?"

The baby's little rosebud mouth pursed, and her tongue momentarily emerged. Her blue eyes looked almost liquid in the dark.

Had it been so long ago, Cathy thought, that she was holding Kenny, nursing him, rocking him in the old pine rocker in the middle of the night? What wonderful times those had been ... alone with her baby in the dark, moonlight gently streaming through the window. She'd sit and think and dream while he nursed, and often, even when he had had his fill and had fallen back to sleep, she couldn't bear to put him down. She'd hold him some more, until her own eyes grew impossibly heavy with fatigue. Then she'd bring him back to bed with her and snuggle with him, until dawn found her, Tom, and the baby all curled up together. Where had those days gone?

Tracy came back, and took the baby from Cathy, placing the infant back in the crib. "You ready to go?" she whispered. Cathy nodded.

Back in the car, Cathy asked, "What about the future? Is there any hope for these babies?"

"The good news is, many of them seem to recover and have no significant long-term effects. A few will have struggles."

"Like what?"

"Hyperactivity, learning disabilities, problems with bonding, neurological problems. You name it."

"This is so sad!"

"They get good care here, Cathy. And if their moms can kick the drugs, they have a chance to be reunited."

Cathy frowned. "Why do they do it?" she finally said.

"Do what?"

"Why do the mothers do drugs when they're pregnant? Don't they know what they're doing to their babies?"

"Addiction is hard. Cocaine, especially, can produce terrible cravings. The mothers choose to ignore long-term consequences for the short-term high."

So sad, Cathy thought. So very sad.

Tracy glanced at her. "Lots of people get into cocaine, Cathy, even well-educated people. I talked to Tom about it recently. This is one reason he's fighting so hard against the dealers. He sees what it's doing to families."

✝ ✝ ✝

When they got back to Trish's house, Cathy went upstairs to shower. Peter was coming about six-fifteen. He had invited her to a party. It would be a good chance, she told herself, to meet some of the other faculty members. Maybe an evening of stimulating conversation would help her decide if she wanted to apply to the masters program at his college.

She had so many options now. She felt so free. Kenny was doing fine, based on her phone conversations with him. Anyway, he'd be off to college in the fall. Finally, she could do something just for herself.

In the two weeks that she'd known Peter, Cathy had changed. She could feel it. She was blossoming under his attention. He introduced her to some art films, brought her flowers, took her to dinner, and attended lectures at the college with her. So intellectual. So interesting! And a perfect gentleman to boot.

She wondered how late she'd be out. Peter had said something about maybe going back to his place afterwards. He probably meant the whole group.

So why was she slipping on her best underwear? And her lace bra?

Cathy shoved those thoughts out of her mind. It was the conversation she was going for, she told herself. She wiggled into her little black dress and sheer black stockings. She put on her pearl earrings and brushed her hair back lightly. Maybe she should color the gray. She sighed. She looked at her watch. Six o'clock. She was right on time.

She transferred her wallet, keys, and some tissues into a small, black evening bag and went downstairs. As she did, she heard the phone ringing and the doorbell chiming at the same time.

"I have the phone!" Trish called out. She must have just gotten home.

Cathy went for the front door. Peter was early.

"Come right in," she said, smiling. "I just have to get my coat."

"Phone's for you, dear," Trish said, walking into the foyer. She handed Cathy the cordless phone.

"Hello? Oh!" As she heard Tom's voice, she turned her back to Peter and walked quickly to the kitchen.

"Won't you come in for a drink?" she heard Trish saying. They were following her.

"How are you, Cathy? I've been trying to get you."

She hadn't talked to her husband in almost two weeks. Her stomach tensed up. "I've ... I've been busy. There's lots to do here."

"So I gather," Tom said. His tone sounded light, friendly.

She pressed her hand over one ear to block out the conversation between Peter and Trish. Peter refused the drink. She saw him look at his watch.

"Are you okay?" Tom said.

"Yes. I'm fine."

"What have you been doing?"

"Sitting in on classes, going to the library. Things like that."

"Oh, evening classes."

Peter caught her eye, distracting her. "No, mostly daytime," she responded, without thinking. She felt her face redden when she realized what she'd said. "Listen, this isn't a real good time to talk," she said quickly. "I was just about to go somewhere."

A long pause followed. "I've been trying to get you every night this week."

"Yes, well, I've been busy. I'm sorry. I can't just sit around in case you call."

"Trish said you were out with ... with some professor?"

Cathy didn't answer.

"An English professor?"

Her defense mechanisms began to engage.

"Same guy? Every night?"

She felt her heart pound, her throat tighten.

His voice suddenly sounded very tired. "Cathy," he said softly, "what are you doing?"

It would have been better if he had been angry. She could have handled anger. Guilt was a different story. "You're a trained investigator, Tom," she said finally in a harsh whisper. "You figure it out!" and she hung up.

CHAPTER 16

NAUSEA ROSE IN TOM'S THROAT. He gently replaced the receiver of the phone. Slowly, a snake curled around his heart, squeezing it like a trapped rat. He shook his head, hard, got up, kicked the chair away, and went up to his bedroom. He took out his navy blue sweats and his athletic socks. He stripped off his clothes, dropped them on the floor and stepped over them. He pulled on his sweats, his socks and his running shoes, and left the house.

The air felt fiercely cold. Thick clouds hung in the sky, reflecting the lights of the shopping center in the distance, creating a dream-like pinkish glow in the eastern sky.

Tom took a deep breath and began running, his heart like a lead weight in his chest. He headed down the sidewalk, not caring which way he went, crossing streets without looking, ignoring the warm glow of the lights of the houses. He refused to notice the bite of the cold on his ears, refused to acknowledge the ache in his chest, refused to feel the tremor in his soul.

He ran and ran, down past the school and on into the next development, down streets he had never driven, past houses that were unfamiliar, his feet drumming the snakes into submission with staccato insistence. It didn't work, but he refused to acknowledge that. He ran and ran until his lungs hurt and his heart felt like it would burst, and then he ran some more. He ran down a dead end by mistake. He stopped. His chest heaved and his blood pounded in his temples. He put his hands on his hips and walked around, trying to catch his breath, kicking at the gravel with his feet.

Suddenly, he bent down and picked up a loose rock. He juggled it in his hand, feeling its weight, its rough edges pressing into his palm. And then he shifted back like an outfielder, launched the rock skyward with all his might, and yelled, "Where are you?"

But there was no answer. There never had been, and a front porch light flicked on, and so he turned and began running again. It started to rain, tentatively at first, and then steadily. It was a cold, icy rain, and it beat into his scalp and plastered his hair down. It ran down the back of his neck until it mingled with his sweat and soaked his shirt. It ran in streams like cold fingers over his eyes and on down his face, and he wondered if this was what it felt like to cry.

✞ ✞ ✞

"Everything all right, Cathy?" Peter said as he climbed in the BMW.

"Yes. Just fine." She bit her lip and forced the memory of Tom's voice out of her head.

The party was in a nice area of Swarthmore, about thirty minutes from Trish's house. Peter seemed in a talkative mood and Cathy was quite happy to listen to him as she watched the night go by. The sky was clear to the north, but clouds were beginning to creep in from the south, and Cathy wondered if it was raining where Kenny was.

Peter told her about his day, about his struggle to instill in the video generation an appreciation for literature. He lamented his students' poor writing skills, and he philosophized on the reasons for it. He blamed it mostly on twelve years of reduced government spending on education. And while Cathy thought about that, he lobbed a bombshell her direction.

"Oh, by the way," he said. "I should tell you. This party? My wife will be there."

"Your wife?"

"Well, actually," he said, grinning, "my soon-to-be ex-wife."

Cathy looked at him. "Peter, I didn't know you were married!"

"Not very married." He laughed. "We're close to a divorce. And don't worry, there's won't be any issues with me bringing you. Nothing unpleasant. We're very civilized." He took a left turn. "At some point we realized we weren't in love anymore. She had an affair, I had an affair, and so we split."

"Do you have children?"

"We never wanted them. She's a professor as well. Nineteenth-century American lit. Our careers are our children." He smiled and looked at her. "See? Nothing messy!"

She tried hard to process that. He was married! But then, so was she. What was she doing?

He turned to her at a stoplight. "I imagine what it would be like if I had met you first." His voice sounded soft and warm, reassuring even. He moved his hand over to cover hers. "I'm so glad you came to Philadelphia!"

They arrived at the house, a large stone Colonial with a front walk lined with boxwoods. Inside, the center-hall design allowed for lots of crowd movement between the living room-family room on one side and the dining room-kitchen on the other. About fifty well-dressed people were standing around with drinks in their hands as Cathy and Peter walked in. Peter must have sensed her intimidation—he grabbed her hand and began making introductions. He brought her a glass of wine and soon she found herself immersed in conversation.

She felt surprised she could hold her own. But her part-time job at the library had kept her up on current literature, she followed the news fairly closely, and Kenny talked sports nonstop. And she was good at asking questions and getting other people talking.

Peter disappeared for a little while but she was caught up in a three-way conversation about feminism in literature. When she saw him conversing with a slim blonde across the room, she thought nothing of it, until the man next to her told her that was Peter's ex-wife. "They're modeling a great divorce," the man said. "Staying married wasn't hard when people only lived until their forties. Nowadays, it's ridiculous to think marriage should last until death."

Would her parents have stayed married had they not been killed in that accident, Cathy wondered?

Peter returned, smiling, and Cathy re-focused on him. An

hour later, he suggested they go home.

By home, he meant back to his place. She assumed he had invited others over, but when they got to his house—a small bungalow in a quiet city neighborhood—she sensed he had other ideas. He put on some classical music, and handed her another glass of wine. They talked, then, for another half hour, and then, her George Clooney-lookalike kissed her.

Honestly, it felt good. Exciting. Stimulating. She hadn't felt that way in years. She yielded to it, kissing him back. She drank in his touch. She wanted it. She needed it. The loneliness and fear that had dominated her became a distant memory. When she opened her eyes momentarily and caught sight of her wedding ring, she shut them again resolutely. She kicked off her shoes. She got comfortable.

He pulled back abruptly. "Excuse me," he said softly. "I'll be right back." Her heart pounding, she watched him go back to his bedroom. What am I doing, a voice inside asked. She refused to answer. All she knew was that Dr. Peter Montgomery made her feel alive.

☦ ☦ ☦

When Tom got home he was soaked. He stripped off his clothes and took a hot shower. He stayed in it until he'd run all the hot water out of the tank.

When he got out, he heard the phone ringing. "Hello."

"Where have you been?"

"Out, Jack. Running."

"Are you okay?"

"Fine."

"You sure?"

"Sure. Why?"

"Tom, it's almost ten o'clock. I've been trying to get you for hours. And it's forty degrees and raining. Not exactly prime jogging weather."

There was a long pause. "What'd you want, Jack?"

"I just wanted to tell you I'd be picking you up at six-thirty in the morning. To go get Kenny."

"Okay. I'll be ready."

He hung up the phone and put on clean sweats. He went down to the family room and flicked on the TV.

☦ ☦ ☦

Peter returned a minute later. He had a small black pouch, from which he pulled a brass box.

Cathy cocked her head, curious. "What is that?"

"Something that will make you feel like you've never felt before." Carefully, he popped open the box and licked his little finger, dipped it in the white powder, and offered it to her. "You want to go first?"

Cathy stared at him, confused.

"Okay then, I will." Peter put the powder into his mouth, on his gum line. Then he put the box down and turned back to her, kissing her.

"Wait, Peter! Wait," Cathy said, pulling back. "What is that?" Her heart began to pound.

"It makes this so good!" Peter smiled and began kissing her neck, her ear, her cheek, and then her mouth.

Soon, she was lying back against the arm of the couch and his weight was pressing her down, trapping her. As her claustrophobia rose, so did her fear. "No. Stop. Wait, Peter!"

"No, no. Can't stop. Not now. I'm feeling it!" Peter said and he resumed kissing her aggressively.

"No!" Cathy shoved him away. Surprised, he fell, knocking the brass box off the coffee table spilling the white powder on the floor.

"Look what you did!" He cursed.

"Peter, I'm sorry … I just …"

"Sorry?" His face was red and his eyes wide. "That was a hundred bucks!"

"Is it cocaine? Are you using cocaine?"

"Of course it's cocaine! What did you think? You are so naive!"

The look in his eyes scared her. "I want to go home."

"Oh, no! Not yet."

Cathy jumped to her feet. His eyes narrowed. "I don't do drugs. I don't even want to be around drugs." Out of the corner of her eye, she spotted her purse on the table right next to the door. "I'll find a way home."

He grabbed her arm, hissing his words. "You can't go!" His grip on her arm hurt. He planted his mouth on her lips and pressed himself against her. "You leave and I'll tell your husband. Is that what you want? For your husband to know what his good little wife's been up to?"

She jerked away from him. "Don't touch me!" she said. When he moved toward her again, she elbowed him hard, in the gut. Then she turned, raced for the door, grabbed her purse, and ran in her stocking feet out into the night.

Behind her, she heard Peter cursing.

Cathy ran for three blocks, then stopped and burst into tears. Hearing a car behind her, she ran again, fear driving her. She zigzagged through his neighborhood. House after house lined the darkened streets, and she ran shivering in the cold, her coat and shoes left behind.

How could she have been so stupid? Why hadn't she seen it? All the time Peter was charming her with his words he was after one thing. Sex. Enhanced with drugs!

Drugs! Images filled her mind. A baby, crying from the effects of cocaine. Her son, bruised and beaten by a drug gang. Her husband, his eyes full of pain.

What was she thinking? What had she been thinking?

Stupid, stupid, stupid.

Ahead, Cathy saw lights. A restaurant. IHOP. She needed to get warm. She needed to feel safe.

She pushed in the door. Inside the air smelled like pancakes. Comfort food.

"Can I help you?" the hostess said kindly. Her eyes were gray, like Tom's, and Cathy saw them searching her face. I must look like a mess, she thought. The hostess looked down. "Honey, where are your shoes? Where is your coat? What has happened to you?"

Cathy began crying again. "Do you have a pay phone?"

"Come here, honey!" The hostess took her back to the office, and explained to the night manager that this guest needed a phone. One look, and the manager agreed.

Cathy fought her tears. Hands shaking, she dialed.

Voice mail. Her own voice mail! Tom's! She'd accidentally dialed home. She hung up quickly, and began sobbing again.

"Let me help you, sweetie." The night manager wore a tag that read "Marie." She put an arm around Cathy. "Some man do something to you, honey?"

Cathy just nodded.

"You want me to call the police?"

"No!" Cathy said.

"You got someone else for me to call?" Marie asked.

Cathy nodded. She forced herself to focus and wrote down Trish's number.

Thankfully, someone picked up. Tracy.

CHAPTER 17

TOM WATCHED THE LATE SHOW, the re-run of the ten o'clock news, and half a movie. He got up and got a six-pack of beer from the fridge and watched an old John Wayne flick while he tried to drink himself to sleep. The last time he looked at the VCR clock it read 4:09.

But he must have eventually dozed off because when the phone rang at five o'clock it woke him up.

"Tom?"

Cathy's voice knocked the cobwebs out.

"I'm sorry if I woke you up. I wanted to catch you before you left."

He could hear she'd been crying. "Cathy? Are you all right?" Why was she calling him at five in the morning? His heart started pounding. "Cathy?"

"I'm okay. I ... I just needed to talk to you. Is it okay, Tom? Can we talk?"

He sighed and sat down. "Yeah," he said, "I think we need to."

She started to say something and then stopped. "Is our phone still tapped?"

"Yes, it is, but whoever is listening at the office is going to turn off the recorder, right now," he said gruffly. "I'm going to get a cup of coffee while the recorder is turned off. Hold on."

"Okay."

He came back in a few minutes. He put his steaming mug of black coffee on the kitchen table, sat down, and picked up the phone. "Okay, Cathy. Go ahead. I'm ready to listen. But first, are you okay?"

"I'm okay."

She told him about Peter. He listened quietly, bracing himself. When she began sobbing, unable to get words out, his mind began racing, trying in advance to form his response to whatever she might say.

She got to the part about the cocaine. "He what?" Tom said angrily. "Used cocaine with you right there?"

"Yes," Cathy said.

Tom cursed.

"That's when I left. I ran out."

Tom felt pressure in his chest, like a fist pressing hard. He opened his mouth and drew in a deep breath, trying to relax. He had to ask the question. He had to know. "Cathy, did you ... did you have sex with him?" He could hardly get the words out.

Cathy's hesitation felt like it lasted a million years. "No."

Relief flooded him.

"But I let him kiss me. And I'm so sorry."

Tom groped for words. "Cathy, you're vulnerable. That's my fault."

"He paid a lot of attention to me. I haven't had that for a long time. I didn't know I was still ... attractive."

"For heaven's sakes. You turn me on all the time! I love just watching you!"

"How am I supposed to know that?"

He took a deep breath. "I'm sorry. I love you. You're the only woman I've ever loved. And that's the truth."

She blew her nose softly. "Tracy and I have talked all night."

"She's a great kid."

"I got so low, Tom, I honestly couldn't remember why I married you."

He heard Cathy pull another tissue out of a box.

"But then I realized it: You've always treated me with respect. And you've always stood for what's right, even when it hurt you personally."

He closed his eyes and drank in her words.

"I'm sorry, Tom. I'm sorry I was so stupid. And I'm sorry I hurt you."

"Cathy, I forgive you. You're stressed and I forgive you. I'm sorry I've been such a lousy husband. But promise me you won't just walk away again, that you won't just give up on us."

"I promise, Tom. I promise." She swallowed a sob. "Tracy said I've been expecting you to make me happy, and that's put too much pressure on us. She talks like Kenny, Tom. She talks about God."

Tom remained silent.

"You know what she told me? 'Happiness is like a skittish colt. If you try to catch it, you never will. But if you sit down in the middle of the field, and start looking for God, if you thank him for the things around you, pretty soon happiness will come nosing up to you, and you can reach right out and grab it.'"

He heard Cathy blow her nose.

"Tom, I want to come home! I'm so scared!"

"I love you, Cath. You need to stay in Pennsylvania because it's not safe here, but I'm going to come up and see you. Can you hang in there for a few days?"

"Yes. Tell Kenny I love him."

"And you tell that Dr. Peter Montgomery that if I so much as catch him glancing your direction I'm going to..."

"Trust me, he's coming nowhere near me. I promise, Tom! I ... I love you."

They hung up and Tom hit the table. "Yes!" he yelled. He hit the refrigerator, the cabinets, the countertop, and the stove. "Yes, yes, yes!" He hit the dishwasher. "Yes!" Then he glanced at his watch: six-fifteen. He'd have to hurry to get dressed before Jack came. He hit the wall over the door as he left the kitchen. Yes! And he hit the wall down the hall and up the stairs, and he hit the bedroom door and bounced it open. "Yes!" he said, and he turned on the radio. Lite rock. Sixties music. Yes!

☩ ☩ ☩

At six-twenty, Jack rang the bell at Tom's house. When there was no answer, he used his key to let himself in. He was a little early.

He stepped inside and almost tripped on Tom's muddy shoes. He reset the alarm system, and listened. He could hear the radio on upstairs. He went in the kitchen and helped himself to a glass of orange juice. He walked into the family room and shook his head. Two pillows and a blanket were scattered on the couch, and the TV was still on. Beer cans and an empty pretzel bag lay on the coffee table. Jack moved the blanket and sat down to wait.

Tom came downstairs at six thirty-five wearing his tan slacks and navy blazer, his gun discreet but available. As he came through the foyer, he glanced outside and saw Jack's car in the driveway.

Tom stuck his head in the door of the family room. "I gotta get me a dog that'll keep out intruders," he said to Jack. "Some big ugly Rottweiler."

Jack picked up one of the empty beer cans on the coffee table. "No, it wasn't a bad night last night. No. Not much. 'Everything's fine, Jack. Just fine. I always drink like this.' "

"Yeah, well. It wasn't my best night. But it's okay now, partner." Tom said. "Cathy called."

"Whoa. Let me guess. She misses me."

"She didn't even mention your name," Tom said with a smirk.

"Must have been a pretty short conversation."

Tom laughed. "Come on, you sorry excuse for an agent. Let's get going. You're running late."

Tom drove his own car to the high school, parked, and climbed into Jack's car. He grimaced as he settled in the front passenger seat. "Man, am I stiff!" he said.

"It's nice to see you getting in touch with your feelings, Tom. How much sleep did you get last night?"

"Had to be at least forty minutes. Cathy called at five."

Jack looked at him, seriously for once. "And everything's okay? You seem happy."

"You know, Jack. Happiness is like a skittish colt. If you try to catch it, it'll run away from you. But if you just sit down, and enjoy the things that are right around you, it'll come up to you ..."

"And you can use the 9 mm to drop it!"

"Yes!"

They both laughed.

"Tom, this is great. Not only are you getting in touch with

your feelings, but you're startin' to make sense when you talk."

"Let's get out of here."

CHAPTER 18

IN THE PACKED GYMNASIUM, THE noise of the crowd, the shouts of the coaches, and the cheering of the other wrestlers bounced off the hard walls like rifle fire on a range. Nervousness and excitement blended in every wrestler's veins until it became impossible to distinguish between the two.

Tom found a place in the bleachers, halfway up, behind the coaches. After dropping Tom and Kenny at the high school, Jack had gone on to Tom's house. He'd stand guard there as a precaution. They didn't want any surprises when Tom and Kenny came home later that night.

Kenny paced behind the row of folding chairs, off to Tom's right. He stretched his arms, loosening the muscles of his back. He jumped up and down lightly on his feet, his eyes never leaving the mat where the 160-pound wrestler from his team was in the process of pinning his man.

It was a district meet. From his seat in the bleachers, Tom could see colorful warm-up suits from eight different schools dotting the gymnasium, forming an ever-changing kaleidoscope. And he could feel the excitement, too—the pit of his stomach felt alive with it.

Winners today would go on to the regionals. Kenny was the heavy favorite in the 171-pound class. After winning the state championship at 160 pounds last year, Kenny had spent the off-season doing weight training and running. And it had paid off; he had been undefeated before his run-in with Angel Ramos.

Time. Kenny pulled off the red, white, and blue pants and

jacket of his nylon warm-up suit and dropped them behind his chair. He pulled the straps of his wrestling singlet up, momentarily aware of the scars on his chest. He adjusted the legs, buckled on his protective headgear, and fixed the strap. Then he walked up to the mat, blowing his breath and shaking out his arms. His opponent—what had Coach Hall said his name was? Perez? David Perez?—was from a high school on the other side of the county. Kenny had never wrestled him before. Perez wore a black wrestling singlet with red striping around the edges of the legs and neck. A broad white band across his chest held the name "Warriors" written in red.

The crowd cheered as the wrestlers approached the inner circle. Kenny was up, ready to go. He stuck out his hand for the customary handshake. He looked into his opponent's face, saw the olive skin, the black hair, and the black eyes, and he felt his heart take a double beat. Shake it off, he told himself. Don't even think about it.

The blast of the referee's whistle started things off.

"Let's go, Kenny!"

"Break him down!" His teammates shouted words of encouragement.

The two wrestlers circled each other warily. Kenny avoided the black eyes, choosing to focus on his opponent's hands instead. Each wrestler waited for a moment of vulnerability that might open the door to a takedown. They were cautious, controlled, like rock climbers searching for a handhold.

Perez tried first. He went low, diving for Kenny's knees. But Kenny reacted, grabbing Perez around the waist at the same time he moved his feet backwards to stay out of reach. Perez twisted out, and they circled each other again. "Way to go, Kenny! Take him down, now!" a man in the crowd shouted.

This time Kenny went for it—a low, diving move with a twist that he had used very successfully all year. But his timing seemed off and as they fell to the mat Perez twisted out and rotated quickly, coming behind Kenny and gaining the upper hand. "Two!" Kenny heard the ref say as he awarded the takedown to Perez. The crowd on the other side of the gym cheered.

"That's okay, Kenny! Let's go! Gotta go hard!" Coach Hall's voice penetrated the cacophony of sound.

Kenny pushed up on all fours and made his move, a lightning quick roll-out to the right against Perez's weak arm, followed by a lunge up and to the left for control. But in the middle of the roll Kenny looked up and saw his opponent's olive skin, and in that split second he hesitated, losing his chance to take control. Perez moved quickly, forcing Kenny back to the mat. Kenny powered over, and found himself face down on the mat with Perez on top of him.

That's two. Coach Hall shook his head. That's two he's missed.

Now Kenny was angry with himself. Suck it up, he thought to himself. Get a grip on it, Kenny. But a slimy wave of fear had begun to swell in his stomach and he had to swallow hard to suppress the feeling.

"C'mon, Ken, get in there!" someone shouted.

The crowd began yelling, "Ken-ny, Ken-ny, Ken-ny!"

Kenny looked down at the olive hand covering his left wrist. He tried to push up, but Perez had him well covered and for a second he felt the suffocating sensation of being trapped. He closed his eyes.

Suddenly a vortex of fear began to spin deep inside Kenny. He heard voices in his head: *Here he is, Jefe, Donovan's kid. Just like you wanted.*

Oh, man. Kenny felt saliva spring to the hinges of his jaw. He took a deep breath and pushed hard trying to throw off the voices along with the boy on top of him. He managed to slide out to the right, to get partially out from under Perez. His face reddened and his muscles bulged from the strain. Then he ducked his head and tried to throw Perez up and to the left. He caught Perez off balance, pushed him part of the way over, but then Perez found a burst of energy at the same time Kenny's hand slipped on the mat and he grabbed the advantage, twisting Kenny's arm up behind his back until it looked like his shoulder would dislocate. A familiar pain shot up Kenny's arm and a loud gasp escaped his lips.

In the stands, Tom stood, his face intent, watching Kenny's reactions.

"Turn it around, Kenny! Turn it around!" his buddies yelled.

You are not a fed, but you are the son of a fed. His blood runs through your veins, eh?

"C'mon, buddy. Power up! Power up!"

Lock it in, lock it in, Kenny said to himself as he heard Coach Hall's voice. Just listen to him. A drop of sweat fell from his brow, exploding on the mat beneath him.

Perez shifted his position, trying to turn Kenny over on his back. Desperation made Kenny's head pound.

"Move it, Kenny! Make it happen!"

In a burst of effort, Kenny twisted violently under Perez and in one motion jerked his arm free and rolled away from Perez. But Perez moved right on top of him. In an instant, Kenny lay on his back. He momentarily felt both shoulders touch the mat. He heard the slap of the ref's body as he threw himself to the mat to judge the pin and a shot of adrenalin charged through him.

"Bridge up! Bridge up!"

Kenny arched his back and stretched his neck up to keep his shoulder off the mat. He hadn't been this close to being pinned all year and he hated the feeling. He doggedly propelled himself over and backward and when he felt Perez's hand slip he jerked free and escaped. It had been a near fall, three points for Perez and a one-point escape for him.

Kenny bounced on his feet. He shook his arms to loosen the muscles. He was breathing hard, sweating. He shook his head to clear it.

"Take him down, Kenny. Let's go. Time to move!"

The two wrestlers were back in neutral position, circling each other again. Perez had tasted blood and seemed anxious to get on with it. He lunged for Kenny's hips, but hit too high. Kenny shifted left and avoided the takedown, but he didn't react fast enough to move on his opponent. Perez got up and they circled again.

A JV wrestler with a foam bat moved up behind the ref as the time clock counted down. Three, two, one. At zero he tapped the ref on the back and the whistle blew, signaling the end of the first period.

Kenny jogged off the mat.

"Hey, Kenny. What's wrong? You're missing your moves!" Coach Hall put his hand on Kenny's shoulder.

Kenny shook his head. "I don't know." His eyes moved past the coach, over his shoulder to the bleachers. He could see his dad sitting up there, watching him intently.

"Well, don't let it throw you. You're down five to one but there's plenty of time left. You can still beat this kid." Coach Hall hesitated. "You feel okay?"

"Yeah, I'm all right." Kenny felt angry at himself, frustrated with his poor performance, with the thoughts that kept distracting him. He bounced up and down a few times, trying to get his confidence back, trying to get the shakes out of his knees.

Round Two. Kenny was up. Perez got down on all fours. Kenny got down next to him, covering him, his right arm loosely around Perez's waist, his left hand on Perez's left elbow. Kenny stared straight ahead, past that head of black hair. Beyond were the opponents' bleachers, where a group of Latinos were cheering for Perez. Kenny shifted his gaze.

The whistle blew, Kenny's opponent twisted forward, and Kenny scrambled to keep control.

"Stay with him, Kenny! Stay on top!"

"Go, Kenny!"

"Turn him over, Kenny! Turn him over!" Everyone was shouting—the coaches, the other wrestlers, the people in the stands.

Kenny moved to the side, powered forward with his legs, and dug his head into Perez's side, trying to flip him over. But he felt an arm slip and twist out of his hand and it broke his concentration. There was a scramble of arms and legs as the two wrestlers fought for control. The muscles of their arms stood out in sharp "V's" and sweat beaded on their backs. Kenny tried changing his grip just as the crowd on the other side shouted encouragement to Perez.

"Fuerza! Fuerza!"

Kenny missed his hold and in a split second Perez reversed him. Two points. The Latino crowd went wild.

Coach Hall was now completely mystified. He looked back at Kenny's dad, sitting in the stands.

How tough are you, kid? The voices swirled in Kenny's head again, rattling him, shaking his concentration. *Mas? You can take more?*

Kenny knew he was in trouble. He began to panic, his face flushing and his jaws tingling with nausea. Focus, Kenny. Focus. But he couldn't hear the coach's voice. Okay, focus on the mat. He stared at the red circle. It's a mat, he told himself. You've seen it a million times. He gritted his teeth, and twisted up and to the left, pulling his shoulder down and out, pushing with his hips at the same time. Perez counter moved, and the two wrestlers became locked in a fierce equilibrium of forces. Kenny's face and shoulders turned red with exertion.

... but because of his father, we do a little more.

Coach Hall had stopped yelling. He sat quietly, concentrating on Kenny, trying to figure out why his best wrestler was down 10-1 in the second period.

Kenny worked for a grip, struggling against the force of Perez's arms. Suddenly, the Latino crowd began shouting, "Vamos! Vamos!"

Coach Hall saw Kenny's eyes glaze for a split second, saw him suck in a breath and then blink, hard. And he knew in an instant the nature of the problem.

The coach looked back at the seat where Tom had been sitting. It was empty. He looked further around and saw Tom standing to the left of the bleachers, hands on his hips, fifteen feet behind him. Their eyes met. They both knew.

The whistle blew marking the end of the second period. Coach Hall jumped up and moved toward Kenny before his wrestler was even off the mat. He reached him as Kenny jerked his headgear off.

"They're not here, Kenny. The people you're thinking about, they're not here. Look at me, Kenny." His eyes were blazing, and they burned into the deadness in Kenny's eyes like flames into a newspaper. "He's just a kid—that's all. Just a kid with a Spanish name."

Kenny was breathing hard. Sweat dripped off his face. His eyes darted to the far side of the gym. Helplessness and fear swirled inside him.

"Look at me, Kenny! Look at me!"

But he couldn't look, couldn't focus.

Coach Hall grabbed Kenny's wrists and held them in front of him. "Look at your hands, Kenny! They're free!"

Kenny looked down.

The coach grabbed Kenny's hands, forcing them behind his back and holding them there. He moved close, until he and Kenny stood toe to toe, nose to nose, eye to eye. "Is this the way you like it, Kenny? Do you like it this way?" He was right in Kenny's face, his breath hot on Kenny's cheeks.

Kenny tried to pull free but Coach Hall hung on, and once again impotence and despair gripped Kenny as tightly as the zip ties that had cut his wrists just a few weeks ago. He tried to look away but the coach's eyes were compelling.

"Are you going to let them keep you this way the rest of your life?"

Kenny swallowed hard, hating the feeling, struggling for control. He forced himself to meet the coach's gaze. And then he began to think. I don't like this. I don't want him holding on to me. He began to fight against the coach's grip.

They stood there, staring each other down, both men breathing hard. The restless noise of the crowd seemed like distant thunder, the tension between them like thick humidity. Finally, Coach Hall let go of Kenny's arms. "You want to get through the tiger's cage? Stare him in the eye and walk straight at him. Go straight at him, Kenny. Do it! You don't have to be the victim anymore."

I don't have to be the victim. Kenny closed his eyes and took a deep breath.

"You're not the victim!"

The whirling vortex inside slowed down. I don't have to be the victim anymore, Kenny thought to himself. I'm not the victim. He liked the way that felt. I'm not the victim anymore, he said to himself again. I'm not the victim!

"Go get them back!" Coach Hall whispered.

And when Kenny opened his eyes, he tasted confidence again. Perez didn't know it, but he was about to wrestle a different man.

Kenny put his headgear back on as he jogged back to the mat. I can do this, he thought. This is wrestling. I can do it.

Coach Hall glanced back at Tom before he sat down. Tom

nodded.

Round Three. Kenny was down. The whistle blew and Kenny exploded out of position, standing straight up, half-carrying Perez on his back. His heart was pounding, his muscles bursting. The crowd roared its approval. Coach Hall jumped straight up. "Yes!" he shouted.

"All right!"

"Go, Kenny!"

"Get him!"

Kenny didn't give Perez a chance to recover. He attacked his hips, knocking him flat down, and Perez was barely able to flip to his stomach before Kenny was over him, taking control.

"Yes, Kenny! That's it! Now work him over!" Coach Hall jumped to his feet. The ref looked over at him. He sat back down.

Kenny dug his feet in, grabbed Perez's arm, and began pushing. Perez grimaced in pain. The crowd went wild.

Kenny wrestled intensely, methodically. The muscles of his upper back and arms swelled as he moved against Perez, putting everything he had into the effort.

"Way to work, Kenny! Way to work!"

Kenny remained unaware of anything but the olive-skinned body beneath him and the drumming of his own heart.

"Get him over!"

"Go! Go! Go!"

He pushed again and suddenly the resistance gave way and Perez lay on his back. A look of fear crossed Perez's face as he arched up desperately, and he began pushing toward the edge of the mat, toward the out-of-bounds.

"Pull him back! Make him wrestle!"

Kenny glanced up, saw the line, and with a super adrenalin charge he reversed the force of his direction, half-pulled, half-carried Perez back into the ring and in one swift move slammed his shoulders to the mat. Kenny fell on top of him, and with his right arm pulled Perez's left leg up to keep him on his shoulders.

The ref fell to the mat, sliding around until he had a clear view of Perez. One, two, he slapped his hand down. A pin!

Kenny jumped straight up in the air. He did it! He did it! Yes!

His teammates were electrified, their ecstasy filling the gym, drowning everything else out. Kenny shook hands with Perez. The ref raised Kenny's arm, winner of the 171-pound class. And Kenny ran off the mat and jumped into Coach Hall's arms.

"Way to go, Kenny! Way to go!"

Kenny was filled with joy. Thank you, God! Thank you! He left the coach and ran back to his dad. Tom was grinning ear to ear.

⑱ ⑱ ⑱

What a night, Tom thought to himself later as he lay in bed, finally yielding to the exhaustion he felt. He'd had practically no sleep these last twenty-four hours. After the meet they had all gone out for pizza. The boys on the wrestling team were all charged up, laughing and horsing around. Kenny could hardly keep his feet on the ground. It had been a long time since Tom had seen him so elated, so full of himself, and it felt so good.

Tom and Kenny got back home at midnight. Jack was waiting for them. He was ecstatic when they recounted the match for him. He'd slapped Kenny on the back and told him he was a terrific kid, plucky as a fighting gamecock. He was as proud of him as if he were his own son. Then they all had ice cream to celebrate.

They couldn't resist calling Cathy, late as it was. And she was there and sounded happy to hear from them. She was thrilled at Kenny's victory. She missed them, she said, and Tom had felt like the wind had shifted and he was no longer going to have to fight like crazy just to keep from being blown out to sea.

Finally. Now all he had to do was run Kenny back down to J.D.'s first thing in the morning and then get back to work on Ramos.

Tom yawned and turned over. For once, he had no trouble falling asleep.

CHAPTER 19

FOR HER FIRST ASSIGNMENT AS an agent, Sandy had pulled night duty at the office on a Saturday night. It was quiet, nothing much going on, and she tried to pass the time by reading the myriad of regulations with which an agent must be familiar. She sat at one of the metal desks, her feet propped up. Directly across from her was a bank of "hello phones," numbers used by agents for informants, answered with a simple "hello."

Even the radio had been quiet that night and Sandy struggled to stay awake. Then one of the phones rang and someone asked for Tom.

✞ ✞ ✞

The first thing he saw was that the clock said 3:10 a.m. The phone rang a second time. Tom jerked himself awake and picked it up. "Donovan."

"Tom? This is Sandy, down at the office."

"Sandy?"

"Yes. I'm new, and look, I'm sorry to wake you up but I just answered the hello phone. Some guy is desperate to talk to you. Like right now."

"Now?" Tom rubbed his face. "Who is it?"

"Luis somebody. He says you have a mutual friend."

"He wants to talk to me now?"

"I'm sorry, sir."

Tom sighed. He looked at the clock again. Three hours of sleep in two days. Great. "Give me the number," he said, sitting up. He wrote it down. "Okay, thanks," he said, finishing with Sandy. Then he dialed the number. "Luis?" he said.

"Hello, Donovan."

Recognizing the voice of one of Ramos's men, the fog began to clear. "What do you want, Luis?" Why did Luis want to talk in the middle of the night?

"I'm in trouble. I need to talk to you."

"I'm not a priest, Luis."

"No, man. They got a warrant out on me. I can't do no time, man."

"Anyone can do time. What's the warrant for?"

"Some trouble with some horse, man."

Heroin? Really?

"But I'm tellin' you, it's a set up. And I can't do no time, man."

Tom sighed. "What do you want from me?"

"I want some help with the prosecutor."

"Why should I help?"

"I got something you want."

"I doubt it."

"No, man. Listen. I got the evidence you want, on our friend."

"Is that right?"

"Yeah, man. On what he did. With the knife."

Tom swung his legs over the side of the bed. This was getting more interesting. "Luis, why don't we get together, say, tomorrow?" He grabbed the pad of paper and pencil from the night table.

"Oh, man. You don't understand. It's got to be tonight."

"Luis, it's three o'clock in the morning!"

"Look, man. I'm taking a big chance here. He's out lookin' for me, y'know? He finds me ... I'm gone. It was his stuff I was selling."

Tom rubbed his head. Think, think. "I don't know Luis. It's hard for me to get away. I'll tell you what. I'll send someone to pick you up and find a place for you to stay. Then I'll talk to you tomorrow."

"No, man. I don't trust no one else." He sounded angry. "Forget it, man. I just thought you'd want this knife. I was there, Donovan. When he did it. To the boy. I saw it happen. I saw him hurt your kid. But hey, man ..."

"Hold on, Luis. Hold on." Tom took a deep breath. He hated to wake Jack up. But this could be good. "Okay, tell me where you are."

Luis said he was in a phone booth at a gas station. Tom figured he could get there in fifteen minutes. "Okay," Tom said. "And you've got Ramos's knife?"

He did.

"I'll be there in half an hour."

"Make it quick, man. I'm freezing my butt off."

✟ ✟ ✟

When the tap on Tom's phone activated, Sandy listened to his conversation with Luis. Interesting! Maybe Agent Donovan was getting his break. But wait, he wasn't really supposed to be out on the street, working the case, was he? She thought for a minute, then decided to call her supervisor, just to be safe. Maybe he'd want to know, even if it was the middle of the night.

✟ ✟ ✟

Tom pulled his clothes on and took his gun off of the nightstand. He looked in on Kenny. The light coming in the window cast a cross-shaped shadow on his body but his face was in the light and Tom could see that he was sound asleep. Then Tom went on downstairs, grabbed his parka from the closet, and went into the family room where Jack slept on the couch.

"Jack. Jack." He shook his shoulder gently.

Jack opened his eyes. "Tom? What time is it?"

"A little after three. I just got a call from one of Ramos's guys. He wants to flip."

Jack sat up and rubbed his face. "Oh, yeah?"

"He wants me to pick him up. Now."

"Why now?"

"Who knows? You know how screwy these guys are." Tom waited for Jack to absorb that. "I'm going to get him."

"Alone?"

"You've got to stay with Kenny." Tom hesitated. He could see Jack really didn't like this idea. "I'll call Smitty. He lives nearby. He can back me up. It'll be okay." Tom pushed his point. "This could be just what we've needed. He says he saw Ramos cut Kenny. He's got the knife. I've got to do it. Just stay here with Kenny. I'll be back as quick as I can."

"Just watch it, Tom, okay?"

"Sure, Jack. I promise." Tom grinned at him and went out the side door, reactivating the alarm as he did.

Tom jumped in his Bureau car and took off. Rain had made the streets slick and he made an effort to slow himself down a bit. The last thing in the world he needed right now was an accident.

Then he remembered he hadn't called Smitty. He cursed out loud. Oh, well, he'd be quick. And careful.

✞ ✞ ✞

Sandy's supervisor certainly did want to know. He called Fitz who immediately ordered three drug squad and surveillance agents who were on the street at the time to the location where Tom was to meet Luis. Then Fitz got in his car himself. What was Tom doing, going out on something like this by himself? Fitz sighed. Typical Tom.

✞ ✞ ✞

Jack lay back down on the couch. He was just drifting back to sleep when the cinderblock hit the front door with a crash that shook the bones of the house and jolted him awake. He jumped up and grabbed for his gun in the dark, knocking it off the coffee table and onto the floor. He scrambled wildly for it. He heard another crash and then the alarm went off. Where's the gun, where's the gun? His mind raced. He heard footsteps in the foyer.

Then he heard a noise, looked up, and saw two men silhouetted in the doorway of the family room. The one on the left carried a shotgun in port arms position. They hadn't seen him yet.

Jack sprang straight at the taller man, grabbing the shotgun and turning the muzzle toward the second guy. There was a tremendous explosion, a blinding flash, and the simultaneous scream of a man as the gun discharged.

"Roberto!" the man with the shotgun yelled.

Jack kept his grip on the gun and pushed hard, shoving the man on his back. Jack went down right on top of him. He shoved the shotgun down crosswise against the man's throat. He could hear a battle raging upstairs, could hear Kenny yelling and a lot of crashing. Kenny! He had to get to Kenny!

Jack pressed the shotgun against the man's throat with all his strength. In the dim light, he could see the man's eyes darting in fear. The man struggled under him, pushing upward and trying to kick Jack off, but Jack wasn't about to let him do it. Then Jack heard Kenny scream out, "Dad!" and adrenalin shot through his body. He had to get to Kenny! He shoved down harder on the gun. "Die!" he said through gritted teeth.

The flick of the man's eyes, up and to the left, registered an alarm in Jack's mind, but before he could react, the butt of a rifle came crashing down on the back of his head. He saw a white flash, and he heard himself yell "Kenny!" and then everything went black.

CHAPTER 20

"HURRY!" THE MAN WITH THE assault rifle reached down and pulled his friend out from under Jack. The house alarm still shrieked and the shotgun blast had surely alerted the neighbors. The man stood up, reached for the shotgun, and placed the muzzle at the base of Jack's skull.

The other man jerked him away before he could find the trigger. "Come on, Jorge! There's no time! Let's go!"

The two grabbed Roberto by the arms and dragged him out. They left the house, threw Roberto in the van, jumped in themselves, and roared off. In the distance, they heard sirens.

✞ ✞ ✞

Tom was almost to the pick-up point when he saw a county cop, his lights blazing, headed the other way. A minute later, he saw another one, headed the same direction. Something must be happening, he thought. Saturday night. Prime time for drunks.

Then he saw what looked like a Bureau car, a standard government sedan, speeding down the road. That seemed curious. He started to flip on the radio, but decided not to. The gas station where Luis was lay just up the road, on the left.

But as he started to make the left turn into the gas station, he looked, and the phone booth was empty. The rain on the windows made it hard to see. He stopped the car, opened the door, and stepped out. He looked around. And Luis was not there.

Another cop car screamed by. Tom looked at it and felt a

sudden rush of adrenaline. He looked back at the empty phone booth and blinked. A dark dread washed over him. Oh, no. Oh, please, no.

Suddenly two Bureau cars swung into the gas station and a guy Tom knew from a surveillance squad jumped out and ran up to him. "You're okay?" he asked.

"Why?"

"The alarm's gone off at your house."

His words jolted Tom. "No!" he shouted, and he jumped back in the car and roared off toward home, the other cars screaming behind him.

When he rounded the curve and saw his house Tom died inside. There were cop cars everywhere, lights flashing, and some Bureau cars. His front door stood ajar, like a mouth open in shock, the doorjamb splintered.

He left his car in the middle of the street and ran to the house. Fitz met him as he came through the door. The shock and concern on Fitz's face stabbed again at Tom's heart.

"Oh, no. Oh, no." Tom's eyes shifted to an ambulance stretcher. "Jack?" He looked at Fitz.

"They bashed him in the head. He's unconscious. But you're okay? We thought ..."

Tom grabbed Fitz's shoulders. "Kenny? Where's Kenny?"

Fitz looked surprised. "What?"

Tom turned toward the stairs. "Kenny? Kenny!" He slowed down when he saw blood on the carpet, then did the rest of the stairs two at a time. Fitz followed right behind him.

"Was he here? Was Kenny here?" Fitz asked.

Tom ran into Kenny's room. "Kenny? Kenny?" The covers were thrown back, the bed empty. Then he ran to his own room, and as he turned to look, his heart sank. The comforter from the bed had been ripped off, the night table knocked over. The digital alarm clock and phone lay sprawled on the floor. The slats of the bedroom closet doors were shattered and splintered. And the distinct smell of chloroform filled the room.

Fitz touched his shoulder. Tom sank back against the doorjamb, his heart beating erratically. He gasped for breath.

"Was he here? Was Kenny here?" Fitz asked again.

Tom stood trembling all over. He opened his mouth to speak but nothing came out.

"Tom?"

Tom closed his eyes. "I screwed up. I really screwed up."

Fitz turned and immediately began issuing orders, to seal off the entire house, do a thorough search, begin a door-to-door of the neighborhood, get additional manpower out. Now they had a kidnapping and no time to lose.

Tom slammed his fist into the wall and cursed Ramos over and over. Sweat ran down his neck and his heart felt like it would explode. He followed Fitz down the stairs.

"Take it easy, Tom," Fitz said, turning to him.

"Ramos! I'll kill him! I swear, Angel Ramos is a dead man, and I don't care what they do to me! I'm gonna kill him!" he shouted. He tried to push past Fitz.

"Calm down! Just calm down." Fitz grabbed him.

"I'm gonna kill him!" He shoved Fitz away and headed for the front door.

Two other agents heard the yelling and turned to help.

"Tom, no! You're not leaving!" Fitz caught up to him, grabbed his arm and threw him back against the wall. He stood two inches taller than Tom and thirty pounds heavier and he used every bit of his size advantage. "You're not leaving!" Tom's head crashed against the wall. "I'm taking your gun. Listen to me. I'm taking your gun," he lifted it out of the holster and handed it to an agent right behind him. "I want you to stay here, with me." Tom didn't try to resist any more. He leaned against the wall, his head spinning.

A county cop in the foyer had watched the scene. "Ramos? Did you say Ramos?" he asked. "Is he any relation to the boy that got killed last night?"

Both Tom and Fitz turned toward him. Fitz let go of Tom, who walked slowly over to the cop. He grabbed his shirt. The officer looked down, anger sparking in his eyes.

"Tom, let go of him," Fitz said.

"What did you say?" Tom said to the cop.

The cop pushed Tom's hands away. "Last night we had a car stop go bad in South Alexandria. There was a shoot-out. One of our officers killed an eighteen year old named Pablo Ramos."

"Oh, no!" Tom turned away. His head sagged. "Oh, no."

Fitz spoke to the officer. "When did this happen?"

"About eighteen hundred."

"I'd like a full report on that, officer. As soon as you can. All the information you can give me." He turned back to Tom. "Tom, come out to the kitchen with me. I need you to tell me your end of this."

"Fitz!" Another agent, Kate Cameron, called out. "Fitz, the neighbor that called 911 saw a white van."

"Somebody on it?"

"Yes, sir!"

"Okay," Fitz said, "now you tell me, Tom, exactly what happened. Start with telling me why Kenny was here."

Tom's tongue felt thick and his throat had closed up, but he managed to get most of the story out before somebody came racing in. "We got a white van on fire behind the high school!"

Fitz looked at Tom. "I want you right next to me. Understand? Stay right next to me."

Tom nodded.

The rain had changed to a misty drizzle. By the time the men arrived on the scene, the fire department had knocked down most of the fire with foam. A few orange and yellow flames licked at the interior. The van stood steaming in the rain, blackened and ugly. It was a white Chevy, Virginia license plates "RKS 668."

"They'll check it as soon as they can," Fitz said.

Tom shook his head. "He's not in there. If Ramos was going to kill him, he'd leave him where I'd be sure to see him." His voice sounded detached, and indeed, he felt like his soul had detached from his body. He stood there silently, gradually becoming oblivious to the cold and the people around him. His eyes became fixated on the water dripping off the van and into a puddle on the pavement. He stared at the water for a long time, watching the pattern it created as the drops hit the puddle. Not again, he thought. Not again.

After a long time, Fitz touched his arm and he realized he was trembling all over. "Let's go home, Tom," Fitz said softly. "There's nothing we can do here."

CHAPTER 21

HE FELT SICK. HIS STOMACH was churning. I'm going to throw up, Kenny thought. Why am I so sick? He opened his eyes. It was dark, pitch black. He couldn't even see his clock. Why couldn't he see his clock? Why was he moving? Why was it so dark? Oh man, was he sick!

He was lying on his belly, on what? A metal floor? Why? He struggled to get up. He felt sluggish and awkward. He made it to all fours just before his stomach heaved violently and he vomited. Over and over his body convulsed until at last his belly was empty, his ribs ached, and he collapsed to one side, exhausted.

He felt someone roll him onto his back and he was oddly unable to resist. Dad? What was going on? Was he wrestling? Where was he? He looked into the blackness, his head spinning. He squeezed his eyes shut and then opened them again.

He felt his left arm being stretched out. Someone was holding him down. There were hands on his thighs, hands on his shoulders. He could feel them, but whose were they?

He heard a click, and a small flashlight flicked on, and a circle of light appeared illuminating just his left arm. He looked on in confusion as someone wrapped rubber tubing around it, just above his elbow, and tightened it. He watched, feeling strangely detached, as if the arm were not his, although he knew it was. And then he saw a hand with a hypodermic needle enter the light. The needle moved toward his arm and he wanted desperately to get away, to move back, away from the needle, but somehow, he couldn't organize himself to do it.

He watched, horrified, as the needle pierced his skin and the plunger was depressed. He looked away and moaned, and a feeling like warm syrup being poured throughout his body flowed through him. His jaw dropped open and he closed his eyes. Oh, Dad ...

✝ ✝ ✝

When the SAC, Alex Cramer, walked into Tom's house it was easy to see he was not a happy man. His jaw was set and his eyes were focused straight ahead as he strode through the foyer, ignoring the agents and cops that swarmed around. This wasn't going to look good, not for him, not for Tom, not for the Bureau. And the image of his own eighteen-year-old son, now safe at home in bed, kept intruding uncomfortably on his thoughts.

As he walked down the hallway, the jacket of his gray pinstripe suit swung open. His Smith & Wesson rode easily on his side.

"Fitz!" His tone was commanding.

"Right here, sir," Fitz responded, sticking his head out of the kitchen.

✝ ✝ ✝

Tom had been leaning back against the countertop, but he stood up as Cramer walked in. He started to shake hands with him, but one look at his face told Tom it would be inappropriate.

"Mr. Cramer," Tom said quietly. Two other agents left the room, leaving Tom, Fitz, and Cramer alone.

Cramer looked from Tom to Fitz. "So what happened here?" he demanded.

Fitz filled him in, neatly and clearly explaining the events of the last hour or so. Tom stood in the corner, next to the stove, trying to stay cool, trying to hide the tension that gripped his body in fits of trembling.

"This isn't good." Cramer responded when Fitz had finished. "This isn't good at all." He walked over to the sink. "How's McRae?"

"Unconscious, sir," Fitz responded. "Possible fractured skull."

Cramer slammed his fist on the counter, and turned

toward Tom. "I told you to do two things, Donovan." He pointed his finger at him. "Stay off the street, and get your family out of here. I knew you'd ignore the first one, but I really figured you'd have the brains to protect your kid!"

Tom winced.

Cramer walked closer to Tom. "You think you can ignore me, Donovan?" He gestured angrily. "We've had an agent assaulted, a boy kidnapped. You managed to endanger yourself, your partner, and your son, all in one fell swoop. I pictured you smarter than that!" He walked a few steps away and then turned back. "What do you think they'll do to your son?"

Tom's eyes were on the floor. Cramer's tongue lashing drove the guilt deeper and deeper, but he had no response. He deserved it. All he could do was ride it out.

"Alex," Fitz interjected.

Cramer held up his hand as if he didn't want to hear it. "I ought to yank your creds right now, Donovan. You've been an agent how long? And you still haven't learned to follow orders?" He turned, shaking his head. The room seemed deathly still.

Cramer turned back to Tom. "You have any other surprises for me? Anything else I should know? I mean, before I have to go out there and explain to the Director, and the Washington Post, and seventy-five thousand television reporters exactly how we managed to let a two-bit drug dealer abduct the son of an FBI agent?" He sat down heavily in one of the chairs at the table.

"No, sir."

Cramer looked at him as if to say there better *not* be anything else, then he blew out a frustrated breath.

"Alex ..."

"What is it, Fitz?" Cramer sounded impatient.

"You don't know Kenny."

Cramer looked up at him. "No, that's right. I don't. And now, I may never get the chance."

Fitz jiggled something in his hand. Tom saw it was a little silver cross.

"Kenny's pretty strong-willed himself. Wrestling is really important to him." His voice sounded low and steady. "The minute he began waking up in the hospital he was talking about wrestling, bugging the doctors, asking when he could wrestle again." Cramer looked at Fitz hard, as if he were going to challenge whatever Fitz said, but Fitz kept on going. "They could hardly keep the kid down long enough to recover."

"Kenny was determined to wrestle in the district meet yesterday," Fitz continued. "Alex, I believe, knowing Kenny as I do, that if Tom hadn't brought him up for it, he would have come up on his own. He would have borrowed a car, or talked a friend into coming down to get him or something. One way or another, with or without his father's permission, I think Kenny was going to wrestle yesterday. I don't think anything short of locking him up would have stopped him."

Tom's heart thumped hard in his chest. He grabbed on to Fitz's words. And even Cramer's eyes softened a little.

Fitz continued. "I believe, in his heart, Tom knew that, Alex. He figured Kenny'd be safer with him than running around on his own."

Yes, Tom thought. Thank you, Fitz. Thank you.

"I think Tom made the best decision he could, given the circumstances, Alex. It turned out terrible, but I might have done the same thing."

Cramer looked over at Tom, looked him up and down, let out a heavy sigh. "But he couldn't even let us know, give us the courtesy of asking, before he disobeyed a direct order?" He nodded toward Tom, speaking about him as if he weren't even there.

"Maybe he should have told us what was going on, Alex, but then, maybe he knew what we'd say."

A long silence filled the room. Tom's hands shook. He jammed them in his pockets. A thousand thoughts raced through his head, his brain spinning like the flywheel on an engine.

Cramer seemed lost in thought, mulling over his choices of reaction, thinking out his next move like the good chess player he was. Finally, he stood up and walked slowly over to Tom. "I came down on you too hard, Tom. I'm sorry."

Tom felt a shiver of relief run down his spine, not that he gave a rip about his career at this point. "Yes, sir," he said.

"He was only supposed to be here seven hours, sir. Just long enough to sleep. I never thought ..." He couldn't finish. He shook his head.

Cramer nodded, then looked away. "I still don't know how I'm going to explain this," he muttered. After a few moments, he turned to Fitz. He looked at his watch. He thumped his knuckles on the table. "It's almost five," he said. "I want status reports from you every four hours, beginning this morning at eight. I want every available agent shaking the bushes, looking for this guy. I want a 'no comment' response to the press. If this thing isn't resolved today, I want to meet with you, Dave Borsten from Hostage Rescue," he glanced toward Tom, "and Tom, at seven Monday morning, in my office. And I want you to find Angel Ramos and let me personally crush his face." Then he turned on his heel and walked out.

Tom looked gratefully at Fitz. "Thank you."

Fitz patted him on the shoulder. "You're a good man, Tom. And so is Cramer. I knew he was looking at it the wrong way."

CHAPTER 22

BY SEVEN THE SUN WAS coming up, the sky outside the windows changing from black to gray. Tom stood at the door of his family room, fingering Kenny's Irish Brigade hat, watching as agents gathered evidence. Oh, Kenny, he thought, how could I have let this happen? He felt all cut up inside, like a thousand knives were twisting in his gut.

The doorjambs were black with fingerprint dust, and two men were bent over the carpet, cutting out samples. A photographer, who Tom figured had already photographed the room from every possible angle, continued snapping pictures. Small circles painted on the wall and on the rug showed where shot lay embedded in the wall. The shattered lamp lay on the floor, its pieces painstakingly mapped on the diagram being drawn by one of the agents. Fitz and another agent stood side by side, reconstructing what had taken place in the room. At their feet lay another bloodstain, one which Tom knew had come from Jack's head. Tom's stomach turned as he looked at it.

Tom knew he had to call Cathy. He'd been hoping against hope they'd find Kenny by dawn, but they hadn't and since it was 7 a.m. it seemed only fair to her. He had to do it.

"Hello?"

"Tracy, get Cathy. And then stay with her."

"Okay."

From the sound of her voice, Tom knew Tracy had caught the seriousness of his call. His knees shook. He didn't want to do this! He braced himself.

"Tom, what's wrong?" Cathy asked.

He told her. "I was duped, Cathy, and while I was gone, they broke in, assaulted Jack, and took Kenny."

"Took him where?"

"We don't know. We have hundreds of agents and cops out looking for them. Hundreds of them."

"Oh, Tom!" She began crying, and then she said, "I'm coming home."

"No, Cathy. You're safer up there. I'll keep in touch with you."

"Tom," she said, sniffing, "I'm coming home. This is something we need to go through together."

And he felt glad.

"Hang on a minute," he said. He put his hand over the phone. "Fitz?" Fitz came back to the kitchen. "She wants to come down here."

Fitz looked at him. Tom could feel his eyes reading his soul and he felt awkward, naked. Did Fitz know about the problems in their marriage? Tom had never discussed it but Fitz picked up on things.

"Where could she stay?" Fitz asked.

"I'd be glad to have her," Kate said. She'd come in the room behind Fitz. "I'm in northwest D.C. Ramos doesn't operate there. We could sneak her in and then she could just lie low. Tom could come and go, if he was careful. I doubt my neighbors would notice."

Fitz thought about it for a minute. "Yes," he said finally. "That'll work."

"And Cramer?" Tom asked.

"I'll fix it with Cramer. You two set this up."

Tom turned back to the phone. "Cathy?" he said. "We've got it arranged. Here's what we'll do ..."

Tom hung up the phone and walked outside. The cold, damp air made him shiver. In the pale light of dawn he could see agents taking plaster casts of the footprints under his bushes and of the tire tracks across his lawn, and he wanted them all to go away. He wanted the yellow tape identifying the crime scene to disappear, and the agents' cars and vans to leave, and he wanted everyone out of his house, and the door to be replaced. He wanted the blood off his carpets, and the shot out of his walls, and the sickening smell of chloroform out of his bedroom. He wanted Jack to come walking in, grinning and telling some hick story. And most of all, he wanted his son back, laughing and smiling, his blue eyes flashing with life.

Kate came up next to him and touched his arm lightly. "Anything I can do for you, Tom?" she asked.

He inhaled sharply and felt his teeth chatter with tension. "I want to see Jack, Kate. I need to see Jack."

"Come on," said Kate. "I'll take you."

✞ ✞ ✞

As Tom and Kate walked through the door of Fairfax Hospital, Tom thought, I've been in this place too much lately. They tracked Jack down. As Tom opened the door to his room, Smitty, staying with Jack, got up and left, leaving the two friends alone.

"Hey, buddy." Jack looked pale and tired in the stark fluorescent light.

Tom walked over to him and shook his hand, gripping it with both of his and trying to read the incident report etched in the lines of Jack's face. "How are you, Jack?"

"I'm madder 'n a bull gettin' clipped." Jack pulled himself up awkwardly to a sitting position, wincing as he did. "They were in that house before I knew it, like an assault team, in the door and right up the stairs. Two of 'em came in after me, and the others were on Kenny. He gave 'em a fight, Tom. I heard it." He shook his head. "Smitty says we don't have him yet?"

Tom shook his head. "No. Everybody's looking for him. But we don't have him yet."

"I'm tellin' you Tom, the minute I get outta here I'm gonna track down Ramos and make him wish ..."

Tom held up his hand. "Hold it, Jack. You're taking the curve a little too fast, buddy. Take it easy."

Jack settled back. "Well, this sure is different."

An awkward silence followed. "You put up an incredible fight, Jack, from the looks of my family room."

"I'm only sorry I didn't kill 'em. All of 'em."

"How you feeling?"

Jack looked off to the side. "Head hurts. I got six stitches back here."

Tom stood up and looked at the back of Jack's head

"Mostly, I'm feelin' real bad. I let you down, Tom, you and Kenny. And I'm sorry."

"What are you talking about? You did everything you could, Jack. Everything."

"I was supposed to be your backstop, Tom. Keep you from makin' a mistake. And protect Kenny. I didn't do either one." He let out a long breath. He looked at Tom, his eyes drooping with fatigue and depression. "I'm sorry, partner. I'm really sorry."

Tom shook his head. "It was me, Jack. I should have known. A call like that in the middle of the night. I can't believe I let them sucker me into it."

"I should've stopped you, Tom. Why didn't I stop you?"

"You shouldn't have had to. I should have stopped myself."

They sat there for a while, listening to the sounds of the hospital, the PA system, voices in the corridor, a squeaky wheel on some cart.

"I never actually thought they'd be that smart, y'know, Tom?"

Tom saw a little metal tube clamp on the floor. He reached down and picked it up and began playing with it. Open and shut. Open and shut.

"You know Ramos' little brother, Pablo?"

"Yeah."

"Fairfax had a vehicle stop go bad last night. They killed him."

Jack cursed.

Tom rested his elbows on his knees and looked at the floor. "I think we're in trouble, Jack."

"You're not givin' up there, are you, partner?" Jack asked softly.

Tom didn't answer him.

"Y'know, Tom, Kenny wouldn't want us to just belly-up on him."

Tom looked away.

"I mean, okay, we made a big mistake. But I don't think we oughta tuck our tails and slink under the porch, like a couple of whipped dogs."

Tom smiled ever so slightly.

"What do you say we suck it up, partner, and go on from here?" Jack continued. "I'm sure Kenny's still givin' 'em all kinds of grief. What do you say we admit we both screwed up, and then get on with the job?"

Tom rubbed his hands over his face and held them over his mouth and nose. "I can't give up," he said. "I've got to get him out of there." He looked Jack in the eyes. "I've got to!"

"I'll be right with you, buddy. Soon as they give me my clothes back."

Tom stood up and patted him on the arm. "You just take it easy. Take care of yourself, okay, Jack? I can handle this for now."

CHAPTER 23

WHEN KENNY WOKE UP AGAIN, he found himself lying on a wooden floor on his belly in his Virginia Tech T-shirt and his boxer undershorts. He still felt nauseous. And cold. Kenny tried to move, but his right hand was restrained. He opened his eyes and saw a handcuff around his wrist. The other end was around the input pipe of a radiator. He felt his stomach pitch and a wave of revulsion rolled over him.

Cuffed? Cuffed? He jerked his hand but the cuff remained secure.

Where was he? He struggled to move but the best he could do was turn halfway over and look around.

He was in a small, dirty room, empty except for two dingy armchairs. Dust lay heavily in the corners and there was a large brown stain on the wall, like someone had heaved a cup of coffee at it. He was cuffed to an old-fashioned radiator, under a window. He could see spiderwebs and dead bugs on the floor, and he could feel a draft of cold air coming in around the window.

He put his head back down and tried to suppress the nausea. No! No! How did he get here? What happened?

He remembered the alarm going off. He'd run to his dad's room. The bed had been empty. Where was Dad? Then someone jumped him, and he remembered a rag with an awful smell covering his face.

He groaned softly at the memory. A bitter chill ran through him, and a voice from the past echoed in his ears. *Next time, we not just play with this fine boy. We kill him.* He closed his eyes. He had to get out of there. Oh, God, help! Panicked, he tried to work his hand out of the cuff. Too tight. The radiator was old. Maybe he could break the pipe. He jerked and jerked but all he gained was a bruised wrist. He sagged back down on his stomach and closed his eyes.

Footsteps. Footsteps and a voice. "Get up." Someone nudged him in the ribs with a shoe, and suddenly Kenny felt infuriated.

"Get up!" the boy said again, and he kicked Kenny a little harder. Kenny grabbed his leg with his free hand.

"Watch him!" A second person ran up, and threw himself on top of Kenny, squeezing his air out. Kenny twisted against him, but he laced his fingers up through Kenny's hair, and forced his head down to the floor, cursing.

Kenny could hardly breathe, this man felt so heavy. He heard a click, and felt a knife against his throat.

"You listen," the man said. His breath was hot. "They say let you get cleaned up and dressed. But I'm not going to screw with you. You want to lie here freezing, smelling like a sewer it's okay. I not going to fight you, man. Comprende?"

Kenny didn't respond.

He jerked Kenny's hair. "Understand?"

"Yes."

"Okay. We try this again. But you give us trouble, and you stay chained like a dog."

He got up and Kenny took a deep breath. Kenny closed his eyes for a minute and forced himself to calm down. The cuff came off. Kenny pushed himself up to his knees and looked around.

The man, who looked about twenty-five, dark-haired and heavyset, stood next to a boy younger than Kenny. He wore a red Bullets T-shirt and tan chinos. He had short, black hair and dark eyes. And in his shaking hands he held a 9 mm semi-automatic handgun, pointed straight at Kenny's chest. He looked ludicrous holding that gun, like a little kid wearing his dad's cowboy boots.

"Get up!" the man said again.

Kenny's legs and back were stiff and sore and he had to struggle to get to his feet. His head spun crazily, and he hesitated a minute before he began to walk in the direction he was prodded.

They took him down the hall to the bathroom and stood in the open door as Kenny used it. The black and white tile in the room was grimy and broken in places, the floor yellow with age. The sink hadn't been cleaned in an eternity, and Kenny tried not to touch it as he washed up. He gulped water from his hands, drinking as much as he could both to calm his stomach and help flush out whatever drugs they had used on him. He still felt groggy, and a sickening mix of fear, despair, drugs, and anger churned in his stomach.

Kenny pulled off his Virginia Tech T-shirt. He splashed his face and used his T-shirt as a towel. As he wiped his shirt over his eyes, he turned and noticed the boy staring at the scars on his chest. He felt his face grow hot. He put his T-shirt back on.

They walked him back to the room. The man handed him gray sweatpants and socks, and Kenny pulled them on. He glimpsed the outside world through the grimy window. He was in the city somewhere. Outside was a commercial building with a flat composite roof. He glanced at his watch. It was 12:16 p.m. Sunday. At home, his friends were just getting out of church.

Then the man forced him to sit down on the floor and he cuffed Kenny's hands behind him, padlocking the cuffs to a short, heavy chain, like a length of tow chain, which was attached to the water pipe feeding the radiator.

As Kenny heard the lock click shut, a dark, black wave of despair spread over him. Oh, God, he thought. I can't handle this! I can't! He leaned back against the ridged metal rib of the radiator and closed his eyes. God, make it go away. Please, make it go away. He bit his lip, hard, to keep from crying.

✟ ✟ ✟

Twelve-twenty, Sunday afternoon. Cathy stared out of the car window at Washington's sunny, clear day, her insides tight with anxiety.

A friend of Tom's, an agent from Philadelphia, had driven Cathy down. She used to resent what she disparagingly called the "agent fraternity." Now she felt so grateful for it. That camaraderie of common purpose and support was of critical importance to her now.

They drove down upper Wisconsin Avenue, past city churches emptying their parishioners into the bright winter sunshine, past restaurants and shops and stores preparing to open. People walked and jogged on the sidewalks. Cathy stared at them. They seemed so whole, and she felt so shattered.

The Washington Cathedral appeared, a classic Gothic cathedral, eighty years in the building. It stood high on a hill, its towers and gargoyles majestically presiding over the beautiful old neighborhoods of northwest D.C.

Once again, Cathy realized she longed for something she could not define: Someone, something to make things right, to bring order out of chaos, and peace to her troubled heart. She wished she could talk to Tracy.

Kate, the agent who had volunteered to host her, lived in an elegant row house built in the 1920s just off Wisconsin Avenue, not far from the Cathedral. An alley ran behind the house, and next to it stood a garage with two old D.C. license plates nailed to the wall. A six-foot wooden fence surrounded the bricked-in patio, and new wooden steps led up to the back door. Tom's friend led Cathy into the house through the back yard, as instructed. Tom sat waiting for her in the kitchen.

✞ ✞ ✞

Kate had given Cathy the front bedroom, the one with the large bay windows and the pineapple-post bed. Violets and bachelor buttons were scattered over the wallpaper, and a blue, lavender, and white rag rug lay on the floor. In the corner stood a walnut vanity from the 1930s, its three mirrors reflecting Cathy's drawn and worried face as she and Tom entered the room. He was behind her, carrying her bags, his stomach queasy, dreading the conversation he knew was inevitable. As he stood looking at her in the mirror, he realized again how much he had missed her, how angry he was at himself that he had failed her in so many ways.

He put the bags down. She turned around.

"Tom ..." "Cathy ...," they both said together.

She turned away from him again and walked toward the window. He braced himself as she turned and faced him.

"How could this happen?"

"It was my fault."

"How could they break into our home, take our son ..."

Tom jammed his left hand in his pocket and rubbed his head with his right.

"I don't understand ..."

Tom flared up. "It's my fault, okay? I was stupid to fall for the ruse. If I hadn't been so anxious to get Ramos." He jammed his fist into the wall, right onto a bachelor button. "I can't believe I fell for it. Why didn't I see through it?"

"Stop, Tom. Stop."

"I was so stupid ..."

"Stop!"

She crossed the room, put her arms around him, and hugged him. "Stop it! I'm not blaming you!"

"Oh, Cath," he whispered, "I'm so sorry."

"I'm sorry, too, Tom. About Kenny, and about the fact I've hurt you. I was an idiot."

He put his arms around her, and they held each other for the first time in a very long time.

After a few minutes she let go of him and walked over to the bed. "We've made a mess of it, haven't we. Both of us," Cathy said. She sat down, and for a minute he was afraid she was going to cry. But then she took a deep breath and said, "We're going to need to sort it out, Tom, but I think that has to come later. Right now, all I can think about is Kenny."

"I agree." Tom swallowed. His throat felt tight.

"How did Ramos know Kenny was in town?"

"The kid Kenny wrestled was Latino. There was a large crowd there, a big group of people shouting things in Spanish. I guess word got back to Ramos. He's well-connected in the community."

"Don't people know he's a drug dealer?"

"Lots of people live double lives. Friends and neighbors see what they want. A guy has money, he's willing to help out, people don't ask where he got it."

She remained quiet. He felt his heart drumming.

"Oh, Tom," she said, tearing up. "Why Kenny? Why did it have to be Kenny?"

"I wish it were me, Cathy. I'd give anything if it had been

me." He rubbed the back of his neck.

"I wish I had been here," she said. "I was so selfish, so angry at you both. I should have stayed home, then I would have been in the house ..."

"And then Ramos would have taken you, too, Cathy. I'm glad you weren't home." Tom's stomach turned at that horrible thought.

Cathy reached for a tissue. He could see she was beginning to cry.

Tom walked over to her, sat down, and pulled her head down on his chest. "Shh ... shh," he said. "Don't get upset. Kenny wouldn't want you to get upset." His stomach churned. "Kenny's so strong." Tom stroked her hair. "You should have seen him, Cathy. You would have been so proud of him! We didn't tell you everything on the phone. He really clutched during the match. He said he had flashbacks and he kept missing his moves. He was down ten to one and he came back. And when he won, he was just elated, just so happy. I haven't seen him that happy in a long time." He kissed the top of her head. "He's strong, Cathy. He's a fighter. He'll hold on until we find him. And we will find him."

After a while, she looked up at him. "And how are you, Tom? How are you doing?"

"Real angry at myself."

"Did you call your mom?"

"No."

"You've got to call her. She'll want to know."

"I will, Cathy. I just can't right now."

He held her for a while longer, and then he said, "Would you like a cup of tea?" She nodded, and he left the room. No doubt, Kate would have some tea around. And it was all he could think to do.

He returned a few minutes later with a cup of steaming tea in one hand, and a mug of black coffee in the other. "Here you go," he said, setting it down on the night table.

"Thank you," Cathy said. She looked a little more composed. Glancing around the room, she said, "Where are your things?"

"I'm not staying here."

"Oh." Cathy looked up at him.

"What's wrong?" he asked.

"Could you stay with me? Or are you angry with me?"

"I didn't know if you'd want me to. I don't want to pressure you."

Her eyes got teary. "I need you, Tom. You've been my rock all these years. That's why it hurt so much for you to ignore me. I had no rock."

Suddenly, Tom could see the pain he'd caused. Her parents had died long before Tom met her. And he'd been MIA for too long, lost in his job. She felt abandoned. Again. "I'm so sorry, Cath." He sat on the bed next to her, shifted his coffee to his left hand, and put his arm around her.

"Tracy says you can't be my rock. That it's putting too much pressure on our marriage."

Tom had no idea what that meant.

"I don't understand all that. Yet. The point is, I need you. And I would like it very much if you'd stay here with me."

"Okay, then, I will." And he felt glad.

"And Tom, I need to know what's going on with the investigation."

"Cathy,…"

"I know, I don't usually like to hear about your job. It overwhelms me. I don't know if you can understand that, but it does. This is different. This is our son. I need to know what's happening. Even if it's hard to hear."

"Okay," Tom said.

"One last thing. I need to know what you're feeling."

He gulped his coffee. It burned his tongue.

"I don't believe it when you tell me everything's fine," Cathy said. "Not when I can see that your stomach's upset and you can't eat, or when I hear you slip out of bed at night and go downstairs because you can't sleep. Something's going on inside you, Tom, and I want to be in on it. I need to be close to you, Tom. I need that."

Tom stood up. He noticed his coffee cup was shaking and he steadied it with his other hand before he turned around and looked at her. "Is that it?" he asked.

"That's it."

"Cathy, I promise I'll spend as much time with you as I

possibly can. I don't know how this is all going to go down. Or how fast. But I'll be here whenever I can."

She nodded.

Unable to stop his trembling, he put his coffee down and shoved his hands into his pockets. "I'll keep you well-informed. You can have as much detail as you want. As for the other," Tom walked slowly across the room and rubbed the back of his head. "I don't know how to do that. I'm not a touchy-feely kind of guy. It's just not me."

She just kept looking at him.

"I don't want to get all tangled up in feelings."

She moved to him and touched his arm. "Whether you want to or not, you are, or you wouldn't have so much trouble sleeping. Now how about letting me in on it, just a little?"

The wisp of gray in her hair caught his eye. He touched it, brushing his hand gently over her face. He could have lost her, his one great love. He slid his hand behind her head, bent down, and kissed her on the lips, so grateful, so thankful, for the warmth of her presence. "I'll try, Cathy. I'll really try," he whispered.

CHAPTER 24

HOURS LATER, KENNY HEARD SEVERAL men enter the room and he turned to see who they were, his chain clanking against the radiator. The first man stood taller than most of the Latinos. His jet black hair was shaggy. Despite his broad face, his eyes were set close together, and a large scar bisected his cheek from his ear down close to his mouth. He wore tan chinos and a white T-shirt, and a gray plaid flannel shirt.

He walked over to the young boy, who sat in one of the chairs, and tapped him on the shoe with his boot. "Unlock him," he demanded, nodding toward Kenny.

"Okay, Luis."

Luis: Had Dad mentioned Luis? Kenny searched his memory.

The boy uncuffed Kenny and pulled him to his feet. As he got up, the blood drained from Kenny's head and for a minute his vision went dark. Then the boy re-cuffed his hands in front, and shoved him toward the door of the bedroom.

They took Kenny down the narrow stairs to the first floor. The deep purple of the evening made the house gloomy and dark. The shadowy rooms seemed like catacombs to Kenny. He wondered what was going to happen. He didn't want to go with these people. He didn't want to be in this house. His head ached. He wanted to close his eyes, and then wake up, and find out it was all just a terrible dream. He kept looking for a way of escape, but Luis had his hand firmly on Kenny's elbow.

They entered a room lit only by a modern black metal floor lamp, which threw a cone of bright light directly up to the ceiling. Kenny could see eight or ten men, standing around talking. Actually, they were around his age, but they looked older. Some had beer. Some were smoking. They all turned and stared as Kenny came in the room. With a squeeze and a shove that seemed like the underhand flip of a baseball, Luis pushed Kenny down into a hard wooden chair.

The air crackled with tension. Kenny's neck muscles grew tight as he looked the men over. Which ones were there before? Who stood by while Ramos cut him? He'd memorize their faces. He'd make sure he'd have no trouble identifying them later. No trouble at all.

After what seemed to be forever, Kenny heard footsteps in the hall. Everyone stopped talking. Kenny looked up just as a man, smoking a cigar, walked in the room.

He had on black dress pants, a gray and white knit shirt, and a leather bomber jacket. The man's black hair was brushed back. It hung slightly over his collar. He would have been handsome had it not been for his eyes. They were small and black, set in his face like burning coals in a barbecue pit. He stripped off his jacket as he entered the room, handing it to a gang member, and he flexed and stretched the muscles of his arms as he approached Kenny. On his feet he wore gray alligator-leather western boots.

When Kenny saw him, when he smelled the cigar, and recognized those boots, his heart rate increased, and blood rose to his neck and face. It had to be Angel Ramos. Oh, God, he prayed. Help me!

Ramos walked straight up to him, pulled him to his feet with his left hand, and examined him as if he were inspecting merchandise. "Well, look who came back."

Kenny's mouth went dry at the sound of his voice.

"You ready for more, eh, kid?" He looked around the room, then back at Kenny. He put his hand on Kenny's neck. Kenny jerked away.

Ramos laughed. He looked at the other men. "He still fights, eh?" He smacked Kenny across the mouth. Kenny shook it off, anger blazing in his glare.

"Anyone tell you why you're here, young Donovan?"

Ramos's voice sounded too smooth. It didn't match the tension that narrowed his eyes into dots. "No?" Suddenly Ramos shoved him across the room, pushing him hard into the wall. Kenny's head went back, crashed into the plaster, but he regained his balance and stood up straight as Ramos approached him.

"Let me tell you." El Jefe was breathing hard. He reached out and cupped his hand under Kenny's jaw, almost like an affectionate older brother, and Kenny felt a thousand icicles fall into his brain.

"I had a little brother just your age. Eighteen. He was sharp, you know? Fun. Last night, he was with our friend Ricardo. They were driving along, minding their own business. Suddenly there are blue and red lights in Ricardo's mirror. The cops. So, like a good citizen, he pulls over.

"But the cops, they don't come up to Ricardo's car. He waits, and waits, and finally Ricardo, he steps out of the car, to see what's going on. So does Pablo. They walk back toward the cops. And Ricardo reaches into his back pocket to get his license. And what happens? The cops start shooting.

"The bullets, they are flying everywhere. There is no where to hide. And Pablo, who has no gun, gets hit. He falls in the street, blood gushing out of his side, his head." Ramos' eyebrows narrowed until they almost touched.

"And do the cops help my brother? No, they stand there, doing nothing, watching as he bleeds to death on the street, like an animal." Ramos was breathing hard, his eyes glowing, his hands clenched.

Everyone else in the room remained still. Kenny could feel a muscle in his thigh quivering. He flexed his jaw and swallowed hard.

Ramos glared at Kenny. "And so my little brother is dead. Because your father killed him!"

Kenny shook his head. "No! My dad was with me last night—he didn't kill him!"

"Your father has every cop in Virginia gunning for us!" His face twisted in anger.

"What are you talking about?"

"My little brother is dead because of Tom Donovan!" Ramos stood so close he filled Kenny's field of vision. Red-faced, he pressed his lips tightly together. A trickle of sweat escaped his brow.

Kenny shook his head and took a deep breath, his anger driving him past where he knew he should be. "Your brother is dead because he was stupid! He shouldn't have gotten out of the car!"

Ramos shifted his weight, pulled back his right hand and let a punch fly that hit Kenny squarely in the jaw, knocking his head back against the wall. Kenny twisted to the right and spit out a stream of blood. He felt Ramos reach for him, grabbing his shirt, and he reacted instinctively. "Get off me!" he yelled. Turning, he raised his bound hands with all his might and caught the boss squarely under the chin. He saw Ramos' head snap back and surprise shattered his expression like fractured glass.

Two men jumped on Kenny immediately, wrestling him back against the wall, the smell of their breath and their sweat thick in his lungs. Ramos regained his balance. Kenny saw his eyes were burning with anger. And over Ramos' shoulder, Kenny caught a glimpse of the young boy, a look of horror on his face.

"Carlos," Ramos said, taking a step backward and rubbing his chin. The boy came forward. "Cuff his hands *behind* his back."

Carlos quickly moved to comply. Kenny stood panting, blood dripping from his mouth, while Carlos re-cuffed him. "You've created your own problems," Kenny said between breaths. "My father is just doing his job."

The boss walked up to Kenny almost casually. His eyes had turned to chunks of obsidian, cold and hard. He put both hands on Kenny's neck, feeling it as if he were checking for a hand-hold. Kenny twisted his head, but the boss held him firmly.

"You know what I do, kid?"

Kenny looked him straight in the eyes. How he hated that voice!

"I teach you something about dying."

Kenny kept his eyes steady although his heart was pounding. Oh, God, he prayed. God help me!

"Then maybe you understand how Pablo felt." He placed

his thumbs carefully overtop Kenny's windpipe, stroking Kenny's neck. Kenny trembled under his touch.

"I take you right down to the point of death, then you feel the panic that Pablo felt, lying there by himself in the street." His words were smooth, like a snake gliding across a rock.

Kenny felt the vise-like hands begin squeezing his neck, constricting his airway. He pulled back, and tried to twist away, but he couldn't break Ramos's hold. He fought, pushing hard with his legs, but he was trapped, and as he sucked in a thin stream of air, his stomach convulsed.

"Scary, eh, kid?"

Jagged, miniature lightning bolts flashed in Kenny's eyes. His face turned red and his eyes widened. Air. He had to get air. He needed air!

"How are you feeling?" The boss tightened his grip.

Kenny took one more breath, and then his windpipe closed completely. His mouth gaped open and his eyes glazed over. Blood screamed in his veins and he felt like his chest would split. His legs collapsed under him and he sank helplessly to his knees. Ramos stood over him, his eyes full of hatred, his nostrils flaring, and Kenny felt like he was staring at the face of Satan.

Kenny's vision dimmed, and suddenly he saw himself step off a cliff, and fall silently through a black void. He saw disembodied hands reaching out unsuccessfully to catch him. He was falling swiftly, without resistance, like a parachutist in a free fall. He smelled the odor of a match that had just been blown out, and heard the scream of an osprey as it dove for a fish. He felt cold begin to creep over his body and he thought, how odd. I'm so young.

Abruptly the pressure released and Kenny felt his throat rip open and his lungs re-inflate. He fell to the floor and rolled over on his belly. He heard the gasping, desperate sound of a drowning man and when he opened his eyes, he saw the world dance before him on the brownish-red rug.

Ramos stood over him. Kenny could see the toes of his boots and the muddied cuffs of his black pants.

"We do this again, kid," Ramos breathed, "many times, until the feeling of dying becomes as familiar to you as the scars on your chest. Until you see my face and bitterly regret the day your father took your mother in his arms and began your life in her. Until you understand that no one fights Angel Ramos and wins. Your father screwed up, kid, when he chose me to mess around with." He kicked the toe of his boot into Kenny's side and left the room.

✟ ✟ ✟

That night Tom and Cathy lay side by side in bed. A silver spray of light from the moon added a bluish cast to their room. Both were exhausted but neither could sleep, and they lay there silently, a thousand thoughts tumbling through their heads.

"What did Jack say to you?" Tom asked.

"He said he was sorry. He feels really bad that he wasn't able to stop them. And he said he wasn't giving up."

"He took an incredible whack."

A car drove down the street, making a metallic, grating noise, like it was dragging its muffler.

"Tom," whispered Cathy, "I'm scared."

"I know." He felt for her hand under the covers. "What can I do for you?" he asked.

"Just hold me."

So he held her in his arms, loving the feeling of her body stretched out next to his, hating the circumstance that put them back together. They lay there wordlessly, watching the shadows move across the wall. And after a long while her breathing became slow and regular, and he could tell she was finally asleep. He lay awake, watching the night progress, trying desperately to avoid sleep himself. Eventually his eyes closed, momentarily at first, but then for a longer time, and his breathing grew deep.

✟ ✟ ✟

Tom could see Kenny walking away from him. They were in a field. The wind blew hard, turning the tall grass into shimmering green-gold waves. The sun looked very bright and the sky was white with glare. Tom hustled, anxious to catch up to his son. "Kenny! Kenny!" His voice was strong and loud, but Kenny seemed not to hear him. "Kenny!"

Suddenly in the brilliant radiance up ahead, to the left of Kenny and slightly behind him, Tom saw a man stand up, emerging from the grass like a ghost. Then, to his horror,

Tom saw the man raise his hand from his side and point a pistol directly at Kenny.

"Kenny! Gun!" Tom screamed, even as he saw the muzzle flash and heard the pistol's sharp report. He grabbed his own gun and, bracing himself, fired off three rounds. Then he blinked hard and watched, amazed, as Kenny simply kept on walking and the gunman disappeared once again into the grass.

How'd the guy miss? Tom asked himself as he resumed running toward Kenny. What happened? "Kenny!"

He had only run a short way when he saw yet another gunman, this time off to Kenny's right, stand up. "Kenny! Gun, right! Kenny!" Tom extended both hands and fired quickly at the second man. Once again, both he and the gunman missed, and Kenny kept on walking at the same pace in the same direction. Tom could see Kenny's hair blowing in the breeze, see the trail in the grass he was leaving, but Kenny seemed oblivious to everything around him.

Tom felt frantic. With no cover, both he and Kenny were completely exposed. Kenny seemed to be dazed. And he, Tom, kept missing the shooters.

In desperation Tom began to run. Why couldn't he catch up? He pushed himself harder, until his lungs were bursting in his chest, and his legs were exhausted.

And then, off to the left, a third shooter stood up. He aimed a .45 straight at Kenny's heart. Bam! Bam! Tom saw the shooter's arm recoil, saw Kenny's shirt puff out as if a bullet were exiting. And still Kenny kept on walking.

Tom's fear and frustration turned his knees to jelly and made his arms feel like lead as he tried to aim his gun. His heart beat wildly, and he saw his hands quiver as he fired off four rounds at the third shooter.

"Kenny! Kenny!" Tom began running again, running faster than he ever had, running for Kenny's life. "Kenny!" Finally, he began closing the gap. Fifty feet, then thirty, then twenty. "Kenny!" Why couldn't he hear him? Fifteen feet. Ten.

Tom put on a final burst of speed. "Kenny!" He reached out with his left hand, grabbed Kenny's shoulder, and spun him around.

Tom's heart stopped and vomit rose in his throat.

The left half of Kenny's face was missing.

✝ ✝ ✝

"Tom, what is it? Tom! Tom!" Cathy's alarmed voice snapped him back to reality. He was sitting up in his bed, sweat drenching his body, coughing and shivering, clutching the sheets tightly in his hand. His eyes darted wildly.

"Tom, easy. Easy, Tom!" Cathy put her arm around him.

Tom closed his eyes tightly, and then re-opened them. He looked around. He was in a bedroom, with Cathy. That's right. Kate's house. "I'm okay," he said finally. He coughed again spasmodically. "I just had a dream. I'm sorry I woke you. Go back to sleep. I'm okay now." Okay, except for the twelve million snakes slithering in his gut. Oh, man.

Cathy laid back down. "Come here, Tom. Lie down."

He stretched out next to her, drawing her close. He waited until her breathing returned to normal and then he slipped out of bed. He grabbed his clothes and went silently downstairs. If you had to wrestle snakes, it was better to do it by yourself with the lights on.

He went down to the kitchen and looked in the fridge. He found a Coke. Then, in the back, he spotted a small jar of maraschino cherries. He poured the Coke into a glass filled with ice and dropped in some cherries. Then he went into the living room, snapped open his briefcase, and took out a legal pad and a pen. He sat down on the couch, propped his feet on the coffee table, and began making notes.

✝ ✝ ✝

Though he felt exhausted, Kenny couldn't sleep. When he dozed his head would drop, constricting his airway and awakening him in a panic, his heart beating erratically, his hands shaking violently, his cuffs rattling against the metal radiator.

He focused on his breathing, trying desperately to get control of himself.

The full moon's light filtered gently but persistently through the dirty window pane above Kenny's head. The young boy sat sleeping in a chair, snoring softly, his gun resting precariously on his lap. Occasionally, Kenny could hear voices from a room across the hall, usually muffled, but sometimes sharp and angry. He couldn't tell what was going on, but they were leaving him alone, and that's all he cared about.

A cough ripped through his throat. He felt lonely, terribly lonely. He thought about his parents. His father must still be alive or why would Ramos fool with him? But his dad would be furious, his mother frantic. And they would fight.

Those thoughts quickly became too painful, and Kenny had to choke back tears. He tried to pray, but words wouldn't come. He found himself wondering if anyone was listening anyway, so he quit trying.

He felt lost, adrift, like a house washed off its foundation by a flooding river, traveling downstream, spinning crazily, completely out of control, battered by debris, at the mercy of a power far beyond itself.

What had his coach said? "The way to get through the tiger's cage, Kenny, is stare him in the eye and walk straight at him." How do you do that when you're chained to a radiator? When the tiger wants to kill you? Kenny shivered.

The moon's light was taking over more and more of the room. Suddenly Kenny wanted to see it, as if looking at it would help him re-orient himself, give him something familiar and normal to grab onto.

The chain his cuffs were padlocked to looked short, but not too short. Maybe he could ...

Yes! He could stand. The radiator felt hot, but not too hot. He swung his left leg up, propping his foot on the radiator, and hopping on his right leg until he stood next to the window. And he found he could see outside.

It was a clear, cold night. The air was transparent, the sky black. The moon was full and high, a pearlized drop of luminescence hanging clear and bright. Around it the stars lay scattered like little white candy dots.

Sometimes in the summer, he and his dad would grab a blanket and go outside, throw it on the ground, lie down on their backs, and watch the stars. The best times were out in the country or at the beach in August, when heaven's own fireworks display, the Perseid meteor showers, would appear.

He stood there for a long time, thinking, savoring those

memories, allowing them to flow over his depression like a balm. He watched the night unfold, the stars and moon moving slowing in a silent, eternal pageant. And a scripture verse came unbidden to his mind. "The heavens declare the glory of God ..."

What had Terry said? "When you hit a crisis of faith, Kenny—not *if* but when—go back to the basics."

He looked up at the sky. Could he honestly look at the universe, the stars, the moon, the planets, and believe they all happened by chance? No way. Just a month ago, running at night with his dad, he'd wanted to say, "Look at it, Dad. God's screaming at you, 'I am here!' " He hadn't, of course, but he'd wanted to.

And now, here he stood, bound, a helpless hostage, looking at the stars through a dirty window. But the same message was emblazoned across the night. He grabbed onto it like a promise.

He leaned his head against the window frame. The sharp edge pressed into his scalp, but it was somehow comforting, as if his soul longed for anything straight and defined. God is real. The stars said it. God is real.

God is real and he is omnipresent. Everywhere. With him, even.

What's more, he is omniscient. He knows everything.

He is omnipotent. He can do anything.

Most importantly, he is love, Kenny thought.

He is love.

Kenny knew well his earthly father's love. He *trusted* his father's love. God's love surpassed even that. And what did that passage in Romans say? Nothing could separate him from God's love. Nothing. Not death, not life, not angels, nor rulers ... and not Angel Ramos.

God's love was right here, right now. Despite Angel Ramos. Kenny could trust God. He *would* trust him. Even in these circumstances. Even if he didn't feel it.

Like Daniel in the lions' den. Like the children in the fiery furnace.

Terry had taught on that recently. What had Shadrach, Meshach, and Abednego said? My God is able, thought Kenny, to deliver me. My God is able. But if he does not ...

He took a deep breath. If he does not, I'll be dead. But ultimately, it'll be okay. I'll be in heaven. Because of his love. Nothing can separate me from his love, Kenny thought. Nothing. No one. Not even Angel Ramos.

Kenny unwound himself from his perch, and sat back down next to the radiator. He crossed his legs and leaned his head back and squeezed the tears away. He tried praying again. He thanked God that his father apparently was alive, thanked him that he, Kenny, had survived so far, thanked him that he was not truly alone. And he asked God to meet his needs for food, for water, for encouragement, for rest ... for faith.

Finding a way to lean his head against the wall, he began to relax. Then he made a plan. He'd do what he needed to do to survive. He'd look for a way to escape, or to facilitate a rescue. And he'd stay positive. God was with him in this tiger's cage. He had to believe it.

He woke up a couple of hours later in a coughing spasm, gasping for breath, coughing and choking so hard he must have broken a capillary, for he tasted blood. He was desperately trying to get control, to quell the spasm, when he felt a hand on his right shoulder. He opened his eyes. The young boy was kneeling down next to him. He had a cup in his right hand and he offered it to Kenny. Kenny gratefully put his mouth around the straw and took a sip—and tasted cherry Coke.

CHAPTER 25

AT 5:30 A.M. TOM went upstairs and took a shower. He shaved, using a new, sharp razor, and slapped on some Old Spice. Then he put on his best suit, a dark blue wool, over a crisp white shirt. He finished with a conservative red, white, and blue striped tie. He wanted to look sharp, to convince everyone, especially himself, that he was okay, in control.

He laced his SIG Sauer 9 mm on his belt, put his wallet in his back pocket and the leather case with his badge and his credentials in the breast pocket of his jacket. Then he leaned over his sleeping wife and kissed her goodbye.

"Tom?" she said.

"Going in to see Cramer. I'll call you later."

"You haven't heard anything?"

"Nothing, hon. You go back to sleep. I promise I'll call if there's any news."

✞ ✞ ✞

"How's McRae?" Cramer asked as Tom and Fitz walked into his office.

"They released him late yesterday afternoon," said Fitz. "There were no complications, as far as they could tell. No fractures. Just a concussion and a split scalp."

"We talked to him at nine o'clock last night," said Tom. "He still had a headache, but said he felt okay. He was going to bed."

"Good," said Cramer. "Let's go in the conference room where we can spread out." Leaving the jacket to his dark gray suit hanging on the back of his chair, he picked up his notebook and a pen and led the way next door, flipping on the light as they entered the room.

Fitz strode right behind him, carrying some charts. Behind Fitz came Dave Borsten, head of the elite Hostage Rescue Team. Officially part of the Washington Area Field Office, HRT had its headquarters at the FBI Academy at Quantico, Virginia, about forty miles south of D.C. The team of fifty highly qualified agents spent much of their time training. They practiced rappelling by stepping backwards out of helicopters, off buildings, and down cliffs—wherever they could find a steep slope and a heart-stopping drop. They practiced room-entering techniques and assault procedures until their actions were as coordinated as the finest clock mechanism. They shot their weapons on the pistol and rifle ranges, and they kept themselves in top physical condition, prepared at all times for the call that would put their training to use.

Tom closed the door behind him. In his hand he carried the legal pad he'd worked on last night.

They all took seats around the table and were just about to begin when the door opened and Jack stuck his head in.

"Y'all have room for one more?" he said with a slight grin.

"What are you feeding these guys?" Cramer turned to Fitz, incredulous.

Tom jumped to his feet and shook Jack's hand. "Jack, what are you doing? Are you supposed to be working?" He helped him over to a chair.

Jack sat down. "I hope you don't mind me bargin' in, Mr. Cramer. I just thought I might be able to add something to your meeting."

Cramer shook his head in disbelief.

"What'd the doctor say, Jack?" Fitz asked.

"He said I shouldn't drive for a few days," Jack said. "So I drove my truck in so if I hit something I wouldn't get hurt."

"You drove?"

"Not really. I had a new agent come get me." Everyone laughed. Then Jack got serious, the grin on his face disappeared and the skin at the corners of his eyes grew tight. He looked hard at Cramer. "They took Kenny right out of my hand," he said, almost in a whisper, "right out from under me." His hand clenched into a fist. "I love that boy like he was my own son. I've got to go after him. I've got to help get Kenny back."

Tom rested his elbow on the table, his fist pressed to his mouth, emotion rising in his chest.

Cramer nodded. "Then let's get on with it. Fitz, bring us up to date."

Fitz stood up and put his charts up on the easel which stood near the end of the table. A diagram of the foyer of Tom's house, with evidence and damage marked, was the first exhibit.

Fitz began detailing what the Bureau knew about the incident. He began by playing a tape of Luis's call to Tom. Everyone listened carefully. Tom relived the nightmare.

"Approximately six minutes after Tom left the house, a crash at the front door awakened Jack."

"Sounded like a cannon," Jack said.

"They used a cinderblock, and busted right through the door. They must have worn gloves—we found no usable fingerprints anywhere in the foyer or on the door. On the second hit, the alarm went off, and we began to mobilize from the office.

"We are surmising at least five entered the house, while one remained in the van outside. Jack's car was plainly visible in the driveway. Two of the assailants found him in the family room."

"Actually, I found them," said Jack.

Fitz flipped to the next chart, a diagram of Tom's family room. "Jack, would you like to tell us what happened?"

Jack told his story. Tom listened, restlessly drumming his thumb against his leg, his anger and grief barely contained.

Fitz took over when Jack had finished. "We have positively identified Jack's blood, here," he pointed to an area near the door. "The blood in this area belongs to the suspect who was shot."

"They called him 'Roberto,'" Jack said.

Fitz nodded. "We believe that is Roberto Garcia, age nineteen. He is a known associate of Ramos, lives in the Arlington area, has priors for armed robbery and possession of cocaine. We have surveillance on that house, and we have alerted local hospitals. There's enough blood there that

Roberto's going to need some medical care."

"The shotgun was a 12-gauge, loaded with double-aught buck shot. We found shot here," he pointed to the chart, "in the walls and floor. And we found Jack's gun here, under the coffee table. It had not been fired."

Fitz went on, detailing the evidence found in the family room. Tom listened restlessly, his mind already on what he hoped to say. But then Fitz's next words grabbed his attention.

Fitz said, "We can only surmise what was going on upstairs. Kenny must have heard the alarm or the crashing. He headed for the master bedroom, and that's where they found him. We got his prints off the wall around the panic button, and prints off the drawer of the nightstand, which was standing open."

"He was looking for a gun," Tom said.

Fitz nodded. "The room looked like a war zone, covers pulled off the bed, louvers of the closet shattered, things knocked off the nightstand ..."

"He put up a heckuva fight," said Jack. "I heard him."

"Under the bed, we found a rag saturated with chloroform. We also found two marijuana joints on the floor. We're checking them for prints and DNA."

"Jack, did you hear anything, anything that would enable you to identify any of the UNSUBs?" Cramer asked, using the Bureau term for "unknown subject."

"I heard a lot of shouting, most of it in Spanish. I heard the one guy I was wrestling call the guy I shot 'Roberto.' And I heard Kenny."

"Anything distinguishable?"

"Just one word: 'Dad.'"

A chill ran down Tom's back.

"Okay, gentlemen," said Cramer. "Those are the facts. Now what do we do? The brother killed by Fairfax, he's having a funeral?"

"Yes, sir," said Fitz. "Tuesday. We will be there. We have the mother under surveillance, as well as the funeral home. We'll get everything we can out of that. Ramos may show up. In the Latino community, missing your brother's funeral would be a big deal. But we don't have probable cause yet.

So we can't pick him up—we can only follow him."

Cramer exhaled noisily and sat back. "And he knows we'll do that, so he's not going to lead us back to Kenny. We have all his known associates under surveillance?"

"Right."

"And how about a wiretap?"

"The judge is being a stickler," Fitz said, "so nothing yet."

Cramer tapped his pen on the table, and then he said, "Tom, I'd like to hear from you. Do you have any ideas?"

"First of all, I want to reiterate that I believe my son is still alive. If Ramos was going to kill him, he'd leave his body somewhere I'd be sure to see it." Tom rubbed his sweaty palm on his pants leg. Now came the test. He hadn't been sure whether he would be a sheep or a goat in this meeting. He picked up his pen, adjusted his legal pad, and leaned forward. Then, step by step, he outlined his plan to draw Angel Ramos out of hiding and get his son back.

When he finished, the room was quiet. Cramer tapped his pen while he thought. "You realize that you could get into a situation where Ramos could pick you off easily. Maybe you and Kenny both."

"If I do it right, Kenny'll be behind cover. And as for me," Tom shrugged, "that's where I'm relying on Dave's boys."

"Well, what do you think, Dave?"

Dave's eyes inspected Tom, as if weighing his mettle. Tom didn't know him well. They hadn't needed to work together before. And he had no idea what Dave had heard about him.

Dave cleared his throat. "I think Tom's life would certainly be in danger."

Tom looked down, his pulse drumming in his ears. He needed HRT's support to sell his idea.

"But I think if it were my kid, I'd be out there wearing a bull's-eye if necessary."

Tom looked up at him, a rush of gratitude pouring through him.

"I think we can overcome much of the risk with good planning, and I'm willing to give it a shot."

CHAPTER 26

WHEN HE WOKE UP AGAIN it was light outside and he was hungry and stiff. He needed to go to the bathroom. The young boy sat in the chair, looking bored and sleepy.

There were loud voices from across the hall again, and Kenny thought he heard someone groaning. Curious. He strained to catch the Spanish words.

The boy looked up as Kenny shifted his position. Kenny decided to break the silence. "Thanks for the drink last night. Carlos? Is that your name?"

"Yes."

"How old are you, Carlos?"

"Eighteen."

Sixteen, Kenny thought. If that.

"And what school do you go to?"

Carlos shifted uncomfortably in his chair.

"La Escuela de las Calles, the School of the Streets. Am I right?" Kenny smiled at him.

Carlos nodded. "¿Usted habla Español?"

"Only a little. From Spanish class."

Kenny shifted his position a little. "Hey, Carlos. Can I get up? Use the bathroom?"

Carlos abruptly stood up and walked across the room. "Gordo!" he called, and he said something in Spanish. A large, heavyset kid came in, and the two of them unlocked Kenny and escorted him to the bathroom. Obviously, they had their orders.

Later that morning, Kenny was dozing when a man walked in the room. He handed Carlos a bag. "Here's lunch.

Everything okay?"

"Si." Carlos looked in the bag, then back at the man. "What's going on?" he asked, nodding toward the room across the hall.

"Nothing. Forget it," said the man as he left the room. Carlos walked back to the chair rummaging around in the bag as he went.

Kenny followed him with his eyes, his stomach juices biting painfully into his gut and saliva springing into the hinge of his jaw. Carlos sat down in the chair, unwrapped the burrito and began to eat. After a few bites, he glanced up and saw Kenny staring at him. Kenny looked quickly away, embarrassed by his obvious need, and Carlos took another bite.

Kenny tried to focus on something—anything—else, but he couldn't help it, his eyes were drawn like magnets to Carlos's burrito.

Carlos caught him looking again. "Are you hungry?" he asked.

Kenny nodded.

"No one has given you food?"

Kenny shook his head. "No. No one."

Carlos stopped chewing, looked at his burrito, then back to Kenny. He sighed. Finally he shrugged his shoulders and got up.

"They gave me two."

"Thanks," Kenny said. He closed his eyes and said a brief, silent prayer of thanks.

Carlos sat down on the floor next to Kenny and fed him bites of burrito and sips of Coke.

Between bites, Kenny asked him about local sports, school, and finally about his family. Anything to keep him talking. "You have brothers and sisters?"

Carlos nodded. "A brother fifteen, a sister thirteen, another sister eight, and Paulito, the baby who is almost three."

"Wow. You're lucky. I'm an only child." They ate some more. "What's your dad do?"

Carlos's eyes flickered. "He was killed. Three years ago. In a construction accident."

"Oh, man, I'm sorry. That must be rough."

Carlos didn't answer.

"I'm sorry, Carlos. Losing your dad, man!"

The boys were quiet for a while, then Carlos asked, "The scars on your chest?..."

"From my first encounter with Angel Ramos. You weren't there?"

Carlos shook his head. Kenny told him the story. Then he asked, "You've known Ramos for a long time?"

Carlos shrugged. "I've been part of the crew for a while. A friend got me in." He sounded proud. "We are like family. We protect each other. Without a gang, out there," he nodded toward the streets beyond the window, "you are nothing. With Ramos, I can be proud. And someone touches me, it is like touching Ramos. They get it back, double."

Another outburst erupted across the hall—loud moaning followed by an angry argument. Two men came out of the bedroom and continued arguing in the hall, fast and furious. Kenny caught about every tenth word.

Kenny watched Carlos's face carefully. "How well do you know Ramos?"

"Ramos is a great man. He helps us. When my friend's mother's check was late, he paid their rent. He bought uniforms for the youth basketball team at church. He does all kinds of stuff. The rest of this," Carlos motioned in general toward Kenny, "I don't understand." Then he went over to the chair and sat down, as if he had to think about something real hard.

Kenny couldn't keep quiet anymore. "He's using you," he said.

"What?"

"He's using you, Carlos, to sell his drugs, make his money for him. That's why he acts so nice. Ramos doesn't do anything that doesn't benefit himself."

"No! He cares about people!"

Kenny sighed. "If he cared about people, Carlos, why would he have you selling drugs?"

"Everybody sells drugs, man."

"And why all the violence?" he said, his voice low but intense. "You saw what he did to me downstairs!"

"You shouldn't have hit him. He just lost his temper, man!"

"Yeah, and last time his knife slipped. Five times. I shouldn't have had my chest in his way. Wake up, Carlos. The man's a snake. And he'll play you like a cat plays a mouse until you get close enough, then he'll swallow you whole. You just wait and see."

"No, you're wrong!" Carlos said angrily. "Shut up! He's my friend."

"Like he's a friend to Roberto, Carlos?"

Carlos glared him.

"I understand a little Spanish, Carlos. Does a good man stand by and watch a friend die?"

"Shut up!" said Carlos, and he walked away.

✝ ✝ ✝

A short time later, Kenny heard voices on the stairs and Ramos walked in the room, followed by three of the younger gang members. Carlos took a position by the door, far away from Kenny.

"Get him up, Carlos," Ramos said. The smell of his cigar and the sound of his voice made Kenny's heart pound.

Carlos unlocked Kenny, avoiding his eyes. He pulled him to his feet, and then re-cuffed him. Ramos walked over to Kenny, grabbed him by the hair, and shoved him toward the boys. Two of them caught Kenny, and as he looked up at them he saw smirks on their faces.

"I want his shirt," Ramos said. "We write a message on it to his father. But his shirt says 'VT'? What kind of message is that, eh? So we need Kenny's help." Ramos patted Kenny's cheek.

Kenny jerked his face away.

Ramos grabbed the chain on Kenny's cuffs with his left hand and gripped his arm with his right, holding Kenny in place. "Tito," Ramos said, "give it a shot."

A short, wiry boy walked up to Kenny. His eyes were bright, his body tense. His hair was cut short on the sides, long on top, and was caught into little ponytails by colorful rubber bands. He pulled back his right fist and hit Kenny hard. Kenny's head twisted to the right and he gasped as pain exploded throughout the bones in his face.

"A good hit, Tito, but no blood, eh? Let's try someone else."

One by one the boys came forward and hit Kenny, on his jaw, his eye, his mouth, until his ears were ringing and bright arrows of light flashed in his eyes, and anger raged within him. But still no one had drawn blood. Ramos held onto Kenny, the smoke from his cigar nauseating him.

"How about you, eh, Carlos?"

Carlos muttered something Kenny couldn't hear, raised his hands and backed up a step.

"What's wrong, Carlos? You think he hit you back?" Everyone laughed, and started saying things in Spanish. Kenny couldn't focus, but he knew they were teasing him. Tito pushed Carlos lightly, and said something in a jeering tone of voice. Kenny saw Carlos's face redden. Then he stepped forward. Kenny took a deep breath and braced himself. Carlos stood right in front of him, his mouth a straight line, his eyes fixed, his hand clenched.

"Do it, Carlos!" Ramos hissed.

The blow hit with a smack, right on his nose. Kenny staggered back as the blood flowed, pouring over his shirt in a bright red fountain.

"Hey, hey! Way to go, Carlos!"

"Good job, primo! Excellente!"

But when Kenny was able to look he saw the shame on Carlos's face. As he straightened himself up, he saw Carlos turn away abruptly and leave the room.

CHAPTER 27

THAT EVENING, AS THE PURPLE shadows edged their
way into the room, Kenny woke up. He had escaped into his
world of sleep. They had taken off his shirt, and he sat bare-
chested at the radiator, his face and chest sticky with dried
blood.

Carlos sat in the chair. His elbows rested on his thighs, his
head lowered. He played with a tiny piece of paper in his
hand. He glanced up, met Kenny's eyes, and quickly looked
away.

Kenny sighed deeply. He bit his lip. "You don't belong
with these people, Carlos."

"Why'd he do it?" Carlos's voice sounded angry,
demanding.

"I told you why. Ramos is a bad guy."

"No. Your father. Why'd he put a hit out on Pablo?"

"He didn't. It's a lie."

"He did. He told the cops to kill him."

"No way! My dad would never do that."

"Why'd they stop him then? Why'd they shoot? Pablo had
no gun! Your father ordered the cops to kill him, that's why."

"No, Carlos, he didn't. That isn't how it works. He'd have
no reason ..."

"He hates Ramos! He wanted to hurt him!"

Kenny was getting hot. He jerked against his cuffs. He was
breathing hard, through his mouth because his nose was
swollen shut on one side. He figured it was probably broken.
"My Dad would never do that! Never!"

"Why does he hate Ramos?" Carlos eyes were flashing,

and Kenny could feel his anger, even in the dim light.

"Ramos is a drug dealer, Carlos. That's my dad's job—to arrest drug dealers."

"He tried to beat Ramos up. In the men's room. At the 'Frisco Grill."

Kenny hadn't heard that story. "Tell me about that," he said. Carlos gave him Ramos's version of the encounter. Kenny listened carefully and then said, "Turn on the light."

Carlos looked at him darkly.

"Turn on the light!"

Carlos got up and turned on the overhead light. The dingy room brightened.

"Now look at me, Carlos, look at my chest."

Carlos walked back over to him and bent down. He looked carefully at Kenny. The parallel lines looked like purplish red thread, covered in many places with dark brown, newly dried blood. Kenny saw Carlos take it all in, then, slowly, Carlos raised his eyes.

"Now you tell me the truth, Carlos." Kenny's voice remained soft. "If someone did that to you, what would your dad have done?"

Carlos's face turned red, and he dropped his head and rubbed his forehead with his hand. He got up, walked over to the door, placed his hand high on the doorjamb and leaned his head against it. Then he abruptly left the room.

He returned several minutes later, looking troubled. Carrying a small, wet towel, he walked over to Kenny, squatted down, and without saying anything, began wiping the blood off Kenny's face and chest. Tears welled in Kenny's eyes.

When he finished, Carlos stood up.

"Thank you," Kenny said, shivering.

Abruptly Carlos pulled off his sweatshirt. Then he unlocked Kenny, released his cuffs, and handed him the shirt.

"Thanks," said Kenny softly.

Kenny put the sweatshirt on. For a brief moment, he wanted to run, to break through the window, or race out of the door. But he sat back down so Carlos could lock him up again. He'd made a connection. Thank you, God, he thought. Thank you.

✞ ✞ ✞

The day of Pablo's funeral dawned bright and sunny, the sky a brilliant blue. Perfect light for surveillance cameras, shooting through the tinted glass of a van.

Fitz refused to allow Tom to go with the surveillance squad, so he sat in the office, listening to the radio transmissions, working on his plan, and hoping to hear from one of the informants he had contacted.

Meanwhile, a navy blue Ford van sat parked down the street from the big church on Trembley Street. Inside, behind the tinted glass, were two agents, a man and a woman armed with still and video cameras, ready to photograph every mourner who showed up for Pablo Ramos's funeral, every car that drove near the church.

"That's him," said the man. "That guy in the black suit, getting out of the limo. That's Ramos."

The woman sat up straighter so she could see better. "And the woman must be Maria Aguilera."

"Got to be." He picked up the radio. "We've got the King Snake at Location One. Entering now," and surveillance cars moved into place in a three-block radius around the church.

High above Alexandria a small plane circled. "You catch that?" asked the agent co-pilot.

"Got it," responded the pilot. "It'll be an hour before they move."

By 10:45 a.m., the street was packed with cars and people. The funeral mass began on time, at eleven. Among the mourners were several Latino agents, who blended into the crowd perfectly, and used the prayer times to carefully eye each and every participant, keeping a special eye on Angel Ramos.

Outside, a bearded agent dressed in jeans and a heavy jacket walked casually down the street and through the parking lot. He looked lost in thought, almost like a homeless man, talking to himself. In actuality he was transmitting license plate numbers of every car near the church to an agent sitting in a parked car some distance away, who logged them.

When the mass finished, the mourners emerged from the church, and the agents began videotaping again. As Ramos moved out into the bright sunshine, he looked straight at the van. "He knows we're here. He's smiling for the camera," said the one of the agents. "Can you believe it?"

As the funeral moved to the cemetery it had a silent, federal escort in the form of two nondescript government sedans that joined the procession. Other surveillance cars moved along parallel roads, keeping in touch by radio. And the plane made passes overhead, covering the scene from the air.

At the cemetery, across from the newly opened grave, on the small road, sat a white work van. Two men with shovels were moving some dirt around some shrubbery. Inside the paneled van, two other agents watched the mourners, videotaping them through a periscope mounted on the roof in a vent. After Pablo was laid to rest, Ramos helped his mother back into the limo. The surveillance cars and the plane followed them back to her house.

✝ ✝ ✝

Kenny thanked God for Carlos. Literally. He kept bringing him food, and would unlock him whenever he could find an excuse. Kenny began to see him as a lifeline. But he could tell Carlos was struggling with his mixed allegiance. His face looked troubled, his eyes worried.

The house had been quiet, too quiet. Something was going on. Was it just Pablo's funeral? Or was there something else? Kenny didn't know.

Off and on Kenny and Carlos would talk, surface-level conversations on safe topics like sports and movies. Kenny told him about his wrestling. But Kenny didn't know yet how Carlos was feeling about Ramos, and how far he might be willing to go to help him. And Kenny knew better than to push it.

Finally, at about four o'clock, Carlos said, "Kenny, I'm going home. For dinner. I bring you back something, okay?"

"Okay, Carlos. Thanks!" He watched him leave the room. Someone would be there in a minute to replace him, someone less friendly. Kenny felt suddenly depressed. He leaned his head back, and began thinking of every song or hymn he had ever sung, trying to find one that might help him combat his black mood. But his brain wasn't working, so he retreated back into his dark, private world, and soon he drifted off to sleep.

CHAPTER 28

THAT NIGHT, AT THE OFFICE, Tom, Jack, and Fitz sat watching videos of the day's events as they were projected on a large screen. Cramer walked in as they were finishing up. "What'd we get?" he asked.

"Ramos showed up, as we suspected," replied Fitz. "He's gone back to his mother's house, and we've had the house under surveillance all evening. So far, we've got nothing."

Once again, Tom felt a wave of disappointment.

"We got everyone who attended," Fitz continued, "on tape and on film." He pushed a button and rewound the video. "Here's Ramos's mother." He clicked on the laser pointer which put a red dot on the screen, and he circled the woman. "And here's Ramos, his sister and brother-in-law, and other family members. As you can see, half the community turned out. It was easy for us to blend in."

Cramer seemed satisfied. "How about your informants, Tom?"

"I've contacted five, sir. Told them I wanted to talk to Ramos, cut a deal. Haven't heard anything back, but then, he's so isolated, it'll take a while for the message to get through."

"Okay, gentlemen. Keep me posted." Cramer left the room.

✞ ✞ ✞

An hour later, Fitz got a call from a member of the surveillance squad. He put it on speaker so everyone could hear. The squad had lost Ramos. They were convinced he was no longer in his mother's house, but didn't know how he'd gotten out.

Tom grabbed the reins. "You were on the front and back?"

"Yes. Full coverage."

"And who did you see, going in and out?"

"No one, Donovan. That's the problem. No one went in, no one came out."

"Well, there had to be someone!"

Fitz motioned for Tom to back off.

"He's saying no one left?" Tom said to Fitz. Incredulity strained his voice.

The surveillance agent picked up the conversation. "I'm telling you, Donovan, no one left!"

"Well what did happen?"

"It was quiet, okay? All night!"

"And no one used a door, or a window, or the garage."

"Only the pizza man, Donovan! That's it! Now, I'm telling you ..."

"Pizza man? Pizza man?"

"Yeah, they got a pizza delivery at 10 p.m. You know, the guy walks up to the door, the guy hands 'em the pizza, the guy ..."

Tom blew out his breath in frustration. "That's how he did it!" He cursed.

"What? There was only one guy. And he never went in the house!"

"Yeah, but did he go behind a bush? Near the front door? So you couldn't see him? Just long enough for Ramos to switch places with him? Did you even think to watch for that?"

"Look, Donovan ..."

"No, you look, Taylor. A junior grade detective would have picked up on that ...!"

"Okay, okay, Tom," said Fitz. "You may be right. Now, be quiet."

✝ ✝ ✝

The smell of the cigar woke him. The room was completely dark. Kenny turned, and in the doorway, he saw Angel Ramos standing, his body outlined in light from the hall. Kenny saw him throw down his cigar, crushing it out on the floor. Then two other men came in the room, one carrying a boom box. They flipped on the light. No one said anything to Kenny.

The three men stood talking, their words angry and tense. Ramos took a small glass pipe out of his pocket, put something in it, and lit it. The smoke curled up toward the ceiling as he took a hit of what Kenny figured was probably crack. He passed the pipe around.

One of the men approached Kenny. He unlocked the cuffs from the chain securing him to the radiator. Kenny immediately felt his heart begin to beat faster.

"Come here, boy," said Ramos, his eyes almost feral.

Kenny fixed his eyes on Ramos and walked straight at him. He stopped about two feet away. Out of the corner of his eye, he saw someone else come in the room. Carlos. He saw him look up, and flatten himself against the wall next to the door.

"All the way," Ramos said.

Kenny took a deep breath and moved closer. He could see the pulse throbbing in the boss's neck, smell whatever he was smoking. The pores on Ramos's face were open, the skin blotchy, as if eliminating impurities from his body took extraordinary effort.

"It's time to put on a show for your daddy, boy."

"Leave him out of it, Ramos. Whatever you do, it's between you and me."

"Tough, eh?" He took another hit off the pipe. His eyes gleamed, his left eyebrow twitched. "They buried my brother today, kid."

Kenny stayed silent.

"What a shame, eh? To die so young." Ramos shifted his weight as if he were bracing to pick up some heavy load. "So we remind your father of what he did." He put his hands around Kenny's neck. Kenny heard a click, as someone depressed a button on the boom box. The boss's fingers felt icy cold around his neck, like strands of frozen rope.

Kenny's muscles tensed and his head started to swim. His eyes blazed with defiance and he heard himself say, "Just do it, Ramos," and he cursed. And as he felt his airway begin to close, he thought to himself, *God forgive me, I'd kill him if I could.*

✠ ✠ ✠

Minutes later, as Kenny sat on the floor, chained again and gasping for breath, wheezing and choking on the stringy mixture of phlegm, stomach acid, and spit in his throat, he felt a hand on his back, and he knew it was Carlos's. When the buzzing in his ears stopped and he could see again, he found the strength to raise his head.

Carlos pulled a blue handkerchief out of his pocket and wiped Kenny's mouth. "What he is doing to you is wrong," he said, his voice cracking. "It is wrong." He stopped. "Roberto is dead."

Kenny nodded, and he pretended not to see that Carlos was crying.

"Kenny ... I ..."

"Carlos!"

Luis stood right behind him.

Carlos quickly rubbed his sleeve over his eyes and stood up to face him.

"Don't forget, Carlos, this kid is not one of us, eh? And if anything happens to him, if he accidentally gets away, if the feds find out where he is, it will be you who will have to answer for it. To Ramos, okay?"

Carlos nodded.

"That's a good boy," and he walked out.

✠ ✠ ✠

Angel Ramos sucked in on his cigar. "We got the feds going, eh, Luis? This is the third message I get, saying Donovan wants to talk."

"Give it up, Angel. It's going nowhere. Let's get back to our business, the drugs."

"But this is fun, eh?"

"Until they catch us. Until they lock you up."

"I could walk down King Street right now, and they could do nothing. They have nothing on me, Luis."

"It has cost us Roberto."

"And we will make them pay for that."

"I don't like it."

Ramos blew a big cloud of smoke out. "Pablo is dead. I will not let Donovan get away with that."

"So kill his kid, and let's get on with it!"

"That is too easy, Luis. I want him to sweat. I like the thought of it."

"You go too far, Jefe. You are going to screw us all up."

"Relax, Luis. We do this my way. I always take care of you before, eh?" He laughed. "Here. Have a cigar. On me."

CHAPTER 29

TOM LOOKED AT HIS WATCH. Wednesday. Day Four for Kenny. He opened his desk drawer, pulled out the small, black book and flipped through the pages, searching for another idea, another informant he could press. He heard an office hello phone ring.

"It's for you, Tom."

He took the receiver. "Donovan."

"Is this Agent Tom Donovan?"

"Yes."

"This is Santini, the bartender at Chico's. You got a present here."

"From who?"

"How should I know?"

"What is it?" Tom's heart pounded.

"Come see for yourself."

"Why don't you just tell me?"

"It's a T-shirt. With something on it. Could be blood. I guess you can figure that out."

Blood? "Leave it alone. I'll be down in thirty minutes."

"I'll try to be here."

Fitz drove and Jack and another agent sat in the back. The winter sun streamed through the front windshield of the Bureau car, making Tom sweat. He unbuttoned his trench coat and restlessly patted his thigh while Fitz negotiated the tangled spaghetti of the Southwest Freeway.

"You know, he's pullin' your chain," Jack said from the back seat.

"Any contact is better than nothing."

"Stick to the game plan, Tom," Fitz said as they approached Chico's.

Santini himself, a short, broad-faced, dark haired man, met them at the door. Tom blinked, waiting for his eyes to adjust to the dark. "The note's here," Santini said. "The present is over there, on the coat rack." He nodded toward the rack behind Tom, to the left of the door.

Tom read the note without touching it, then he turned to the coat rack. Beyond the abandoned trench coat hung Kenny's Virginia Tech T-shirt, covered in blood. Tom's heart began to pound, but outwardly he stayed completely cool.

"Thank you, Mr. Santini," Tom said. "These agents will have some questions for you. Call me if you get any other messages." Tom handed him a business card, and walked out the door, Jack right behind him.

The minute the door closed behind them, Tom started cursing.

"C'mon, Tom," Jack said. "You knew he would do this. Let's walk it off. The boys'll be a while."

✞ ✞ ✞

That night, when he got to Kate's, Cathy approached him as he hung up his coat. "How'd it go today? Any word. Do you know yet where Kenny is?" she asked.

"It went okay," Tom replied, avoiding her eyes, "and no, we don't know."

"What happened?"

He really didn't want to talk. "Things just aren't moving, that's all. I'm going to take a shower." He went upstairs and let the drumming of the shower isolate him from everything and everyone around him, and maybe, especially, from himself.

✞ ✞ ✞

While he was upstairs the phone rang. Cathy picked it up.

"How's Tom?" Jack asked.

"Jack, what happened today?"

He told her.

"Why won't he tell me these things?" She looked across the room. On the wall hung a print of two stocky Hereford cows, staring over a fence, surrounded by swirling snow. The term "bullheaded" came to mind.

"He probably doesn't want to upset you. Maybe I shouldn't have told you."

"Don't you start, Jack. Don't you dare! Without you, I won't know anything," she said. "Look, thanks. I'd better go."

"I'm sorry if I caused a problem here. I was just worried about Tom."

"You're fine, Jack. Thanks."

✝ ✝ ✝

He lay on the bed on his stomach, his arms up under the pillow. She could see the muscles of his upper back and his biceps standing out. His skin was tan against the white sheets, his hair still wet from the shower. His eyes were open, and he stared into nothing.

"Why didn't you tell me?" she said.

"About what?"

"The shirt. Ramos slipping the surveillance."

He sighed.

"Tom, you should tell me these things. I asked how your day went, remember?"

"I didn't want to upset you. How'd you find out?"

"Jack called. While you were in the shower."

"I wanted to protect you from that. I didn't want you to have to deal with it."

"Tom, I don't think that's true."

He turned over and looked at her.

"I think *you* didn't want to deal with it. That's why you didn't tell me."

He looked away.

She sat down on the edge of the bed, her head drooping. She blinked back a tear.

Tom turned toward her. He reached out, and pulled her down onto his chest, embracing her. "I'm sorry, Cath." He stroked her hair.

"It's okay."

He continued stroking her hair.

She looked up at him. "I called your mom."

He closed his eyes. "She okay?"

"She's amazing. She's determined to have faith, she says."

Tom sighed. "Thanks, Cath. For calling her."

✟ ✟ ✟

By Wednesday night, Kenny was really starting to go crazy, having been cuffed to the radiator for four days with only an occasional "torture break," as he called it. His body ached all over, his hands and shoulders especially. His head throbbed. But hardest to deal with was the confinement. He found himself beginning to have vivid daydreams of running, across fields, around tracks, through woods, on the beach.

He slept restlessly, in fits of dozing. Periodically he would awaken and stretch his aching legs and shift his weight on his hips, and one by one he'd count his fingers to check the circulation in his hands. Then he'd rotate his shoulders, trying to relieve the terrible pain that gripped them like steel gloves. Finally, when he had done everything that he could and still felt no better, he'd resign himself to his portion of hell on Earth and try once again to sleep.

In the middle of the night, he heard voices.

"Carlos!" someone yelled. Carlos, who had been sleeping in the chair, quickly jumped up and walked toward the door. Luis strode down the hall. "Get the kid up. We're moving. And watch him, Carlos."

Carlos came back frowning. "They want you downstairs. We're moving," he said.

"Be tough with me in front of them. Rough me up a little."

Carlos looked at him, puzzled.

"Act like you realize now you were wrong to be nice to me. You've remembered your loyalties. I'll go along with it," said Kenny. "You've got to be careful, Carlos, or they'll hurt you."

✟ ✟ ✟

"I said move it!" Carlos yelled as they reached the bottom of the stairs. He shoved Kenny, and Kenny twisted away angrily.

They took him downstairs to a garage. Gordo plastered tape over his mouth and the constriction made Kenny begin to panic. He began counting backwards in his head to calm himself down. Then two men picked him up and threw him into the trunk of a large sedan, a Ford, blue, license plate VMW 738. Kenny memorized it quickly. Then the trunk lid slammed shut and Kenny lay alone in the darkness.

Oh, God, what now, he thought. He shook from the cold and from anxiety.

It wasn't a long drive. Kenny moved around among the assorted tools and dirty rags in the trunk until he had a clear place to lie. He leaned his head against a canvas tool bag. He could hear muffled voices from the front, speaking Spanish. He could feel the car stop and go as it wound through the city streets. It stopped for good, and a few seconds later the trunk lid popped open, letting the cold night air pour in.

Hands reached in and pulled Kenny up and out of the car. "Hurry!" someone hissed, and Kenny found himself in the middle of a phalanx of gangbangers, being hustled along a sidewalk toward a dreary Cape Cod house. They were in a cramped neighborhood of identical houses, the monotony broken only by the variety of trash in the front yards and the number and age of the cars parked on front lawns, across sidewalks, everywhere possible.

They entered the house and Luis led them past a darkened living room where two men watched a flickering blue TV, and up a narrow, enclosed stairway, into a bedroom that contained one chair and an iron bed with a stained, bare mattress. Carlos uncuffed Kenny, shoved him onto the bed, and re-cuffed his hands to the bars of the iron bedstead. Then the others left, leaving Carlos to watch him.

Carlos gingerly pulled the tape off Kenny's mouth. They both winced, one in pain and one in sympathy, but Kenny felt glad to get it off.

"What's going on, Carlos?"

"I don't know. The cops were on to us, maybe."

"Where are we?"

"Alexandria. Near Del Ray. Not far from my home."

"What time is it?"

"Three in the morning. They had to move you in the dark."

Kenny sighed. "So what's next?"

"I don't know, amigo."

CHAPTER 30

TOM LOOKED WITH EXASPERATION AT the drifting mounds of paperwork on the conference room table. There were printouts on the vehicles spotted at the funeral, video tapes, reports of the surveillance teams and of contacts with informants ... on and on it went. He threw a pen down. Forget the paperwork! All he wanted was his son.

He restlessly walked around the table, chewing on the end of a paperclip, trying to think of what else he could do to get Ramos to deal.

"We just gotta play him like a trout," said Jack. He sat in a chair, with his feet propped up on the table, looking at a report. "You gotta know what they're bitin', then flick that lure out there and see if they'll surface."

"Well, I'm pretty sure about what he'll bite on. But how can I get it in front of his face?"

Jack stood up. He rubbed the stitches in the back of his head. "Y'know, I wonder what ever happened to good old Roberto?"

Tom looked at him, frowning slightly. "Hey, Jack. We ought to check the rolls of that church. See if there's any Latino doctor that might have been willing to do Ramos a favor."

"Yeah, that's a good idea! I'll get somebody on that right away." Jack got up and left the room.

A minute later, he stuck his head back in the room. "Hey, Tom. A Fairfax cop is on the phone, line 7. He wants to talk to you. He was one of the guys at your house that night."

"Okay."

Tom walked out to his desk, picked up the phone, and talked to the cop for about five minutes. Then he hung up. Jack came over.

"What's up?"

Tom shrugged. "The cop was doing some paperwork. A couple of weeks ago they busted somebody for possession. The guy seemed scared, anxious to talk. Said he bought the coke from a kid named Carlos, who worked for a guy named Ramos. The cop just wanted to pass that along, for whatever it's worth."

Jack raised his eyebrows.

"I don't remember a Carlos, do you?"

"No. I don't. Maybe he's new. What difference does it make? We're getting nowhere! All this ..." he cursed and gestured around the room, "... and none of it makes any difference!"

"It'll happen, Tom."

Tom glanced at his watch: five o'clock. Tom didn't want it to be five o'clock because that meant the day was almost over, and his son was still not back, safe and sound, challenging him to a basketball shoot-out in the driveway. Tom jammed his hand in his pocket. It was so frustrating!

He felt like rousting somebody. Anybody. As if Fitz would let him.

Maybe he should make the rounds of the bars. Put the word out himself. Not rely on his informants. *I want to talk to Ramos. I want to deal.* He could make a dozen bars tonight. Maybe he should.

His beeper went off. He looked down. 5545. Spark the informant's special signal. Tom's heart thumped as he dialed a public phone in a bar where they often met.

"Spark?"

"Somebody wants to talk to you. Direct. Got a number?"

Talk? Direct? Yeah. Yeah. Good! The first good news of the day. Tom felt blood surging through his body. He gave Jack the high sign across the room.

"Here's one." He gave Spark the number of a "hello" phone in the office. Ten excruciating minutes later, it rang. Everyone stopped what they were doing.

Tom automatically looked at the recorder. The tape was

rolling. He let the phone ring three times, and then picked it up. "Hello?" he said.

"Buenos dias, Donovan."

Instant adrenalin rush. Ramos! Tom signaled for a trace.

"Don't bother trying to trace this, Donovan. I'm on my car phone. You should try them. They're nice."

"I want to talk to you."

"So I hear, so I hear. But it's too late, Donovan. I warned you."

"What's the game?"

"No game. I tell you before what I do."

"If you'd wanted to do that, you would have done it at my house."

"No, no. You don't remember? I tell you how I do it—slowly, methodically, and I make him scream."

Tom fought his rage. "Look ...," His hand was sweating.

"It's too late, Donovan." Ramos paused. "But I have a little tape for you. It's a game we play. So he learns what Pablo felt like, dying in the street like a dog. Listen."

Tom heard a muffled voice, which he knew was Kenny's, then words Tom couldn't really understand, and then an awful, gurgling, choking sound. Tom felt his face flush and his head began to spin. He gripped the phone. He heard the sound of someone gasping desperately for breath. Kenny? Kenny? Tom wanted to jump through the phone.

"You like it?" Ramos asked.

Tom struggled. Cool it. Cool it, he thought. "Let's talk," he said. "I think I can get you something you want."

"It's too late, Donovan." Ramos hung up.

Tom dropped the phone and slammed his fist into the table. Sweat dripped off his forehead. His ears were ringing and he was hardly aware that Fitz had come up to him. He cursed.

Fitz put his hand on his shoulder.

"I wish," Tom said, "that I'd killed him when I had the chance!" He shook off Fitz.

Everyone in the office was looking at him. Someone rewound the tape. Jack walked toward him.

Tom looked around, his eyes blazing in anger. "I don't want Cathy to know about this! You understand? I don't want her to know!" He walked straight toward Jack. "So you just shut up about this, Jack! You got that?" he said, pointing his finger at him. Then he grabbed Jack's shirt, and got right in his face. "Just shut up!" he yelled, and then he shoved Jack aside and left the office.

Everyone was stunned. They had never, never seen Tom mad at Jack. Ever.

Fitz listened to the tape again. He shook his head, and handed the earphones to Jack.

☦ ☦ ☦

He was sitting on the back of a bench outside the office overlooking the Anacostia River, his feet on the seat, oblivious to the cold and the descending darkness.

Jack quietly walked up to him. "Y'know, Tom, this neighborhood's not a safe place to be after dark by yourself."

Tom didn't look up.

"Mind if I sit down and watch the tires float by with you?"

Tom moved over, and Jack joined him. The sky was clear and the river looked like a black no-man's land, sort of a natural demilitarized zone between Buzzard's Point and the far shore. Behind them the street remained busy, full of people headed home for the night.

"In all the years I've been here at the Point, I haven't figured out which is more entertaining. Watching trash float down the Anacostia or watching the junkies push dope right out in the open. It's the only place I've ever been where it's considered a privilege to have an office without windows."

A car horn blared right behind them. Tom looked over at his partner. "I'm sorry, Jack. I should never have ... done that."

"It's okay, partner."

They were quiet for a while. Lights from the traffic winked on and off across the river.

"Tom, I listened to that tape. Several times."

Tom threw something to the ground.

"There's a couple good things about it."

Yeah, right, Tom thought.

"First, Kenny's still alive. That's for sure."

Tom shifted on the bench.

"Second, he used Ramos's name. He said 'Just do it,

Ramos.' He identified him for us. That opens up a lot of possibilities for us. Wiretaps. Subpoenas. Lots of stuff."

Tom started listening.

"Third," said Jack, "check out the language Kenny used. He cussed. He never uses that language, Tom. Never. Who does? You. I think he was getting a message to you. I think he was saying, 'Dad, I'm okay. I'm still fighting.'"

Tom grabbed onto the hope. He looked at Jack.

"He hasn't caved in. The kid's still hangin' in there."

Tom shook his head. "I couldn't hear him. I was so mad."

"He's okay, Tom. Ramos may be messin' with his body, but he hasn't gotten to his mind. Or his spirit."

"I wasn't thinking about it that way."

Jack scratched the back of his head. "You remember a couple of years ago, when you and Kenny and I went down to Quantico, and we were running the Yellow Brick Road, just for the fun of it? Early spring, probably two years ago."

Tom nodded.

"When we finished, we were walking back through the woods, and the trees were leafing out, and it was beautiful. The dogwoods were in bloom, and the redbuds were all pinkish purple, scattered around like nature's post-it notes, saying 'Yep, winter's over, boys. You made it.' The sun felt warm and we were sweaty and tired and glad just to be alive.

"Well, we were walking along and I saw something odd, something I'd never seen before in the woods. We'd had a couple of big, late winter storms, and a lot of trees had been blown down. There were two big pines that had fallen. On the way down, they'd caught a young oak sapling, about four inches in diameter and about twenty feet tall. They'd carried that little tree right down to the ground, but the odd thing was, they hadn't broken it and they hadn't uprooted it. That little oak was still alive. Its trunk was bent ninety degrees where it came out of the ground, and it was pressed flat by the pines, running along the ground for twenty feet or more. But it was alive. The pines were dead, but the oak was determined to survive, even though it might be crushed down.

"When I think of Kenny with Angel Ramos, Tom, I think of him like that little oak. He may be flat to the ground, he may have a couple of dead pines holding him down, but he's surviving. He's doing what he can to stay alive. And I've got to believe, Tom, that he's gonna make it. I've got to believe it."

Tom felt a tiny flicker of hope in his soul. "Thanks, Jack." He blinked. They were both quiet for a while, then Tom said, "I'm sorry about ... inside."

"It's okay, Tom."

CHAPTER 31

HE FELT GRATEFUL FOR THE bed. Just being able to stretch out on his back, flat, gave him incredible relief. He had asked Carlos for a Bible, and he had found one! Kenny had spent the rest of the day reading as best he could, propping the book up, changing pages whenever he was allowed to be free for a moment. He felt better than he had since Sunday, and that night he fell into a deep sleep, his first in a long time.

A hand rubbed across his belly woke him up. A chill coursed through his body. The room was dark, just enough yellow light from the hall spilling in to enable Kenny to see Ramos sitting on the edge of the bed. But he didn't need to see him—the smell of the cigar was enough.

Ramos took a long drag, the end of his cigar glowing, the smoke momentarily enveloping his face. A scene straight from hell, Kenny thought. Kenny grabbed the bars of the bedstead to brace himself, but Ramos seemed in a mellow mood. And at least he was smoking tobacco.

"Ah, you are awake, eh? You are like me, lying there, thinking." His voice sounded quiet, almost contemplative. "You know what I think about? At night? After I have been with a woman, and I am lying there, waiting to sleep?"

Kenny remained silent.

"I think about how I kill you, and I see, in my mind, all the ways."

Ramos reached around slowly and pulled a .45 out of his waistband. It was a huge gun. He put the barrel of it right behind Kenny's right ear. Kenny cringed as he felt it press against his skin.

"Sometimes I see the gun, right here, behind your ear, and your brain flying everywhere like wet, gray, stuffing."

Kenny trembled.

Ramos put the gun away. Then he put his hands over Kenny's throat. "Sometimes I dream about choking you, my hands cutting off your air until your eyes plead with me to stop and you squirm in my grip. We practice that, eh?" He chuckled

Kenny swallowed hard as Ramos took his hands away.

"But my favorite way, Kenny, my favorite way to think about it is this." He pulled out his knife, and Kenny's eyes got wide. "In my mind I see how it will look when I cut your throat and your neck turns red with the blood." He took the knife and traced a pattern across Kenny's throat.

Kenny felt it cut his skin, felt a thin trickle of blood drip down his neck. It was like ... it was just like .... His knees began to shake and his stomach quivered. He looked up and saw Ramos's black eyes gleaming at him. Ramos had a half-smile on his face.

Kenny closed his eyes and struggled to control himself. Please God, please ... don't let him. He grabbed the bars tighter.

Ramos laid the knife flat against his cheek and that familiar fear intensified inside Kenny, sucking at him, drawing him deeper and deeper into a pit, and he felt himself sliding, sliding, but then something happened inside him, something snapped, and he heard his coach's voice: "You don't have to be the victim anymore. You don't have to be the victim." God is with me, Kenny thought, right here, right now. If God is for me, who can stand against me? Who?

"I love the idea, Kenny," Ramos continued, "and the only reason I wait is I want your father to watch, to see the fear in your eyes and hear you scream. I want him to watch you suffer and die, and then I kill him, too." Ramos looked away, as if the image satisfied him, and he pulled on his cigar.

Kenny watched the cigar glow in the dark. He took a deep breath, and then he took a step of faith. "So what?" he said, surprising even himself.

"Eh?"

"So what?" said Kenny. His voice sounded hoarse, but somehow he was able to keep it steady. "So what if you kill me? You think my dad's going to go off in a corner somewhere and suck his thumb for the rest of his life? He's tougher than that."

Ramos looked at him curiously.

"And so what if you kill him, too? You think the FBI is going to say, 'Oh, well, that's over' and go away? Give me a break, Ramos. I thought you were smarter than that." Kenny loosened his grip on the bedstead. The swirling fear slowed down. In a minute he'd have his footing again. He could feel it.

"No, Ramos, you may think you've got our lives over a barrel, but you've screwed yourself up, big time, by kidnapping me."

"What do you say?"

"You kill an agent or his son, and you'll be living in trenches the rest of your life. You won't be able to lift your head without getting shot at." Yes, he was on a roll.

"Ah, but you are wrong. Because they have no proof I am the one. I always keep, how you say, a 'buffer' between me and the cops."

"Oh, is that right? Hmm. Let me see. You play that tape for my dad?"

Ramos nodded.

"You were pretty high that night you choked me. Did you listen to that tape? Before you played it?"

A glimmer of doubt seeped into Ramos's eyes. Kenny saw it. And he went for it.

"Do you know what I said? I said, 'Just do it, Ramos!' I used your name."

Ramos cursed him but Kenny didn't stop.

"That gives them probable cause. Now they can get search warrants for your house, your mother's house, your girlfriend's house. Any evidence in those places, Ramos? Any little shred of evidence you may have forgotten? Evidence of kidnapping, or your drug dealings? Or maybe, murder?" Kenny paused.

Ramos stood up quickly. He threw down his cigar and

crushed it on the floor. Kenny saw him clench his fists.

"And wiretaps," Kenny continued. "They'll get authorization now, and they'll be listening, all the time. Of course, they'll issue an arrest warrant for you. Go through a red light, the cop runs wants and warrants, and bingo! You're in the can."

Ramos moved toward him suddenly, kneeled over him on the bed, grabbed Kenny by the hair, and smacked him in the mouth. "Shut up, you! Shut up," Ramos yelled.

But Kenny wouldn't shut up. "Now, let's see, what else," Kenny swallowed the blood and cleared his throat. "The T-shirt. I suppose you did remember to wear gloves? Sometimes they can get fingerprints off fabric, Ramos. And if a stray hair of yours got on the shirt, well, they'll use that, too. Oh, I should tell you. They can also get fingerprints off bodies, so if you do decide to choke me to death, be sure you wear gloves. Or wash my neck. Come to think of it, your prints are probably all over me already." Kenny sighed. "You'll have to dump me in the river. Like you did Roberto."

Ramos cursed. He grabbed Kenny's neck and pressed him into the mattress. Kenny struggled to breathe, but he managed not to panic. Ramos let him go, with a jerk.

"Yeah, the way I see it," Kenny continued, "your life is over in the U.S. Agents, cops, citizens—everyone will be looking for you. You won't be able to go to the movies, take a woman to a dance. No more casual dinners at Chico's or, where was it, the 'Frisco Grill?

"No more Latino Festival. You won't even be able to go to church, Ramos. You can try changing your name, getting new papers, whatever, but some things, like fingerprints and DNA, you won't be able to change. And anywhere you go, someone could hear that accent, look at that face, and say 'Who was that Latino they wanted for killing that kid?' You might even make America's Most Wanted. No, you can stand there and think about the fun you'll have killing me, but that's the last fun you'll have, Ramos. In America, you're history."

Ramos screamed at him. He grabbed Kenny, smacked him across the face, and then he stood up abruptly and walked out of the room.

✟ ✟ ✟

"Tom!" Jack came into the conference room. Tom was in his shirtsleeves, looking at a list of search warrants on Ramos they had either already obtained or were about to obtain. "Tom, you want to hear something interesting?"

"Sure."

"Smitty went over to that church to check on that doctor business. When he got there, the priest was talking to a teenager. He handed the kid a book, a Bible, maybe. Smitty really didn't think anything of it. But when he walked up to the priest and flashed his creds, the kid turned white as a sheet and took off."

Tom looked at Jack curiously.

"The kid's name was Carlos."

"Carlos?"

"Yeah. Carlos. A Bible. A new kid working for Ramos. It could fit."

"You're right, Jack. Did you tell Smitty to check it out?"

"The priest went out of town. Smitty's trying to track him down."

"If he can't find him, tell Smitty to check out every kid over ten named Carlos in that church."

"Right, Tom. Fitz is gettin' the rest of the warrants. He wants to get together with us and map out some strategy. We're gonna get these guys. The trail's gettin' hot!"

A young agent stuck her head in the door. "Tom, phone. He says it's important."

Tom jumped up, and went to the hello phone. He forced himself to sound calm. "Donovan."

"Hey, Mick." Spark sounded scared. "I need to talk to you. About what you talked to me about the other day."

Tom signaled Jack. "Yeah, uh, look, let me call you right back. In ten minutes. This, uh, isn't a good place to talk."

"I know what you mean, Mick. Here's the number."

Tom waited the ten minutes. Spark had to believe he was calling away from the office. Then he dialed the number he'd been given.

"Okay, Spark. What is it?"

"Ramos wants to talk to you. He may be ready to deal."

"Great! Good job! What happened?"

"I dunno, Mick. It was a no go, then all of a sudden ..."

"Where?"

"He wants me to pick you up. He wants to talk on the move."

"In your car?"

"Yeah."

"Are you cool with that?"

"Yeah. Listen, I think this guy's a sleaze, but I'll do it for you."

"Thanks, Spark. What time and where?"

"He wants me to pick you up tonight at ten, at the corner of Duke and Market, in Alexandria."

"Okay."

"And Mick, he says no heavy jackets. No weapons, no wires. Come clean, or he'll blow us both up."

"Yeah, yeah." He cursed. "I'll come clean, Spark, don't worry."

CHAPTER 32

"IT'S TOO RISKY, TOM." FITZ paced across the conference room.

"We knew it would be risky!"

"But you, alone with them, in a car? They'll blow your brains out right there! I don't like it."

"Fitz, I need to do this. It's the only break we've gotten."

"No, Tom. There's got to be another way. Suggest a restaurant, someplace we can stake out."

"You don't know these guys! They'll spook if I start screwing with them."

"What's going on?" Alex Cramer walked in. Tom immediately stood up, trying to shake the tension out of his shoulders. He listened while Fitz filled Cramer in.

"So, I was just telling Tom, I thought it was too risky for him, and that he ought to go back to them and suggest someplace we can wire and watch."

Cramer thought for a few minutes, then he asked Tom a few questions. He put his hands on his hips and walked over to the display of police department patches on the wall. Then he turned around.

"Let's let him do it, Fitz. I think he's right, these goons'll scare off easily if we appear to have the opportunity for control. And I think this case warrants extra risk. If he's willing to do it, let him."

✞ ✞ ✞

Tom stood at the corner of Duke and Market smoking a cigarette, his first in more than twenty years. The cigarette signaled the surveillance team to stay away. He was wearing tan slacks, an oxford cloth shirt, and a tweed wool sports jacket, open at the front. His shirt pocket held a standard, black government pen with a tiny transmitter hidden in its shaft. The technical squad would try to follow him in a van, taping whatever they could get. And the code word, in case Tom felt his life was in immediate danger was "double-cross." Tom didn't plan to use it.

He was shaking from the cold. It was another clear black night, thirty degrees outside, and the weather forecasters were talking about the possibility of a big storm in a few days. But what did they know? Tom looked at the stars, and wondered if Kenny could see them, too.

An old Chevy Caprice pulled up. Spark sat at the wheel. Tom flicked down his cigarette, stepped on it, and opened the door. Spark glanced quickly toward the back seat, then back to Tom. Tom saw the glance, and got into the front seat without looking back.

They had just entered the George Washington Parkway, headed south, when the man moved forward. Tom felt a knife at his throat. Tension gripped him.

"Buenas noches, Donovan."

"You're not Ramos," Tom said, staying perfectly still.

"He sent me, to hear what you have to say."

"I thought I was going to talk to Ramos."

"You got me, Donovan. Take it or leave it."

Tom blew out a breath, trying to manage his anger. "Okay."

"First, I check you," said the man. The knife went away. The man leaned forward, staying just outside Tom's field of vision, and ran his hands all over Tom's body, his chest, his back, the waistband of his slacks, his thighs, checking for wires or guns. Tom gritted his teeth, and managed to stay still. The man patted his breast pocket, found the pen, and threw it on the floor at Tom's feet. Tom didn't react.

A cop car drove by and Tom looked away covering the side of his face with his hand. He hoped it wasn't one of his buddies. This wasn't a good time for a friendly encounter with the locals. He heard the man behind him shift in his seat.

"Okay, Donovan. Now what's your offer?"

Tom took a deep breath. "I want my son, alive. And I'm willing to pay. A lot."

"How much?"

"A million cash, and two million in heroin."

The man whistled softly. "Where did you get that money, Donovan? I didn't know they pay agents like that."

"I can get it."

"How?"

Tom sighed. "Okay. Look. I'll admit it. I'm desperate. I want my boy." He tapped his knuckle nervously on the side window. "A month ago we did a big raid with DEA in Southeast. A black gang, with connections in New York. The money and the drugs we seized are in the Evidence Room downtown. I've got access to it. I think I can get the stuff."

Out of the corner of his eye, Tom saw Spark staring at him.

"How sure are you?"

"I'm sure. I've been around a long time. They trust me."

The car remained quiet for a while. Tom's heart pounded in his chest. Would he buy it?

"How do I know you're not setting us up?" the man in the back seat said.

"Look, what do I have to do to prove it to you?" Tom said, angrily. "I told you—I'm desperate." He hesitated. "I love my son. I want him to live. I'll do anything, anything to help him." Tom stopped again. "Do you know what they'll do to me if they catch me? I'll lose my job, go to prison. And how long do you think I'll last there? I'm taking a big risk here! But my boy is worth it. He's ... he's my only kid." Tom squeezed his hands over his eyes like he was about to cry. Then he sniffed. Fortunately, his nose was running from the cold. "Besides," he said. Then he let loose a stream of profanity directed at the FBI. "They couldn't care less about my son. They're doing nothing to find him."

The man in the back grunted. Tom stayed quiet, letting him think. He wished he could get to that pen.

"Go back to town," the man said, and Spark turned the car around.

As they approached Prince Street, the man ordered Spark to take a left. They were entering a low-income housing development. "Okay, Donovan," he said. "In two blocks, I want you to jump."

"What?"

"You heard me. Jump. Roll out of the car. I'll tell Ramos what your deal is. We'll be in touch."

Somehow Tom managed to kick the pen under the seat.

"It'll just take a second for me to stop," said Spark.

"He jumps! Now, Donovan. Go!"

Tom took a deep breath, opened his door, and jumped out. He hit the pavement, hard, on his shoulder, and rolled toward the curb. His head smashed into the bumper of a parked car, and a gash opened above his right eye. He quickly got to his feet, and walked to the sidewalk.

Stay away, stay away, guys. Tom mentally instructed the surveillance team. Ignore the blood. He quickly activated all the signals—jacket open, smoking a cigarette. Stay away. And, just as he suspected, within two minutes he saw Spark's car. They had doubled back, to see if Tom would be picked up.

Tom took out his handkerchief and pressed it over the cut on his eye. He watched Spark's tail lights disappear into the night. He walked on quickly because he was freezing, for twenty-five minutes, smoking constantly, until he got to a bar he knew well. The bartender's name was Sonny.

"What happened to you?" Sonny asked. He led Tom to a back room where he opened a first-aid kit. Sonny volunteered as an EMT in his spare time.

"A little automobile accident, that's all," said Tom. "It was parked. I wasn't."

"You need stitches, man."

"You got a butterfly bandage?"

"Yeah."

"Stick it on."

"Okay, Tom. But you need stitches."

He walked out thirty minutes later. He'd refused Sonny's offer of a beer, and had sat at the bar sipping a Coke loaded with cherries, applying pressure to his cut. And now, he figured it was safe to go home.

He walked outside, threw a cigarette down on the street and crushed it, and buttoned up his jacket. Thirty seconds later, the government sedan pulled over and picked him up.

✝ ✝ ✝

He debriefed with Fitz and Jack and Cramer for an hour. Fitz drove him to Kate's and he crawled upstairs to bed. Cathy had waited up.

"How'd it go?"

"I got in the car. I told him what the deal was. I got out."

"How'd you get cut?"

"I ran into the bumper of a parked car getting out."

"Getting out? Of Spark's car?"

"I got out kind of suddenly."

He dropped down into the armchair. He felt exhausted. He didn't even feel like getting undressed.

"What was Ramos like?"

"Wasn't Ramos. He sent someone else. Luis Aguilera, I think."

"And what was he like?"

"Typical scumbag."

"Were you scared?"

"Of him? No."

"Well, were you nervous? Angry?"

"In the car? No. It was nothing."

"Tom ..."

"Look, what's the big deal? It went okay. What else do you want to know?" He got up and jerked off his sports jacket, and started unbuttoning his shirt.

"I've been sitting here waiting for you, worried about you, worried about Kenny. Now I want to know: What happened out there? How do you feel?" When he didn't respond, she pressed harder. "Tom, don't you realize how much I'd like to be out there, looking for him? When you don't talk to me, I feel completely cut out! He's my son, too!"

He sat back down in the chair with a thud. He covered his eyes with his hand. He could feel Sonny's bandage. His head was throbbing. His shoulder was killing him. He sighed and tipped his head back.

"Cathy, Cathy, Cathy. I'm sorry." He stopped. He took a deep breath and blew it out, hard and he forced himself to respond to her. "In the car I felt angry. The jerk put a knife to my throat and I wanted to kill him." Tom got up and walked over to the window. "When he patted me down and I felt his hands on me I wanted to explode with rage. It was all I could do to stay still. I hated it, Cathy.

"I played my part well. I sounded weak and desperate. Even Spark thinks I'm ready to turn on the Bureau. And I felt good about that. But then the scumbag jerked me around, made me jump out of the car, and it made me so mad," he turned around, "and all I've been able to think about is, Kenny has to deal with this all the time. Every day. And I'm furious about that, and I want to kill someone."

"I'm sorry."

"Oh, and one more thing. I liked smoking again." And he left the room and went down the hall to take a shower.

CHAPTER 33

LOUD ARGUING FROM DOWNSTAIRS WOKE them up. Kenny looked at Carlos, alarmed, and Carlos went out the door to the top of the stairs to listen. He came back a few minutes later.

"Luis is furious," he said. "Ramos has been seeing his sister. Last night, Ramos beat her up. Again."

Kenny shook his head. "Nice guy."

"Something else is going on, but I can't tell what."

They listened for a minute more, then Kenny said, "Hey, how about letting me up, amigo?"

He was in the bathroom, washing up, when they heard heavy footsteps on the stairs.

"Let's go, let's go!" said Carlos, shoving Kenny just as Luis entered the hallway.

A stream of Spanish followed. Kenny could see Luis was still angry. Red-faced, he gestured violently. He grabbed Kenny's elbow, marched him back into the bedroom and threw him on the bed. Kenny's head hit the iron bedstead with a clunk, and he braced himself for more.

Carlos moved without being told to cuff him up.

"Luis, Luis!" Ramos stood at the bedroom door, smoking a cigar. He walked toward the bed.

"We don't have to be rough! I thought that was wrong, eh?" Ramos laughed. "Come here, Carlos. I want to talk to you," and the two of them went out in the hallway.

Luis leaned over Kenny, his eyes flashing. "Don't try anything today. Do you hear me?"

Kenny nodded.

"If you do, Carlos is in danger. Understand? Ramos is watching you both."

Carlos came back in the room. He looked pale. Ramos walked over to Kenny.

"Be good, eh?" He took his cigar and knocked off the excess ash by rolling the lighted end across Kenny's neck.

Kenny arched his back and grabbed the bars as the searing pain scorched the side of his neck.

Ramos laughed. "See, Luis? We have an understanding. No need to be rough." He patted Kenny's leg, and walked out of the room.

Luis looked from Carlos to Kenny and back again. He pointed a finger at Carlos. "Don't unlock him, for any reason!" He started to leave, then turned and said, "Give me the key, Carlos. Just to be sure."

Carlos gave him the handcuff key and Luis walked out.

As soon as he left, Kenny cried out from pain, squeezing away tears.

"I'll get ice, as soon as they leave," whispered Carlos.

The ice helped. A little, anyway.

"What did he say to you?" asked Kenny when he could finally speak.

"There's something big happening," Carlos whispered. "A lot of money involved. Ramos wants everyone to be there with him. So they're leaving us alone, except for Gordo downstairs." Carlos swallowed. "I hate what he does to you. I hate it."

The morning dragged by, one boring minute after another. Kenny drifted off to sleep several times. Around noon, Carlos appeared with a large supreme pizza in one hand and two drinks in the other. "Oh, too bad. You are awake. If you were asleep, I could eat yours," Carlos said grinning.

"No chance, bandido. I'm starving."

Carlos set the pizza down on the bed and the drinks on the floor. Then he took a key out of his pocket.

"What are you doing?" asked Kenny.

"Luis took the key," said Carlos, "but he forgot. There are two cuffs, and two keys, and both keys work."

"Carlos ..."

"They won't be back for a while. I can't do much for you,

but this I can do."

What a gift. Kenny sat up, rotating his aching shoulders. He felt his neck gingerly. A blister had formed where Ramos's cigar had burned him. "Wow," he said. He swung his legs over the side of the bed, stood up, and stretched. He glanced toward the door. The sound of the TV blasted up the stairway. Carlos read the concern on his face.

"Gordo's playing video games. He doesn't care what we're doing." He opened the box of pizza and Kenny took a slice.

"Thanks."

The food tasted so good. Kenny was on his third slice when Carlos suddenly asked, "What's keeping you going, Kenny?"

"What do you mean?"

"Ramos hates you. He hurts you. You are chained here, away from your family. But you still joke with me. I hear you humming. You don't give up. Why?"

Kenny shrugged. "You are helping. I am so grateful for that." He closed his eyes, took another deep breath. "But also I believe in God." Faith, he thought. The assurance of things hoped for, the conviction of things unseen.

"God?"

"Yeah." In his mind, Kenny traveled back to August, just six months before. It seemed like an eternity. "I knew this girl from school. She ran cross country. She got cancer. Lost her hair. Lost her leg. Got real thin. But she had the most amazing attitude." Kenny stopped, remembering Jen. "I started asking her questions, because I was curious. How could she be so happy? She began talking to me about her faith, and then one day I understood. I believed! It was like ... like a blindfold came off and I could see. A whole new world opened up to me. I knew God was real. I knew that he was good and I was not. And I knew that Jesus had died for my sins. I just knew it. And I loved him for it."

Carlos said, "This girl, she lived?"

Kenny shook his head. "No." He remembered her funeral and the multitudes of kids that showed up, her parents and her siblings and their mixture of grief and joy, and the music —incredible music. "She died on her seventeenth birthday."

He continued, "Jen is in heaven, now, with Jesus, happier

than she has ever been. If Ramos kills me, I'll be there, too."
He wiped his eye with the back of his hand. "In the
meantime, there's some purpose in this." He gestured with
his hand. "I don't know what, but God's doing something
through this, in me ... or in my parents, and maybe in you."

Carlos frowned. "In me?"

"He loves you, too, Carlos. He wants you to know him."

"When my father is hurt, my mother, she prayed and
prayed. Day after day. He still died." Carlos jutted out his
jaw. "I think there is no God."

"There's a God, Carlos, an amazing, beautiful, perfect
God who loves us. I don't know why some people live and
others die, why some prayers get answered and others ... it
seems they don't. I don't get it, but I trust God. Sometimes
when I'm lying here, I feel his presence as clearly as I sense
yours. He's real. Believe me. He is very real."

Kenny lay back down on the bed, cuffed his own left wrist
to the bedstead, and said to Carlos, "Lock me up, bandido,
before our buddy gets back." He smiled. "We don't want to
get on his wrong side. Of course, with Ramos, both sides are
the wrong side!"

✝ ✝ ✝

Tom came racing into the conference room. "He's going for
it!" he said. "Spark just called—Ramos wants to deal!"

"All right!" yelled Jack.

"Tom, that's terrific!" said Fitz.

"I've got to call Cathy!"

"Hold on, hold on," said Jack. "When are you meeting
him?"

"This evening. Seven fifteen."

"Where?"

"A movie theater on Duke Street."

Jack turned to Fitz. "I'll set up the backup."

✝ ✝ ✝

Tom handed the ticket seller at the movie theater twenty
bucks and took the ticket and the change. He was dressed in
jeans and a sweater, no coat. No weapons, no wires. He
wanted it to be obvious.

He went inside and found a seat in the middle of the
second to the last row, as instructed. There were only nine

other people in the theater, and three of them were agents. Tom's eyes adjusted to the dark. He sat perfectly still, waiting, trying hard not to watch the screen, to focus on hearing.

The slight squeak of the chair behind him alerted him. Then he felt the blade of a knife scrape across the back of his neck. A deep chill ran through his body. Was it the same knife?

A hand reached forward and patted him down. He wanted to explode.

Hot breath. "When can you get it?"

Ramos. Tom looked straight ahead. It took all his control not to turn around and kill him. Shove his fist down his throat. Stick Ramos's own knife in his gut up to the hilt.

"Early tomorrow morning," he whispered. "Hardly anybody will be around."

"Okay, then. Give me a number. I call tomorrow night, 2 a.m. I tell you where to meet me. I give you thirty minutes. You give me what you say, you get the boy."

"Thirty minutes? That's not much time. I'm coming in from Fairfax remember."

"Oh, I know where you live, Donovan." Ramos chuckled. Tom wanted to rip his heart out.

"Okay, I give you forty-five. For traffic. Because I'm nice." Ramos ran the knife up and down Tom's neck again. "Don't screw-up, Donovan. Your boy, he's getting tired. I don't think he last much longer, y'know? You get one chance. Do it right. Come alone, no guns, no wires. Bring what you say. Got it?"

"I'll be there." Tom handed back a slip of paper with a phone number written on it.

A slight squeak, and Ramos was gone. Tom sat there for fifteen more minutes, trying to calm down. Then he got up and left. Tomorrow night. He'd see his son tomorrow night.

CHAPTER 34

"AND SO THE WIND COMING in from the northeast," the TV forecaster swept his hand over what looked like a giant comma on the weather map, "will be bringing all that Atlantic moisture right in over us here. We can expect three to five inches of rain, and wind gusts up to thirty miles per hour. The ocean temperature is now forty degrees, so our temperatures will be in the low forties." He turned and smiled at the camera. "It's a classic nor'easter, folks, and it's a big one. Expect small stream flooding, heavy downpours, high winds, and maybe even some hail."

Fitz snapped off the TV.

"I don't like it. I don't like it at all," Dave Borsten said. "We won't be able to get the chopper up. Or the plane. Visibility's going to be lousy. It isn't good. It's a no go as far as I'm concerned."

Tom squirmed in his seat.

"What if when he calls, Tom tells him he can't get out, he's got car trouble, or he got called out on a case?" said Cramer.

"Or he wasn't able to get the stuff," Fitz added. "Something was going on at the office, and he couldn't get into the Evidence Room."

"Yeah, or maybe ..."

"No!" said Tom, his voice like the sharp crack of a rifle. Cramer, Fitz, and Borsten all turned to look at him. His heart beat hard. "We have to do it. Tonight."

"Tom ..."

"Tom nothing. I know these guys. When Ramos said we

had one shot at this, he meant it. And unless he postpones it, we've got to go. Even if we can't get the chopper up."

"We won't be able to adequately protect you," said Borsten.

Tom's eyes widened. "So what?" He stood up and paced behind the table. "This is my kid whose life is at stake. If we try to screw with Ramos, he'll kill him. Without hesitation." He turned to look at the men. "We've got to do it, tonight." His voice was low, passionate. "Protect me as best you can. I'll take my chances with my life. I'm not taking any more chances with Kenny's."

The room was stock still. Everyone turned toward Alex Cramer. As Special Agent in Charge, it was his call. The tension in the room seemed to pulse. After what seemed to Tom like an eternity, Cramer glanced at Fitz. "All right," he said. "We're on for tonight. We'll do the best we can."

Borsten shook his head.

✝ ✝ ✝

Just after midnight, Tom paced up and down a quiet corner of the office, chewing on a straightened paper clip, thoughts flashing through his mind. He'd made a two-hour visit to the office early Monday morning, just in case Ramos had someone watching. He'd emerged with an attaché case and a gym bag. Yes, he had the drugs and money. Go tell your boss. Actually, the bags were empty now, but the Director had approved the use of the drugs and money, and inside the office some poor guy stood over a copy machine laboriously copying the front and back of each bill. Someone else would be in charge of the drugs, but their use as bait would be monitored just as carefully.

Twelve hours ago, he'd kissed Cathy goodbye. He'd held her close for a long time, her head pressed against his bulletproof vest. She had cried. All week she'd been amazingly calm, but today she'd cried. When he asked her why, she'd said it was because she realized that she could lose both her son and her husband in one awful moment, or she could get them both back. It was the scariest day of her life.

So he'd kissed her and promised her that he'd call her the minute he had Kenny. "And Kate can bring you to him. We'll have to take Kenny to a hospital to be checked, even if he looks fine. It'll probably be George Washington or Fairfax, depending on where I meet Ramos," he'd said, "and you'll be able to see him there. In just a few hours, Cathy. Just hang in there a few more hours. Then you'll have your son. And your husband. We'll all be back together."

Even Kate had hugged him and wished him well. He went out the door, knowing he was about to pull off the most important mission of his life.

The members of the Hostage Rescue Team, dressed in their black Nomex raid suits, were gathered in the office, in the large bull pen downstairs, ready to go. They wore full body armor and had their ballistic helmets, night vision goggles, and weapons ready.

Five contingency plans had been developed, dependent on whether Ramos wanted to meet Tom inside, outside, in a public place, and so on. Tom had stretched their set-up time by getting Ramos to give him forty-five minutes to meet him, but even at that, they knew it'd be tight.

Tom went over the basic plan in his head for the millionth time: Ramos would call with the drop point. Once they knew that, the sniper-observer teams would take up positions. As Ramos moved toward Tom, the SWAT team from the Washington Field Office would establish a perimeter and block his escape. The HRT members who were not on the ground at the drop point would be in cars, just beyond the perimeter, ready to chase Ramos in case he got through. Tom, appearing to be alone, would hand over the drugs to Ramos, but hold back the money until Kenny was safe. Once Kenny was behind cover, a squad of agents would come forward, grab Tom to protect him, while HRT went for Ramos. Every other available agent in the office would be used for back-up beyond the immediate perimeter. Their priorities were: 1. Secure Kenny. 2. Protect Tom. 3. Get Ramos.

Tom liked the plan and if it weren't for the weather, he'd be totally confident they could pull it off. The loss of the chopper meant Ramos had a chance to get away. At this point he didn't care. He just wanted his son.

✞ ✞ ✞

When the phone rang at 2 a.m. everyone froze, and Tom

broke into a sweat. He let it ring twice, then picked it up.

"Donovan," he said.

"You get it?" Ramos asked.

"I got it," said Tom.

"You know East Potomac Park? Hains Point?"

"Yes," said Tom. He looked at Borsten, already madly jotting notes.

"You go to Buckeye Drive. There is a streetlight there, right at the curve, and a big tree with a notice of a Latino Festival in Mount Pleasant. You be there. In forty-five minutes."

"Right. I'll be there."

✝ ✝ ✝

"We lucked out. It's close," said Fitz.

Borsten began issuing orders. "Call the Park Police. Tell their guys we have something going right outside their headquarters. Tell 'em to stay away. And don't let them give you any nonsense!"

"Turner, get Harbor Police. I want two small boats. And I want two guys to approach Hains Point from the river side, and two from the channel side. Right now! Tell them to find out what counter-surveillance we're dealing with."

"I want eight guys ... A-team, where's my A-team?" A dark-haired agent moved forward. "Mack, I want you to take your team, by boat, to the end of Hains Point and start moving up to where Donovan's gonna be. Belly crawl if you have to." Mack nodded, his eyes shiny and bright against his blackened face, and he moved quickly to carry out Borsten's orders.

"Okay, now, let's see, what else." Borsten ran his hand through his hair.

Jack moved close to Tom.

"How are you doin', buddy?" said Jack. "Nervous?"

"I'm ready, Jack. It's gonna go down. I can feel it."

"Tom!" Cramer walked toward him.

"Yes, sir!"

"Time for you to head out."

"Okay."

Cramer grabbed his hand and shook it. "Don't take any unnecessary chances, Tom. And good luck."

"Yes, sir. Thank you."

"We'll do everything we can to back you up. I want to meet this boy of yours. Tonight."

"Yes, sir."

☦ ☦ ☦

Outside the wind was blowing strong and hard. The rain was coming down like a million slant bars under the street lights. The windshield wipers couldn't even begin to keep up.

Smitty was at Tom's house in Fairfax, making it look occupied in case Ramos had someone watching it. When he got the call from Fitz, he pulled a hat low over his face, got in Tom's car, and drove slowly toward Washington. He stopped at an all-night gas station, went into the men's room, and changed jackets and hats with Tom waiting for him there. "Make it happen, Tom" he said. "You can do it." They shook hands. Tom got into his own car and continued on to East Potomac Park, his stomach alive with tension, his hands sweating even in the cold. I'm coming, Kenny, he thought. I'm coming.

CHAPTER 35

EAST POTOMAC PARK WAS A flat, low tongue of land. On one side lay the Potomac River, on the other, the Washington Channel. Ohio Drive skirted the perimeter and was bordered by a wide sidewalk. A concrete seawall, topped with an iron guardrail, ran along the edge. It was a three-foot drop to the water below.

Tom went over these facts in his head as he drove toward the drop point. The park itself consisted mostly of long, flat, grassy stretches studded with well-trimmed trees. In the summer, people played soccer, had picnics, and even staged polo matches there. Visibility was pretty good, and Tom figured Ramos had chosen it because he guessed it would provide few places to hide back-up if Tom was double-crossing him. Tom wondered if Ramos had remembered that one of the only two buildings on the spit of land was Park Police headquarters.

But Ramos had been right about the visibility, and Borsten was none too happy about that. He'd finally decided to put one sniper-observer team on the roof of the Park Police building, and one strapped to the seawall, peering over the edge. They'd knocked out some of the streetlights in the area to give additional cover.

Borsten wanted to place one more sniper unit in the area. He had a boat deliver a team dressed in ghillie suits to the end of the Point. The ghillie suits made the men look like walking bushes—it was an idea borrowed from the ancient Scots, an earth-colored suit covered with mesh, into which were woven branches of bushes and twigs from trees and leaves, that served as camouflage. The suits were very heavy, but they made a man nearly invisible in the woods or bushes. After climbing up the seawall, the team began the long crawl toward the rendezvous point.

The early observers reported no counter-surveillance—Ramos was either confident or stupid. Borsten decided to take another chance—he ordered a seven-man assault team into a scruffy van, and had them sneak in to the Park Police building on the Point, leaving the van parked outside like a junky maintenance vehicle.

Borsten stationed back-up agents near the Jefferson and Lincoln Memorials, on either side of the 14th Street Bridge, across the Case Bridge, and in nearby L'Enfant Plaza. By 2:35, everyone was in place, and Tom sat in his car by himself under the light.

The time went by slowly, too slowly, and Tom wished he had a cigarette. The wind was fierce, stripping leaves and branches off of the trees. Tom could hear the waves of the Potomac crashing into the seawall—the river was frothing at the mouth. And across the Channel, in the marina, the rigging of the boats clanged against aluminum masts.

At 2:45 Tom got out of the car. He wore tan cargo pants, his bulletproof vest, two shirts, and a heavy wool sweater that would be soaked in minutes. No weapons, no wires. Believe it, Ramos. He put a gym bag, containing bags of heroin borrowed from DEA, at his feet. He chained an attaché case full of money to the lamppost next to him. He rehearsed his lines: *I'll tell you where the key is when Kenny's in my car. Kenny first, Ramos. Then I'll give you the key.*

Finally he saw lights. His heart rate quickened. Come on, Ramos. Do your thing!

The car drove toward him. Tom shivered. He flicked on a small flashlight, pointing it straight to the ground. His signal. The night was so black, he wondered if the snipers' night-vision goggles were good enough to pierce that darkness.

The car, a black Lincoln, stopped about fifty feet away. It pulled up at an angle to Tom, so that he could see the front and right side.

Tom strained to see. Rainwater dripped from his hair and into his eyes. The wind buffeted him and he had to brace himself.

The front passenger door of the Lincoln opened, and someone stepped out, someone with an assault rifle. He looked around. Then the man turned on a hand-held spotlight and swept the area, checking the grass, the benches, the trees. Tom was glad HRT had stayed back. Way back. Finally the back door opened and a man got out. Tom realized it was Angel Ramos. He moved aside. Tom saw Kenny step out of the car, and even through the rain, in the dark, he could see it was his son. The way he carried his shoulders, the shape of his head ...Tom blinked away the rain and his heart jumped. It was Kenny! Kenny!

"Ramos?" Tom yelled over the storm. Kenny heard him. Tom saw him turn toward the sound of his voice. "I got the stuff. Let him go now!"

"I send someone ...,"

Tom strained to hear Ramos.

"... to check ...," and his voice trailed off.

"What?" yelled Tom. "Come on, Ramos, let's do this. Let's do it!"

"I send ...," but before Ramos could finish, Tom heard a sound, and saw something out of the corner of his eye that gripped him like an icy hand. Headlights. From two cars. Headed straight toward them. At a high rate of speed.

Ramos heard it, too, and he turned to look and suddenly Tom heard shouting in Spanish, and gunfire, aimed at Ramos.

Then Tom saw Ramos shove Kenny back in the car and dive in after him. Tom began running, hard, screaming, "No! No!" The other cars swept by Ramos's car, shooting, the bright bursts from their guns lighting the night, the sound roaring in Tom's ears. He ran through the rain, slipping on the wet grass, running, running, his heart pounding wildly in his chest. No, come back, come back!

One of the other cars circled back around, driving over the grass, shooting at the rear of Ramos's car. Tom saw the car accelerate quickly, fishtailing on the wet road. No, no! He began running and yelling, his arms and legs pumping, hard. Suddenly he saw bursts of automatic weapon fire from Ramos's car, directed at him, and bullets whizzed past him.

Something hit him in the chest and knocked him off his feet.
He rolled over in the wet dirt, stood up, and began running
again, yelling "Kenny! Kenny!" But Ramos's car sped off
and pulled away into the night, its taillights like red, demonic
eyes as they disappeared into the blackness.

Tom slowed to a walk and then stopped, his lungs aching.
His mind began playing tricks on him, and he couldn't tell
what he was seeing: the grassy stretches of the park or an
alley with high board fences. The sound of the guns still
echoed in his ears and he began shaking. He blinked his eyes.
Could he see men? Men or trees? He felt confused. Where
was he? And where did everyone go? Where did the men go?
He thought he heard someone calling his name. "Tommy!
Tommy!"

Jack grabbed him by the arm. "Tom? Are you okay?
Tom?"

A sense of helplessness and despair poured over him and
he staggered back, and Jack steadied him. "What
happened?" Tom said.

"We don't know. It wasn't us. That's all we know." Eight
agents surrounded him, their weapons maddeningly
irrelevant.

Tom stared into the night, into the blackness that had just
swallowed up his son. "Why'd they kill him?"

"They didn't kill him," Jack said. "They just shoved him
back in the car."

He turned and looked at Jack as if he didn't know who he
was, and said again, "Why'd they kill him?"

Jack carefully searched his face, and saw that Tom's eyes
were focused somewhere else. He took his friend's arm,
turned him around, and said, "Come on, Tom. Let's get you
out of the rain."

They began walking back to a van.

"Jack, is Tom okay?" Fitz's voice came on the radio.

"He needs to get warmed up," replied Jack. That was
enough for now.

"I'm sending another van over. We've got blankets and a
heater going."

The van met them coming across the grass. Jack helped
Tom get inside and out of his wet clothes. Tom was

trembling and shaking so badly he couldn't even undress. "Tom, you got hit!" said Jack, as he fingered the bullet hole in Tom's sweater. There were holes in his shirts, too. And his body armor was damaged, but it had done its job. "You're going to have a heck of a bruise." Tom seemed not to hear him. Jack looked carefully at Tom's chest and gently probed his sternum. "You're okay, now, buddy. You'll be warm in a minute." Jack wrapped blankets around him and sat him down next to the heater.

Tom's eyes focused on Jack. "What happened?" he asked.

"We don't rightly know, Tom. We're still tryin' to figure it out." Jack patted his best friend on the back and thought how completely inadequate that gesture was. "I'll be right back."

⚜ ⚜ ⚜

When Kenny heard his dad's voice, his heart jumped to his throat. Dad! He'd found him!

Suddenly, he heard shots from his right. Ramos shoved him back in the car, and Kenny tried to fight, but there was no chance to get away. He yelled, "Dad! Dad!" as Ramos forced him back into the center of the back seat. The car started moving and Ramos slid in next to him, screaming in Spanish. Two cars flashed past, firing guns. Jorge, who was sitting on Kenny's left, wasn't even all the way in the back seat when Luis floored it, and the car fishtailed and took off.

Kenny twisted his head around, trying to see his dad one more time, and he thought he saw him running in the darkness. But then the other car circled around, and he saw headlights behind them and bursts of gunfire.

He hunched down. Just at that moment, he heard an engine roar and a terrible boom! The back window exploded. Glass flew everywhere, all over Kenny. Jorge, next to him, screamed and lurched forward. A huge wound opened in the top of Jorge's head, near his ear, and blood poured out.

Kenny squeezed his eyes shut. The car streaked across Memorial Bridge, headed back to Virginia. The smell of blood and death filled Kenny's nose, and the wind and rain and cold poured in through the open window and down his back.

Luis swung onto the GW Parkway. The cars following them had peeled off somewhere around the Lincoln Memorial, and they were alone on the black road. Ramos and Luis were yelling at each other in Spanish. Kenny kept his eyes closed and prayed frantically.

Suddenly, Luis swung the car to the left, up and over the low curb, and stopped it on the grassy shoulder. Luis got out of the driver's seat, jerked open the back door, grabbed Jorge's body, and pulled it out of the car. Kenny saw it roll over and over down the grassy incline. Luis got back in the car, and they sped off into the night.

☥ ☥ ☥

Jack asked a young agent to come into the van and sit with Tom. Then he called Fitz on the radio.

"He's been shot, Fitz, right in the vest."

"I'll be right over with an EMT."

"Yeah, he'd better be checked."

"Were they able to get him?" Jack asked when Fitz pulled up. An EMT stepped inside the van.

"It happened so fast. SWAT didn't have time to close the perimeter. One of the HRT units thought they had him going around the Lincoln Memorial, and everyone went chasing him. It was the wrong car."

Jack cursed. "What a night."

"How's Tom?"

"Stunned. Like a steer that's just been hit over the head by the butcher."

Fitz rubbed his hand over the back of his neck.

"I'm all right! Now leave me alone!" Tom's voice rang out from inside the van.

Jack looked at Fitz. "I'd better get in there."

Jack climbed back in the van and sat down next to Tom. "Let 'em check you, Tom. You've been hit."

"Did they get him?" Tom asked, but Jack's face gave him the answer and he groaned and leaned his head back.

"Sir, come with me. We have an ambulance outside."

A string of profanity followed.

Jack said, "Tom, you need to go to the hospital. You need to have your chest looked at."

Tom didn't answer.

Jack looked at the EMT. "How about if I take him?"

"It's not regulation, but okay. If a supervisor agrees."

Fitz not only agreed, but got his own car and he and Jack went with Tom to the hospital, leaving Borsten in charge of the ongoing pursuit. A police officer met them and got Tom in an ER exam room right away.

Fitz motioned for Jack to step out for a minute. "I'm going to call Cathy. She needs time to adjust before Tom gets there. And I want to check in with Borsten."

"What a hellacious night." Jack said.

"How's he doing?" Fitz asked when he returned.

"X-rays look good so far. Doctor suggested he stay for a day, for observation. Tom said a few things to him my momma would've whipped me for, and the doc backed right off. Amazing." Jack shrugged. "Did Borsten get Ramos?"

"No."

A nurse approached them. "Are you gentlemen with Mr. Donovan?"

"Yes, ma'am," said Jack.

"You can go on in. The doctor's signing the release papers now."

CHAPTER 36

FITZ TOOK THE ROCK CREEK Parkway back to Kate's, cutting up Massachusetts Avenue. A number of large trees were down in Rock Creek Park, and standing water in the road splashed high above the car as he drove through the low places.

Tom slouched in the front seat, silent, staring at the raindrops sliding like tears down the windshield. Fitz told him everything they knew about what had happened, but Tom didn't respond. He had pulled deep within himself.

Fitz pulled into the alley behind Kate's house, blocking the garage, and cut the engine. The house looked dark. Tom's watch read 4:45 a.m.

Fitz and Jack sat still. Tom knew that they were waiting for him to move, but he didn't have the energy to open the car door and get out. Maybe by staying in the car he could keep the night going, give himself one more chance to make it right.

Tom sat with his head leaning back against the headrest. He'd been trying to figure out how he would explain what happened to Cathy. He hadn't come up with anything. He dreaded going inside.

Finally Fitz spoke. "How are you feeling, Tom?"

Tom winced. He cleared his throat. "Okay, Fitz. I'm okay." Even as he heard his voice saying those words his heart sunk to his boots. A feeling like molten lead spread through his body. He was not okay. He was anything but okay. In fact, he wished he were dead, that the bullet that had struck his vest had found its mark.

Out of the corner of his eye, Tom saw Fitz glance back at Jack.

The muscles in Tom's jaw flexed over and over while he stared straight ahead.

"Tom," Fitz said quietly, "I've been with the FBI for a long time. This was the toughest thing I've ever had happen to me. And it wasn't even my son. Now how are you really feeling?"

Tom turned his head. Feeling? He didn't want to feel. He wanted to get those snakes back in the box, put a rock on the lid, and let them slither all over each other in the dark. He didn't want to deal with them. But the snakes kept slinking out, and right now one was squeezing the blood out of his heart and another one was slithering through his brain.

A deep shudder ran through him. Tom shifted in his seat. "I was so close." His voice broke. "I was so close." He swallowed hard. "There he was, standing right next to the car. He expected me to help him."

"You did everything you could."

"I couldn't make it happen. The most important event of my life, and I couldn't make it happen."

The despair in his voice reverberated through the car, like the low-frequency boom of a mortar you can feel in your chest from miles away. The three men sat perfectly still. Outside the wind buffeted the car, and Tom could hear the unlatched door of a neighbor's garage slamming shut, over and over.

"Tom," Jack said, "do you understand they didn't kill him? You kept asking me, 'Why'd they kill him?' Do you understand, they didn't kill Kenny, Tom? He's still alive! There's still hope."

Tom thought for a long time before he responded. He stared out the window. He put his right hand to his forehead. It was shaking. "I got confused, Jack. I thought I was ... I guess I was having a flashback."

"A flashback?"

Tom sighed. He dropped his hand to his lap with a thud. Then he began to speak in a low voice.

"My dad," he said, "was a cop. Boston. Charlestown District. Big Irish area. He was a big guy, over six feet, and

around two hundred pounds. Officer Patrick Donovan."
Tom paused, as if he were savoring the name. And then he
closed his eyes, and the world faded away, and the sound of
the rain dripping, dripping, constantly dripping carried him
across a cable of time stretched taut with emotion, back over
forty years, to another alley and another rainy night.

⚜ ⚜ ⚜

He was a seven-year-old boy then, the oldest in his family,
and Tom liked nothing better than to be called "Pat
Donovan's boy." "That's Patrick's boy," the men outside the
hardware store would say. And his chest would swell with
pride, and he'd run a little faster or jump a little higher to
show them he was worthy, that he was, indeed, the son of
Officer Patrick Donovan.

Patrick had black hair and blue eyes and a grin that made
Tom's heart quicken. Always ready to play with Tom, he'd
swing him up over his head, wrestle with him on the floor, or
throw a baseball to him in the alley behind their house any
time he had the chance.

But it was as Patrick Donovan, the policeman, that he had
burned the strongest image in Tom's heart. Tom loved to see
him in his uniform—he had a wide black belt and a shiny
silver badge, handcuffs, and a big revolver. Tom liked his billy
club the best, because his dad used to play with it. He'd walk
down the street whistling and swinging that thing, twirling it
between his fingers. Sometimes he'd hold it up chest high.
Tom would hang from it and his dad would challenge him to
do chin-ups. "One more, Tommy-boy!" he'd say and Tom
would struggle and pull to do one more, just to see his dad
smile.

One late afternoon in early spring, when the trees were
just beginning to bloom, and the day was warm with
promise, Patrick Donovan took a break from his patrol and
stopped at the house to pick up something he'd forgotten.
Tom had hoped he'd come home to play, and he was crushed
when his dad said goodbye again. He begged his dad to let
him go with him, just for a little while. Of course, Patrick
knew he wasn't supposed to, but his beat was in their own
neighborhood and all the kids tagged along with cops once in
a while. So he gave in.

It was about 4:30. They walked along, laughing and joking. Patrick told Tom stories about his childhood, about his brothers and the trouble they all used to get into growing up in the city. His parents had brought him to America from Ireland when he was five, and he had a lot of stories.

It had rained the night before and the air was fresh and moist blowing in off the bay. Puddles still lay on the sidewalk. Daffodils were blooming in many of the small yards they passed. It was Lent, and they could smell fish frying as they walked past the houses.

They crossed Hamilton Street and went on down Coleman. There was a short alley there that ran between some row houses and dead ended into the brick wall of a warehouse. Six-foot-high board fences lined the alley, and there were some trash cans along the sides.

As they got to the alley, a little calico kitten ran out and Tom stopped to play with it.

Down the alley, two men were working on a car, trying to change a tire. They were swarthy, dressed in suits, and Tom could remember thinking they looked out of place. "Hey, officer!" they yelled. "Can you give us a hand?"

His dad answered, "Sure!" and told Tom to meet him down there. Later, when he thought about it, Tom realized the men probably never even saw him.

The kitten ran off, and Tom started down the alley. He could see his dad talking to the men. He saw him squat down next to the tire and jerk the tire iron to free up the lug nuts.

Suddenly Tom saw another man step out from behind a fence. Tom saw the glint of steel as the man pulled out a pistol and put it to his dad's head, just below his right ear. Tom saw his father react with alarm.

Two more men appeared. One took his dad's service revolver. Tom would find out later they were part of a gambling ring his dad had testified against five years earlier.

Tom slipped behind some garbage cans, only about twenty feet away. He could hear their voices, and his dad had turned so he could see the shock on his dad's face. Tom's heart beat so loudly he was terrified the men would hear it.

Officer Donovan was on his knees by the car. The men made him lace his fingers behind his head. They were cursing him. One man—Tom would recall later he had on a brown suit and had a gold cap on his front tooth that glistened when he talked—put the barrel of his pistol right up under Patrick's jaw, tilting his head up so they were staring into each other's eyes.

"I want to hear you beg," the man said.

"Blackie, you don't want ta do this," Tom's dad replied. His brogue always got worse when he was tense. "They'll find you. You'll get the chair."

"C'mon, copper, beg for your life."

The other men looked nervous. They kept glancing down the alley. "Get it done!" Tom heard one of them say. But Blackie ignored them. He stood over Officer Patrick Donovan and licked his lips, as if some coarse appetite was about to be satisfied.

"Now, Blackie, listen," Patrick Donovan said. "Y'know I was only doin' my job. It was nothin' personal. Don't do somethin' now you'll regret later. Somethin' that'll land you on death row."

"You're on death row, you stupid mick!" He laughed as he said it, and his laugh sounded inhuman. And then, as if in slow motion, Tom saw Blackie drop his hand slightly, and pull the trigger.

Patrick's head jerked and a red gaping hole appeared where his eye and his forehead used to be as Tom watched in horror. Patrick's remaining eye was wide open and he fell back, hit the car, and slid behind the back wheel. His body twitched and convulsed as Blackie shot him three more times.

Tom covered his ears to block the roar of the gun but he could not take his eyes off his dad. He crouched in his hiding place as the men ran down the alley. He watched as the life flowed out of his wounded father and into a puddle of oily rainwater under the car. Tom was frozen in place, frozen in time.

Within minutes he heard sirens. Police, ambulances, people from the neighborhood swarmed around. It was beginning to get dark and no one saw Tom. No one was looking for a scared little boy who had just seen his childhood destroyed. And Tom's voice was stuck in his throat, his body completely immobilized by shock.

Tom watched them as they hovered over his father's body. He watched as they took photos and dug slugs out of the ground. And he watched them as they threw a sheet over his dad and put him into a hearse and drove away.

It began to rain. Still Tom couldn't move. He sat there, rain dripping down his face, his clothes sticking to him, watching the drops splatter into the pool of oil and water and his father's blood. The horror of what he had seen seared Tom's soul with the intensity of white hot iron.

✞ ✞ ✞

A gust of wind came up and shook the car. The neighbor's garage door slammed again, and Tom opened his eyes. Off to his left he saw Fitz staring out of the window, blinking back tears.

Tom gently touched his own eye and his own forehead. His skin was whole and warm, and he wished he could touch his father's face, and close his father's wound, and restore life to this man he loved so much. He dropped his head and stifled a sob.

Then he continued, his voice choking with emotion. "I stayed there for hours," Tom said, trembling. "My mother must have been frantic, but no one knew where I was. Finally, in the glow of a street light I saw my uncle. 'Tom! Tommy!' he called. I couldn't answer, so I just stood up. 'Oh, Tommy!' he said as he swept me into his arms. He had on a plaid shirt, and I remember the smell of wet wool and the scratchy way it felt when I put my head down on his shoulder. He carried me back through the dark, empty streets to my home.

"I remember them stripping off my wet clothes, putting me in my bed, spooning some hot soup down my throat. I remember my mother sitting next to me, tears running down her cheeks, her hand holding mine. The house was filled with the voices of my aunts and uncles, and the weeping of my grandmother. There was the smell of candles burning and I saw a priest walk past my bedroom door.

"I stayed in my bed for a week, unable to walk or talk. Neighbors and relatives came and went, doctors came to see me. Finally, on the seventh day, I got up. And when I got up,

I knew I wanted to spend my life fighting the kind of people who killed my father."

Tom stopped and looked straight at Fitz. "I've been trying to replay that scene ever since, Fitz, trying to make it come out right. The good guy wins, the bad guys lose. And I've been very successful. Until now. Now I'm watching it again, watching it go down bad, only with my son and not my father. And I feel as helpless and as terrified as a seven year old behind some trash cans in an alley."

The three men sat, staring into the dark, engulfed in an electric silence. Finally, Fitz spoke. "I never knew that, Tom, about your dad."

"It isn't something I like to talk about."

Fitz reached out and touched Tom's shoulder. "I'm sorry. That's an awfully heavy burden for a seven year old to carry."

"I've done okay. At least up to now." And before anyone could say anything else, Tom abruptly opened the car door and got out.

"I think I'll just stay here tonight," said Jack softly. "I'll bet Kate has a couch that'll fit me."

"Did you know this, Jack? About his dad?"

"Just the basics. From Cathy. Like he said, it isn't something he likes to talk about, even with her. She had to get the details from his mother." Jack shook his head. "Cathy told me he testified against 'em, and even at age seven his testimony was so clear it sent the trigger man to the electric chair."

"Call me," said Fitz, as Jack got out of the car. His voice sounded strained. "If you need anything, if Tom needs anything, call me."

CHAPTER 37

THE HOUSE WAS ALMOST DARK inside. Kate had waited up for them.

Tom sat down on a kitchen chair right inside the door to take off his boots. He could smell the earthy, moist odor of humus from the park. His fingers felt stiff and awkward as he worked at the laces.

"How are you Tom? Can I get you anything? A drink? Anything?" Kate's voice was gentle.

"No, Kate. Thanks." He looked at her. "Where's Cathy?"

"She went on to bed. She was pretty upset. She wanted to come to the hospital, but I thought ..."

"It's okay." Tom stood up and left the room.

Jack and Kate watched him go. "Kate," Jack said, his face drawn with emotion, "I need a hug. From a friend."

✝ ✝ ✝

Tom's legs felt like lead as he climbed the twelve steps to the second floor. He walked down the hall and switched on the light in the bathroom. He unbuckled his belt. He dropped his slacks, pulled off his jacket and his shirt, and threw them all in a pile on the floor. He kicked off his boxers and turned on the shower.

For Tom, a hot, steamy shower was normally a relief after a long day's work but tonight it was just water coming down, a means to an end. Get the dirt off and get to bed.

When he entered the bedroom it looked like Cathy was asleep, turned on her side with her back toward him. He desperately needed to be touched, to feel her skin against his, but he was afraid to approach her, afraid that if she were angry, if she turned away from him, her rejection would be the final shove that would propel him into the snake pit that had always waited for him.

He slipped quietly in behind her. He could see her in the ambient light of the room, her shoulders lifting rhythmically with her breathing. His loneliness overpowered him and he moved forward, gingerly putting his hand on her hip. She didn't move away. Encouraged, he slipped his arm around her waist and pulled her to him, until her back was touching his chest and he could bury his face in the fragrant scent of her hair. She still did not move. He touched his face, his chest, his hips, his legs to her as if she could somehow strengthen him, anchor him in the storm that was swirling inside him. And he felt her move and adjust her position until they lay like two spoons in a drawer, alone together. His heart was pounding and his jaws ached from tension, but he held her, silently noticing her breathing adjust to his, grateful for the synchronism.

After a little while she stirred as if she had finished a dream and was now noticing him. She turned toward him, her features soft, and wordlessly looked into his glistening eyes. Her body felt warm against his, smooth, and comforting. She looked him over, studying him, and then she took his face in her hands, and kissed his neck just behind his right ear. He could smell her fragrance, feel her soft breath in his ear. He felt his throat constrict. She pulled his face toward hers and as he closed his eyes she kissed each one, tasting the saltiness of his grief, the warm wetness of his tears. She kissed his cheeks, his lips, his nose, his eyes again, and then she gently pulled his head down until he was resting on her warm breast, and he heard the reassuring cadence of her heartbeat as it regulated the timing of his life.

And in the safety of her arms the box split open and the thousand snakes that Tom had fought all those years came sliding out. His shoulders heaved and his chest quivered as a deep, guttural sob emerged from the depths of his soul, and a flood of tears began cascading down his cheeks. He tried to catch his breath, to stifle the feelings, but Cathy held on tight and suddenly the seven-year-old-boy and the forty-seven-year-old man were weeping and grieving in her arms. All the unspent grief, the unacknowledged pain of all those years merged with the anguish of the night, and he was overwhelmed with emotion.

His sorrow washed over him like a rogue wave, buffeting him until his body shook as he tried desperately to fight it. Cathy held him close as the wave crashed over his head, sending him spinning into a chasm. Images of his father, the gaping red hole in his face, his vacant, staring eye, merged with his vision of Kenny, handcuffed, at the mercy of another group of swarthy men. He heard voices, Spanish voices, Italian voices, cursing and laughing. And he felt the sickening paralysis of dreams, the complete inability to control his arms and legs, to rescue his own father, to save his own son.

He began to panic as despair washed over him like salt water over a sand castle, destroying every turret, every wall of the fortification he had so painstakingly built over the years. He heard himself cry out, "Oh, God!" and in his mind's eye he saw himself tumbling over and over underwater, caught in a riptide, helplessly being sucked out to sea by a force much bigger than he.

He heard himself crying, and the sound of his own grief was a foreign language in his ears. He lay sobbing in Cathy's arms until her silent tears merged with his on the front of her nightgown, and they both lay exhausted. They locked their bodies together, clinging desperately to each other. They had not spoken at all, and they hadn't needed to.

CHAPTER 38

SOMEHOW THEY HAD MADE IT back to Alexandria.
Luis dropped them off in the alley. Ramos shoved Kenny
into the house, through the back door. Kenny stood shaking
in the bright light of the kitchen, his teeth chattering,
freezing in his wet clothes.

Ramos yelled in Spanish, screaming orders, and the men
hustled to obey him. His face was red, his eyes narrow, and
his commands were accompanied by sharp gestures. Kenny
was desperate to get away—away from Ramos, from Spanish
words and handcuffs, gunfire and speeding cars, and away
from Jorge's blood, that had formed a sticky mess on his
sweats. With every breath he could smell death. He couldn't
think, much less pray. He felt dizzy and, oh man, he had to
get away. Every time he closed his eyes he saw flashes of light
and Jorge's head exploding.

Ramos turned toward him. "Tito, get him out of these
clothes! I don't want to look at him!" Ramos shoved Kenny
across the room, past Gordo, his face frozen with fear.

"Come on!" Tito grabbed Kenny's arm and moved him
into the front room. He picked up a flannel shirt and a pair
of jeans from a pile on the floor. Then he uncuffed Kenny's
hands. "Get changed. And be quick!"

When Kenny felt his hands come free, tears came to his
eyes. He had to get away! He took two quick breaths. He
pulled off the soaking wet sweatshirt and his stiff, bloody
sweatpants. His hands were shaking, the cuffs swinging
loosely from his right hand. He pulled the jeans on. Tito
stood right behind him. Gordo lingered near the door,

watching.

Kenny snapped the jeans and picked up the shirt and put it on and began buttoning it up. Thank God, the clothes were dry. He reached down to the pile of clothes and picked up a sweatshirt, and put it on, too. He was so tired of being cold.

"Hurry up!" said Tito.

Kenny pulled the sweatshirt down over his chest.

"Now give me your hands ..."

Kenny started to put his hands behind his back, then he panicked at the thought of being cuffed again. He had to get away! And before he even thought out what he was doing, he jerked his hands away, turned, and hit Tito square on the nose. He saw Tito fall back onto the floor. Then Kenny ran, right past Gordo. As he pulled open the front door, he heard Tito yell, "Get him! Get him!"

He plunged outside, the cold night air hitting him like a smack in the face, and he jumped off the porch, leaping over all three steps at once.

"Get him! Get him!" men shouted frantically. Kenny could hear their feet on the concrete, hear their sharp cries of anger behind his back.

He ran down the front walk, off the curb, between the cars parked in front. The wet asphalt was slick and black beneath his feet, the night air cold and sharp. The men behind him were grunting and running hard, and he clenched his jaw and put on more speed.

He headed for the mouth of the cul-de-sac. If he could get to a big road, where there was traffic, maybe a cop, or a lighted house, or a gas station. Anyplace, anywhere he could get help.

He cut between two parked cars. The main street was just ahead. If he could make it ....

He never saw what he tripped over. It could have been a kid's bike, or a tricycle left out on the sidewalk in the rain. Or a wagon. Whatever it was, it was metal, and hard, and it sent him sprawling across the wet grass of someone's lawn. He tasted dirt, and he knew it was all over.

Immediately they were on him, pinning his arms and legs down, the weight and heat and smell of their bodies pressing the wind out of him. He fought against them and managed to get a hand free. But he stopped struggling when he felt a gun right behind his ear.

They jerked him to his feet and hustled him back to the house, his arms held tightly by two men, his legs reluctantly retracing his path, his heart shattered.

As they entered the door of the house Ramos began beating him, cursing him in Spanish. Then El Jefe stepped back.

Kenny stood, doubled over, struggling to breathe, his mouth gaping, his eyes glazed. Then slowly, he lifted his head. The tiger's cage, he thought. The tiger's cage. He met Ramos's stare.

Ramos turned to the gang. "He is getting to me, this kid. He is like his father. He doesn't know when to quit. He gets to me!" Ramos was breathing hard, his eyes glittering with anger. He wiped his mouth with the back of his hand.

Carlos stood pressed against the wall, fear plastered on his face.

"You want your hand uncuffed, boy? Okay. I can make that happen." Ramos reached down, grabbed Kenny's shirt, and sent him sprawling on the floor. As Kenny put his hands out to catch himself, Ramos stomped on the kid's left hand, his boot landing hard. Then he put his whole weight on it.

Bones broke. A chilling cry ripped from Kenny's throat. He struggled to move, to crawl away from the pain, and he ended up on his knees, curled over his hand, choking and crying. Ramos stood watching, his hands on his hips, his eyes glowing, as if he were admiring a piece of work. "Okay," he said to the stunned gang members. "He wants his hand uncuffed. Now he can have it that way." Ramos laughed.

The men looked away, down at their shoes and vaguely across the room. One of them took a long drag on a cigarette and let the smoke out in a long silent stream. A short thin boy edged toward the door.

Ramos looked at them and laughed again. "You're all afeminado." Then he picked up Kenny's right hand, which still had the cuff on it. He dragged Kenny across the kitchen floor to the sink. Ramos opened the cabinet under the sink and snapped the open cuff onto the water pipe, leaving

Kenny sprawled awkwardly on the floor.

Then Ramos looked around the room. "There," he said. "Now I think we have no more trouble." He looked at his watch. "We go in one hour. Five-thirty. Be ready." And he left the room.

✞ ✞ ✞

He must have been out of it for a while when he became aware of someone gently lifting his head.

"Kenny!"

He struggled toward consciousness.

"Kenny!"

Kenny opened his eyes. Carlos crouched before him, holding a white pill to his lips.

"Take it. It'll help."

Kenny opened his eyes wider.

"It's a pain pill. Take it."

Kenny took the pill, sipping water from a cup Carlos held for him. Then Carlos picked up an ice bag, which he placed on Kenny's left hand. "Keep it there, okay?" Then Carlos bent down and put his mouth right next to Kenny's ear. "Give me the number, Kenny. I want your father's number."

Kenny squinted at him. "I'm getting tired, Carlos."

"I know, Kenny. Now give me the number."

Kenny's eyes flickered. Carlos shook him gently. "Your father's number, Kenny."

"536 ... 536-8749."

"Donovan, right?"

Kenny nodded.

Carlos wrote it down on a piece of paper and stuffed it in his pocket. "Be strong," he whispered. "Don't give up. God is with you." Kenny just stared at him. "Promise me, Kenny. Promise me you won't give up!"

Kenny nodded. Carlos touched his shoulder and quietly left the room.

Carlos slipped out the back door and through the yard. From an upstairs window, Angel Ramos watched him go, sparks of anger glittering brightly in his eyes.

✞ ✞ ✞

Someone uncuffed him. Kenny forced his eyes open. "Carlos?"

No, Tito. Kenny heard the sound of tape ripping and Tito plastered a wide strip over his mouth. Then Tito grabbed his right hand and pulled it behind his back. Pain exploded through his body and Kenny heard himself scream, his voice muffled by the tape, before he passed out.

When he woke up again he knew he was in the back of a truck, and his hands were taped behind his back. But he didn't care. He didn't want to know who he was with or where he was going. He just wanted to escape, back into unconsciousness or sleep. Then he heard in his mind Carlos's words, "Don't give up, Kenny," and he prayed silently, Oh, God, don't let me give up. Please, Lord. And he closed his eyes.

✞ ✞ ✞

The bouncing of the truck over the rutted road woke him up again. Each bounce sent sparks of pain through his hand and up his arm, taking his breath away. Finally the truck stopped, and Kenny heard the back door open, and someone grabbed him and pulled him out.

He tried to open his eyes. Where were they? The sky was brightening in the east, though the sun still hid under the thick clouds. The wind felt cold.

Kenny took a deep breath. He could see fields and woods and open spaces. They were in the country, somewhere. A line of cedars, dark green in the dawn, stood down a fence row. The fields were fallow, full of waist-high weeds bent over with the weight of the rain that had beaten on them last night. Kenny shivered.

"Come on," someone said, and they walked Kenny toward an old farmhouse. It was a typical, turn-of-the century house, two stories, white clapboard, with large windows on the front. Beyond it, down to the right, was an old barn, and a few other outbuildings. He could see no other houses nearby.

The gang members picked their way over the muddy yard, their shoes slipping on the wet dirt beneath their feet. Gordo seemed to struggle in the mud. He kept glancing over his shoulder.

Kenny followed them past the old oak in the front, up the three wooden steps, across the wide porch, and into the house.

They marched him to a room on the first floor, and Kenny slid down the wall, and sat on the floor, and he closed his eyes. The pain!

How would Carlos find them? Carlos! He groaned and drifted back to sleep.

CHAPTER 39

SEVERAL HOURS LATER, WHEN DAYLIGHT had intruded upon them, they shifted their positions and pulled apart. Tom turned on his back, and stared at the ceiling, seeing the dark panorama of the night before play out again and again.

Cathy propped herself up on one elbow, and she took her finger and traced the edges of the ugly purple bruise on his chest, as if she were outlining the pain in his heart. He felt tears spring to the corners of his eyes.

"What are you thinking of, Tom, right now?" she asked.

He closed his eyes and opened them again. "Oh, Cathy," he said, "I miss my dad. I've always missed my dad." He choked up. "And seeing Kenny last night ... I am sad, and angry, and I feel out of control." He turned away from her and she began rubbing his back. "You know," he said, his voice hoarse with emotion, "I always thought that if I put one more bad guy in jail, solved one more case, that feeling would go away. I realize now, it never will."

"You can't just bury grief like that, Tom. You've got to talk about it to get over it."

He turned over on his back again. Tears slid from the corners of his eyes.

"I love you, Tom. I love you."

✟ ✟ ✟

Jack, Cathy, and Kate sat around the table in the kitchen. Kate had made a pot of fresh coffee, hoping the smell would encourage them all. No one felt like eating.

"He said he'd be down in a few minutes," said Cathy.

Jack walked over to the window and looked out. The thermometer read forty degrees. It was still blustery and gray outside, though the wind had died down. The rain continued off and on, and Jack thought for a moment how nice it would be if last night had been just a bad dream.

They heard a light tapping on the door. Fitz. Kate got up and let him in.

"Looks like you guys slept as well as I did." He walked into the room. "How are you, Cathy?" he said, hugging her. He carried a package in his hand.

"I'm numb, Fitz."

"How's Tom?"

"He's awake and dressed. You can go on up and see him if you want."

"I will."

"Anything new?" asked Jack.

"A rival gang saw Ramos's car and recognized Luis Aguilera driving. They followed them, and when they turned into Hains Point, they realized it was a perfect opportunity to pay Ramos back for something.

"The car we stopped was the other gang's car. They are cooperating. They're scared. They want to be sure we know they weren't aiming at Tom's son. They gave us some information and about an hour ago we found the place we think Ramos held Kenny at the beginning of last week. We're hoping we'll find something that will lead us to where they are now." Fitz hesitated. "We also found a body, one of Ramos's gang members, on the GW Parkway near Memorial Bridge."

"But no Kenny."

"No Kenny. We think that's good news. Maybe Ramos will try again. If he didn't see us."

Everyone tried to absorb that thought.

"Fitz, you want some coffee?" said Kate.

"No, I'm going on up to see Tom."

✞ ✞ ✞

Tom was sitting in an armchair with his back to the door. His hands were folded into a triangle in front of his closed eyes. He was deep in thought. He heard Fitz and looked up.

Fitz touched Tom's shoulder. "How are you?"

Tom hesitated, then shook his head.

"Cramer wants you to talk to one of the counselors."

"Okay."

"He's coming over in a while." Fitz pulled up a chair and sat facing Tom.

"What do you know about what happened?"

He told Tom everything they knew up to that point. Tom listened without reacting. Then Fitz opened the bag in his hand and pulled out Kenny's Bible, the one with his name imprinted on the front. "I stopped by your house and picked up some things. I don't know why, but I thought you or Cathy might want to have this right now. Kenny's written all through it."

Tom took the Bible and rubbed his hand over the burgundy leather cover. He could almost feel Kenny's fingerprints on it. He opened it, saw his son's handwriting, and felt fresh tears spring to his eyes.

"I brought this, too." Fitz opened his hand. On his palm lay a small gold cross.

A tear slid down Tom's cheek. "That was my father's," he said, his voice breaking. He picked up the cross, folded it into his fist and pressed his fist to his mouth.

"Tom, you know you did everything you possibly could have done."

"But I didn't get him back."

Fitz didn't respond.

"You know, Fitz," Tom said, "after I saw my father murdered, I got so angry. How could I trust God? From that day on, I refused to go to church." He looked up at Fitz. "A priest told me I was going to hell but I didn't care. I think it's ironic that my son, who has my father's eyes and my father's smile, also shares my father's deep faith."

Tom clutched the Bible to his chest. "All those years when Kenny was a kid I never took him to church, never mentioned God. I used to feel guilty about it because I knew my father wouldn't have approved. Yet my son grew up and got connected somehow. And it's almost like my father overruled me, and reached down from heaven, and gave his grandson the gift that was the most important to him."

"That's what's helping him right now, Tom. His faith."

"I don't understand why God let this happen."

"We won't, this side of heaven, know why." Fitz shook his head. "It just doesn't make sense. Not the way we see it."

Tom remained quiet for a minute, then he said, "All morning long, I've been hearing my dad's voice. Something he used to say to me when I'd complain. 'And now, d'ya think ya know better'n God, Tommy? With him bein' way up there, and you bein' way down here?'"

Tom stood, put the Bible on the nightstand, and walked across the room, still gripping the cross in his fist. He looked out the window at the gray day. Raindrops slid down the bare branches of the bushes, and the tires of passing cars made swishing sounds on the wet street.

He turned around to Fitz. "I've shot my wad, Fitz," he said. "I've done everything I can, everything I know, to get Kenny back." He looked away, and shrugged.

"Are you giving up, Tom?" Fitz said gently.

"No," Tom said. "I'm not giving up. But I just feel like this is beyond me, way beyond."

He felt Fitz's eyes on him, carefully searching his face, trying to see beyond the exhaustion.

"And what do you think your dad would say if he were here, Tom? What would he tell you?"

Tom looked up at the ceiling. "The same thing my son would say. Do your part and leave the rest to God." Tom looked at Fitz. "And I have no idea what that means." He sat back down.

"He loves you, Tom, and he loves your son."

Tears flowed again from Tom's eyes. Inside he felt fractured, like a crystal glass broken and swept into a box. "He's been haunting me my whole life."

"Who, Tom?"

"Jesus. In my dreams I see his eyes. I see his hands. And I turn and walk away. Every time."

"It doesn't have to be that way. It's not too late."

"He's punishing me. For my pride."

"No, Tom. No. Open your fist."

Tom complied.

"Look at the cross, and then tell me who is being punished," Fitz said.

The phone rang. Someone downstairs picked it up.

Fitz put his hand on Tom's knee. "He took the punishment for your sins, and for mine. He took it, Tom, because he loves you. The same way you love your son, and were willing to die for him last night."

Tom raised his eyes.

"Can I pray for you?"

Jack came racing up the stairs. "Tom! Tom!"

Tom stood up. So did Fitz.

Jack said, "Tom! That was Cramer. Alexandria Chief of Police just called him."

Tom's heart started pounding.

"A Latino boy got whacked last night. A .45 right in the back of the head. He had your name and number in his pocket!"

Tom's eyes widened.

"His name," said Jack, "was Carlos Ramirez!"

"Carlos, the new kid? With the Bible?"

"Could be."

"Who's Carlos?" said Fitz.

"A member of Ramos's gang. We think," replied Jack. "The detectives are going over to question the mother now."

"Tell them we want to be in on that," Fitz said.

"I want to go," said Tom. "Fitz, I want to go."

Cathy came upstairs. "Tom, what does this mean?"

"Fitz?" said Tom.

"What about the counselor that's coming over?" said Fitz.

"Cathy'll talk to him. And I can talk later."

Fitz looked at Tom. "All right. But you have to stay quiet. If this kid was involved, we want to keep the lines of communication with his family open. We don't want to appear threatening, okay?"

"Agreed," said Tom. Then he turned to Cathy. "Hon, I don't know what this means. It could be a lead. It could be nothing." He grabbed his gun, slid it on his belt, and reached for his jacket. "I'll call you as soon as I can." He handed her Kenny's Bible. "Hang on to this!"

He started to leave, then stopped. He turned back to his wife, took her in his arms and kissed her. Then he kissed her again. "Thank you."

She looked at him. "Be careful!"

"Yes!" he said as he ran down the steps.

CHAPTER 40

THE ADDRESS LED THEM TO a neighborhood of small houses crammed one on top of the other like crackers in a box. All kinds of cars—old sedans, souped-up trucks, big old Ford station wagons—jammed the street. Olive-skinned children played in, around, and among the vehicles as if they were equipment on a playground. Fitz eased the government sedan carefully down the street. The children looked up, eyes wide.

Mrs. Ramirez's house looked like it hadn't been renovated since it was first occupied after World War II by some returning GI and his family. The old asbestos siding was cracked and broken, and the underlying tar paper showed through in places. The shrubbery, overgrown and untended, gaped in spots.

The three men got out of the car. Tom walked on toward the house, and Fitz grabbed Jack's arm.

"If he gets hot, if he starts to say anything to Mrs. Ramirez, I'm counting on you to help me get him out of there."

"No problem. And after that, bullridin'll look so easy, I may take it up as a hobby."

Two detectives and three agents, including a Spanish-speaking agent named Alicia Melendez, were already inside. The two detectives had asked their questions. Now, it was the FBI's turn.

Mrs. Ramirez sat on the couch with Alicia. The couch was covered in an ugly brown fabric with bright orange and yellow flowers. A preschooler hung onto his mama, staring at the visitors.

In her mid-thirties, Mrs. Ramirez looked older. Overweight, her dark hair streaked with gray, she wore a black skirt and a white blouse. Part of a waitress's uniform, Tom guessed. She dabbed at her reddened eyes with tissues.

Tom looked around. The room was sparsely furnished with shabby furniture. A few toys lay scattered around. A single bare bulb in the ceiling fixture and the blue glow from the large television in the corner provided the only light. A crucifix hung on the wall. Through an open door, Tom could see dirty dishes piled in the sink. A sickly looking gray cat licked the topmost plate.

"Señora Ramirez, estos hombres son del FBI," Alicia began. Mrs. Ramirez, these men are from the FBI.

She nodded, looking at Alicia through teary eyes.

Alicia continued in Spanish. "Mrs. Ramirez, we need to ask you some questions about Carlos. Can you help us now?"

"Si." Her voice remained expressionless, as if she herself had died last night.

Alicia looked back at Jack and Tom. Tom stood leaning against the wall, chewing on a toothpick. Jack stood right next to him. Fitz, who was still wearing his raid jacket, sat across from the two women, in an armchair.

"Mrs. Ramirez, do you know where your son was last night?" Fitz asked.

Alicia translated.

Mrs. Ramirez spoke rapidly in Spanish, looking only at Alicia. Tom got the feeling Fitz intimidated her.

Alicia turned to the interviewer. "She says Carlos was out. She knew he was running with the wrong crowd. She didn't trust this man, Ramos. But she says he was like a father to the boys in the neighborhood, and she couldn't keep Carlos away."

"Mrs. Ramirez, when did you last see Carlos?"

Alicia asked the question, then said, "About four-thirty in the morning. He came home. He woke her up. He wanted some pills, some pain pills, leftover from when her husband got hurt. And some ice. She asked him 'Carlos, what are you doing?' He said a friend of his had gotten hurt. He said he had to help him, then he would come back. She argued with him, but he went anyway."

"And do you know where he went with these things?"

Mrs. Ramirez shook her head and responded in English: "I stay here, with the little ones. Carlos, he go out on the streets by himself. I don't like it. I know it come to this. But what I s'posed to do? The boy is sixteen!"

Tom shifted on his feet. Fitz glanced at him.

"Mrs. Ramirez," said Fitz. "We have reason to believe the gang Carlos was with is holding a kidnap victim. We're trying very hard to find him. Would you have any idea where they might have been hanging out?"

She shook her head. "Ever since his father died, Carlos, he is lost. He stop going to school. He come home, face all bruised, like he is in a fight. Then, one day, he start talking about Ramos. Ramos this, Ramos that." Mrs. Ramirez began to cry. "But he would never tell me where they go, what they do, how he gets the money he brings home. I didn't know where he was anytime. And lately ..." She wiped her eyes.

"Lately?"

"This past week, he act so strange. He steals food. I find him sneaking out with some of my husband's old clothes, and a blanket. I say, Carlos, why you need this? But he won't tell me. He kiss me and he say 'Don't worry, Mama. I bring it back.'"

Tom took a deep breath. He ran his hand over his chest, where the slug had hit him last night. It was so painful. He saw Jack look at him.

Jack raised his eyebrows, asking if he were okay.

Tom nodded.

Mrs. Ramirez blew her nose softly and then continued. "One night, he say, 'Mama, could you make that soup I like?' And he take that with him, too. Now why he do that? I don't know ... something goes on, but I don't know what."

Tom shivered.

Alicia asked Mrs. Ramirez a few questions about where she worked, her other children, Carlos's friends, where he had gone to school. Then one of the other agents picked it up.

"Do you know anyone else who might be able to tell us

where Carlos was going? Kids in the neighborhood, his friends ... anybody else?"

"Many kids know Ramos. Whether they can tell you where he goes ...," she shrugged, and then she rattled off the names of half a dozen neighborhood children.

"Thank you, Mrs. Ramirez," said Alicia. "I'm giving you my card. If you think of something else, will you call me?"

Mrs. Ramirez nodded as she blew her nose, and the agents turned to leave. Tom stood for a minute, his hands on his hips, and then he walked over to her.

Jack turned to intercept him. Fitz grabbed his sleeve. His look told Jack to wait.

"Mrs. Ramirez," said Tom. "I'm Tom Donovan." He sat down on the couch next to her. He took a deep breath. Alicia moved closer and began translating his words. "It's my son who's been kidnapped." He hesitated, letting that information sink in. "Mrs. Ramirez, I think Carlos was trying to help my boy. The clothes, the food, the medicine ... I think Carlos took that stuff for Kenny."

Tears began streaming down Mrs. Ramirez' face, and she bit her trembling lip. Tom looked down at her hands, which were twisting the tissue she held.

"I think Carlos got killed because he was trying to do the right thing last night, trying to call me, and let me know where Kenny is." His voice was soft and gentle. "Do you understand?"

She nodded.

"So Mrs. Ramirez, when you think of your son, don't think of him as a bad kid, a kid who got mixed-up with a drug gang." He hesitated, waiting for Alicia. "Think of him as a hero. Someone who gave his life for a friend. That's the way I always will." His voice choked up and tears filled his eyes.

Jack and Fitz exchanged glances.

Mrs. Ramirez ducked her head and sobbed, and Tom gently hugged her. "I'm sorry you've lost your son," Tom said, then he got up to leave. And as he did, a motion from the kitchen caught his eye, and before he could even be alarmed, a young teenaged boy walked out.

"Señor Donovan," he said, "I can show you where Carlos

went."

"Miguel?" said Mrs. Ramirez. "What did you do?"

Tom stared at him.

"I'm sorry, Mama. Carlos was upset last night. Mama, he was crying! I got curious. I had to see what was going on. So I followed him." He looked straight at Tom. "I know where he went."

Jack and Fitz moved toward them, their faces intent on the boy. "You can show us?" Jack asked.

The boy nodded.

"Mrs. Ramirez," said Fitz, "is it okay if he goes with us?" Alicia translated.

"He won't get hurt?"

"I promise you, we'll keep him safe."

"Okay," she said weakly. "Okay."

☗ ☗ ☗

"Alicia, you take my car," Fitz said. "Put Miguel in the back. You're driving him to school, or something. Let him point out the house. Don't go too close. Okay?"

"Right."

"We'll stay a few blocks away. Call us when you're clear."

Alicia and Miguel took off. Fitz, Jack, Tom, and the two other agents crammed into the Chevy. Jack leaned forward and tapped Fitz on the shoulder.

"Let's find us a mailman."

Fitz looked back at him.

"I think there's a package that needs delivering."

"Good idea."

It was eleven in the morning. Somebody must be around. Sure enough, four blocks away they saw a postal service truck.

"Hope he's not one of the disgruntled ones," muttered Jack as he got out. "Cover me, boys!"

Tom smiled in spite of himself.

Jack approached the mailman, flashed his badge and quickly explained the situation. He came back to the car. "Mike, you're about his size. Go for it!"

Mike got out, and switched jackets with the mailman. He put on his hat.

Alicia called. "WF-3, it's in Dove Court, off Third Street.

At the very end of the cul-de-sac. It's a white frame Cape Cod. The house to the left has a chain-link fence in the front."

"Okay. Take Miguel home. We're going to try a ruse. We'll call you."

✝ ✝ ✝

Mike took off in the mail truck. He had his radio tucked under the mailman's jacket. He found Dove Court, drove in, and went to the last house. He parked the truck, and picked up a package from the back. "WF-7 to WF-3. I'm about to deliver a package to 2249 Dove Court. Looks like nobody's home," he said, depressing the mic under his jacket.

Mike walked up to the door. He knocked. He got no answer. He knocked again. There was still no answer. He came down off the porch and peeked in the front window. The house was dark.

He depressed the mic under his jacket. "It's vacant."

"Check out the back."

"Okay, One."

The backyard was a mess, with paint buckets and trash everywhere. He walked up to the kitchen door and peered in the window. Trash littered the floor. He could see the kitchen sink. The door to the cabinet underneath was open, and he could see something bright. Cautiously, he shined his flashlight through the window toward the sink. His heart jumped when the light illuminated handcuffs, still attached to the pipe.

"Bingo," he said into the mike.

"Do we need SWAT?"

"No. They're gone."

"Back off," said Fitz. "Come back here. We'll get the search warrant. WF-8?"

"Here," responded Alicia.

"Meet us in front of 5516 Turner Place once you're clear."

CHAPTER 41

MIKE RETURNED IN A SECOND. He switched jackets again with the mailman, gave him back his truck. "Thanks a lot," he said, and the man drove off. Then he slid back into the car with the others. "It's empty. Looks like they cleared out in a hurry. There's trash all over the place. No vehicles around."

"How'd you know it was the place?" Tom asked.

Mike glanced at him, then looked away. "I saw something, under the sink." He looked at Fitz. "Handcuffs. Hooked to the water pipe."

Tom tightened his jaw.

Alicia drove up and Fitz got in her car to use the car phone. Within a short time, he had a telephonic search warrant. Exigent circumstances.

"Okay, we're clear. I've got some backup coming to handle the evidence, but if we want to do a walk-through, we can."

"Let's do it." said Jack.

The rooms contained very little furniture. The kitchen was filthy, fast food wrappers, soda cups, and beer cans thrown carelessly in the corner. A roach crawled across a pan encrusted with burnt chili in the sink. The door of the refrigerator stood open.

Tom saw the handcuffs, and his stomach turned. Fitz pointed to a zip-lock plastic bag filled with water. "An ice-pack?"

Tom nodded.

"Let's look upstairs," said Fitz.

There were two bedrooms. One had mattresses on the

floor. The other contained an iron bed, and even from the doorway, Tom could see that the white paint had been completely worn off of two of the bars of the bedstead.

"The campfire's still warm, partner," said Jack. He pointed to a copy of yesterday's Washington Post.

Fitz walked over to the bed and looked at it from several angles. Then he lifted up the mattress, and pulled out a black Bible. He looked at Tom.

"You want to see what he was reading?" said Fitz. He had opened the book to where the edge was turned down. "'The Lord is my light and my salvation; Whom shall I fear? The Lord is the defense of my life; Whom shall I dread?...Wait for the Lord; Be strong, and let your heart take courage.' "

Tom listened, his heart heavy. Why'd he ever waste time arguing with him?

"Psalm 27," said Fitz. "The hostage psalm. Some of the guys in Lebanon hung on to that for a long time."

"Hey, guys, check this out!" Alicia called from the hallway. The men followed her voice. She was standing over a pile of clothes in what was originally a linen closet. "Look." She pointed to some sweats.

"What is it?" asked Fitz.

"Lots of blood."

Tom turned and walked away, fighting to keep from throwing up. Was it Kenny's blood? Glancing once more in the room where his son had been held, he went downstairs, careful not to touch the handrail, his steps jerky and unstable. At the bottom of the stairs, he saw Jack.

Their eyes met. "You all right?" his partner asked.

Tom nodded.

Jack had just opened the coat closet. He turned back to it, shining his flashlight into the interior.

Tom stood breathing with his mouth open, fighting his nausea. He saw Jack bend forward and reach into the closet. When he straightened up, Jack had a pair of workboots in his hand. "What'd you find?"

Jack had turned the boots over and was staring at the soles. "I need an evidence bag."

Tom quickly retrieved a large paper bag. Jack placed one boot inside, then turned the other one upside down again.

"Paper towel?"

Tom found one and laid it on the floor in front of Jack, who was squatting down, his penknife in his hand. Jack took the blade, and flipped a little of the soil clinging to the tread of the boot onto the paper towel. Then he carefully put the boot inside the bag with its mate.

"What is it, Jack?" Tom stared at the black dirt.

Jack had picked up a small sample and was rubbing it between his thumb and forefinger. "Holy smokes."

"What?" Tom's heart had begun pounding.

"Cardova." Jack looked up at Tom.

Fitz appeared. "What's going on?"

Jack stood up. "I found this in some boots." He gestured toward the black dirt.

"Looks like what's in my wife's garden," Fitz said.

"It ain't, though. If I'm not mistaken, it's Cardova, a special kind of soil, made mostly of graphitic schist."

"Graphitic?" Fitz asked. "Like graphite?"

"Yep. It'll write on paper almost like a pencil. And it feels slick."

"What's the point?" Tom asked. He felt like his head would burst.

"Point is, this stuff is rare. Only found in a few places within a two-hundred-mile radius of here." Jack frowned, still rubbing his fingers together. "What if these guys had some place planned out as a retreat, some place they could go if things got bad. And what if one of 'em had been there and dragged the soil back here?"

"That's a stretch," Fitz said, rubbing his chin.

"But it's something," Tom said.

"How do we pursue it?"

Jack responded, "First, we got to get these boots down to the lab and confirm what I'm guessing."

"And then?"

"We look at the maps. In college," Jack said, "while everybody else was looking at girls in magazines, I was staring at soil maps."

"That explains a lot," Tom muttered.

"Cardova's gonna be off toward the mountains. Culpeper County. Fauquier, maybe."

Fitz shook his head. "I don't know. I'm not seeing these guys heading off to the country. I'm thinking they're still around here. They're urbanites, remember?"

Tom's heart dropped. What Fitz said made sense.

Fitz continued. "Let's regroup. What's our next move?" He tapped his pen against his leg.

"These boots need to go to the lab," Jack said doggedly.

"Right. Sure. I've got the evidence team coming to take this place apart."

"They need to go now."

Tom saw Fitz grimace. Jack wasn't usually annoying.

"Okay," Fitz said. He called the rest of the agents into the dining room. "Jack, you tell Sean here exactly what you want done. He'll run them downtown."

Jack and a young agent moved toward the kitchen. Jack had the bag of boots in his hand. But it was the look in Jack's eyes that registered with Tom.

"Alicia," Fitz said, continuing, "you and Mark check out the other kids Mrs. Ramirez gave us."

She nodded.

"Smitty, you contact the local police. Find out who the bad boys are in the neighborhood. Then follow through with probation and parole. Let's see who's desperate enough to stay out of jail to remember something about the folks who lived here." Fitz went on. "I want a door-to-door right away ..."

"I'll organize that, Fitz." Brad Everett was a Principal Firearms Instructor and he had worked the drug squad at the Washington Field Office. He had just arrived on the scene to help with evidence, along with Caryn Wheeler and several others.

"Okay, good. Is there a phone in here?"

"In the living room, Fitz."

"All right. Caryn, you contact the phone company. Find out what they can give us on calls from this number."

"Okay."

"We want a tape register—all calls in and out, not just the long distance calls."

"Right."

"I'm going to talk to Cramer. I think I'd like to plan a

simultaneous bust on every location we can associate with a gang member. Let's shake things up. We'll see if Alexandria can help us out. You want to be in on that, Tom?"

"No," said Tom quietly. "You can bust in doors without me." He rubbed the back of his head.

Fitz looked at him quizzically. "All right." He kept handing out assignments. When the others had left, he turned to Tom. "You okay?"

"You know what I'd like to do, Fitz?"

Fitz shook his head.

"I'd like to take a drive out to Culpeper, or wherever, with Jack. Check out that dirt."

Fitz frowned.

"I know it's a long shot."

"Why would a bunch of gangbangers go all the way out there?"

"I'm not sure they would. But I like checking out things that don't fit. And, I could use a change of scene."

Anybody could understand that.

Fitz nodded. "Whatever you want, Tom."

Jack reappeared. "You feel like a road trip?" Tom asked him.

"You bet."

"You guys are both tired," said Fitz. "Let me send Mike with you. Let him drive, okay?"

✞ ✞ ✞

Kenny sat slumped up against the wall. Oh, God, please help me, Kenny thought as he emerged back into the painful reality of the farmhouse. He opened his eyes. They were leaving him alone, thankfully, letting him sit on the dining room floor while they were busy with their heated debates, their crack pipes, and their beer.

Where was Carlos? Oh, Father God, where is Carlos? Kenny was starting to feel desperate, desperately lonely, desperately thirsty, desperately in need of one friendly face, and when he began to feel himself tipping toward chaos he closed his eyes and prayed, and dove back into the ocean of his unconscious as fast as he could.

Chapter 42

MIKE CORNELL NEGOTIATED THE BACK country roads with finesse, steering the Bureau car toward Warrenton, the seat of Fauquier County. It was closer than Culpeper, so Jack had suggested they start there.

The dashboard clock told Tom it was noon. Sitting in the front passenger seat in an attempt to overcome his nausea, he stared out of the window at the largely unspoiled countryside. The gently rolling hills were dotted with placid cows. Turn-of-the-century white clapboard farmhouses nestled under stands of ancient oaks. He could see laundry flapping on lines in the backyards, sturdy, weather-beaten barns, and tall silos. A woman in jeans and knee-high boots, her hair contained by a bandanna, emerged from a barn with a bucket in her hand, and headed for the row of calf houses where baby Holsteins stood tethered. The scene looked so peaceful.

So, yeah, like Fitz said, why would a Salvadoran street gang drive all the way out here? And why did he, Tom, feel so drawn to Jack's crazy idea?

"I can't believe I'm saying this," said Tom, "but tell me about the rocks, Jack, and the soil." He glanced at his partner in the back seat.

"Ha!" Jack grinned at him. "I knew you'd come around."

"Just tell me."

"Okay, so we're in Virginia. You got five basic geologic regions. You've got the Coastal Plain, then west of that, the Piedmont,"

"Which starts at the fall line," Tom said, interrupting.

"Right, then west of the Piedmont you got the Blue Ridge, then the Valley and Ridge region, then the Allegheny Plateau. So the rocks and soil are different in each region, right? And they're all folded over each other, and moved around by tectonic events that took place over a billion years ago."

Tom nodded.

"So there's all kinds of rocks in Virginia and all kinds of soil. Now, it's important to know what kind of soil you got if you're a farmer, or if you want to mine, or ..."

"... or build a building."

"Right. So geologists map them. When I was working on my master's degree, I worked in the Piedmont, tromping all over the place studying soils. Basically, you got three kinds of soil: sand, silt, and clay. Sandy soil, you can see the particles. Like at the beach. Silt is finer and the particles are flat, giving it a slippery feel. Clay has the smallest particles of all, which is why it packs down so much and feels plastic-y."

"Bad for gardens, good for bricks."

"You got it!" Jack rubbed his hands on his pants legs.

"What tipped you off that this soil was special? It just looked like dirt to me."

"It looked like more than that to me. When I rubbed some of it between my fingers, it slid. I could feel the graphite in it. Cardova is a silty soil that comes from graphitic schist."

"What's schist?"

"A metamorphic rock. A rock that's been changed by pressure or heat. Graphitic schist is not common. If the lab proves me right, we can narrow down where those boots were to just a handful of places."

Tom nodded.

"It's still a long shot, Tom. I'm not arguing that."

"I know. The boots may not even be connected to the gang."

They let that dismal thought occupy them for a moment. "I don't know why this is driving me," Jack said, breaking the silence, "but it is. Maybe I'm just tired. Maybe it's something else." He reached forward and clapped Tom on the shoulder. "I just want to find your boy."

✝ ✝ ✝

Kenny's tongue felt thick and his eyes were hot, and he wondered if he had a fever, and how long you could have a fever before you got convulsions. And he had just started to panic when he felt a hand on his shoulder and he looked, and saw Gordo.

Gordo looked nervously around, then he squatted down in front of Kenny and gently took the tape off Kenny's mouth. Tears came to Kenny's eyes, and he licked his dry lips. Then Gordo picked up a McDonald's cup, and held it to Kenny's mouth. It was full of cool water, and it swirled around Kenny's tongue and slid down Kenny's throat and filled his belly. "Thank you!" He shivered with gratitude. "Where's Carlos?" Kenny whispered, but Gordo didn't answer.

✞ ✞ ✞

Special Agent Ed McLaughlin held down a one-man office in Warrenton, acting as liaison to several sheriff's departments. Tall and ruddy, his light brown hair was flecked with gray. He had on tan pants and a tweed sports jacket with leather patches at the elbow. Tom liked him the minute he opened his mouth.

"Good afternoon, boys. Sorry to meet you under these circumstances." He shook hands all the way around. "Let's go talk to the man who actually knows something."

He led them out of the door, across the street and up the hill to an old county office building. Inside, McLaughlin led them to the glass-doored office of the county's chief soil scientist. "This is James Finn," he said. "Introduce yourselves."

Finn looked like he'd stepped out of the L.L. Bean catalog. Dressed in khakis and hiking boots, his shirtsleeves rolled up, he could have been a park ranger or trail guide. Tom was starting to see how geology attracted people who loved the outdoors. He understood how Jack would have chafed at a job in the lab.

Jack, meanwhile, kept glancing at his watch. Tom wondered why. That nervous energy wasn't typical of him.

"So how can I help you?" Finn asked.

Jack explained what they were looking for. "I'm hoping the lab results will be in soon," he said, "confirming my suspicions."

That explained the watch-checking.

Finn began pulling charts off the wall, big plats attached to wooden poles. He laid them out on a table. "If you're right," he said to Jack, "you probably want to go into Culpeper County. That's where most of the Cardova is, up back behind the high school, in that area. But we've got some too, in a few places." He took a pencil and marked a few areas on the map. "Tell you what, I'll print something out for you."

"Better make five copies," Jack said. Then he turned to McLaughlin. "Any chance we could get some deputies to help us?"

"I can ask."

Finn came back with copies of the map, with the places where Cardova soil had been identified circled in red. Tom looked at his copy. How could these small, scattered patches of dirt help find his son? Suddenly he felt like the floor was dropping out from under him. He caught his breath.

"Tom?"

Jack's voice brought him back.

"We can do this." Jack put his hand on Tom's arm. "Let's go."

They divided into three teams: McLaughlin and Finn. Mike and a sheriff's deputy. Tom and Jack. They agreed they'd meet back in Warrenton at five o'clock. Before they left, Jack made one more phone call, to the lab. He hung up, grinning. "Cardova," he said, "just like I thought."

Tom's spirits lifted.

"Geology is fractal," Jack said as they drove to their first location. "Full of repeating patterns that show more and more detail the closer you look at 'em. You see a fold in the rock where a highway's been cut through, and I guarantee you, there's a fold within that fold, on down to the microscopic level."

Tom knew Jack was just talking because he was pumped up, but he tried to follow what he was saying.

"In geology, you got to decide what scale you're going to study. But all of 'em are equally complex. I think of law enforcement the same way."

Tom glanced over at him.

"Fitz, he's focused on the big picture, trying to find patterns that'll lead to Kenny. We're looking at dirt. But there's as much to be learned there as what Fitz is doing."

An hour and a half later, they'd driven by four areas of Cardova soil, finding nothing but some gentle-eyed cows chewing their cuds, not even an outbuilding to investigate. Jack's initial enthusiasm was beginning to wear down. They had one more patch to go, then they'd have to move on to Culpeper County.

The sun was sinking in the west like a giant peach, slipping behind the cobalt mountains of the Blue Ridge. The sky overhead was the color of lapis lazuli, deep and clear. In the west, Tom could see pinkish wisps of clouds, the trailing remnants of the storm that had buffeted the area last night.

Jack found the last map location. It was the smallest patch of Cardova on their list, and it appeared to be in the middle of a large, abandoned farm.

They drove up as close as they could. The farm lane snaked through a stand of trees, obscuring the house and whatever outbuildings there were. "We're gonna need a search warrant to get in there," Jack said, "and we got nothing to justify it."

Tom shook his head at that miserable truth. "Maybe I could just sneak up there a little ways. Scope things out. And if it looks promising ..."

"... and the defense attorney asks you in court if you had a search warrant before you stepped on the property, you will have blown the whole case."

"I don't care about the case! I care about my son."

"And you know I know that."

Tom sighed.

"Guess we should go back." Jack turned the car around.

"We have time to get a Coke?" Tom asked. He could really use the energy.

"Sure."

A few miles down the road, Jack pulled into the parking lot of a Shifflett's store, one of a dozen or so country stores that dotted the county. It looked like a fairly new building, with two gas pumps out front and ruts in the parking lot where a truck had run over the asphalt before it was set. Signs advertising the Virginia Lottery were plastered on the front windows.

"You mind going in, Jack?" Tom could hardly face getting out of the car. It felt like admitting defeat.

"Not at all. You just relax, buddy."

Tom leaned his head back as Jack went in. He closed his eyes. When he did, in his mind's eye he saw his son, beaten and bruised, and he jerked his lids open. *Oh, Kenny.* His stomach turned.

To his right, two black men dressed in work clothes leaned against a truck. Driven by desperation, Tom opened his car door and walked over to them. "Gentlemen," he said. He flashed his badge. "Tom Donovan, FBI."

"Evenin'," the taller man responded, and he stuck out his hand. Tom felt an almost childish sense of relief. Maybe law enforcement wasn't the enemy so much out here.

"I wonder if you might have seen some strangers around here. Dark-haired guys. City people."

The men looked at each other. "Don't know. Don't think so."

"Take a look at these pictures. They might look something like this."

The two men bent over the mug shots like they were yesterday's sports scores. Finally one of them looked up, his eyebrows raised.

"What you want 'em for?"

"Kidnapping," Tom replied.

"A child?"

He swallowed. "My son."

There was a long pause. The man closest to Tom let his breath out slowly between his teeth. "Yes, sir. We'll keep an eye out. That's for sure."

"Thanks, guys." Tom handed each of them a business card. "I'd appreciate it if you'd call me, collect, if you hear or see anything that might help."

"Yes, sir, we surely will."

Jack came out of the store with two bottles of soda in his hands. He looked surprised when he saw Tom.

"Thanks," Tom said to the men. He took one more look around, and began walking toward the car.

The sky had darkened to the blue-black color of a bruise. Here and there a silver star sparkled like a promise, and the blinking lights of an airplane marked its silent journey across the night. Tom tugged on the handle of the car door to get in.

One of the men called out, "Hey, Mister! Mister Donovan!"

Tom stopped. The man pointed to an ancient pick-up coming down the road. "Here comes old Billy. Billy Sears. He knows just about everything going on 'round here."

Tom walked slowly over to the pick-up as it entered the lot. When Billy rolled down the window, Tom identified himself and told him what he wanted. Jack joined him.

Billy got out of his truck. Tom figured he had to be seventy-five. Eighty maybe. But he had the big, strong hands of a farmer and a kind face. He scratched his jaw. "Y'know," he said, "last night I couldn't sleep. My dog started barkin', woke me up. Finally walked out on my porch, just to look around. Sky's just startin' to get light. And the dangdest thing, I thought I seen lights headed up the lane at the old Tyler place. Ain't nobody been livin' there for years, but lately I been thinkin' someone's there on and off."

"Wait a second," Jack said. He jogged back to the Bureau car, grabbed the map he'd been using, and thrust it in front of Billy. "Can you show us where that place is?"

"Well, you got a circle right on it!" the man said. He pointed to the farm they'd just tried to look at.

"Who owns it?" Tom asked. His heart began to pound.

"Don't rightly know. I heard some city feller bought it, holdin' it for development. But I don't know."

In the country, people pick up on things. That's what Jack had said. Tom looked at Jack and saw in his face the hope he was feeling. "What's there?" Tom asked.

"There's a quarter-mile lane leadin' up to the house," Billy said. "Then you got an old house, smokehouse, barn, shed. Oh, and a pond. And woods behind it."

"Let's see if Mike is in radio range," Tom said.

He was. He and the deputy arrived moments later. Meanwhile, Tom used the pay phone outside of the store to call McLaughlin's number and tell them what they needed.

"Who owns the property?" Tom told McLaughlin's secretary, and he gave her their location.

"We should move the cars around back," Tom said.

"This is still a pretty remote chance, you know," Jack warned, but the brightness in his eyes conveyed a different message.

"It's fractal, Jack. An infinitely repeating pattern. I'll explain that to you later," Tom said. He turned to Billy. "You mind hanging out with us for a while?"

"No, sir. I don't."

Tom walked over to the two black men, still smoking by the building, shook their hands and thanked them while Jack, the deputy, and Billy moved their vehicles behind the building. The deputy asked the manager for access to his office and use of his phone, and he agreed.

But they still needed probable cause for a search warrant, and Jack had some ideas on how to get it. "Let's call the power company and see if there's been a hook-up order lately," he said.

Before they moved on that, his pager went off. "It's Fitz," Jack reported. He called Fitz back, then said to Tom, "Someone in that Alexandria house called a number out here."

"Let's pursue that!" Tom said. Minutes later, he stood in the manager's office wiring up a small tape recorder to the manager's phone. Then he explained to Mike what he wanted him to do and he gave him the number.

"Ready?" he said.

"Let's do it."

Tom could feel his scalp tense up as Mike lifted the handset and dialed.

"Hello?" someone said, answering. A male voice. Young.

Tom and Jack could hear the conversation over a small remote speaker.

"Hello, this is the phone company," Mike said. "We're installing new digital equipment in the area and we're checking on service. Have you had any problems with your service lately?"

"What?"

We need more words, Tom thought. More words, Mike.

He made a circular motion with his hand.

"Are you the customer at this number? We need to know, for our records ..."

"What? I don'...."

Definitely Latino. Tom leaned forward.

They heard some shouting in the background, and then a different voice.

"Hello? Who is this?"

Tom's blood ran cold. He grabbed Jack's shoulder. Angel Ramos. He'd recognize that voice anywhere!

"Hello, I'm from the phone company." Mike bent forward, concentrating on his lines. "We're checking on service ..."

"Everything's fine," said Ramos and he slammed down the phone.

"Holy ..."

"Jack!"

"I do okay?" asked Mike.

"You just lifted up a rock and found the King Snake!" said Jack, his eyes wide. He could hardly believe it.

The door opened and the deputy came in.

"Just got this in from the sheriff. Owner's name is Edmund Perez ..."

"Perez!"

"The lawyer!" said Tom. "Ramos's lawyer!"

"And the wrestler, Tom. Wasn't the wrestler's name Perez?"

"I never put that together!"

"Electric company had a hook-up order about six months ago. Want the residence number?"

"Let me guess," said Jack. "843-8890."

"That's it!"

"Yes!" Tom yelled. "Yes! Rocks matter, Jack. Just like you said! Rocks matter!"

CHAPTER 43

LOUD ARGUING WOKE HIM UP. Angel Ramos and Luis were about to come to blows, right in the middle of the room. Several others stood around, some with clenched fists.

Kenny bit his lip against the pain in his hand. Where was Carlos? He looked around, then tuned in to the argument. He struggled to clear his head, and tried to follow the Spanish being flung around the room. What was the big deal? Did it have to do with him?

It was more than him. Just from their expressions, and the intense look on the other gang members' faces, Kenny could tell this was a showdown between Ramos and Luis. But he couldn't tell who was winning.

Suddenly Luis began shouting in English. His face twisted in anger and the veins in his neck bulged. "I tell you, you had no right ... You should have dumped the kid long ago, then none of this ..."

"Shut up, Luis! You are not El Jefe! You are not the one to tell me ..."

"It is your pride, Ramos, only your pride. You are thinking of no one else."

"Luis ..."

Ramos had his back to Kenny, but Kenny could see the redness in the back of his neck as he flushed with anger. His shoulders were tensed and his arms slightly crooked, and Kenny knew that posture all too well.

"He knew the rules. He was going to ruin it for us all." Ramos gestured around the room, his cigar leaving a trail of smoke in the air.

Across the room, Tito fingered something nervously in his jacket pocket, and Kenny knew instinctively it was a gun. The others in the room were focused on the fight in the middle. Gordo was nowhere to be seen.

The arguing continued. Luis spit on the floor. "He didn't deserve to die, Ramos. He was a kid ..."

Wait, what? Who was a kid? A chill ran down Kenny's spine, and his heart began thumping and before he knew what he was doing, he was pushing himself up along the wall to a standing position. What was Luis saying? Who was he talking about? The hair on the back of Kenny's neck was standing up, and he didn't know why.

"Shut up, Luis!" Ramos took a step forward.

"You didn't have to kill him, Ramos." Luis' face was black with fury. "Carlos is dead because you are too proud ..."

Carlos is dead? The words exploded in Kenny's brain, and he closed his eyes and blew out a breath. Carlos is dead?

"... to admit you screwed up when you grabbed Donovan's kid ..."

Carlos? Carlos?

"... that you got us all in too deep. And you made Carlos pay ..."

Oh, God, no!

"... with his life ... and now Carlos is dead ..."

Kenny's face flushed and he broke into a sweat and his heart was pounding and suddenly he couldn't stand still. Carlos is dead? Carlos? Dead? He yelled "No!" at the top of his lungs, and he leaped for Angel Ramos, hitting him square in the small of his back with his head, and as he did, he heard the pop! of a gun, and felt a burning streak across his ribs. Angel Ramos went down with Kenny on top of him. There was yelling and screaming in Spanish, and two more shots, but all Kenny could hear was "Carlos is dead, Carlos is dead ..." over and over in his head, like a tiger clawing at his soul.

"Get him off! Get him off me!" Ramos pushed him off, and Kenny rolled away, a wet patch of blood on his shirt. Kenny looked up. The ceiling was spinning.

Ramos reached for his gun, but it wasn't there. He turned, and saw Tito standing over Luis, a .22 pistol in his hand.

"Give it to me!" he yelled. He grabbed Tito's gun and turned back to Kenny.

Kenny saw Ramos point the muzzle of the gun toward him and he clamped his eyes shut. He heard a click, but the gun didn't fire. He opened his eyes.

Ramos pointed the gun and tried again. Still nothing. It was jammed. Furious, he swung the gun at Kenny, who flipped over on his belly and squeezed his eyes shut. The gun hit him in the side of the head and he cried out. The gun clattered to the floor beyond him.

Ramos cursed and kicked Kenny in the ribs. The toe of his boot turned red with Kenny's blood. "He's bleeding to death. Luis gets his way!" Ramos kicked Kenny again. "Get him out of here! He's bleeding all over the place. Throw him in the pond."

Hands grabbed Kenny and lifted him up. His eyes were open, but he was completely disoriented, and he fixated on the drops of his own blood falling, exploding on the floor beneath him.

They took him to the front door, and he felt the icy cold air as they opened it. "It's dark!" he heard one of them say. An owl hooted in the distance.

"I can't see nothing!" said the other man.

"Let's take him upstairs. We can dump him in the morning. Ramos doesn't need to know. And this boy, he is goin' nowhere."

Up the stairs, the worn, dirty paint becoming spotted with red now, and then into a room, and there they dumped him unceremoniously on the floor.

Kenny stayed very still, barely breathing.

"Should we watch him?" said one of the men.

"Where you think he'll go? Look at him. He's dying. Besides, it's too cold up here."

"We keep an eye on the stairs, just to be safe."

"You worry too much."

They left the room, and Kenny took a deep breath. He was alone, and he was cold, and he didn't care. He didn't care about the searing pain in his hand, or the hot, wet, wound on his side, or even his hunger or thirst, or the homesickness that had become like a corpse chained to his soul. Carlos was dead. Carlos was dead. Oh, God, no!

Kenny felt the warmth of his own blood pooling underneath him. I'm dying, too, he thought. For sure this time. A tear slid from his eye. Oh, Carlos! I'm sorry.

Then he closed his eyes and waited to die.

✝ ✝ ✝

"Cramer and Borsten are with me. The rest of HRT is on the way." Fitz was heading west on I-66, talking to Jack on his radio. "The Fauquier Sheriff will be there soon. We've gotten permission to use the education building of Hope Springs Baptist Church, right near that Shiflett's Store, as a command post. The Sheriff will meet you there. The pastor's on his way over with the key."

"Good, Fitz, sounds good."

"How's Tom?"

" 'Bout like you'd expect. Like he's sittin' in the chute at the rodeo, waitin' for the gate to jerk open."

"Tell him to hold on."

✝ ✝ ✝

"Feel free to use anything you need," said the pastor, flipping on the lights. The stucco-covered education building had one large room, several classrooms, a kitchen, and bathrooms. Though small, it would work. "Let me know if I can do anything for you."

"Thank you," said Tom.

"You know anything about that house?" Jack asked Billy.

"Sure. Been in it a thousand times."

"Great!" said Jack, and he handed him some paper and a pencil. "Will you make us a map of the interior? Rooms, windows, doors, closets—as best as you can remember?"

"You got it," said Billy. He licked the end of the pencil and went to work.

The sheriff spoke to Tom. "I got every available deputy coming down here, including the emergency response team. We'll be glad to help however we can."

"Right now, I'd like to get somebody over there to watch it. Jack!"

Jack turned around.

"What if they move again?"

"Yeah, you're right."

"I can get ya to it," said Billy. "I'm 'bout done here."

"Can you get us a clear view of the house?"

"Yep. And they'll never know you're there."

"How close?"

"Two hundred yards. Up on a hill. It'll be a clear shot."

"You can get us up there without being seen?"

Billy laughed. "I been huntin' around here all my life. I guess I can sneak you guys up there, if you know how to be quiet."

"Mike!"

Mike looked up.

"Go with Billy. Don't do anything but watch the house. Use the radio if you see anything, especially if it looks like they're moving."

"Right, Jack."

⚜ ⚜ ⚜

Fitz, Cramer, and Borsten arrived at the church. Fitz grabbed Tom's hand. "Your instincts are superb, Tom!"

Tom shrugged. "It was Jack."

"Fine job," said Cramer. "By the way, I talked to the U.S. Attorney before I left. He can't wait to get this case!"

"When I called Cathy to tell her the news," Fitz added, "she really wanted to come down."

Tom raised his eyebrows.

"I told Kate to bring her. She can stay here, at the church, where she'll be safe."

"Good," Tom said. "And HRT?"

"They'll be here any minute."

Cramer and Borsten had discussed tactics all the way down, and the plan was nearly set by the time they arrived. First, they would gather as much intelligence on the situation as they could.

Tom, Jack, Fitz, Cramer, and Borsten stood around a large table, poring over the maps, making sure all the bases were covered. As soon as the rest of the agents arrived, a team armed with powerful telescopes, binoculars, night vision equipment, and parabolic microphones were sent to the hill overlooking the farmhouse. Their job was to watch the movements of the men in the house, observe people coming and going, try to locate the room where Kenny was being held, and to gather any other data that would help ensure the success of the mission and the safety of the agents and Kenny.

Vans, buses, and cars filled the small church parking lot. The Hostage Rescue Team, in their black raid uniforms, stood clustered in small groups, going over equipment and procedures. The four teams that would actually assault the house were at an abandoned house behind the church, quietly practicing over and over the techniques they would use. In the meantime, a light plane began making passes high over the old Tyler place.

CHAPTER 44

IT BEGAN LIKE THE LOW rumble of thunder in the morning, a distant grumbling that crept into his awareness only gradually. Semi-conscious, Kenny heard it, and it prodded him toward wakefulness. He resisted, but it came again and again, closer and louder each time, until he could no longer ignore it.

They who wait for the Lord shall renew their strength.

The sound of it struck a chord in his soul.

They shall mount up with wings like eagles;

He opened his eyes.

They shall run and not be weary;
They shall walk and not faint.

He lifted his head. He looked around. He was alone. In an empty bedroom. With windows.

They shall run …

Kenny's heart thumped.

They shall run …
They shall run!

Maybe it wasn't time to die. Maybe it wasn't his time. His adrenalin kicked in. Kenny put his head on the floor and pushed up with his knees, then he curved his back and pulled himself upright. His head spun. He waited for it to clear. Help me, God. Help me run and not faint.

He looked over his shoulder. There was no one around. No one. Help me run.

Kenny picked a window. He lurched to his feet. Pain coursed through him and he started to vomit, but he choked it back down. He stumbled to the window. Outside he could see only blackness and the faint outline of trees. Wedging his shoulder under the frame, he pushed up. Nothing. Stuck. He gritted his teeth. He slammed his shoulder upward, ignoring the pain, and did it again, and on the third try, the window opened, just four inches, but enough. And Kenny gave it one more good push and up it went, the cold air spilling in.

He looked out. It was a long drop. A light from a downstairs window revealed some bushes right below. Maybe they'd cushion his fall. Anyway, what choice did he have? So he breathed a quick prayer, laid his belly on the sill, and rolled out. And as he sailed through the air, he felt as if he were outside himself, seeing himself fall in slow motion.

He hit the bushes with a thud, on his back. The jolt sent excruciating pain through his arms and hand and he bit his lip to keep from crying out.

Kenny had to wait until the pain subsided so he could breathe. He rolled onto his belly, moved away from the light, and staggered to his feet. He could feel warm, new blood under his shirt. But he lifted his eyes, saw the woods, and stumbled toward them. He'd always felt safe in the woods.

✝ ✝ ✝

"I'm glad you came down." Tom and Cathy were alone, in a Sunday School classroom off the main room. He held her in his arms. Beyond her he could see a poster with John 3:16 written on it: "For God so loved the world, that he gave his only Son, that whoever believes in Him should not perish but have eternal life." He closed his eyes.

"Tom?"

He opened his eyes. She looked at him, searching his face. "How are you?"

He gently pressed her head back down on his chest. He took a deep breath. "I'm scared," he said. His knee started to shake.

She squeezed him gently.

"I'm scared he's going to kill Kenny at the last minute. I'm scared our guys are going to kill Kenny by accident." His voice choked. "And I'm scared I'll have flashbacks like the other night." He stopped. The other knee was shaking now.

She hung on.

"It's like walking into hell again," he whispered. "And the

only reason I'm doing it is because my son's already in there."

"You can do it, Tom. I have confidence in you."

He shivered. "He could die," he said.

She held him close, so close that they were breathing in unison, and then she caught her breath, and he could tell she was trying not to cry. "I don't want him to die," she said, her voice cracking, "but if he did, you know what? He'd be in heaven. With your dad." She caught a sob. "He believes that, Tom. That's what Tracy said. So we should, too."

He stroked her hair and she looked up at him. Tears filled her eyes. He kissed her.

✞ ✞ ✞

"We're moving another intelligence team around to the back of the house. There's been no movement in or out," said Borsten.

"Okay," said Cramer. He looked around the table. "We're agreed—we're going to use a ruse instead of a direct assault."

Everyone nodded except Borsten.

"Dave?"

"I'd rather go in direct."

"If we create some confusion at the front door, one of the adults—Ramos or Aguilera—is sure to appear." Fitz's voice remained patient. "We still haven't located Kenny in the house, right?"

Borsten nodded.

"So that gets one of the adults away from him. I think it's worth it."

A general murmur of consent followed, and Borsten reluctantly backed down.

Cramer continued. "We block roads here, here and here. We establish two concentric perimeters—we use the SWAT team in the inner circle, about twenty yards from the house and the rest of the agents behind them. We don't want anyone getting away from us this time!

"We have three snipers covering the house. HRT will have four teams right next to the house, and three more teams in the woods. We begin the ruse, all goes well, and we take 'em." He looked at the others. "Sounds good to me. Any objections?"

There were none. Tom took a deep breath. "Just one question," he said.

Everyone turned to him.

"How long before we go?"

Cramer looked at his watch. "It's nine now. We've been on them for two hours. Let's say we watch them 'til nine-thirty. And then we go."

"Even if we don't know exactly where the boy is?" asked Borsten.

"Nine-thirty. That's it." Cramer looked around. "Okay, who's our actor? Do we have a volunteer?"

✞ ✞ ✞

"Hey, amigo, Ramos isn't foolin' around, eh?" The wiry young Latino puffed on a cigarette nervously. "Did you see what he did to Tito? For nothing! Tito didn't do nothing!"

"Yeah. Maybe we better move the kid, eh? Even in the dark. We better do what El Jefe said," his friend whispered.

"Yeah, you're right. I finish this, then we do it, eh?"

They felt the cold air coming down the stairs as they went up. They began to hurry. When they got to the door, the room was empty.

Cursing, the men ran over and looked out the window.

"Se escapó!" He slammed the window shut. "We'd better look outside, before El Jefe finds out."

But as they turned to leave, their faces dropped. Angel Ramos stood in the door, his coal-black eyes flashing with anger.

✞ ✞ ✞

"Alex!" Borsten's voice sounded urgent. "We've got a report of gunfire, two shots, three minutes ago, at 9:16. In an upstairs bedroom."

"Let's go! Let's do it now."

CHAPTER 45

TOM SAT IN THE FRONT seat of the Bureau car, next to Fitz. Jack sat in the back. They were parked on the edge of the road, near the entrance to the old Tyler place. They were silent, intent on listening to the crackling of the radio that chronicled the assault on the house where Kenny was being held. Every once in a while, Tom's knee would begin to shake. He would take a deep breath and will it to stop.

The sky looked black. The wind had died down, and HRT was happy because they could get their air units up. Every once in a while, Tom could see the blinking lights of a light plane.

Agents in field pants and raid jackets had been delivered to nearby roads and were hiking in to form a circle around the house. The farthest distance from the house to a road was less than a mile, so within fifteen minutes, if everything went well, the house should be surrounded.

HRT had positively identified Ramos in the house, and had determined there were at least seven other people present. But Kenny's location had still not been pinpointed, and that was a concern.

Alex Cramer and Dave Borsten were on a hill, overlooking the farmhouse, ready to watch the operation as it went down. "How about the chopper?" asked Cramer.

"It's on the ground, cranking, less than five minutes away. And I've got a six-man team with it, in case we have a runner."

Cramer nodded.

"Leader One, this is A-team. We have the target location

in sight."

"Standby A-team," said Borsten. "Teams report as you achieve the target location."

"B-team ready."

Tom could see in his mind's eye the black-clad teams moving almost silently over the ground. Stealthily they would surround the house, covered by the three snipers stationed strategically on hills overlooking the farm. The snipers would shoot only if they were given the green light by the bosses, or if they had to protect the life of another person.

One by one the teams reported in, until only the D-team was missing. Finally they, too, were in place, and the farmhouse was surrounded by HRT, standing off in the woods, just out of view.

Borsten took a deep breath and glanced at Cramer. "We're ready, sir."

"Move them up."

"All teams move to final positions. All other units stand by."

Tom had watched them practicing near the church. He knew the teams would move right up next to the house, ready to break in through the windows and doors when the time was right. They'd throw flashbangs inside, devices designed to disorient the occupants with brilliant explosions and loud noise. Before Ramos and the gang knew what was happening, HRT would be in the house, taking control, alert for weapons and violent resistance. Unlike the image often portrayed by Hollywood, they'd shoot only if it was absolutely necessary. Most importantly, they'd grab Kenny, and get him out of there as quickly as they could.

Tom's knee started shaking again.

"All right, Borsten," said Cramer. "Let's do it."

"All teams stand by. Everett," said Borsten into the radio mike, "you're on."

Brad Everett had nerves of steel. He gave a thumbs up as he drove past Tom and the others in the car. Dressed in casual clothes, and accompanied by an agent posing as his wife, he looked like just a guy lost in the country. He swung into the old Tyler place's lane, and his taillights disappeared as he bumped down the lane.

Tom leaned forward, put his head in his hands, and wished he were a praying man. He looked over at Fitz, who looked like that was exactly what he was doing. Tom straightened up, and drummed his thigh with his thumb. Come on, Ramos. Fall for it. And keep your hands off Kenny.

☩ ☩ ☩

Everett's car lurched up the lane. He stopped the car, grabbed a map and the classified ads from the local paper, took a deep breath, and opened the car door. "Wish me luck," he said to his partner.

"Break a leg," she replied, smiling at him.

He went up the porch steps and knocked on the front door, studiously avoiding looking at the HRT agents hiding in the bushes on either side. Look natural. Look confused. Look cold. You can do this.

The door opened. A heavyset Latino teenager looked out.

"Hi, uh, I'm looking for the Barrett place. Is this it?"

"What?" The kid opened the door wider.

"Do you have a refrigerator for sale? You see, it says here ..."

"Gordo, what's going on?" Ramos came to the door. And as soon as his silhouette appeared in the door frame, everything broke loose. Everett dove for the bushes and HRT rushed the door. Three agents took Ramos down. Two more put Gordo on the floor.

"Get down! FBI, get down!" other agents shouted. Boom! Boom! Flashbangs detonated and smoke billowed. The sound of glass breaking announced the windows were defeated.

"FBI, get down!"

"Back door breached!" Good news on the radio.

Two teams raced up the inside stairs.

"FBI! FBI!"

"We got 'em! We got 'em!"

"Second floor clear! Two down up here!"

It was all over in less than ninety seconds and not a shot was fired. Every gang member was overpowered, every room was secured. For HRT it was a simple mission—no booby traps or tripwires to deal with, no explosive chemicals, no foreknowledge by the suspects. Piece of cake. No problem.

✞ ✞ ✞

"Command One, this is Team One."

"Go ahead," responded Cramer.

"The target location is secure. You can come on in."

Kenny? Why didn't he mention Kenny?

"We'll be right there."

Cramer and Borsten got in their car and drove toward the house, while Fitz did the same. Nobody said anything. The important information hadn't been delivered, but nobody dared acknowledge it.

They pulled into the front yard of the house and wordlessly Tom, Jack, and Fitz stepped out of the car. Tom's stomach was so tight he could hardly breathe. Borsten and Cramer had pulled in, too, and Borsten had gone in to check with the team leaders. After what seemed like forever, Borsten came jogging back.

"He's not there."

"What do you mean?" Cramer asked.

"We got one dead on the first floor, a gang member. And two more gang members dead upstairs. But the boy's not in there." Tom sagged back against the car. "We checked the whole house."

"Then where is he?"

"I don't know. And Ramos isn't talking."

"What do you mean he's not talking?"

"He wants to see his lawyer. He says he's not talking."

Cramer cursed and marched off toward the house.

Fitz touched Tom's arm. "Hang in there, Tom. We'll clear this up."

Tom stood up straight and turned toward the door of the car. His hands were shaking. "I'm going to get in the car, Fitz. I'm going to open this door, and get in the car. Because if I'm out here when they bring Ramos out, I'm going to kill him."

✞ ✞ ✞

Two HRT members held Ramos in the pantry off the kitchen. Two more agents guarded the door. Each of the other gang members had been taken off by two or three agents to be questioned separately. Ramos stood sullenly in the small room, his hands cuffed behind him, his dark eyes fierce with anger.

Cramer pushed past the guys at the door like a through freight. "Get out," he said to the HRT agents. They left. Without asking why.

Cramer pushed Ramos back hard against the wall. "Where's the boy?"

"What boy?"

"You know what boy!" Cramer shoved Ramos against the wall again.

"I don't know, man ..."

Cramer cursed, and grabbed Ramos's collar and twisted it.

Ramos gasped for breath. "I know my rights, man."

"Your rights? Your rights?"

"I want to see my lawyer."

"You'll be lucky if you see daybreak." Cramer was breathing hard. He and Ramos were eye to eye, so close Cramer could feel his breath. Cramer pulled his gun from its holster, and he stuck the muzzle down the front of Ramos's pants. Ramos's eyes widened in surprise as he felt the cold steel against his belly.

"Now you tell me," Cramer said, his voice barely a whisper, "you tell me where that boy is, or you're gonna spend the rest of your life wondering what dress to wear!" and Cramer saw Ramos swallow hard, his Adam's apple bobbing. And he liked that.

Ramos's eyes darted toward the door, but there was no escape. He rolled his eyes toward the ceiling, and took a breath. "He gave up. He was too weak," he hissed.

Cramer prodded him. "Where is he?"

"He was getting more and more tired, you know? Sleeping all the time. And so, a while ago, he just gave up. He died." Ramos shrugged. Cramer looked at him carefully. "I tell my muchachos, throw his body in the pond. So now, he feed the catfish, eh?" and he smiled.

Cramer stared hard at him, trying to look behind his eyes, and he felt like he was staring into hell. He mustered all the self-control he had and he slowly withdrew his gun. Without looking away, he yelled for the other agents, who re-entered the room. "Get this scumbag out of here!" he ordered.

Borsten waited in the dining room, where the body of Luis Aguilera lay on the floor. He looked up as Cramer walked in. "We've got three of them saying Kenny died, and Ramos told 'em to throw his body in the pond."

Cramer nodded. "When can the divers start?"

"They can do a blind grid search as soon as their equipment is on site. But daylight will be better."

✟ ✟ ✟

Tom saw Cramer coming, walking slowly, and he felt his heart twist, and tears came to his eyes, and he put his head in his hands. Jack put his hand on Tom's shoulder.

Tom sat silently as Cramer told him. He wanted to see the house. After Ramos and his gang had been loaded onto transport vehicles, Fitz walked him through. Jack stayed right next to him.

Tom kept his hands in his pockets. He didn't touch anything, and he didn't say anything to the agents who were working in there. But he felt their stares of pity like cigarette burns all over his body.

Back outside, in the cold night air, with the stars scattered above him, he took a deep breath.

"What can I do for you, Tom?" said Fitz. "You want to go see Cathy? Go get some rest? It's a long time 'til dawn."

He shook his head. He turned to his buddy. "Jack, will you go talk to Cathy? I've got to stay here, and I'd sure appreciate it if you would."

"I don't like leavin' you alone, Tom."

"Please, Jack. She's close to you. Please go stay with her."

Jack looked him over. "Okay, if that's what you want," he said finally. "But Tom, it ain't over 'til it's over. And it ain't over yet."

Tom nodded and Jack left.

"How about some coffee, Tom? You want to sit in the car and have a cup of coffee?"

"I'll just take a walk, Fitz. Down to the pond."

"I'll walk you down."

But Tom shook his head again. "No. I'll be all right. I just need to be alone for a while."

"I don't think that's a good idea."

"I'm all right! I need to be alone."

Fitz let him go.

CHAPTER 46

THE POND LAY OFF BEYOND the barn, down a gentle slope in a pasture. Tom stepped over the broken-down fence. The field grass felt wet beneath his feet, the underlying ridges and ruts and the slippery soil making the footing unsteady. Like life. He was used to it, now.

The air felt cold, and he could see his breath. He tried not to notice how black the sky was, how beautiful the stars. It wasn't fair. Not to Kenny.

The farm pond looked like a black mirror lying on the ground, and Tom imagined it had seen its share of cows wading in to cool off in the summer, drinking its cold water. Already the scuba team was there, probing the rushes that grew along the edge with long poles while waiting for their gear, which was being flown in by helicopter.

And Tom sat down on a fallen tree, at the edge of the woods near the pond, and watched them. He began thinking about his life, and why things had turned out this way. What was the point of it all? What was the point of his dedication to his job, of his attempts to live a good life, to provide for his family? To go through all of that and then lose his son? Why was he even alive?

These were deeper thoughts than he was used to thinking. As he had told his wife, he liked to do and not feel. But now he didn't have the choice. There was nothing he could do and he was drowning in feelings. He shivered in the cold, propped his elbows on his knees, dropped his head into his hands, and let the feelings come.

And he didn't know if he was praying or just talking to

himself, but he said, "God, I know you don't owe me anything. I've been thumbing my nose at you for forty years, and I'm sorry about that. But God, if you feel like doing something for me, just out of the goodness of your heart, I'd like to see my son again. Dead or alive. I'd just like to see Kenny one more time." His cheeks grew wet with tears.

In his mind he went back through the years, pulling images of Kenny from his memory like photos in an album. Kenny as a newborn, his black hair plastered to his head, screaming indignantly at the doctor. Kenny at age five, climbing up the rocks of a mountain overlook in Pennsylvania, climbing so high Tom eventually had to climb up after him and bring him down. And then in elementary school, playing football with neighborhood boys much older than he on the grassy parkway in front of their house while Cathy cooked dinner and worried.

Kenny. Always a fighter. Always ready for a challenge.

After a while, Tom noticed he was cold. He got up to take a walk around the pond.

There were no street lights or shopping center lights for miles around, and the moon was not up. The black night enveloped him like a shroud, and indeed, he felt dead inside. He imagined that if he were lying on the ground and someone tipped him up, his soul would slide out of his feet and into a body bag, where it could be zipped up and carried off. Maybe his boots were the only thing keeping him together. Lace 'em up. Keep 'em tight.

He began walking to the left, away from the divers, on a grassy berm that formed the eastern edge of the pond. His eyes were drawn to the inky water, but he was afraid of what he might see there. So he kept glancing back and forth, between the water and the berm, wanting to look but not wanting to see.

And then a thought occurred to Tom, and he turned it over in his mind. What had Ramos told Cramer? About Kenny? The thought gripped him, and he turned it over again, and again, until gradually it became more than a thought, it became a glimmer of hope. And the more he dwelled on it, the more likely it seemed, and suddenly he turned away from the pond, and moved up the hill, slowly at first, picking his way over the field, but then faster and faster, until he was moving at a half-jog, his breath coming in frosty spurts.

Fitz, Cramer, and Borsten were standing by the car and looked surprised as he ran up to them.

"Alex," he said, grabbing Cramer's jacket. He was breathing hard. "Alex, what did Ramos say to you when you asked him about Kenny?"

Cramer looked down at Tom's hands on his jacket. Then he looked at Tom's eyes. "He said he died."

"No, no. What did he say, exactly?"

"Tom ..."

"What did he say?" Tom could feel their pity on him and he shook it off. Come on, Cramer. Come on.

"He said Kenny got tired. And he gave up. He gave up, and he just died."

"Two other gang members confirmed that," Fitz added.

"We know he'd been badly hurt, Tom, and without medical care ..."

But Tom's eyes were wide, and he almost smiled. "Alex, he wouldn't give up. Kenny wouldn't give up! Ramos was lying! Kenny wouldn't give up."

And he let go of Cramer and started running toward the house. The three men stared at him. He turned around, held up his hands, and said, "I need to go in the house. I won't touch anything. I just need to go in!"

"Tom's losing it!" said Borsten, shaking his head, but Fitz and Cramer looked at each other, and in concert they started toward the house.

☩ ☩ ☩

Jack brought Cathy and Kate over to the farmhouse. There was not much to see, but Cathy had wanted to be there, and there was no reason why she shouldn't be. Jack was trying to think of some word of hope he could give her, but he seemed fresh out of words. He knew anything he said would fall flat, so he finally just took Cathy in his arms, standing there by the car.

He looked over at Kate. She was leaning up against the car, one arm crossed in front of her, the other hand up at her mouth. He thought he could see tears in her eyes. She'd gotten close to Cathy over the week, Jack knew. She'd been strong, supportive, but it was finally beginning to get to her. Even though she'd never had kids, it wasn't hard to empathize with Cathy and Tom.

Jack wasn't really sure where Tom was, but some quick motion caught his eye, and he looked, and saw Tom talking to Cramer and Fitz. Tom looked excited, and a little spark went off in Jack's heart. He gently pulled back from Cathy.

"Y'all stay here for a minute, will you?" and without saying anything else, he jogged off toward the house.

CHAPTER 47

THE MOOD IN THE HOUSE was somber. Agents went about collecting evidence, trying to be satisfied with the fact that all the gangbangers were on their way to jail and none of the agents had been hurt, and trying to ignore their frustration that Kenny had not been found, and the fear that that raised within them. An agent's son. That hit too close to home.

But it was hard to ignore Tom, and his enthusiasm seemed, frankly, a little crazy. They tried not to react to him. Poor guy.

Tom stood in the dining room, thinking out loud. "They were all in here. There was a big argument. Luis gets shot. And they said Kenny was sitting on the floor against the wall ... over here, right?"

An agent looked at him.

"Right?"

The agent sighed. "Yeah, Tom. They said he died right over there."

Cramer, Fitz, and Borsten came in.

"And Ramos told them to dump him in the pond, so they carried him ..." Tom moved toward the front door. He looked intently at the floor. "These spots ... are they blood?"

"They said he'd been hurt, Tom. Hurt his hand."

"Why do they go upstairs? Why do the spots go upstairs?"

"Tom ..."

But Tom leaped onto the staircase, taking the stairs two at a time, carefully avoiding the blood spots.

There were two large bedrooms upstairs, one with an add-on bathroom. The room on the left had just one window, facing front. Tom scanned through it. Two agents were in there, dusting for prints. It didn't look likely. He ran into the other room.

The room was empty, except for the bodies of two gang members, both shot in the head, lying near one window.

Tom looked around. In the middle of the room was a stain on the floor. It had a chalk circle around it. "Is this blood?"

"There are two guys shot in here, Tom."

"But why would the blood be in the middle of the room? They look like they dropped where he shot 'em."

"Tom ..." Cramer was right behind him.

"And why'd they get shot, anyway? Tell me that." Tom felt a surge of energy run up his spine. "Because they let Kenny get away, that's why!"

Cramer and Fitz looked at each other.

There were four windows in the room. Tom started with the one on the front wall. It was painted shut. He moved to the side of the house. Dust covered the sills of both. "I'm not touching anything!" He held his hands up. He went to the wall at the back. One more window, the one near the two dead gangbangers. Tom bent down to see the sill from an angle. The dust had been disturbed. And what ... what was that mark?

"Fitz! Fitz, come here!"

Cramer caught on. He radioed Dave Borsten. "Ask your men who were watching the upstairs bedrooms if a window went up or down."

Fitz paced over to Tom. "What are you looking at?"

"Can you open the window?"

It was a double hung window and Fitz hit it pretty hard.

Boston radioed back. "Yes, sir. One window was open. It shut at 9:17, right after the two shots."

"Ah ha! Yes! Fitz, look at this!" Tom pointed to a small brown stain on the windowsill. "Look!"

Was it blood? It didn't look like much ...

Then Tom stuck his head out. It was a long drop down to the ground. But there were bushes below ....

He raced down the stairs, with the three men right behind him. He ran out the front door, just as Jack got to the house.

"What's up, Tom?"

"Come here, Jack! You got a flashlight?"

Tom ran around to the back of the house. Jack flicked on his light and scanned the back wall. "What are we lookin' for?"

"The bushes, shine it on the bushes."

The light pierced the darkness.

"Yes! Look at that!"

"What?"

"Broken branches. Look. The bushes have broken branches!"

"Are you saying," said Borsten, "that Kenny jumped out of that window? There's no way ..."

"Oh, yes! Oh, yes there is. You don't know my son!"

"Where would he go? Our men came through the woods, Tom. So did the back-up agents. We've been all over back there. There was no one there!"

"Maybe he's hiding. Maybe you missed him. Maybe ... who knows? Alex ..."

"No way!" said Borsten.

Cramer looked from Tom to Borsten and back again. Tom's eyes were shining in the light. Cramer didn't have to think long. "Dave, get your men out here," he said. "We're going to check these woods. Again."

⚜ ⚜ ⚜

Fifty feet behind the house stood a fence made of wire and locust posts. There was a small gate, broken down, lying half on the ground. Tom ran straight for it, Jack right behind him. "Look for prints!" Jack yelled.

"Ground's too hard."

They went through the gate. "Which way?" asked Jack. The woods stretched out before them, the tall oaks like black sentries in the night. As the flashlight moved, the trees' shadows swung around crazily. There was no obvious path, just a dense stand of pines and oaks and tulip poplars, hollies and dogwoods.

Come on, come on. Think. Which way?

"Straight away from the house," Tom said.

They advanced into the woods. Tom could hear HRT behind him getting organized in the yard. He wasn't waiting.

"Kenny! Kenny!" The forest floor was relatively clear of undergrowth. He could see pretty far. "Kenny!"

"What's this?" asked Jack. But it was only an upturned stump looking a little like a curled up body in the dark.

They moved on back. "Kenny! Kenny!"

"Tom, let's wait for HRT. Before we mess up something."

But Tom didn't even respond. He moved quickly away from the house. *Where are you? Come on, Kenny—where are you?* His eyes strained to see. *Come on ... come on!* In front of him was a holly tree. He pushed past it, hardly noticing as its sharp leaves scraped his face. *Come on, boy!* He walked on, in a half-jog. Some old blackberry brambles grabbed at his legs. He kept on going.

Some fifty yards into the woods he came to a ravine, a steep one, with water flowing down in the bottom. He stopped and looked at it. Jack caught up to him.

"Look around!" said Tom.

"Here!" said Jack. He pointed to a footprint in the mud, just one. Headed uphill. Could be an HRT guy, or it could be ...

"Let's go!" said Tom.

"Uphill?"

"Come on! Kenny!"

It was steeper than it looked. Tom had only gone a little way when he stopped. He was puffing. *Could Kenny have climbed this hill? Hurt?* Tom could smell fresh pine. Up ahead, two large trees lay on the ground. *Probably came down in last night's storm. Come on, come on. Oh, God, which way?*

"I'll check downhill from where we turned," said Jack.

"No! I need your light. Follow me!" Tom took a deep breath and turned uphill again. "Kenny!"

✞ ✞ ✞

He was a little boy again, on his first bike with hand brakes, a silver Columbia five-speed. He was so proud. He whizzed down the hill past his grinning, clapping father.

But he was going too fast. He squeezed too hard, locked the brakes, and sailed over the handlebars, his mouth wide with surprise. He hit the ground, hard. He was hurt, crying, scared. His dad came running up...

"Kenny! Kenny!"

Wait. That wasn't right. Dad's voice was wrong. Try it again.
His dad came running up...
"Kenny! Kenny!"
"Dad?"

✞ ✞ ✞

Tom stopped in his tracks. What did he hear? The wind blew gently through the tops of the trees. Had he heard something? Something else? "Kenny? Kenny?"
"Dad?" Kenny said. "Dad?"
When he saw movement under a fallen pine tree, Tom's heart leaped into his throat. "Jack, here!" Adrenalin surged through his body and he charged forward, pushing branches away. His son! "Kenny!" Tom threw himself onto his knees and grabbed his son, grabbed him in a giant bear hug.
"Kenny, oh Kenny! Son!" He held him tightly, hugging him, the son he thought he'd lost. Kenny was alive! Tom could hardly believe it, but here he was, in his arms! "Kenny! I knew you wouldn't give up!" He heard Jack calling the others on the radio.
Kenny buried his face in his dad's jacket. *The familiar smell, the feel of the cool nylon ...* Kenny looked at him with glistening eyes. "I knew you'd find me!" *His father's strong love could fix anything.*
"Holy son of a gun! Kenny, you made it!" Jack knelt down. He pulled off his jacket and draped it over the freezing boy.
Tom grinned at Jack. Tears ran down his cheeks. "We got him, Jack, we got him!"
Jack was laughing and crying at the same time. "You bet we did!"
Fitz ran up, followed by Cramer. "Oh, thank God!"
Cramer yelled, "Medic! Medic!" Suddenly, he remembered the radio in his hand. He cleared his throat and pressed the mic button. "Borsten, we need a medic in the woods, right now! We got the boy. He's alive! I'll spot you. Bring the chopper in for a med-evac."
"Let's get this tape off his hands," Jack said.
"Here's a medic." Fitz said.
Frank Littleton, an EMT, came crashing through the leaves and dropped down next to Kenny.

"We need to free his hands," Jack said, moving the coat away.

"Can you support them?"

Jack gingerly put his own hands under the black and blue lump that was Kenny's mangled hand while the medic cut the tape off and handed it to a member of the evidence team.

As his hands came loose, Kenny reached forward and grabbed onto his dad's jacket with his good hand. "He killed Carlos, Dad!"

"I know. We got him. We got 'em all."

"Lay him down," Frank said.

As Tom did, Jack gently placed Kenny's mangled hand on his chest.

Frank checked Kenny's breathing and his pulse, and shined a flashlight in Kenny's eyes. He turned the flashlight onto Kenny's face. "There's a lot of blood vessels broken in his face."

"He's been choked," Tom said, his own voice cracking. "His voice sounds hoarse, too."

"Okay, we'll use a neck brace." Frank saw something else, some blood dried in Kenny's hair, and he felt the area of Kenny's scalp above and behind his right eye. "There's a lump here. He got hit." He touched Kenny's face to get his attention. "Kenny, what hurts?"

Kenny looked at Frank blankly.

"Besides your hand. What hurts?"

"Here." Kenny pointed toward his right side.

Frank lifted up Kenny's shirt. "I need some more light."

Jack and Fitz leaned over Kenny with their flashlights.

"Were you shot?"

"Yeah."

"Holy ..." Jack said.

Tom closed his eyes.

Frank leaned down further. His hands probed gently until he saw Kenny react. "It's not bad," he said, finally.

Tom exhaled, relieved.

Agents carrying a backboard and a medical kit came running up. Behind them were Kate and Cathy.

"Kenny!" Cathy cried.

"He's fine, Cathy!" Tom said. "He's going to be fine."

Frank found a neck brace in the medical kit and carefully fitted it on. Then he began splinting Kenny's hand to immobilize it. "This may hurt a little."

That was an understatement. Kenny stiffened and arched his back, grimacing in pain, and all Tom could do was hang on. "It's almost over, Kenny. Almost over."

Frank checked his pulse one more time, then said, "Okay, we're gonna lift him! Excuse us, Mrs. Donovan. Tom, you stay put, we'll get him."

Cathy backed off, tears of joy streaming down her face. Gently four men slid Kenny into the backboard. Quickly they wrapped blankets around him, and secured him with straps.

Tom stood up, and turned to Cathy. She threw her arms around his neck. "Tom, oh, Tom!" she said. "You did it!"

Tears flowed down his cheeks. "No, Cathy. This was a gift, a gift from God." He wiped his eyes on his sleeve.

"I'm ready to move him!" said Frank.

"I'll be right next to you, Kenny," said Tom. He stood up and he turned to Jack. "Thanks, Jack, for everything."

"Great job, Tom. I've always said there's a certain tenacity about you."

"Yeah, something about a mule ... or a pit bull."

"Ready, Tom?"

"Yes!"

✟ ✟ ✟

The roar of the chopper greeted them as it landed in a square illuminated by flares in one of the pastures.

All of the agents still on the grounds had gathered in front of the house. They clapped and cheered as the backboard bearing Kenny went by. Their faces were bright, their mood jovial. They were happy for Tom and happy to be released from the tension they had shared.

Tom and Cathy, Jack, Kate, Fitz, Alex, and Borsten stood watching, buffeted by the wash of the copter blades, as the EMTs loaded Kenny into the chopper. Tom was shaking in the cold wind, his cheeks still wet with tears. A crew member motioned Tom on board.

Cathy released his hand so he could leave.

"You got room?" Tom shouted to the crew member, over the noise, pointing toward Cathy.

He nodded.

Tom grabbed Cathy's hand again. "Come on," he shouted. "I want you with me!"

Inside the chopper, Kenny lay on the stretcher, eyes closed, getting oxygen through a mask, an IV in his arm.

"Morphine!" Frank shouted to Tom, pointing at the IV.

Tom nodded. He sat down in a seat near Kenny's feet, buckled his seatbelt, and put one hand on Kenny's leg, holding Cathy's hand with the other.

Frank, monitoring Kenny's vital signs, gave Tom a thumbs up.

As the copter lifted off, Tom looked down. He saw the farmhouse, surrounded by agents, and he could tell they were cheering. Down by the pond he could see the scuba guys packing up their stuff. He saw Cramer and Fitz and Borsten standing on the front porch of the house, their relief clearly visible in their body language. He saw Jack and Kate standing off to the side, waving. As they got higher, he saw tree tops and miles and miles of forest stretching on to the horizon. And as the houses and people and cars grew smaller and smaller, he couldn't help but notice how different everything looked from way up there.

EPILOGUE

SHE WAS STANDING OVER BY the water fountain, dressed in a black pants suit and teal blouse.

Jack walked up behind her.

"Hey, Katie!"

She looked up. "The name's Kate, Jack."

"I knew a Katie once, back home. I put a frog down her dress." He grinned at her, his brown eyes crinkling at the corners.

She tried not to smile. She pointed her finger like the muzzle of a gun, stuck it in his ribs, got right up in his face, and said, "You try that on me, buster, and I'll get you for assault on a federal officer and sexual harassment!"

"Hmmm," he said, scratching his chin and looking up toward the ceiling. "Might be worth it."

She laughed.

"Say, Kate," he said, leaning his hand against the wall. "What are you up to this weekend?"

"Ugh, painting. I've let it go too long. This weekend, the living room gets it."

"You doin' this by yourself?"

"Yep. Why?"

"Well, how'd you like a little help? From someone who's very experienced?"

"Depends on who it is."

"Someone who's kind, thoughtful, intelligent, brave, hard-working ..."

"Humble ..."

"Oh, yes. He prides himself on being humble."

She laughed again, and he liked that.

"Seriously, Kate ..."

"I didn't know you could be serious, Jack."

"It's a limited-time offer."

"Oh, okay."

"So seriously, Kate, how'd you like someone, me, to come over and help you. Then, when we're done, I'll take you to this little place I know, a country-western bar."

"Country-western?"

"Boots required. I promise you you'll have fun. Money back guarantee. Only for you, it's free."

She looked up at him and pushed a wisp of hair out of her face. He noticed her eyes were green, and when she laughed, which was often, they sparkled like fireworks on the Fourth. Down home.

"You know, Jack," she said. "I'd like that. I'd like that a lot." And when she smiled at him again, Jack suddenly felt sixteen again.

✝ ✝ ✝

It was a black velvet night. The stars were scattered like diamonds, millions of them, across the sky. Tom lay on a blanket on a hillside at Sky Meadows State Park in Fauquier County, his son on one side of him ,and his wife on the other. They were watching the Perseid Meteor showers putting on a spectacular display.

The night was peaceful. A soft breeze blew from the west. In the distance, Tom could hear the cry of a whip-poor-will. Forty yards away, a representative of the Northern Virginia Astronomy Club was explaining how to use a telescope to a little kid. Tom could hear his voice, but he couldn't quite make out the words.

Kenny had just had his second operation to repair the damage Angel Ramos had done to his hand. It had been touch and go at first, and the doctors had been concerned, but Kenny healed well, and now, the doctors were optimistic he'd regain full use of his hand, once this last cast came off.

In just a few weeks, he'd begin college at George Mason, not far from his home in Fairfax. Kenny had decided to stay in town. He could wrestle there just as well and he'd be closer to the trial of Angel Ramos.

Tom was thrilled that Kenny would be home this year. He'd have another year with him.

Another meteor. They looked as bright as fireworks, streaking across the sky.

"The heavens declare the glory of God," Kenny said softly.

"Yes," Tom replied, and he imagined his son smiling at his response.

"Hey, Dad?"

"Hmm?"

Kenny's voice was soft. "Do you think I could make it, as an agent?"

Tom's eyes widened. He quickly looked toward Cathy. She looked asleep, her head on his shoulder. "Why?" he said, keeping his voice low. He glanced at Cathy again.

"I've always wanted to be an agent. Ever since I can remember."

Cathy groaned.

"Oh, Kenny," Tom said, trying to restrain himself. "I think you'd make a great agent."

Cathy turned away. Tom squeezed her.

"It's just that ... somebody has to stand up to these guys or they'll take over. And I liked that feeling, of not letting them win."

Cathy groaned again, louder. "I'm surrounded!" she said.

"Surrounded and outnumbered," said Tom. He kissed her. "Get used to it." He turned toward his son. "I think you should go for it, Kenny. Finish college, then go for it." He chuckled. "Just don't tell your mother. Pretend you're majoring in English."

"I've known this was coming," Cathy whispered. "I've just been in denial."

"That's good," said Tom. "It's a good technique." And he squeezed her again.

Off in the distance, a truck horn sounded.

"Yeah, Dad, I think I will. I think I will go for it."

Yes!

And as Tom laid his head back down, he saw in his mind a big, Irish cop whose laughing eyes and flashing grin were permanently displayed on the walls of his mind. Yeah, Dad, he thought, you're gonna love this kid when you finally get to meet him. You're gonna love him. And he closed his eyes, full of gratitude—and peace.

Now that you've read *The Tiger's Cage:*

Enjoy more novels from Linda J. White, available at amazon.com, christianbook.com, barnesandnoble.com, and wherever books are sold:

Bloody Point

Young FBI agent Cassie McKenna searches for serenity by retreating to her sailboat on the Chesapeake Bay after her agent-husband is killed in a car wreck. But serenity proves elusive. A series of violent events around the Bay seem far from coincidental, and when her former FBI partner, Jake Tucker, is assaulted and left for dead, Cass knows it's time to get back in the game.

> "[A] powerful combination of page-turning plot and real-life characters who struggle with the 'Why, God?' questions we all sometimes ask."
>
> Marlene Bagnull, author and director, Greater Philadelphia Christian Writers Conference and Colorado Christian Writers Conference

Battered Justice

FBI Special Agent Jake Tucker works hard to be an excellent investigator and a great dad to his two kids, even if he is divorced. Having Cass McKenna as his partner helps with both goals. When a shot in the dark takes out a colleague, Jake and Cass set out to find the shooter. They discover a shadowy trail of drugs and criminal conduct connected with a casino—and the battered, bloody body of Jake's ex-wife, Tam. Jake is sure Tam's new husband, a powerful state senator, killed her. But Lady Justice can be battered, too, and soon Jake finds himself in a new fight—a fight of faith, the fight of his life.

> "Linda White is a masterful storyteller who continues to impress. Her latest novel, 'Battered Justice,' grabs your attention from the first page. This edge-of-your-seat thriller weaves murder, romance, deceit, and faith together into a suspense-packed story with characters that have you hooked

through the last page."
    Dr. Sharon S. Smith, SA, FBI Ret.

Seeds of Evidence

FBI agent Kit McGovern's vacation to her grandmother's Virginia island home is interrupted when the body of a young boy washes up on the beach. Who is he? How did he die? And why has no one reported him missing? Kit's only clues are the acorns in the boy's pockets and the tomato seeds in his gut. Teaming up with D.C. homicide detective David O'Connor, Kit follows plant DNA evidence to track the killer, clues that lead them into the dark world of human trafficking.

"[A] suspenseful story sown with fascinating investigative details, planted on a picturesque island, and cultivated by characters you care about."
    Sarah Sundin, author of "With Every Letter"

Words of Conviction

Terror grips Senator Bruce Grable and his estranged wife when their five-year-old daughter is kidnapped from her bedroom. The perpetrator provides the clues to solving the crime: his words. FBI agent MacKenzie Graham, a forensic psycholinguist, analyzes the kidnapper's notes. But will her analysis solve the case in time? And could Grable's guilt have contributed to the crime?

"I have just two words to say about this book: READ IT!"
    Ann Tatlock, author of the Christy Award-winning
    "Promises to Keep"

Acknowledgements

In December, 1992, I had a middle-of-the-night thought: *What if* a tough, aggressive, FBI agent found his life spinning out of control because his son was kidnapped by the drug gang the agent had been investigating? How would he react? When I shared it with my husband, Larry, he replied, "That's a great story. You ought to write it!" I thought, *me*?

Soon, Larry began dragging me over to the FBI Academy, where he was a video producer-director. He introduced me to agents and asked them to share their expertise. They were most gracious and I began putting words into a document on my computer—a mighty Commodore 64. (Seriously. I used to hit "save" and go brush my teeth, that thing was so slow.) A year later, I had a newer computer and "The Tiger's Cage" was complete. I'm most grateful to Larry for kickstarting my novel-writing career.

Supervisory Special Agent Amelia Martinez, now retired, and I shared many lunches together in the Boardroom at the Academy. She gave me a fascinating, informative window into an agent's world. Whenever I'd get stuck on a plot point, Amelia would bail me out. None of my female characters have quite achieved Amelia's flare—her stories at times left me wide-eyed!

I will never forget Marlene Bagnull's words to me in 1993 at the Greater Philadelphia Christian Writers Conference, which she directs. It was my first conference and I sat terrified as she began critiquing the first pages of Tiger. She said, "You're not just a housewife from Somerville—you're a writer and a good one!" She helped me dream the dream. I'm just one of the many, many writers who owe her a debt of gratitude. Thank you, Marlene, from all of us.

I revised that original Tiger manuscript in the summer of 2015, sharpening the text and adding the forensic geology element. I'm most grateful to James Sawyer, soil scientist for Fauquier (pronounced "faw-keer") County, Virginia, where I live. He suggested using Cardova as a plot point. Thank you! It's perfect!

I couldn't have produced this book without my husband's work in preparing it for publication. My Beta readers, as always, saved me from many an error. Hilary Kanter copyedited the book for me. My grown children and my co-grandmother, Marsha Chappell, cheered me on. And I am always grateful for the expert advice given me by my literary agent, Janet Grant, of Books & Such Literary Management.

Thank you, dear reader, for investing your time in reading "The Tiger's Cage." May you be assured of God's sovereignty in all your circumstances, and of his boundless grace and love.

About the Author

Linda J. White writes FBI thrillers and is a national award-winning journalist. Her husband, Larry, worked at the FBI Academy for over 27 years. They live in rural Virginia and have three grown children, three grandchildren, two cats, and a Sheltie who loves to herd them all.

Linda is available to speak to library groups, book clubs, and other organizations.

Web site: lindajwhite.net
Email: rytn4hm@verizon.net
Facebook: Linda J. White Books
Twitter: https://twitter.com/rytn4hm
Visit Linda J. White's Amazon page

Made in the USA
Middletown, DE
24 March 2016